PRAISE FOR
ALL SUPERHEROES NEED PR

"Finally, my God! Elizabeth Stephens is the Blerd of my dreams! This novel is a fizzy, fast-talking takedown of celebrity culture, fandom, and the fine print of heroism—with enough heat to melt vibranium. Stephens delivers an absolutely swoony, steamy love letter to the power of reinvention."

—Nikki Payne, author of *Pride and Protest*

"The book we need, the writer we need, the hero we need, the new series we absolutely need! *All Superheroes Need PR* is unique, and fantastical, and funny, and so sexy it's absolutely on fire! It brought me places where I desperately needed to go, it gave me everything I wanted and more, and it healed the part of me that has been sad since the Beast turned into a human. I want a million more novels set in this universe! Elizabeth Stephens is a jaw-dropping talent, and I'm in awe of her mind!"

—Ali Hazelwood, *New York Times* bestselling author

"You are *not prepared* for Roland and Vanessa. Bro sees her and is like 'I am obsessed and *mad* about it, but also, what if I kidnapped you? Oh, that's not socially acceptable? I *guess* I'll contractually bind you to be Lois Lane to my (grouchy, flame-filled, violent) Superman! Also, I'll call you my *wife, real fast*.' I LOVED THIS BOOK!"

—Katee Robert, *New York Times* bestselling author

"Awkward charm and unhinged possessiveness is a marriage built to last, and no couple does it better than Roland and Vanessa in *All Superheroes Need PR*."

—Natalie Ashee, author of *Sucker*

"What a fun, fun book! I'm so excited to read more in this series. Superhero romances exist, but it's a painfully underserved genre and this was such a fun idea. Great world-building, too, that reminded me a bit of *The Boys*, with superheroes almost being celebrities. Also, so great to see diversity and non-white leads. Will definitely be picking up this author's next book!"

—Kimberly Lemming, *USA Today* bestselling author

"I'm obsessed. *All Superheroes Need PR* was the perfect blend of contemporary and paranormal romance, and it made for a fun and refreshingly original read. This book has it all—intense action, humor, and a scorching romance (pun only a little intended). A must-read!"

—Laura Thalassa, *USA Today* bestselling author

"Elizabeth Stephens did her big one with this delightful romp, where she turns fake dating on its head with a villain who decides he'd rather be a good guy and the PR professional tasked with changing his image. This book is one of my favorite reads of the year! It has adventure and romance, all wrapped up in a spicy package. This page-turner will have you giggling and swooning. Stephens doesn't hold back on the charm or the angst as Roland, a.k.a. the Wyvern, and Vanessa find their way to happy every after. I loved this book!"

—Kenya Goree-Bell, author of The Blood Legacy series

"Best book of the summer, hands down."

—Nisha Sharma, author of *Dating Dr. Dil*

"I genuinely loved this book so much. It was fun and fresh and sexy and sweet, and I was kicking my feet the whole time. Elizabeth has got a reader for life now."

—B.K. Borison, *New York Times* bestselling author

"A deftly crafted and imaginative blending of fantasy, romance, and humor, *All Superheroes Need PR* is an original and fun read from cover to cover. Author Elizabeth Stephens showcases a genuine flair for the kind of distinctive and engaging storytelling style that is aptly suited to engaging her readers' enthusiastic attention with distinctive characters and surprise-laden plot twists."

—*Midwest Book Review*

"This delightfully quirky enemies-to-lovers romance made me grin from ear to ear. I was utterly charmed watching Vanessa's adorable clumsiness turn ex-villain Pyro into her personal hero."

—Kami Tei, Amazon editor

ALL SUPER-HEROES NEED PHOTO OPS

OTHER TITLES BY ELIZABETH STEPHENS

Supers in the City

All Superheroes Need PR

Stand-Alones

The Bone King and the Starling

Beasts of Gatamora Series

Dark City Omega

Shadowlands Omega

Xiveri Mates Series

Taken to Voraxia

Taken to Nobu

Exiled from Nobu

Taken to Sasor

Taken to Heimo

Taken to Kor

Taken to Lemora

Taken by the Pikosa Warlord

Taken to Evernor

Taken to Sky

Taken to Revatu

Population Series

Lord of Population

Monster in the Oasis

Immortal with Scars

Twisted Fates

The Hunting Town

The Hunted Rise

ELIZABETH STEPHENS

Published by Montlake, Seattle
www.apub.com

EU product safety contact:
Amazon Media EU S. à r.l.
38, avenue John F. Kennedy, L-1855 Luxembourg
amazonpublishing-gpsr@amazon.com

ISBN-13: 9781662523601 (paperback)
ISBN-13: 9781662523595 (digital)

Cover illustration and design by Elizabeth Turner Stokes

Printed in the United States of America

To the Black book community. I see you, and I am so grateful for how you see me.

HEADLINES

The Wyvern's transformation has taken the world by storm—or, more accurately, by flame. The Supernatural Defense Department has yet to release a statement explaining the Wyvern's new horns and height, but the Champions of Earth Coalition has remained firm that "the Wyvern is still our hero."

The Wyvern has once again shown the world that heroes will always prevail by defeating the Marduk in an epic battle over Chinook Bay. The supervillain founder of the Villains Network of America has not been seen publicly since.

Caught on camera by the award-winning photographer newly hired by The Riot Creative, Monika Neumann, the Wyvern can be seen wielding a sword with a fiery blade as he breaks up a fight between six rival biker gangs in a Fayetteville Walmart parking lot. No one was injured.

One person who does not seem to be troubled by the Wyvern's new look is Ms.—soon to be Mrs.—Vanessa Theriot! The Wyvern and his longtime girlfriend and PR director are set to tie the knot next year. With the Wyvern's social media following now at two hundred million, it's clear that fans around the world cannot get enough of this superhero couple.

Prologue: The Forty-Eight Hour Festival

Monika

I'm watching Taranis through my lens like a stalker. I shouldn't be. I'm here to shoot a *group* of superheroes, not focus on just the one. Even if I were to focus on just one, it should be the ginormous pink-skinned monster with twin horns who spits fire whenever anyone looks at his girlfriend—sorry, fiancée—sideways, but I'm not.

Instead, I'm focused on Taranis, the world's *favorite* superhero. At least, he was. He may be tied for first now that the Wyvern has turned into a monster, through a process he and other Champions refer to as his *reversion.* But Taranis doesn't seem to mind sharing the spotlight. He's just so *kind.* And pretty.

I swallow hard, snapping a couple shots as he reaches down to help the Olympian stand up. She doesn't need it, of course. She's among the most famous and most powerful of the Champions, but it's still a sweet gesture.

She says something to Taranis as he yanks her up, and she tumbles into him, catching herself on his broad chest, which is covered in glittery, skintight baby-blue spandex. My ten-freaking-pound 400mm lens swivels on top of my tripod.

It's rare that I get to bring out equipment this heavy, since I usually shoot in the middle of hostile environments and in much closer range. A 400mm lens is too bulky and unwieldy, requiring both hands to shoot, if you can even carry it for that long. Now, mounted on my tripod to capture the full gathering of eight superheroes, it's perfect.

With my Nikon Z9 and giant-ass lens, I'm able to catch all the microexpressions on the Champions' faces—more importantly, all the ways their powers flare with their emotions, in fascinating unconscious gestures—from thirty yards back.

Pele, who can manifest and control lava, accidentally scorches the tarmac under her heels when she's shoved back in a playful gesture by Ceto. Ceto controls water, and when she spits some out of her mouth now, it moves like an arrow loosed from a bow, hitting Taranis in the side of his face. He gawks at her in the cutest fucking way, and when he laughs and steps back, electricity titters across the tops of his shoulders. I catch all of it, and it honestly makes me a little teary to see eight of the forty-eight most powerful beings on this planet behaving like children.

My heart clenches in my chest at the sight of Taranis, in particular.

Like 99 percent of the planet, I've had a crush ever since I first saw the shaky footage of him crawling out of his pod as a child twenty-two years ago. His was one of forty-eight pods that fell from the sky that day and changed the world forever. The beings who emerged from each shattered pod looked human enough, but they carried an ethereal, otherworldly aura that made each of them so beautiful, I found them hard to look at. I still do.

These forty-eight alien kids wielded extraordinary powers but had no memory of where they came from or even really how to use them. So, after a confusing initial six months of governments panicking and scrambling to decide what to do with our superhuman guests, the children were placed with human host families, and the Supernatural Defense Department was set up to help manage—*cough,* control, *cough, cough*—them. The only problem? Some didn't want to be controlled.

The child who became the grown-up we now know as the Marduk was the first to defect from the SDD when he was in his early teens. He pulled several of the Forty-Eight with him, and together they formed the Villains Network of America—the VNA—and began using their powers to cause chaos all over the world. The Champions of Earth Coalition—the COE—was established as an offshoot of the SDD to counter the villains. And just like that, the Forty-Eight became instant celebrity brands, with the VNA and the COE competing with massive contracts and endorsement deals to "win" unaffiliated Forty-Eight beings over to their respective sides.

Today, the balance stands:

Champions: seventeen.

Villains: seventeen.

Unaffiliated: fourteen.

The Wyvern evened out the balance between the Champions and villains earlier this year when he ~~fell in love with Vanessa~~ took a contract with the COE. And now eight of the Champions stand together like kids underneath a banner that glimmers high above them in the airplane hangar, celebrating the day the Forty-Eight crashed here. It's a fun festival, one I always enjoyed as a teen when it was first established—but I have to wonder why they decided to keep the photo shoot advertising the festival at this location . . .

The airplane hangar looks . . . rough. It's only been three weeks since the Old Sundale Airport was destroyed when the VNA kidnapped a newly reverted Wyvern and Vanessa, and her crazy family helicoptered in to save the day. Even a few of her coworkers were there, which really pissed me off since I'm technically a full-time contractor for her agency, The Riot Creative. I mean, come on. Why didn't I get an invite to the party? It sounded chaotic and bloody fabulous—quite literally.

Now the historic airport is half caved in, a majority of the antique airplanes destroyed or missing. Even the tarmac still has burn marks and bloodstains on it. But Mr. Singkham, head of the COE, and Ms. Lemon, head of the SDD, thought it would send a powerful message to the VNA to keep the photo shoot here, even if the festivities would mostly take place in downtown Sundale over the course of the next week.

"Are we ready, Monika?" Mr. Singkham shouts over the distance separating us. I'm glad I have my 50mm lens fitted to my backup Z9 ready to go, and give Mr. Singkham a thumbs-up as I approach the group to take shots from much closer.

Mr. Singkham's typically stoic face breaks into a grin as the infectious energy of the Champions permeates the air. Even the Wyvern grins a little bit as he watches the antics of the other Champions, holding Vanessa crushed to his side. His larger-than-life proportions make the average-size woman look like Tinker Bell next to him. Yet she still looks up at him adoringly, like he's a cute cuddly teddy bear instead of someone who looks like he got lost on his way across the River Styx and should be guarding the gates of Hell.

Crouching in the middle of the runway, I adjust my settings to be able to focus on both the people—and aliens—in the foreground as well as the signage billowing over the scorched hangar. I give Mr. Singkham another thumbs-up.

He sweeps a hand over his dark hair. His tie is an homage to his homeland, decorated with the red, white, and much thicker blue stripe of the Thai flag, though I'm sure any average American will just assume it represents the United States. "Shh! Everyone, please give Monika your attention!"

I snap a couple shots of the cluster of eight Champions and four humans, who include Vanessa, Mr. Singkham, Ms. Lemon, and Sundale's mayor, Mrs. Tambor. She was the one who roped Vanessa into the frame even though Vanessa's technically working on-site as the Wyvern's PR manager. But she's also his fiancée.

As the *Sundale Daily* so aptly put, the Wyvern and Vanessa's work romance "took the world by storm," and I'm not at all surprised that the mayor hopes to capitalize on Vanessa's presence here. They have no fewer than eight events over the next week—even more than Taranis and the Olympian—to mingle with VIPs and take photos with citizens.

This is apparently the largest Forty-Eight Hour Festival Sundale will have ever hosted over the fifteen years it's been active. So large that after the Wyvern's reversion, the festival was extended to last a whole week.

And I'm expected to take cutesy pictures throughout all of it. I'm a *war* photographer, *mein Gott*. Not a tabloid gossip-column reporter.

With a grimace, I review the last few frames. They're awful, as I expected they would be. But I just needed to test the focus and shutter speed while Pele held a ball of revolving lava in her hand, Taranis's chest crackled with electricity, and the Wyvern's horns caught fire—simultaneously.

I approach the group, wind whipping the scent of smoke from the hangar to flood my nostrils—just another dagger to the gut, reminding me of the battle I missed. Forcing a neutral expression, I stand in front of Mr. Singkham. "Can you move up front? I can't see you past the Olympian's shoulder."

I then move over to the mayor and pull her forward. A tall, heavyset Jamaican woman, she stands sheepishly amid the crowd of Champions, apologizing to Ceto and the Olympian as she brushes shoulders with them.

Rearranging the group, I flank her left side with Pele and place the Wyvern, and then Vanessa, on the end. I then gather a fortifying breath before stepping up to Taranis. "Would you mind standing here, next to Ms. Lemon?"

He turns his gaze to Ms. Lemon and gives her a sultry wink that makes my own stomach tighten, even though he's not looking at me. He whispers, "Nothing would give me greater pleasure."

The mayor's got dark-brown skin, but damn, I can feel her blushing from here.

A brush of cool air hits my right side, and I jolt at the sight of ice crusting suddenly on Taranis's cheek. He laughs and the ice cracks and falls away as sparks—actual, electrical sparks—flare across his face.

His brown skin turns to silver under the lightning he generates, and his sharp fade highlights the shape of his head. He has a perfect jawline.

A *perfect* jawline. Just slightly too brutal to be called pretty but that, regardless, I'm fairly certain any woman in the world would still kill for.

"Boreas . . ." he says in a mock threat.

The Champion who can control ice and snow rolls his eyes from his position in the back row. A tall, lanky male, he's got light-brown skin a shade darker than Taranis's, freckles, and bright-red hair. The combo makes him seem like he should be controlling spring and summer elements, rather than the wintery ones he does have dominion over.

"Quit your flirting. Let's get this over with," Boreas grunts.

"*Shameless* flirting." The Olympian rolls her eyes.

Stunning, this woman. I place her on Taranis's other side. She elbows him in the ribs, and I bark out a laugh that draws several sets of eyes to me. Just not Taranis's; he's too busy smirking back at her. When I guide her to stand shoulder to shoulder with him, he sends electrical shocks into her arm, covered in green-and-yellow spandex. Again, I chuckle.

Satisfied with their placements, I return to my tripod. I take more photos, arranging and rearranging the group another dozen times before finally taking individual portraits of each of the Champions, plus a few cutesy candids of the Wyvern and Vanessa that I know will dominate the interwebs in the coming days.

When all is said and done, I send the group to break while I gather my equipment and review some of the photos.

Huh.

I backtrack to one picture and zoom in on Taranis's face. It's hard to see clearly in the little digital viewfinder, but it looks like Taranis's immaculately arched brows are slanted toward his nose in an angry line and his full lips are pinched. His eyes, which I've seen shine blue in photographs, now shine purple—yes, I said that right, *purple.* They glow brilliantly, hypnotically, and are trained on the Wyvern's back. The Wyvern pays no attention to him, facing away from Taranis as he gives his fiancée a kiss on the top of her head of tight brown and blond curls. Also . . . are Taranis's fists clenched?

Huh.

If I didn't know any better, I'd say Taranis looks pissed. But luckily, I do know better, and I know that in addition to being the most handsome male in the world, he's also among the nicest. Must be just a weird moment.

I delete the photo and continue through the rest of the collection, stopping at the last picture that I took. It's one of the Champions all laughing. I sigh. Okay, it may not be taking pics in the heat of battle, but it's not the worst gig. Not even close.

Chapter One

Taranis

Three months later

I stare down at the front page of the *London Champions Daily* with my back teeth clenched and lightning skittering along my temples. I know he can see it.

Frederick Yu's face gets redder and redder. The color creeps up from the collar of his starched shirt to his weak jaw. Never trust a man with a weak jaw. I should have fucking known better. Freddie here's been nothing but a disappointment from the start.

"Sir, with all due respect, it's been three weeks . . ."

"Three weeks that I haven't seen one front page with my name on it. You have to scroll for a full minute on any news app to find the first mention of a Champion that isn't the fucking Wyvern!"

Freddie hesitantly approaches my desk. I work from home, though the areas where I live and work are separated by thick concrete walls and a biometrically coded entrance. Nobody comes into my office without my permission. And nobody goes into the livable areas of my home ever. Not that I use the space to relax. I don't relax. I amass power, and I can't do that if people stop taking my calls because I can't out-fucking-smile the goddamn pink monster and his fucking fiancée!

Freddie shuffles his feet, holding his tablet against his chest in a white-knuckle grip. He looks at me as if he'd like nothing more than to bash me over the skull with it. It's a look I know well by now, but only one of the thirty or so idiots I've fired in the past year has actually had the stones—well, the tits—to swing.

My designer at the time tried to slam her laptop over my head after I asked her if she'd developed spontaneous color blindness when she designed my new uniform. As she lifted the device, I exploded it in her hands, which caused a jagged piece to tear through one of her palms. She needed thirty stitches and a couple bones reset, but that didn't stop her from trying to sock me good with her other arm. She missed, in any case, then accepted the settlement my COE lawyers shoved down her throat, and moved on.

I watch Freddie, hoping he'll make the same mistake. My desire to take my aggression out on his stupid face is impossible to think past. I crack my neck.

Instead, the fucker takes half a step back. He shakes his head and cards his fingers through his short black hair, causing it to stick up straight. "We are the best PR firm in the country—"

"You *were* the best PR firm in the country." I drag the Business section of yesterday's paper to the top of the pile.

Hot for PR: *An Analysis on the Power of Public Relations from Rising Industry Powerhouse The Riot Creative.* That's Vanessa Theriot's firm. The headline makes me want to explode the power grid for the goddamn city, starting with the COE headquarters, which is where that puny little multimillion-dollar marketing agency keeps their offices. They're supposed to be *boutique,* for fuck's sake. Not absconding with every decent headline, plastering the Wyvern's face across every front page. Getting her fiancé every fucking brand endorsement I have and then some. He models *underwear* now. He's a goddamn pink monster!

"You aren't going to be able to do better than us," Freddie blusters, his bright cheeks pink, his narrow eyes doing their best impression of a threat.

Electricity crackles along my skin. I can feel it pulse through my temples like a budding migraine before seeping into my eyes, where it undoubtedly glows, turning my irises from purple to red, a warning to Freddie that he may leave this room not only fired, but electrocuted as well. *If only I could simply . . . explode* him, I think with a frown. My powers do have their limitations.

I can control electricity. Cell phones and machines using electrical power, for example, I can turn on and off and operate, to a certain extent. I can also generate electrical currents, forming balls of energy and launching them at my enemies. What I can't do—and what I really wish I could do at present—is generate an electrical current *within* a person. Or being.

I've seen the Marduk do this, not with electricity but with wind. Felt it. The swelling of my lungs; the threat that he could explode them, tearing me apart, if he wanted. That happened the first time I battled him, over a decade ago now, and was the first moment it occurred to me that even though my face was a creation that could bring humans to their knees, I was truly the one enchained, caught in a perpetual act of genuflection. These pathetic humans love my face, my gifts, my body, and so they've bound my limbs with these fetid, feral contracts requiring me to perform *good* acts for their benefit. And in exchange, what do I get? Money? Things? Human toys to act for my pleasure? Fame?

No. None of these things are what I really want. In meeting and battling the Marduk that very first time, seeing the way he carried himself, untethered by contracts and unburdened by the desire to please these pesky little human creatures, I understood for the first time that power is the ultimate goal. The Marduk may head the VNA, running and ruling his villains, but the Champions are all still governed by *humans*. Why is that, when we are the power holders? I want the power the Marduk possesses—but I want it over the COE, who's held my leash for so long. So I'm going to take it.

While I amass what I need to coup in the shadows, however, I still have to play the part of shimmering, shining hero. And I need these useless humans working for me to keep and hold my place in the hierarchy in the meantime. To best amass power, I need the humans to view me as irreplaceable.

But in the past four months, I've been effectively replaced by a pink goon and his stumbling, shy idiot—an idiot whose PR firm is making me the even greater fool.

Snarling, I hold Freddie's gaze for longer than I'm used to staring at most humans. I find their faces repulsive. So much sweat on their skin. Nervous tics and flinches. They exude uncertain energy at all times—uncertain about their standing among other humans, even less certain about me—and I find it exhausting. I may share the same skin they do for now, but once I get new skin, access to the full array of my potential powers, and my weapon, I will ensure I no longer have direct face-to-face dealings with humans going forward. Unless they get in my way.

I hiss between my teeth, "I'm not sure I can do worse."

Freddie's lips press together so tight, they disappear into his mouth. I cock my head toward the door.

"Simone, Simon," I bark, and my assistants open it automatically. Freddie glances over his shoulder at the pair, and I watch with a sick sort of satisfaction as his ego deflates. It makes me happy, watching egos get crushed like this. One of the few things that brings me any genuine pleasure these days.

"My mother always said, *'Even if you are caught in the mouth of a tiger, you will survive if you keep your calm.'* But *you* are the tiger, Taranis."

"Thank you." I offer him my most indifferent grin, no idea what he's talking about.

"Mark my words, Taranis: You will one day try to swallow the wrong person, and you will choke to death." He points his tablet in my direction, and I short the device for the simple spite of it. He won't notice it no longer works until he's long gone.

"Simon will escort you out," I say, waving my hand dismissively at the blond boy on the left side of the doorway.

Simon nods once and says in his usual soft, pliant voice, "Right this way, Mr. Yu."

He steers Freddie toward the door Simone holds propped open. It's heavy, but she doesn't falter, even though I can see her skinny arm shake. I grin—well, as close as I ever get to it. My lips are peeled back and my front teeth are bared; my back teeth are clenched. I watch the back of Freddie's head as he's escorted into the foyer, where Simon hands him his coat and takes him to the waiting elevator. The two men disappear.

"That's enough, Simone."

She closes the door and steps into my office fully. I don't miss the way she exhales and rolls out her shoulders.

"Who's next on the list?" I ask her—a question I should have probably found an answer to before firing my current PR director.

Simone diligently approaches and withdraws a piece of paper from the portfolio under her arm. She sweeps her short loc'd bangs out of her face. She keeps her locs tight and dyed a caramel color, styled in a bun on the back of her head. It contrasts nicely with her dark complexion. Inoffensive, not distracting, professional in every way. Outside of the goons assigned to me by the COE, she's the employee who's been with me the longest. Approximately eight months and counting. I wonder if she'll last the year. None of my other assistants ever have.

I take the paper she slides across my desk, which is made of concrete. The paper is mostly blank. I frown. "What is this?"

"This is the list of available PR firms that are COE approved that we could reach out to today to take on your contract."

COE approved. Because I need their fucking approval for everything. I snarl.

She hands me a second sheet with many more words scrawled down it in a list. Ninety percent of them are in red or orange.

"What's this?"

"The ones listed in orange are available firms with good reputations that are large enough to take on your contract but aren't approved by the COE . . ."

"And how long does approval take?"

"Four to six weeks. Usually companies have to submit a bid including a sample contract, short-term proposal, and a budget. They go back and forth with Mr. Singkham until eventually a contract is agreed upon, and only then will Mr. Singkham let you sit down and meet with them. The process could take months if you're unsatisfied with the first few clients they bring in."

Let you. The rest of the words blend and blur, but those two stand out in sharp clarity. Mr. Singkham letting me do anything feels . . . like something I should have taken care of a long time ago.

But I will. Soon.

I release a dissatisfied huff. Simone doesn't flinch. I'd like to keep her on, because she isn't skittish like so many others I've hired, but if she doesn't give me better news, and quickly, she's going to end up as collateral.

I clear my throat as I put the papers down and place my hands on top of them. However, before I can speak and send electricity skittering over her skin, Simone chooses that moment to stand up a little straighter, adjust the glasses balanced on the end of her nose, and save herself.

"I know it's not my place, Mr. Taranis, but I did have one other suggestion *not* on your list."

I wait. The rope of the guillotine is taut.

She sets down her binder and gestures at my newspaper-covered desk. "May I?"

I give a small tip of my head, and she moves rapidly, her fingers flitting over the papers, dragging a few of my *least* favorite to the top. The ones where the Wyvern shimmers in his new fucking suit, in his new fucking *skin*, his perfect little bride-to-be standing right beside him in half of them.

I grip the cold edge of my desk, wondering if I'll be able to break this one with a touch. I went through three wooden desks before I migrated to concrete. So far, it's held up to my ire. She better get to the fucking point.

"Look here." Her finger moves, not over the headlines but over the tiny, tiny text between the caption and the photograph that reads photo credit: Monika Neumann. "It's on every paper. Online publications too." She reaches into her pocket and withdraws her phone. She already has the latest headlines pulled up, and as she scrolls down, I notice that same name listed beneath every photo in every article.

"And their social media—well, his social media; hers is more personal—you can see here that his following had two major explosions. One after the Forty-Eight Hour Festival, when you were all photographed together and this image surfaced." A picture of the Wyvern, the pink monstrosity, staring down at Vanessa adoringly, his hand tipping up her chin as he leans down to kiss her. The worst part about the photo? You can see my blurry fucking outline in the background, talking to Ms. Lemon, the witch.

"And of course, his first major post. Three million likes. And this was *before* his transition, when he didn't have even ten percent of your following."

I know what photo she's going to show me next. It's a picture of the Wyvern as a Black man with glowing brown skin and fire in his gaze, traveling up a tunnel carrying no fewer than six humans draped over his broad frame. It was a daring rescue after an avalanche. I hadn't been called in for it, nor would I have wanted to go if I had been. But with power over fire, he'd been an easy candidate. And he'd delivered.

"All of the rescue photos were taken by the same person. She was on-site with him."

"In the snow?"

"Apparently, from the reports I've seen produced by The Riot Creative detailing the incident, she snuck into the tunnel after him."

I frown. "She could have died if the tunnel collapsed." Likely would have. Humans are so frail. Pathetic.

Simone nods. "Correct. She's known for taking big risks." She opens her little binder and pulls out a stack of photos—these featuring neither Champions nor villains.

"Jesus Christ," I mutter as I comb through the images. Some of them are . . . hard to look at. Even for me.

Armed militants wearing uniforms I don't recognize, whose badges are written in various scripts I don't speak, hunkered down behind large bags of sand, machine guns peeking out from over the tops. The camera nestled among the guns captures the moment a militant is shot in the head, eyes rolled back, blood spatter visible as it shoots out the back of his skull.

"For fuck's sake."

Another image shows the desert, soldiers posing next to the mutilated body of a man in a different uniform. I glance at another picture, this one of a white man with short blond hair and a filthy beard trapped in a tire. It's on fire.

"Get these off my fucking desk."

She does, gathering them up before setting others down in their place. "Those photos are all Monika's. She's a war photographer. They say she's the best of our generation. She has exhibits too." The new photos Simone shows me are mostly portraits taken from unusual angles or in the reflections of other objects.

"Your point? Other than to make me want to lose my lunch?"

She takes a fortifying breath and gathers all her glossy little pictures back up into her leather notebook, which she holds against her chest. "I think that with the right photographer, you might be able to use even the most average PR firm. After all, The Riot Creative is small. They may be good at what they do, but they aren't *that* good. The significant differential here might just be the right photo ops. A picture is worth a thousand words, but Monika's seem to be worth a million likes."

I flick my gaze up at Simone, thinking that in this moment, I *wouldn't* like to gut her. It's an odd feeling. "Good," I say.

She exhales, her lips twitching in the smallest makings of a smile.

"Very good, Simone."

By now, Simon has returned and stands just inside my office, clutching his own binder to his chest and watching his coworker in awe.

"Who is her present employer?" I ask.

"I'm not certain if she's on an independent contract or if she's a full-time employee of The Riot Creative, but they are her primary employer—not the COE."

"That'll make things easier."

"Yes, sir."

"Set it up."

"Do you want me to set up a meeting between the two of you in private first, or move directly into a contract buyout with The Riot Creative CEO?"

I sit up and make a frustrated sound. The backs of my hands crackle with blue energy. "I want to meet with Mr. Singkham and Ms. Theriot first."

"Of course," she says, not batting an eye even though that was not one of her two suggestions.

"And I want you"—I point at Simon—"to set up meetings with the next three PR directors on Simone's list. The short list, not the red one," I say, disgusted.

"Done."

"Go." I wave my fingers at Simone and Simon and, as they leave, lean back in my seat. I pull up Monika Neumann's social media, finding it surprisingly sparse of any personal content. It's mostly photographs advertising her gallery; each of them has thousands of likes.

There's the occasional shot of her posing in her gallery alongside others—posts that were clearly a collaboration. I find something off-putting about her as I swipe through one of the few self-portraits I find, though I'm not sure why. It's not her looks, which are predictably human and, in that, unexceptional.

She has dark-brown skin and evidence in her features of an East Asian heritage. Her hair is cut short, straight across at her chin and falls there in waves. She's got bangs, round cheeks, narrowed eyes, puffy lips, and a wide nose. A bigger girl, her tits and thighs are thick, and she's got a waist. In the self-portrait I'm staring at, she's wearing a short dress that hugs her body from cleavage to mid-thigh.

I don't see many curvy girls online dressing sexy, I realize with a frown. The few that pop up in my feed, which is dominated by news—news about *me*—are usually expertly dressed and covering up all their soft bits. But not Monika. She's not hiding. She's *confident*. More confident than I want her to be, given the conversation I'd like to have with her.

Returning to her self-portrait, I see that it's a brand deal she has with Nikon advertising some model of camera. The caption reads *Out from behind the lens*, and the first picture is of her, seated sideways on a fluffy ottoman so that her profile is visible. It's a black-and-white photograph, and she's looking into the distance at something that's got her smiling.

I roll my eyes. I mean, what's she possibly smiling at? Her horde of cats? She's got *cat lady* written all over her. The rest of the pictures in that gallery are all the same: annoyingly sentimental, making her look unusually confident, content, and even *sweet*. As if she likes the life she has and has the life she likes. I can't stand her already.

I'm about to exit the irritating app when I notice a single image that's *not* a photograph, but looks more like a flyer. Monika's face appears on the front, surrounded by a frame that is made to look like paper lanterns. I click on it.

> Bridging Cultures and Celebrating Success: Jinju Lantern Festival Kicks Off at the South Korean Embassy October 5th
>
> I am so excited to be joining Ambassador Min-hyuk at the Korean Embassy to celebrate the Jinju Lantern Festival kickoff this fall! I still can't believe I've been

> counted among the guests of honor alongside some of the most influential South Koreans living in the US—including one of my personal icons, Elizabeth Cho, who founded the Gallery Reconstruction Project to provide space, and funding, for emerging artists to get their start. I am a personal recipient of one of Cho's grants and can honestly say that I don't know where I'd be without them . . .

Yada yada.

> As well as supermodel Grier Kim-young, one of the first biracial Black Koreans I ever met, outside of my own family oc, and who I had the pleasure of photographing almost a decade ago now.
> Americans and Koreans and all are welcome! Come see me! I will be displaying some of my photographs as part of the South Korean Embassy's Bridging Cultures series . . .

"SIMON!" I shout, forgetting that I already dismissed him. I angrily send him a text, which he takes two full minutes to reply to. I frown. Simone would have been faster.

He calls me instead of texting. I pick up the phone, hostility clogging my throat, which diminishes only somewhat when he begins speaking in response to my text right away. "Yes, Taranis. I spoke with PR and there was an invitation sent to our team for the event, but they declined as it doesn't serve our interests."

Our. Our, our, our. Who the fuck is *our*?

"Would you like me to have them go back and accept?"

"Yes . . . no. No, actually. Don't change anything." My mind is working. I scroll back through her feed to the picture where she looks so happy, staring at her cats. "Check for me if Monika Neumann is single."

"She is."

"How do you know? Did you check?"

"Oh, I am . . . I, um . . . Well, you see . . . the thing is that I kinda asked her out when she was photographing you and the other Champions for the Forty-Eight Hour Festival shoot, and she, uh . . . she said she doesn't date."

Jesus Christ. I rub my hand down my face, wondering how it is that I ended up on this planet. Among all higher life-forms that exist across the galaxies, humans must surely be the dumbest. "And she wasn't just telling you that to get you to go away?"

"Well, I . . . have kind of been following her since. On socials. I mean . . . not in a creepy way. I just really like her photography . . ."

For the love of god—a.k.a. *me*.

"And no, she's not, um . . . seeing anybody."

"Good. Then get the other meetings set up. I have a plan."

Because a contract is always nice, but the real way to ensure a woman's cooperation is to approach her as a man—not that I am one of those. Human women are fickle and easy to manipulate, and it will be more effective to ensnare her through charm than through contracts. A little smile I've perfected over the years, and she'll be mine.

The COE will be mine.

Humanity will be mine.

As for the Marduk and the villains?

We'll either cement our alliance, or I'll move to plan B and kill him.

And this all begins by taking control of the news cycle, and Monika Neumann.

Chapter Two

MONIKA

"Hey, Monika, can you come in here for a second?"

I glance up from where I'm standing at Margerie's shoulder, poring over the images on her computer—pictures and videos I sent her over the past week. Tons of photos of behind-the-scenes wedding-planning blah. Even though it's not at all what I like documenting, I can't deny that these pictures are good, and that Vanessa's ecstatic *ooh*s and *ahh*s over every damn picture fill me with a simple kind of satisfaction.

She's not *ooh*ing and *ahh*ing now. Called away half an hour ago, she left her VP Margerie's office in good spirits. Now she's back and looking stressed.

"Uh, sure," I answer, confused by the strain on Vanessa's face. Her cheeks are pink, making her look younger than she is, her pretty brown curls full and windswept around her shoulders. She's wearing a demure dark-gray button-up and black slacks with just a touch of color on her nails, which are bright pink. She watches me from the doorway of Margerie's office like somebody's standing just out of sight with a gun to her head.

My short black hair tickles my jaw as I tilt my head, trying to make sense of what might have her so on edge—and more importantly, what it has to do with me.

Margerie hasn't looked up from her computer. "Go, go. You're no help anyway. You took all these superromantic pictures, but you don't even like any of them." She scoffs like it's criminal of me to not want to spend my days following Vanessa and Roland around from dress fitting to cake tasting, taking nauseatingly cute pictures of them smearing frosting on each other's cheeks. Cue shudder. *Cue jealousy.*

"I'm not a romantic," I grumble. "I don't like the hearts-and-flowers kinda stuff."

"I got that."

If she knew what I *did* like, she'd probably have even choicer words for me. Or take me straight to her church and drown me in a bucket of holy water. I don't know why it surprised me when I found out that Margerie goes to church. As she's a trans woman, I sort of assumed she wouldn't, and that got me realizing she was the first trans person I'd ever met, and that got me wondering if, despite being the daughter of a South Korean diplomat and a German with Malian roots, born in Seoul and raised in Berlin before immigrating to the United States for university, maybe I was a lousy citizen of the world? And then I realized I was being too hard on myself—I didn't have *any* friends. I'm a workaholic. And that got me depressed.

As a sexually active—my mother would say *promiscuous*—person, I didn't even have time to slot in the regular sexcapade these days. A hot, successful, single thirty-six-year-old who wasn't even getting laid? I wanted to weep. It's been six months since I last had sex, and even that was regrettable and forgettable. The woman did not eat the coochie—at least, not mine—and her strap-on game left a lot to be desired.

Now I'm following around a hot, happy couple getting ready to celebrate their love, trying to tell myself it isn't the worst thing in the world. I'm one of only thirty guests of honor invited by the South Korean ambassador to celebrate a major Korean cultural festival, and I don't even have a date. Womp, womp. Cue the world's tiniest violin.

"Monika?" Margerie glances over her shoulder at me, her red hair electric in the soft natural light streaming in through the picture window behind me. "Vanessa's been calling your name. You having an aneurysm? Because I can give Emily a ring. She's the COE doc."

I swat her on the back of the head and scowl, turning toward Vanessa and snapping out of my pity slump. "What's up?"

Vanessa's wearing a similar scowl to mine as she stares down at her phone. She tucks it into her back pocket and waves me toward her. "So . . ." Her voice falters as she escorts me out of Margerie's office through the bullpen. The Riot Creative offices currently occupy one floor, though they're expanding to take over the one beneath this one in the coming months. As part of that expansion, Vanessa's asked me about taking on another photographer to apprentice—an idea I abhor. I work alone.

And have no friends . . .

Or a date to the ambassador's party—an ambassador who is friends with my mom and won't hesitate to report back to Berlin that I showed up to the party of the century alone . . .

Scheiße.

"This isn't about the apprentice thing, is it?"

"No, no. No!" She shakes her head like she's shaking out of something, and looks at me askance. "You told me already you weren't into that. I wouldn't bully you or ask you again."

I blink at her, a bit stunned. She's so different from the other clients I typically work with, who are either hyperdemanding or don't know what they want and are happy with anything. Vanessa Theriot is smarter than she lets people know, highly strategic, and also *nice*. Most of the members of her team are. It's sick, really. I'm not used to being around such niceness. It makes my skin itch.

I smirk, my annoyance dissolving a little bit. "*Bully?* Have you ever bullied anyone in your life, Vanessa?"

She smiles, her eyes seeming to uncloud from whatever'd been bothering her. "I bully my brothers sometimes?"

"By 'bully,' you mean you ask them to do things for you and they do them?"

"Yeah?"

"Right." I laugh and shake my head as we arrive at the elevators. "That tracks. Where are we going?"

She huffs, "Well, here's the thing: It seems that your exclusivity clause to the Wyvern isn't as exclusive as we thought. Jem is reviewing our contract with the COE now, but there appears to be some fishy wording that basically gives Mr. Singkham the right to offer secondments to other Champions."

I frown. I had my own lawyers review the contract, and they didn't flag anything like that. Though . . . I can't say I'm *wholly* put off by the idea. If other Champions have work for me, it might be kinda nice to take a break from the wedding photography.

Keeping my voice neutral, I say, "Okay. Did they have anyone in mind?"

The elevator doors ding open. I step inside. I have chills on the backs of my arms, though I'm not sure why. I tend to run hot and am wearing a loose long-sleeve black shirt, but I'm feeling warmer and warmer the farther and farther up we go. Heat rises? Nah. That doesn't track.

"Well, we've gotten a few requests for you. Like the shoot you did for the Olympian after the Forty-Eight Hour Festival. That was ad hoc, and you were paid separate from our contract. The other, longer term requests, we've shot down—but there's one that's come through over the weekend that's been pretty . . ." Her face screws up.

"What?"

"Just . . . annoying. And Mr. Singkham is urging us to consider seconding you to him, or even splitting up your contract fifty-fifty."

"Who is it?"

Vanessa's gaze slides to mine. She's shorter than I am by a few inches, and almost dainty by comparison, but right now she's looking at me like she wants to fight. She reaches toward me—past me—and slams on the emergency stop. Red lights flare and a siren sounds. BEEDOOBEEDOOBEEDOO.

"What the fuck, Vanessa?!" I shout, slamming my hands over my ears.

"Frickity frick frick!" she screams. "I didn't know the alarm would go off!"

I turn toward the door and smash the bright-red button below the floor numbers, but the alarm doesn't stop and the flashing lights just flash brighter. "Fuck! It's broken."

"HELP IS ON THE WAY!" a robotic male voice shouts into the cacophony. *"HELP IS ON THE WAY!"*

Vanessa tries to reach the control panel but stumbles. "Waugh!" Her arms windmill, and as she falls, she headbutts the railing lining the wall.

"Oh shit!" I scramble over to her as she hits the ground and rolls onto her back. Beneath the blazing red lights, I can already see a purple welt forming in the center of her forehead.

"Is it gonna leave a mark?" she wheezes.

"Uh . . . no. No, definitely not." Dropping to my knees, I scramble over her, accidentally kneeing her in the gut.

"Ooph!" she gasps.

"Sorry!" I shout over the alarm. I crawl to the opposite wall and reach for the phone hidden beneath a glass panel I didn't notice before. "CAN YOU TURN OFF THE FUCKING ALARM! We pushed the button by mistake!" I scream into the receiver.

"HELP IS ON THE WAY! HELP IS ON THE WAY!"

Meanwhile, static crackles over the line, and all of a sudden, the elevator jerks beneath me. "Fuck." I look at Vanessa, my heart in my ears.

She's got tears in her eyes, likely from the pain of trying to brain herself on the wall. I've seen this girl fall over flat surfaces too many times to count. The fact that she's still alive is a testament to the Wyvern's superhuman ability. "Are we gonna die because I pushed the button?" she mouths, though I can only half hear her over this infernal racket.

The elevator jerks again, and my stomach pops up into my throat before I get a chance to answer her. Then BAM! The lights and the siren and all the power goes out. *Scheiße!* We're shrouded in darkness. I wasn't panicking before, but I'm panicking now. The silence is pronounced now that the siren is dead, and I fucking hate the dark.

When I was on assignment in the DRC, covering the governmental takeover of Goma by rebel militants, the DRC army convoy I'd been traveling with was overtaken, and I survived along with two other soldiers by first running for our lives and then hiding out in a large concrete drainpipe in the ground for two days.

That was my last assignment in active combat zones. After that, I started working for an American newspaper covering mostly riots, protests, and the occasional political event. That's also how I was reconnected with South Korean Ambassador Min-hyuck. A close personal friend of my mother's, the two women worked together when the ambassador was stationed in Germany almost two decades ago.

The moment I decided to leave combat zones behind me, much to my parents' collective relief, my mom contacted Ambassador Min-hyuck, who started hiring me exclusively for all her major events—an agreement we still have, though now I only accept when her events don't interfere with my work at the COE.

"Scheiße," I whisper, and the memory of that smell in that tunnel of our collective stink drags me back to another place, another time. I hear gunfire, the explosion of the IED that took out our truck in the first place. I flinch. My bones all lock. My heart slams against my sternum. I feel the pressure start to close in and can hear Vanessa speaking, but only at a distance.

"Are you okay?"

I nod, but my fucking throat is clogged. My mind is clear. Rational. Knows that I'm not where my body feels that I am, but when the elevator next lurches and Vanessa screams, I can feel that sinister drag, *like the drag of a mutilated body through sand, still unfortunately breathing—click click, I take his picture, and with his remaining energy he looks at me like I'm a viper.* Sweat breaks out on my forehead, and I drop the phone. It dangles from the coiled black cord uselessly *like a corpse hanging from a telephone pole in Gaza. The body is Palestinian, hung there by Israeli troops after a broken ceasefire. I don't know much behind the politics. I just stand beneath the swinging sandaled feet, looking up through my lens, and shoot.*

"Let me see if I have service and try to call—" Vanessa starts, but before she can finish her sentence, and before I lose myself entirely to the mist, the massive elevator doors start to crunch . . . crunch . . . crunch open.

Light.

I blink against it. Yellow mingling with an even brighter blue. I look toward it like it's salvation.

We're halfway between floors and, like a good millennial, all I can think about is *Final Destination 2,* until the blue light fades and I can actually see our savior. Then I can't think of anything at all. My brain is stolen right out of my skull, all the juicy bits and thinking parts gone.

Crouched there on the floor above, head ducked so he can look in at us, is *not* the fire-breathing-almost-Mr.-Vanessa-Theriot-superbeing I expected to have found us. Instead, my heart is arrested and my budding panic attack is crushed by the most beautiful face I've ever seen in real life.

Since the Forty-Eight Hour Festival shoot, I've seen him only one time, and in passing in the lobby of his apartment building—and mine. We damn near collided with one another, but he elegantly sidestepped me, while I lost my balance and crashed into our doorperson, Taylor's, desk. Even though he'd seen me just a week before, there was no recognition in his eyes at all.

But he sees me now. And it's rearranging my insides.

His vivid purple eyes stare straight into my soul, picking it apart, finding and rooting out all the loose strands holding it together and pulling. Hard. I'm so glad I'm already on my knees, hanging on to the wall for dear life, because when he winks at me and says, "Hey, beautiful, you need saving?" my soul simply dissolves.

"What?" I say, reduced to my mushy parts.

"Taranis," Vanessa spits, sounding decidedly less enthusiastic than I feel.

"What?" I repeat, this time to her, even though I'm utterly incapable of breaking Taranis's gaze. It's fixed on me, so soft and sweet it feels depraved.

"Taranis is the one trying to steal your contract."

"What?" I say for the third time. I turn to see her moving up into a standing position, but as soon as she's upright, the entire elevator car lurches again. She stumbles, knocking the back of her head against the wall.

"Sorry about that," Taranis says.

"Ssi-bal." I glance at her feet. Crap on a stick, she's not even wearing heels. I tsk. "Roland is gonna freak out when he sees your face. Stop hurting yourself."

"The fuck?" a gravelly voice roars, lacking all the smooth, silky edges of Taranis's voice. A pink shadow appears behind Taranis. "You hurt Vanessa?"

Claws appear on Taranis's shoulder, the charcoal gray clashing with the subdued colors of his clothing. Taranis rolls his eyes. "I did no such thing. You've been with me the entire time."

The elevator lurches down another inch. Vanessa falls again. "Stop messing with the elevator!" she groans, rubbing her back where she slammed into the rail.

"Taranis is helping us, Roland, calm down! Without him, we'd still be stuck, slowly going insane." In my case, rather quickly.

With a few final grumbles, the Wyvern backs off, claws slowly uncurling from Taranis's shoulder. In the meantime, I amble to my own feet, trying to be graceful because I can still feel his eyes on me.

"Thank you, Ms. Neumann." Ms. Neumann. He knows my name. Holy shit. "And *stealing* is a harsh word, Ms. Theriot. I'm only requesting we share her." There's something so deeply salacious in the way he says the word *share,* it leaves my stomach cramping. I should just lie down.

Vanessa doesn't seem to have the same reaction. She scoffs, impervious. "You don't share. Not according to any of the contracts you have with the COE."

"I'm willing to learn new things."

"Since when? You've been filing complaints with Mr. Singkham against the Wyvern ever since he reverted—"

"That's only my PR team. And can you blame them? Your team has been making them look awful," he interrupts with a laugh, and I jolt at the sound. Deep and smooth, with just the slightest smoky-whiskey edge. It's not possible for a man's laugh to be that attractive. Like a long-dead composer scribbled out his most beautiful score in the margins of this man's voice—this being, this *super*being. It shouldn't be allowed. Yet here he is, laughing again as he holds on to the jammed door, leans across the divide into the elevator, and offers Vanessa his hand.

"Roland can help me," she says, surprisingly rudely—for her, anyway.

"So little trust. I did just save you from going insane, didn't I?" He winks at me.

Vanessa still hesitates.

Taranis rolls his eyes. "Considering the Wyvern's powers aren't exactly helpful here, I encourage you to see reason. I can either get you out safely, or he can help by turning the elevator into a kiln."

"Ugh. Fine," Vanessa mumbles.

"Wait!" I hiss, lunging to intercept Vanessa just as Taranis grabs her wrist. "Haven't either of you seen *Speed*?" Both of them stare at me like I've lost my marbles. "Or *Final Destination 2*? Come on, you have to know what I'm talking about. Don't get split in half!"

Vanessa's hand is locked in Taranis's, and they both give me a funny look.

"I . . ." I start, but no other words come out as Taranis's brows suddenly soften and his perfect, blemish-free light-brown skin smooths. So perfect he could be carved from stone, he makes Michelangelo's *David* look like a pox-riddled Pilgrim.

"Actually, maybe she has a point." Vanessa extracts her grip from Taranis's and glances at the opening around his body. "Maybe we should wait for maintenance."

"As you wish, my ladies." Taranis's eyes flare, and he winks at me again. He has naturally thick, curly eyelashes. Perfect eyebrows. I feel weirdly self-conscious of my unplucked brows, and rub the heels of my hands over them before carding my fingers through my hair. I remember I haven't washed it in two weeks. It's greasy at the roots and dry at the ends. What a splendid combination. Also, if I was warm before, I'm sweating now. *Sweating* sweating. Like I just ran laps. Taranis smiles wider, his head slightly cocked.

The elevator lights suddenly turn back on, with no bright flares or concerning adjustment period. Just off . . . then on. The sound of machines working whir to life, and with one short jolt down, followed by a smooth rise up, we're suddenly at the floor Taranis is kneeling on. The elevator dings to announce our arrival.

Taranis is still on the ground on one knee, a dangerous position for me to see him in after having spent so much time reviewing engagement photos this past week. I stuff my sweaty palms into the pockets of my cargo pants, unable to break his gaze, even as Vanessa skips past me into the open and waiting arms of her giant pink monster.

His horns almost touch the high ceilings, and when he catches her against his chest, which is so thick that it looks like he's smuggling barrels, she looks half his size. It's kinda hot. I've never felt particularly dainty at five nine, size 16, and usually end up sleeping with women smaller than me or dudes who weigh as much or less than I do, but I imagine that it might be fun to be tossed around by arms that thick just once.

"Does the dress fit, Monika Kim?" My mom always calls me by her last name whenever speaking with me. My dad finds it adorable, like a pet name, since in Korea we don't have many of those for parents to use to refer to their children. But I always felt like it sounded scolding, even when I was a child. Now even more so as I remember an unanswered text on my phone. My mom sent me a dress to wear to the event. Size 6. Burn. Burn burn burn. Even with his powers over fire, the Wyvern doesn't touch my mother when it comes to fire.

"You won't get cut in half now. I promise." Taranis stands and reaches toward me. The fool that I am, I forget to wipe my sweaty palm before I take his smooth, dry, massive hand in mine.

The moment our fingers touch, I swallow a gasp behind sealed lips, pressed together so tight that it hurts. Holy shit. A surge of energy tunnels from his skin into mine. Maybe he's electrocuting me?

He clears his throat, the connection severed with the loss of our touch. He frowns briefly before sucking in a quick breath and turning those glowing purple eyes back up to mine. He smiles. "Monika, I know we've met before, but I'd like to reintroduce myself." He guides me out of the elevator by gently pressing his hand to my lower back.

He's taller than I am. Not by a foot or two, like the Wyvern is compared to Vanessa, but a good distance. It feels nice. So does that gentle stirring, a low current unlike the heat it had been before. It stirs my gut and my conscience as a sweet realization sweeps me. A damning one. Whatever he's going to say next, he already has me. I'm a fly sucking the nectar without realizing I'm already caught in the trap. Or maybe even worse—I do realize it, and I'm totally fine with whatever happens next.

"I'm Taranis. I've been admiring your work for a while, and I'd really like to work with you. I'm not trying to poach you, as Ms. Theriot would have you believe," he says with another of those deeply charismatic chuckles that make my knees turn to soup. "But I have an upcoming assignment, and even though it might be a little dangerous, I think . . ." He drones on and on, but it doesn't matter. It really doesn't.

Working with Taranis closely *and* doing something dangerous? The latter would have had me alone. And then he has to go and kill me stone dead.

In his sweet, sweet voice, Taranis says, "I also was invited to the South Korean Embassy for the Jinju Lantern Festival kickoff next month. I saw your name listed among the guests of honor and . . . I know I'm not Korean, and I don't want to take the spotlight away from any talented Koreans in attendance, like yourself, but I was thinking since you're already going I might come with you . . . as your date?" He clears his throat, sounding just the right amount of contrite for me to know this is real and not some crazy ploy to get me to take the bid. "Sorry. I know that's insanely forward and you're likely already taking someone, given, I mean . . ." He glances down my body. I'm wearing a baggy black shirt, chunky black sneakers, and fucking cargo pants. "Sorry. I take it back. Of course you have a date already . . . boyfriend. Are you married? I'm so sorry. I didn't see a ring. I—"

"I WILL GO WITH YOU AS A DATE." I say the words at maximum volume, which is strange because I'm speaking in a normal-ish tone. The whole thing is a disaster coated in chain mail. I can't break through the compulsion to keep talking as loud as I possibly can and say, "SORRY. YES. SORRY."

He blinks at me, but he's somehow smiling anyway. "Yeah?" he says, his eyes aglitter. It takes me that moment to notice he's wearing a pale baby blue sweater, beneath the V of which I can see a silver strand glimmer, tan pants, matching baby-blue-and-tan sneakers, and a watch layered among other chunky silver bracelets that collectively look more expensive than my most expensive lens—hell, more expensive than all of them, plus my car.

"And what about coming with me on this mission? It's dangerous, I'll remind you, but I've seen some of your other photographs, and compared to what you went through in the Democratic Republic of the Congo, Syria, or Afghanistan, it should be nothing."

"Oh yeah. Yes. Definitely. I'd love to."

"Monika!" Vanessa's voice is shrill, and I jolt, looking past Taranis at Vanessa standing there with her hands on her hips. "You can't just say yes. You need to see the terms!"

What? Wait. What am I doing? I shake my head. "Of course. I, um . . . will need to talk about it with my lawyer," I say to Taranis. "Not the date part, but the pictures . . . I just need some time to consider . . ."

But he's already pulling something out of his back pocket. I don't get a glance at it before he leans in and brushes his lips over the upper shell of my ear. He puts the smooth, dry paper in my hand. A pen finds its way to my other hand, and a shiver travels between the paper and the pen up through my hands that expands throughout my entire body when his fingertips graze the outsides of my arms.

My eyes all but roll back. No person on this planet has ever had this effect on me. So I don't hear Vanessa or the Wyvern or even the warning sirens between my own temples blazing. Instead, I sign where he points.

He takes the paper back. And right before he brushes a dry kiss over my cheek, he says, "No, you don't."

Chapter Three

Taranis

That was too easy.

Chapter Four

Monika

The disappointment on Vanessa's face was a real test of my resolve after we sat down and worked out a new schedule—that was after Jem, the in-house Riot Creative attorney, about had a heart attack when she saw the amended contract I'd signed while lost in Taranis's pearly purple gems. And his touch. That was some freaky shit. I've never touched Roland directly and have half a heart to ask Vanessa if that's what it feels like anytime she touches him. But right now, with the sour, disappointed way Vanessa looks at me, I'm not asking her shit.

I'm in the doghouse.

The contract I signed was stupendously stupid.

Among the other challenges dealing with my time and how Taranis wants to handle competing requests is the fact that he gets first right of refusal of all the photos I take of him.

If I was working with an independent client looking to get photos taken outside of action settings, like a portrait, that setup would be the norm. But when I'm taking pictures in action settings and dealing with clients repped by agencies and brands, it's usually up to the brand, the firm, the organization, and the company to determine which photos will be used. It's strange even that Taranis's contract with the COE doesn't include that clause. That he somehow got so many personal amendments granting him so much autonomy.

Because the superheroes are all technically brands of the COE, I send the pictures I take to the PR teams for those Champions directly—like I do with Vanessa and the Wyvern—and those teams decide which photos to keep, post, share with media outlets, and sell to other distributors. That's not my bag. I don't care.

But . . . I do care if my pictures may be hitting the interwebs hours or even days after the events I'm photographing take place. My job as a photographer for the COE—why I took the full-time contract in the first place—is to be *the* cutting-edge documentarian of the most amazing actions of the Forty-Eight. And I can't really do that if I'm not able to share any of the pictures I take—or share them late.

But it's fine. I'm sure it's fine. Taranis is so nice. I'll talk to him, to his team. It's been ten days and I haven't gotten to meet anyone from that team yet, but I'll have to eventually—today, hopefully.

I glance at my phone again. It's five till five. A car is supposed to pick me up at five exactly. The message I got last Friday from someone named Simone read:

"First assignment Tuesday. Pick up at five."

I have no idea what the assignment is, and I'm a little frustrated I haven't gotten a brief, that the only details I *have* heard were from Taranis himself when I made the potentially poor and very clearly libido-driven decision to sign a paper without reading it and join this escapade, which he called *dangerous* and nothing else. If I hadn't spent the last week bored out of my mind, I would have reneged. As it is, my boredom is apparently stronger than my pride. My libido is, too, but I've known that for a long time.

I have my camera bag holstered, but I wear my Nikon Z9 fitted with a 50mm lens around my shoulder like a cross-body bag. It's good for night shots, which I *assume* I'll need, given the hour of my pickup, but just in case, I've got a zoom lens in my bag, another Nikon Z9, a 24mm lens, and a 200mm lens, plus my Nikon Zfc with a 16mm lens in my cargo pants as a backup and my iPhone in my other pocket as my backup to my backup.

I fiddle with my camera strap. I'm wearing all black again and the exact same camera I wore when I went on my first mission with the Wyvern. He hadn't reverted yet. He was just a guy with scraggly hair, a scruffy beard, zero fashion sense, and total dominion over fire. He'd used that incredible power and his superhuman strength to rescue dozens of people trapped beneath an avalanche like it was no big deal. He hadn't taken any interviews afterward. Hadn't wanted to pose for photos with the saved. He'd only wanted to get back to Vanessa. I don't meet many like him in my profession.

That mission was my first foray back into action photography—something war journalism–adjacent. And even though I'd since accompanied the Wyvern on a few other missions—and the Olympian on one—they'd all paled in comparison. Surrounded by all that snow, my pulse pounding as I snapped shot after shot, I'd felt . . . home. Which is why, despite my irritation and mounting misgivings, I don't hesitate to pick up the phone on the first ring when I see an unknown number flash across it at 5:00 p.m. exactly.

"Here," a male voice says, one I've never heard before.

My adrenaline surges and I slide off the eccentric cushioned yellow stool at my kitchen island, knock twice on the butcher-block countertop for good luck, and head to the elevator, which opens up directly into my foyer. My flat is bigger than I need, but once I saw that elevator setup, like a ritzy penthouse, I couldn't help but put in an offer.

I hit the lobby with a spring in my step. "See you later, Taylor!" I shout at the door attendant.

Most folks think of a door attendant as an old Alfred type. At least, that's what I expected. I didn't expect the morose, black-wearing, Wednesday Addams equivalent who greeted me on my first day here with a sneer. Taylor is Eeyore, if Eeyore were a Black nonbinary twentysomething with a straight black bob and a little more sass.

They look at me with a flat grimace. "What are you so excited about?"

"I've got a date!"

Taylor gives me their drollest look—probably the most personality I've seen from them this week. "With who?"

"Danger!"

Taylor sulks and turns back to lean their forearms on their desk, all gleaming white marble in this opulent lobby. They huff out the side of their mouth, tufts of black hair blowing away from their face. "Boring."

I laugh as I reach the revolving doors. *"Mein Gott, ich hoffe nicht."* I wink back at Taylor over my shoulder and shout, "Don't wait up!"

"Your enthusiasm sickens me." Their dismay chases me out into the warm, windy night.

Pushing my hair back from my face, I come to a quick stop at the sight of the massive dark-green Humvee double-parked in front of my building. It isn't that I've never been in a Humvee before—I have. It's that, usually, the vehicles I travel in tend to match their surroundings. A well-marked press van in Gaza. A beat-up Toyota on the streets of Port-au-Prince. A bulletproof SUV during riots in Tehran.

But a matte-green Humvee elevated above all the other cars on the block of sunny Sundale? I snort. The sun is still lingering in the sky as it makes its slow descent, and the bright orange of the sunset glints against the black windows. Overkill, much? But when the back door opens and a tan face pops out and waves at me angrily, I roll my eyes and jump in.

"Hi," I say to the man sitting beside me and the backs of the heads in front of me. All men. All armored and armed. All wearing black except for the man in the passenger's seat wearing a shimmering baby-blue uniform. He doesn't turn around when I get in the car. None of them do. The faceless driver just pulls away from the curb, and we go rumbling down the road.

Since no one bothers acknowledging me, I don't say more. If that surprises any of the men in the car, it shouldn't. I've been into battle before, and I've been around men going into battle before—if that's what this is—and I know how this all works. The machismo and testosterone aren't worth beating a head or a fist against, so I've learned to read the air and get what I need in as few words as possible.

"Gear?" I say to the guy seated next to me. He's a Hispanic man underneath all that black fabric, and gives me a mean look.

"You were late."

I wasn't, but I don't respond to that. "Do I need a vest or not?"

"Give her her fucking gear, or am I gonna have to hear her ask a third goddamn time?" The voice that lashes out into the car startles me. I don't recognize it, and I glance around like I'm looking for speakers through which this terrible voice sounds. "Fucking incompetent pill-popping jocks. Don't even know why the COE bothers sending you sorry fucks. You only ever slow me down or get in my way."

Unlike me, these men don't seem to understand that arguing with a man is pointless, especially one who sounds like the prickliest of all pricks. The one in the driver's seat says, "We're with the SDD, not the COE, and we're here to protect you."

The voice scoffs, and it's a bitter, angry sound that I feel all the way in the depths of my chest. My mom may not talk nice to me all the time, but she's never sounded half as violent as this. "Tell that to the last SDD *bro* with a missing leg."

"We're not even here for you," says the guy next to me, and as he leans forward, I realize two things: He's speaking to the guy in the passenger's seat, and that guy is Taranis.

Whaaa . . . ?

"This is a simple fucking power grid fix. We're here to make sure you don't blow anything up you're not supposed to, and make sure *she* stays safe." The guy next to me jerks his thumb over his shoulder toward me, clearly considering me a nuisance. "And that she stays out of the way and doesn't take pictures of anything she shouldn't."

"The SDD isn't happy with her on your tail," the driver adds.

"I don't work for them. Now, stop fucking talking. Can't stand the sounds you make. And when we get to the train station, keep your goddamn guns holstered. Don't need to get accidentally shot by one of you trigger-happy fuckers."

The guy next to me slams his elbow into his door as he leans back. Not sure if it's intentional or accidental, but it punctuates his next words when he says, "You keep it up and you just might."

Taranis snorts and looks over his shoulder at the man on my left. The expression on his face is utterly mesmerizing, only because I don't recognize it. Like the voice that spoke earlier, the one that's *his*, there isn't one single thing about it that harkens back to the man—the *male*—who rescued me from the elevator, who I've seen before a handful of times, who I've photographed laughing alongside other Champions who aren't half as charismatic.

I blink and keep blinking, watching as Taranis's eyes glow a cataclysmic purple, the buttons on the dashboard brightening with them. I suddenly worry about the cell phone in my pocket and remove it, slipping it into the seat back in front of me, rather than risk carrying it or putting it in my pack, where it might explode.

Taranis's voice bottoms out into the lowest whisper, "You think your friend lost his leg by *accident*?" He chuckles and turns to face forward.

All the words thrown back and forth are hard to absorb. I hesitate, wanting to document the look—that exact look—on Taranis's face, but he's turned forward again, and I get the feeling that this version of him isn't something he'd approve of being published to the world. And if his last words rang with even a hint of truth, I'd also like to keep both my legs.

I'm nervous at the sudden way my reality has been tipped, but as the man sitting beside me hands me a bulletproof vest marked Press, I, too, become a different me as I slip it over my head and fasten it tight around my body. I pin my hair back with thick silver clips while the adrenaline in my body thickens my blood to molasses. Everything slows. We drive for another half an hour in silence before we pull into an underground parking garage in East Sundale, one that was once used for commuters traveling to and from Old Sundale Station.

Fifty years ago, this area was the center of commerce, and Old Sundale Station was the city's primary train station. Then the Forty-Eight were discovered, and Sundale bid to have the US regional Champions' offices here. Sundale beat out larger cities, but the influx of new commerce—plus the COE headquarters themselves—required more space than what the then–city center could afford. So they moved Sundale twenty miles west, and what was once known as Sundale became East Sundale. Just like that. Because Taranis's pod fell right in the middle of Sundale, in Memory Park, and the world loved him first and loved Sundale for the happy accident. Back when he was a boy and I was a girl with posters of him on my wall, taking portraits with a disposable camera.

The car bounces over potholes and trash spread out over the ground of the entrance in a thick blanket, as if placed there intentionally to ward off newcomers. Now Old Sundale Station is known to be a hub for squatters and even a meeting spot for gangs and other criminals. The parking garage even has its own name: the Gallery. A name I find particularly fitting, given my background, as we enter it.

A bottle or two hits the outside of the Humvee as we descend to the lower levels of the garage. I feel like Judge Dredd making his way through Mega-City One. I snap a few pictures through the windows. They won't render well, and I likely won't use them unless this turns into a longer story and some outlet, or the COE itself, wants to use these photos to set the scene. Though if this is really only about restoring the electrical grid for the Old Station—why it's out, I've got no clue, and why any higher-ups would order it turned on, given that the station is no longer in use, I've got no clue either—I can't imagine these pictures will be of much use for anything.

"Taking pictures of the dark there, sweetheart?" the guy next to me says. I can feel the energy radiating off him, and want no part of it, so I just ignore him and keep my focus on the world outside the thick glass window.

As the car finally slows, coming to a stop on the lowest level of this subterranean city, a dozen people skitter out of the rays of the Humvee headlights before the car stops, the headlights power off, and Taranis opens his door. I follow.

My feet hit the concrete, and my adrenaline has fully settled. I've got the resting heart rate of a sea turtle. I've got my camera bag looped over my back, my zoom lens and my 200mm lens in my cargo pocket—though I don't expect to be able to use the latter in this low-light setting—and the 50mm lens attached to the Nikon around my neck. Fearing Taranis's explosivity, I'd left my iPhone back in the car, which means I'm relying solely on my smaller Nikon Zfc, now safely tucked into the front of my Kevlar as a backup.

Farther away, I can see folks watching us around the lit rings of open fires, some in trash cans, some set up in metal dishes of all kinds. There must be two hundred people down here.

I snap a few shots with my 50 while the driver, a dark-skinned man who's almost as tall as Taranis, moves ahead of our cluster to the wide service doors. He has a key.

"Come on, *Press*." A fist shoves me from the back, and I stumble toward the dark opening beyond the doors. I don't let him get a rise out of me. Taranis, even though he sees, sneers at the guy—or maybe at the both of us—but says nothing.

Taranis steps through the doorway first. I follow, the dickwad right behind me. The driver with the key is last to enter the service corridor before shutting and locking the door behind us.

Lights flicker on, illuminating the darkness. Recessed high in the walls, only half seem to have bulbs, but even the broken bulbs are still glowing—purple. Taranis glows the same color too. I take a few pictures, watching the tall, athletically built superperson walk down the wide, dry corridor like he's bored, even though, in the distance, you can hear all kinds of sounds that would make a grown man piss if he were caught here alone. Wailing, the sound of a faraway engine running, a cough, a scream, a thud.

The wide corridor has no places to branch off and makes no turns. Eventually, we're spit out through a set of service doors that match the first we passed through, and I'm shocked to see the world open up before us and so glad that I came on this assignment, even if it's just routine electrical work.

The Old Sundale train station is beautiful.

The space is half the length of a football field, and the glass ceiling vaults high above our heads. Most of the ceiling is still intact, but there are a few panels missing, letting in the cool night air. Moonlight streams in. It looks to be full from where it hangs directly above us, partially obscured by clouds.

I snap a few photos, spellbound by the space, until I remember who I'm *actually* here to photograph: Taranis. The Champion in front of me with the attitude so sour he's either having a really, really bad day, or he's the world's most clever con artist.

Turning my gaze to ground level, I watch as Taranis struts out across the tiled floor. It's covered in debris, a few dried leaves, plastic bags, scattered trash, a few broken bricks that look like they might have fallen from the ceiling. It doesn't matter what's covering the floor, though. He could be wading through knee-high shit and still look like the King of Olympus. That was Zeus, wasn't it? Wielder of lightning? Seems fitting.

I glance at a couple photos I've taken and silently toot my own horn. The exposure on these, with moonlight cascading over his glittery uniform, is exquisite. The impulse to send them right away to Vanessa and her team is strong, but I have to keep reminding myself that this isn't the Wyvern, that Taranis has his own PR team, and that sending anything to anyone right away isn't part of the agreement.

I linger near the door, waiting and watching. One of the guys—the dickwad from the back seat—shouts, "Mind giving us some light?"

Taranis makes a disapproving click that would have given my Korean *halmeoni* a run for her money. At the same time, lights around the perimeter of the room start to buzz and emit a bright-purple glow.

Taranis's skin illuminates in tandem, and small sparks of electricity flare over his skin, across his back, over his shoulders, and down his arms to his exposed hands, which flex and clench automatically. I capture it all, watching in fascination as he makes his way right, toward the dark opening where trains once came and went.

Shaped like a backward D, the curved edge of the room to my left is where the entrances to the train station once were, a few staircases leading up to broad landings where coffee shops and restaurants once sat. It's immediately clear why we came in through the strange entrance in the lowest, scariest level of the Gallery. The entrances to the Old Station aren't just boarded up; they're boarded up and reinforced from the inside with huge concrete barriers. Between the boarded-up doors and the barriers are piles of barbed wire. It looks like some folks tried to make it through at some point and stopped. There are a few sections where the boarded doors are broken inward, but nowhere where the barbed wire or concrete barrier has been breached.

"According to the map, the main breakers are in a room a tenth of a mile down that tunnel," the driver says. He points down the left-branching train tunnel. It's pitch black until Taranis illuminates the light bulbs recessed into those walls. Still, there aren't many of them. I can't see more than twenty, thirty feet, maybe, down the tunnel before it curves away.

"Let's get this done quick," the dickwad says.

"I'm not a fucking electrician," Taranis spits. "I can restore power to the grid surrounding the station, but as soon as it trips again, it'll just go back out. And I'm not gonna fucking come down here every goddamn day to reset it."

"Nobody gives a shit," dickwad continues, approaching the edge of the platform. "This is for a PR stunt *you* requested: *Taranis gives light to the people living in darkness.* Your girl is gonna snap a few pictures, and then we can go. Nobody cares if the Gallery doesn't have power tomorrow."

My sneakers plod quietly over dusty tiles as I follow the trio. I capture Taranis's angry look as he glares at the SDD men, and capture as the two men jump off the platform down onto the concrete between the tracks. As I take their picture, I frown, noticing something odd. I double-check the viewfinder. Huh. In the photo, I can see footprints in the dust on the ground between the tracks. Fresh footprints. Fresh ones *not* left by either SDD goon or Taranis.

I open my mouth, then snap it shut, debating whether to speak up or not. I'm not an operative on this mission. I'm only a photographer. It's a difficult position to remember to be in. Press is there to see and record, not change. Watching people brutalized by police during riots. Watching gangs burn down schools. Watching the Wyvern carry bodies through those icy tunnels . . . struggling. It's hard not to help. But that's not my role.

"Got something to say, pip-squeak?" the dickwad says, looking up at me over his shoulder.

I didn't realize I'd made a sound. I hesitate, then eventually ask, "Are there people living down here?" My voice echoes.

"Nobody down here but us."

"What about those footprints?" Standing at the edge of the platform now, I gesture ahead of the men. They go quiet as they examine the disrupted dust between the tracks.

Taranis hasn't said anything at all for the past several moments, but he abruptly cuts in now. "Where are the rats?"

The question confuses me, though I don't voice that confusion. Instead, the driver asks, "What?"

"Is this a trap? Did the SDD put you up to this?"

"What are you talking about?" the driver says with a sharp shake of his head. "Do you see something?" He draws his gun. I take a picture as he points it down the tunnel.

Taranis stands a few feet down the platform from where I do, and ignores the SDD guys in favor of shouting down the tunnel, "Do you want a show? Is that what this is about?" His face roars with brilliant color, the lights in his eyes and under his skin beaming like lavender sapphires. The lights lining the tunnel crackle. So does the electric third rail. Orange sparks fly off it, causing both men to jump.

The driver hisses between bared pearly white teeth, "Stand down, Taranis!"

But Taranis isn't listening. Instead, he's rising into the air, floating like he's suspended by strings. "You want a show, I'll give you a fucking show! Come into the light, you duplicitous freak!"

I drop my camera bag, pull out my other Z9, quickly set up a tripod, and start capturing video from the platform. Nothing happens. Taranis continues to hover there, staring angrily down the tunnel. Leaving my bag behind and proceeding with only my primary camera and the backup in my Kevlar, I drop down from the platform onto the tracks and wait . . . and wait . . .

Just as I start to think Taranis may, in fact, be a total and complete crazy person, I hear it. A faraway sound that sends chills crawling from the crown of my head down my shoulders, to my spine. *It's a giggle.* A woman's giggle, so light and innocent it makes her sound like a child.

Taranis flies forward, moving with a speed that would shock me were I not built as battle hardened as a tank. Instead, I move forward at the fastest speed I can. I shove past the two idiots, slightly concerned at being shot from the back and hoping to high hell this vest protects against machismo and stupidity as well as bullets as I dart into the darkness.

The purple lights still glow against the walls but are spaced so far apart I have to pass through rings of darkness to reach the next. It eerily feels like I'm descending into Dante's inferno as I blast forward, stale air stroking my face. The volume ahead increases, as do the sounds of running feet at my back. Behind me, I can hear Tweedledee and Tweedledum struggling to catch up, and ahead, I can hear the sounds of a battle beginning. Taranis's cries are punctuated by a woman's wild laughter, and I know before I round the next corner *exactly* who's making a sound so haunting.

Taranis hovers at a fork in the tunnel, brawling with another hovering superbeing—a villain who is one of the most feared—while a second villain, the one who'd been making that awful giggling sound, stands on the ground, looking up at the pair with a smile. *Bia.*

Bia was among the first unaffiliated Forty-Eight that the Champions and villains actually campaigned over in a real battle of the brands. With power over animals, the COE called her Aja, named after an orisha associated with nature. They offered her millions and millions of dollars, but whatever the VNA gave her she liked better. In less than a week, she dropped the name Aja and announced herself to the world as Bia, who in Greek mythology is the personification of violence. The news never was able to unveil what exactly the Marduk had offered her to join the VNA, but she's been one of his closest allies ever since.

I come to a dead stop, drop to one knee, and snap her photograph. That's when I notice that while she's just standing there, she's not doing *nothing*. There's a sound . . . a horrible tittering, clattering, scraping sound—a subtle white noise behind the much louder sounds of violence coming from the villain and the Champion tearing each other to pieces thirty feet from me. All around Bia's feet, an army of *rats* is forming. *Mi-chi-nyeon.*

I lower my camera from my right eye just in time to catch Bia's maniacal gaze. She has curly brown hair and dark-brown skin, and is looking at me with bright-green eyes that shine light onto her cheeks. She's considering something, and I don't want to know what it is. When she finally waves at me, too slowly not to terrify, I don't need further instruction—or warning.

We must have arrived at the service room with the electricity boxes Taranis was originally looking for, because there's a door hanging ajar in a little recessed area halfway up the tunnel wall. Flanking it is a short ledge lining the tunnel walls, barely wide enough to shuffle down sideways. Whatever. I'll take it.

I spot a short ladder that will bring me up to the ledge. It's closer to Bia than I care to be, but with no other choice, I dare to run toward it. Bia stands there watching me with an amused and utterly sinister expression as I haul myself up onto the high ladder, spin around on one knee, and crouch on the short foot-wide ledge, gripping the edge for dear life.

Bia simply watches me, and I take a chance. I show her my camera. Snap her photo. She grins even wider. The Forty-Eight are all alike, at least in this. They all *love* having their picture taken. It's so strangely human.

Bia turns her attention away from me down toward the tunnel, and I whip out my backup Zfc, setting it to record from the edge of the platform. I use my 50mm to capture everything else I can in photographs.

While Bia stands below, a horde of what must be tens—if not hundreds—of thousands of rats amasses around her feet while, hovering over her head, Taranis fights the villain parents tell naughty children stories about that are sure to haunt them in their sleep.

The Meinad is a white woman with olive skin, curly black hair and bloodred lips. Her eyes shine red in every photograph of her ever taken, just as they do now as she attacks Taranis with massive claws that are taupe at the base and black farther along—red at the tip now, wet with his blood.

Electricity shoots off his skin as he throws a punch that hits her square in the jaw. She shrieks and the sound . . . the sound is nauseating. Literally. My stomach punches up into my throat and I hurl over the edge of the platform. Even Taranis is thrown back. He hits the concrete tunnel wall a dozen feet to my left above my head.

I manage to get one single photo of him trying to shake off the sound as the Meinad closes back in and scores his chest with her claws, cleaving gashes into his perfect skin that look deep and painful. Bright-red blood weeps down his uniform.

"Hey, you fuckers!" a voice shouts to my right. I don't know if it's driver or dickwad. What I do know is that it's a mistake.

A short hail of bullets blaze, several of which smack the Meinad in the side and in the leg. She screeches again and the bulletfire is cut short when both men fall to their knees. I take their photos, horrified and nauseated myself, this time because of the sound, but also because I can sense what's coming.

Bia lifts both of her long-fingered hands above her head, palms facing the sky, and says so very sweetly, "Time to dine, my sweets."

The rat army around her feet charges forward and overtakes the soldiers too quickly for them to fall back. They try to defend themselves with their bullets, but what are hundreds of bullets against thousands of rats? The men fall and then scream in agony as the rats feast.

Taranis doesn't help the men at all. Instead, he uses the distraction they've provided to his advantage and shoots lightning from his chest and from both arms, two bolts hitting the Meinad in the chest and a third hitting Bia in the thigh. Bia collapses, and when she looks up at Taranis, her features have transformed and she's suddenly wearing the snout of a giant rat.

The Meinad attempts another assault but is battered back by lightning strike after lightning strike. Taranis pummels her into the opposite wall and looks like he'll go for the kill, until hundreds of bats suddenly rush down the tunnel and swarm him. Electricity radiates off his skin, keeping some of them at bay but not all. The Meinad is given another opportunity to lunge. I capture everything with my camera.

"Don't forget our other guest, sweethearts," Bia says, setting her sights to me as the cries of the two men on the tracks devolve to gurgling pleas. Half the bat army suddenly moves in my direction, and I quickly move down the ledge to the electrical closet, gather all my breath and courage to my chest, and step back into the darkness.

Scrambling to grab hold of the door handle from the inside, I manage to wrench it closed, the heavy sound of metal scraping over concrete almost as horrible as the sound of the Meinad's screech. The door slams shut one single heartbeat before thousands of bats pound against the other side of the metal.

I hold on to the cold handle, praying it doesn't give up the ghost while listening to the thuds of tiny bodies, their pounding and scratching, clawing and little squeals on the door, mere inches from me.

It lasts . . . and lasts . . . and they don't give up. But I don't either. My arms are shaking. I've got sweat coating my hairline and lubricating my tits, smashed underneath my bulletproof vest—a vest that does absolutely nothing to deter rats, if the two men still lying on the tracks are any indication.

I don't have time to pray. Don't have the thoughts for it. I know the moment I'm feeling. I've felt it before. Back in that pipe in the DRC, drinking the last of the water from my canteen. The panic of potentially dying for the job, *on* the job. But back then, sitting huddled with those soldiers, there was nothing I could do. Here and now, it's entirely up to me. If I relax my arms and give up, the rats and bats will come in. If I get tired, I get eaten.

I'm not sure if it's better or worse than having no control at all, and as I stand there, vowing to myself that I will not fucking die here, my mind starts to wonder if this is how drowning people feel. Not only a sense of panic at impending death but also a feeling of absolute horror that they died because they weren't strong enough to keep going. That fatigue won out and cost them everything.

The human body isn't meant to endure it all. It just can't. But the will it has to do just that is incredible. Which is what I'm still thinking when I realize the pounding of rats and bats against the metal door has stopped. I don't know how long I've been standing here. It could be minutes. It could be hours. It felt like years.

My arms shake. My legs shake. My core muscles quiver. My neck, shoulders, and back all sear with agony the moment I move. My grip on the door handle spasms as I hallucinate the sound of banging, but it's just the clack of my camera bouncing off my Kevlar and hitting the pocked metal. Taking several deep, staying breaths, I pull open the door an inch, and when nothing tries to kill me, I heave it open the rest of the way. It scrapes even more brutally against the concrete than it did before, this time dragging with it dozens of little rat and bat corpses.

A breeze hits me, carrying with it the scent of blood. The purple lights are off. The darkness is almost complete.

My attention is pulled to the right, back toward the platform that brought us here, but there's nothing in the air. No bats, no Champions. The ground of the ledge might have a few rat and bat bodies littering it, but the tracks themselves are clear of both rats and villains. Taranis is gone. The only thing on the ground are corpses.

Calmly, I exhale. Far too calmly. So calm that I know my therapist is going to have a fucking field day when I tell her about this, how curiosity, rather than abject fear, compels me now to turn around and head back into the utility closet.

To quote Taranis, *"I'm not a fucking electrician,"* but the problem with the electrical grid seems pretty obvious from where I'm standing.

There's a huge box—several of them—but the door to one in particular hangs ajar. Feeling my way around, I open it all the way, and right there in the middle are three massive red handles, all pulled down. I lift all of them up. The lights flicker and return, just like that.

As I drop my camera back to my chest and drag my wrists across my damp hairline, I step back out onto the ledge into the tunnel and know that the power outage was intentional. The point was to draw him here. But to what end? Did they kidnap him? I don't know. Did they kill him? I start to worry.

A shudder nips at my heels and spurs me to move, to get help. I don't want to look at the dead men lying across the tracks, missing some of their . . . parts. But it's my job. As I take a series of shots that will count among my most gruesome photographs yet, I notice my camera. My Zfc. It fell off the ledge but is lying face up near one booted foot, spattered in blood.

Dropping onto the tracks, I pocket my backup camera and snap a few final photos of the dead and of the thousands of tiny, bloody rat footprints tracking away from them. I don't have my phone, so I can't call anyone for help, but I remember that the men held keys to the service corridor, which I'll need to get back to the car—and the car keys, at that. I retrieve both from one of their vest pockets. I have blood on my hands, which I wipe off on my pants. I keep going.

Under the watchful eyes of the flickering orange lights lining the tunnel, I make it back to the platform. Taranis is there, and I feel a small spark of relief to see him pacing slowly back and forth. He's simultaneously trying to peel pieces of bloody uniform out of the grooves on his chest. I heard his footsteps before I could see him, but seeing him and the look he gives me—pure contempt sprinkled with confusion—still surprises me as I pull myself back up onto the platform ledge.

"You're still alive?" he has the audacity to ask.

I hold out my arms, refusing to dignify that with a response.

He huffs, "I'm leaving. Find your own way out."

"Sure, but first can you approve these pictures? I want to get them to the editor and out as soon as possible." I hold out my camera, and when I get close enough, he snatches it from my grip.

I watch the mean expression on his face sharpen and then relax, bit by bit. "You took all of these?"

I assume the dumb question to be rhetorical, and give him a bland look.

He grunts, his gaze flicking away from mine back to the little screen. "Is this everything?" he asks next, handing the camera back to me.

I consider showing him the film from the recording I took with my backup camera, and the other footage from my camera still mounted on its tripod filming the tunnel, but decide against it. The camera fell. There's a high chance I'll have to scrap all but a few stills, if I'm lucky. And the only thing my mounted camera caught was Taranis and me coming and going and the other two SDD guys just . . . going.

"Just these and the recording from the platform," I say, gesturing to the fixed camera. "Though this one didn't see much."

"Fine. Send those you showed me to my team immediately. You can call the SDD if you want to get help for those idiots who were with us."

"'Help'? You mean *body bags*?"

He shrugs. "Don't care. Tell the SDD I did what I could to help y'all, but you were the only one with the grit to make it. Or don't. I don't give a fuck." He takes a few steps away from me, spitting curses as his gaze refocuses on his injuries. He's got wounds covering his face, his neck, and chest, and ordinarily I might grant a little grace to someone so badly injured, but I know his wounds have no bearing on the way he's speaking to me now.

I feel so strange. Not . . . *angry* that I've clearly been manipulated. That he told me what he needed to tell me to get me to agree to take his picture in what is one of the worst contracts I've ever signed, including the BS contracts handed over to me when I was young and green, just starting out, a young, talented Black female photographer white men with money thought they could manipulate. And I don't feel shocked like I did when I first got in that armored car this afternoon and heard the way he was speaking to the now dead.

No, it's clear who this male is. Who he's always been. I just didn't see it. I saw the version reflected in the posters on my childhood bedroom walls. I saw *Taranis*, the brand. But this thing here? This is who he really is. This is what his soul looks like. Who he is beneath this beautiful veneer of humanesque skin. I wonder whether his alien face is just as handsome or if it more accurately reflects his inner ugliness. Whatever the case, I won't be surprised if he eventually reverts, whatever his face looks like.

It was too much to hope that the world could have a hero like the one he's presented himself to be. Someone wholly good, so beautiful on the inside that his outside could only reflect it. I feel a little . . . dumb for having been so severely duped, but in my surprise not surprised at all. After all, Taranis is only proving the old adage that if anything seems too good to be true, it is. Because even perfect veneers can have rotten cores.

"All right."

He gives me a lingering look over his shoulder, eyes narrowing as if I've grumbled an insult at his back he didn't quite hear. He finally grunts. "Don't forget about your NDA. You tell anyone I let those SDD guys die, and I will kill you and make it look like an accident."

"I believe you."

He turns to face me fully then, his gaze so narrowed I'd think his eyes were shut if I couldn't see the bright-purple light blazing out of them. The orange lights on the wall flicker purple too. He opens his mouth to speak, then shuts it, then shakes his head as if shaking off a thought before he repeats, "You can find your own way out."

"I will."

"I'm not going to help you."

"I know."

He sneers at me, his upper lip curling away from his teeth. Then he turns from me and shoots up into the sky in a blur, disappearing through one of the broken windows.

I just watch him go, a strange weight leaving me as I realize I no longer find myself obsessed with him like a seventh grader scribbling the name of their crush in the margins of a notebook. I also didn't stutter when he talked to me. It's like, in the span of an afternoon, he became anyone and no one simultaneously.

Cameras all packed, I shake my head and sigh as I head to the service door, alone. I use the blood-covered keys to quickly make my way down the eerie service corridor, making sure to lock the doors behind me. I slip back into the garage, skin damp with sweat and cold, manage not to get killed by a flying bottle aimed at the Humvee, crawl into the driver's seat, and—with the help of the internet—figure out how to make the giant car start.

Since I don't have the number for anybody at the SDD, I call my PR contact for Taranis at the COE to let them know about the dead guys in the tunnel and chat over editing. Several of the photos have gone online SOOC—straight out of the camera—and I've granted permissions to the photo editors on-site to use the others as they see fit. Tomorrow I'll do my own edits and see whether I might want to use any for my gallery's upcoming exhibit—not that I'm optimistic he'd ever grant me any such permission.

The COE team asks if they can send a medical team to check on me, which I decline, but with the promise that I'll come in to the office for a debrief and a medical check tomorrow.

I jerk up on the parking brake as I finally reach my flat. I park the Humvee in an illegal zone, hoping it gets towed, and make my way through the glass doors of my apartment building.

Taylor sees me and sits up straight, pushing their bangs out of their face and squinting through their thick-rimmed glasses. "Your date went well, I take it?" they say, their facial expression unchanging.

I bark out a strangled laugh that sounds about as bedraggled as I feel. "You could say that."

My hands have started to get the shakes. My shoulders and back sear. My mind is still moving easily, zipping through the events of the evening, putting them into boxes, trying to decide which photos to edit, whether any are worth putting up on my gallery wall, what to do with the fact that I'll have to ask Taranis permission to use some. Are we still going to the Jinju Festival together? Will my dress be tailored in time? What stage heart attack will my mom have when she sees photographs of me wearing it? Will Ambassador Min-hyuk be cool if I show up with Taranis on my arm without warning? If I warn her and he bails—which I have no doubt he most certainly will, given what I know now about his character—will she freak out even more? Will she tell my mom that I'm a liar? If she does that, Mom will likely fly to America first thing, convinced the American culture is having a terrible effect on me, and drag me to Berlin by the earlobe.

"Seriously, though . . . you okay?" Taylor does something unprecedented then: They stand up and come around the desk. I've never seen Taylor get up for anything.

I stand in front of the elevator without pushing the button and cross my arms over my bulletproof vest, my bag's strap feeling like it weighs an additional thirty pounds. "Yeah. I was on assignment. It was . . . intense."

"That blood?" they say, pointing at my arms.

I nod.

"Fuck."

"You said it."

"Then I'll say it again. Fuck."

Smiling, I exhale and nod once more, meaning it this time. I push the button heading up, and Taylor comes over to me, with their sleek nails painted neon purple, and reaches out like they'll put their hand on my shoulder. I laugh outright at the grimace that takes over their face, and shake my head. "Please, spare us both."

They exhale, deflating like a balloon. "Thank god."

I get into the elevator, feeling a little better even if my hands are shaking just as much. "Thanks, Taylor."

They wrinkle their nose. "I'd tell you to stay out of trouble, but . . ." The elevator doors close between us.

Up in my flat, my whole body burns as I sink into my textured bright-yellow couch. I turn the TV on—I'm not even sure what I'm watching. A reality dating show? Maybe? My mind can't focus. It keeps spinning and spiraling out. I realize that I still have blood on my hands and on my clothes, and go to take the hottest shower of my life. As I remove my Kevlar vest, my backup camera falls out. I'd completely forgotten about it.

So clean I've got steam wafting from my skin and hair, I return to my couch, backup camera cleaned of blood as best as I was able. I take a moment to go through my camera bag and pull out the tripod-mounted camera too. Then I take a deep, steeling breath before I start to filter through the recordings.

As predicted, the tripod-mounted camera caught nothing interesting except for a grueling before-and-after comparison of Taranis going down the tunnel and then reemerging from it, looking like he'd been attacked by a giant cheese grater. I don't look *that* bad, but my before-and-after isn't great either.

The smaller camera that fell from the ledge during the rat attack didn't catch much, either . . . visually. But . . . I turn up the volume. Then turn it up louder.

My heart pounding anew and my shaking hands steadying in a way that spells trouble, I plug the camera into my computer and isolate the sounds of the screaming men, the flurrying of bat wings, and the scurrying of the rats until voices become apparent. I hit record on my computer and let my jaw slowly unhinge as I listen again and again and a tenth time.

"The fuck are you doing ambushing me?" says a voice that is unmistakably Taranis's and unmistakably angry.

"The Marduk knows you're holding out on him."

"We have a deal—"

"And you're a little liar."

When Bia's melodic voice chimes in from slightly closer, I recognize the other voice as the Meinad's. "And a thief."

"The Marduk knows you already have it, and if you don't deliver it when and where he told you to meet him, *our* next meeting won't be so pleasant." The giggling makes me shiver, even where I'm sitting on my comfy couch in my warm apartment building.

The sounds on my camera fade out after that, and in the picture, I see Taranis whoosh by overhead without once looking down to even check to see if either of the men on the ground who'd come here with him—to protect him—were still breathing.

As I sit back, heart hammering with realizations, two things become abundantly clear to me:

Vanessa was right. I should never have taken this contract.

And Taranis is, indeed, a bad person.

In fact, I'd go so far as to call him a villain.

Chapter Five

Taranis

"You're sure this is a good idea?"

"I haven't booked all of her time, only some of it, and only at my discretion."

"Still, having a photographer on your heels half the time could be a problem."

"You let me worry about my *problems*. You worry about yours. You're not any closer to crushing the humans and bringing in the Elders, and it's only been, what? Twenty-two years?"

The world's most notorious supervillain shifts in his seat like he's too large for it. The Marduk is the biggest fucker I've ever seen, short of the reverted Wyvern. Meaty around the trunk, meaty in the neck, meaty in the arms and thighs, and covered in tattoos, he looks like he could throw a car. Luckily for me, I'm on his side. At least until his side ceases to serve me.

He pulls on his long, blond beard. The tattoos on his white skin look ghastly, but he's clearly not one to give a fuck about his appearance. He watches me with narrowed black eyes. His eyes are always black whenever he sees me. Mine, however, remain a neutral purple. Hate me all he likes, I don't have the energy to hate him. I *nothing* him, just like I nothing most everything and everyone.

"You don't even want your true Tratharine form back," he sneers.

True and false. I want the power that comes with reverting to my native alien form, but I do enjoy the perks this human face gives me. Still, I smile and lie, "What can I say? Monster isn't my dream look."

"It's your true face."

"This one takes me places."

"Burn it."

"My face? Nah. Like I said, I'll keep it, thanks."

"Burn down the world that it gives you."

"That was supposed to be the Wyvern's job as the first among us to revert, and since you and your little minions failed to convince him to join your side, it looks like you'll have to find another way to overthrow humanity and open the portal that allows your Elders to pass through."

The Marduk growls and leans forward in his flimsy seat. He slams his fists down on the intricately tiled table, which groans underneath his unwavering grip. "*Our* Elders. Just because you forsake your Tratharine past doesn't mean it will not catch up to you."

It's four a.m. and the coffee shop we're at is empty. It's owned and operated by an Ethiopian woman with braids in her hair and a skip in her step. She is so cheery it feels like a slight. The only thing that makes it possible to overcome is the fact that the skips in her steps falter every few feet when she trips over something. She is tall, no curves to speak of—unlike Monika, who has curves for days. The young Ethiopian woman is also gangly and clumsy. The Marduk doesn't seem to notice her at all even though she's the only other person here.

"The past is not so interesting to me as the future," I confess, shaking off thoughts of Monika and her lush curves spattered in blood as she hauled herself up onto the station platform, crawling out of the dark. I . . . hadn't expected that. "I want freedom from these humans."

"Then we want the same thing. It's just a shame the Meinad and Bia needed to remind you I'm not to be fucked with." His gaze moves over my face, where I still bear lingering scars from where that fucking dickhole scratched the shit out of me. The scars will fade completely in a few days, but I can't say I'm not annoyed. Especially considering that I'm going to the fucking South Korean Embassy party on Friday and I don't particularly want to be photographed looking like Scar.

I clench my teeth, disliking the implication that I'm a wild thing needing to be tamed—or worse, a toddler needing a time-out—and place my hand flat and meaningfully on the colorful tiled table between us. "I'm only here because you're a fucking psycho who coordinates his clandestine takeover of the entire world at the crack of dawn on a Monday morning from a coffee shop."

My gaze moves over his shoulder to the woman as she busies herself around her shop like we're not even here. The Marduk and I have met here a few times already, and though it confused the shit out of me the first time I met him here, and not at his more sinister-looking lair down at the old docks, I've never asked him about it. Annoyed, I lean forward and watch the woman trip over the leg of a chair before frowning down at it, smiling, giving it three pats like it's a small dog, and returning it to its place.

"Did you hypnotize her?" I say.

"That's not my purview. No."

"Is she blind?"

"Is that truly what you want to waste your time here interrogating? The coffee shop girl?" His face twitches. All over. Every muscle spasming like he wants nothing more than to reach across the table with his powers and inflate my lungs till they burst.

He's more powerful than I am, and that knowledge hurts. That's why I'm here. I need more. I need everything. And only when I have it will I take out the COE with his help, take *him* out if needed, and exist as I was always meant to: as a god of this world, worshipped by all, beholden to none.

That means ensuring that the Elders don't make it to this planet. And *that* may mean going toe to toe with the Marduk. Something I'm not prepared to do right now. Not if I don't want to end up with pieces of my pretty face scattered all over this coffee shop.

"You're worried about my little photographer, but wouldn't it make more sense for your little coffee shop girl to be the spy? You do meet all kinds of . . . acquaintances here. She could be taking notes."

"No, there's only one spy present." His eyes narrow. He says the word like it's an insult, but I don't care.

I smile lazily. "If you're confident she isn't going to take our picture and plaster it to her six followers on social media, then I guess I'll trust you on that." I watch as she refills the disposable lids and napkins at the little station set up near the exit, dropping half of them in the process.

As if sensing me watching her, she glances up as she reaches the large water cooler and, seeing me staring, gives me a little wave. I raise an eyebrow. It seems to throw her, because she wobbles on her step stool as she pours a pitcher of water into the larger dispenser. Water spills over the rim, and whoops—the pitcher slips from her fingers and comes crashing down.

The Marduk shuts his eyes for longer than a standard blink, his jaw grinding, but he doesn't turn around to see if she's all right. Not that I expect him to. He cares even less for humans than I do. The Marduk landed on this planet when I did, twenty-two years ago, but where I landed as a confused creature unsure of myself and this world, the Marduk landed with his memories intact of the world we came from: Tratharine.

The first time I ever agreed to meet with him as a teen, the Marduk had spun me a wild fantasy of a planet distant from this one forged in violence. The Elders, the ruling body of Tratharine, had set their sights on Earth. They want it for a new home, to expand, to extend their vast dominion over many planets across the universe. And we Forty-Eight are the tools they used to do it. We Forty-Eight form their army.

Reversion is meant to happen to each of us Forty-Eight during our tenure here on Earth. Once reverted, those of us with no memory of Tratharine are set to regain them so that we share the same loyalty the Marduk already does to the Elders and the same bloodlust to enslave or end the humans.

But the Marduk hasn't reverted yet. The only one among the Forty-Eight who has is the Wyvern, and he doesn't seem particularly interested in aligning himself with any army. In fact, the key to his reversion was a *woman*—a human woman to whom he has devoted everything, all in the name of a thing I do not understand and I know the Marduk doesn't understand either: love.

The keys aren't fully understood. At least, not by me. But the little information I've gathered from the COE is that each of us Forty-Eight has an earthbound key that will help us recover our memories, our true forms, and lead us to our weapons.

I know the Marduk fears these keys. If others revert as the Wyvern has and fall in *love*—uck—with their keys, the Marduk's mission is doomed. He's already doomed, as far as I'm concerned. The Wyvern is more powerful than the Marduk is one-to-one, and there are, as of now, as many Champions as there are villains willing to fight them. But the Marduk must know something I don't, because he remains steadfast to his original purpose and determined to see the Elders' plan through.

I feel no such loyalty. I am loyal to only one being in the entire universe: me.

"You all right there, miss?" I call in my most seductive tone, without breaking the Marduk's gaze. Curious because his face gets redder and redder beneath the patterns of tattoos swirling over his arms, hands, neck, and up his jaw to his beard-covered cheeks.

"Sorry!" she shouts, popping back up, drenched in water. As she looks at me, she trips over her stool again. "Don't mind me, Mr. Taranis!"

I smirk. "She knows who we are."

"She's inconsequential. Now, stop stalling." The Marduk's gaze blazes, shining dark light over his cheeks. "I know you have it. The Meinad and Bia's message wouldn't have gotten through to you and you wouldn't be here now if you didn't. Give me my weapon."

"A deal is a deal."

He kicks something beneath the table. It's a duffel bag—well worn, by the look of the frayed black stitching. "I have yours, but you aren't leaving without handing over mine first."

We Forty-Eight fell to Earth with our weapons, but they were taken by the SDD. The Marduk and his minions were able to break into the building some years ago and abscond with several, but the COE still holds several more. Less, now that I've stolen one of them.

The Marduk told me that these weapons, when combined, will open a doorway for the Elders and the other Tratharine to pass through so they can claim this world as another of theirs. They will also help us reduce the humans to servants or eradicate them altogether.

The Marduk knew I'd have no trouble stealing his weapon from the COE. I didn't. And in exchange, among the weapons he stole from the SDD, he claims to have mine. I know the chances he's lying to me are high, but still, curiosity compelled me to oblige.

I reach into my inner jacket pocket and pull out a flimsy stretch of rope, the one I nearly got my eyes gouged out over by the Meinad. "Your weapon, *my liege*." I toss it onto the table between us, and the unremarkable black whip lands with a soft thud, unremarkably.

Yet the Marduk's eyes go wide. He looks down at it like it's a golden chalice offering up immortality. "You *did* have it. Why did you not give it to me when I first asked you for it?"

"I was busy," I lie. The truth is that I needed time. He is already more powerful. If he knows how to use his weapon, even if he gives me mine, that may make the deficit between our respective powers even more unsettling. I had his weapon, but I wasn't sure I wanted to give it up. Bia and the Meinad, however, did indeed successfully convince me.

"Bastard," the Marduk hisses when I don't elaborate. He shoves back from the table. "We're done here."

"Mine better be more interesting than that dirty old shoelace."

The Marduk doesn't react except to smile. It's a creepy fucking smile. "You'd be surprised at just what terrors I can bring with this 'dirty old shoelace.'" His irises buzz with energy that swells between us, an invisible wave threatening to unseat me.

I clench my teeth and cling to the edge of the table as the wave rolls over me, leaving the hairs on the backs of my arms standing on end and my lungs feeling slightly breathless. Annoyed, I snap, "Enjoy yourself, then. It still does you little good, shaped like that."

"Likewise." He kicks the bag under the table again, and I reach down and grab it. It's lightweight, yet metal clanks when I shake it.

"The fuck is this?" I ask him.

He stands up and starts to show me his back. "You figure it out."

"Fucker."

"If you want to know what your weapon does, meet me here same time next week, and we'll make another trade," he tosses over his shoulder.

"For what?"

"Another weapon. I'm sure it'll be no trouble for you at all to steal from the COE again."

It won't, but I have no intention of helping him arm his guard. "We'll see," I evade.

He shrugs. "Or don't. There's always information you can trade."

I have traded him information about the COE's activities before, but it is still risky. If I continue to help him cut off the COE's investigations into his activities, eventually the COE might start to suspect a leak. I don't need their eyes turning to me. Not yet. Not until I have the strength needed to stage my coup and wipe out their leader.

"We'll see," I repeat.

"Suit yourself. You know how to get in touch with me."

I feel the burner phone in my inner jacket pocket, that slight weight, and nod.

I grab my clanking duffel bag while the coffee shop girl scuttles into the back kitchen, the wafting aroma of freshly roasting coffee beans filling the space behind her, and follow the Marduk toward the door.

Out on the sidewalk, I shout to him while he stalks away from me toward the sunrise, pulling up his black hood. "Next time, I'm not meeting you here at four a.m. Pick a different time."

"No. We meet before the café opens to the public."

"Then we'll meet somewhere else at a human time."

"No," he seethes. Wind whips past me that causes chills to crawl up the back of my neck and sear my lungs. "Never forget: We aren't human."

Chapter Six

Taranis

The weight of the duffel bag in my hand both excites and upsets me as I descend onto my balcony, having opted not to go through the front door of my penthouse. I don't need to be caught on camera with this, even though it doesn't look like much at the moment, and I don't want questions from my morose doorperson.

I am excited by the prospect of what the bag contains, yet disappointed by the size. Shouldn't my weapon be a big, intimidating hunk of a thing? A massive blade as broad as I am tall?

I snort as I open my balcony door and head to my office. Though Simon and Simone aren't in yet, I'm still cautious. I lock the door just in case and place the bag down on my desk with care, curious when I hear the inner rattle again.

Standing over my desk, I unzip the dirty gym bag. The sound of the zipper catching makes me jump. I grin at myself. I'm the god of fucking lightning. What do I have to be scared of?

I separate the zipper and push the sides of the bag down to reveal the only contents within. My head cocks. My face screws up.

What the fuck?

Chapter Seven

Monika

"Mr. Singkham, while I appreciate the faith you have in me . . . with all due respect," I blurt out, "you can't be serious." It's Monday morning. Eight a.m. Way too early for this shit.

I'm gripping the edges of the armchair while he leans toward me across his desk, his black eyes hungry. "You're the only one who can get close enough to Taranis to discover if his treason is a new development or if he's been acting against COE interests this whole time. We need to know how deep the treachery goes."

"As a *spy*?"

"You *are* pretty equipped for it."

I glance at the pink monster sitting in the armchair beside me, looking interested but otherwise entirely unsurprised.

After discovering that compromising audio my backup camera had caught, I turned my recording over to Mr. Singkham directly. He cautioned me not to divulge its contents to the SDD, and we didn't get another chance to talk about it, given that I spent the next three days in and out of SDD debriefs and COE medical consults. I was fine. SDD was pissed and Mr. Singkham was nervous. I knew why. Ms. Lemon was a terrifying woman, and I had a funny feeling that if she found out

Mr. Singkham's best and longest-standing Champion had been passing notes to the other side this entire time, it'd be Mr. Singkham's head.

My SDD meetings done and dusted, Mr. Singkham called me into his office at my first availability Monday morning. Today. He also surprised me by calling the Wyvern in to join us. Immediately after Mr. Singkham showed the Wyvern my recording, I'd expected the monster male to express outrage or shock. Instead, he'd simply stuck out his bottom lip, nodded along, and said, "That tracks."

In response to his insinuation that I'd make a good spy, I turn toward the Wyvern and give him my best incredulous stare. He ignores me and huffs smoke out of his nostrils while he examines his claws, one ankle hooked casually over the opposite knee. "I don't like the way Emily's guy buffs these. I like when they're shinier."

"How can you be so cool about all this?" My voice cracks open like a skull slammed against pavement—i.e., *my* skull, after Taranis realizes immediately that I'm spying on him. "I can't spy on Taranis! You've met the guy, right?"

"We've all met the male—" Mr. Singkham starts, but I shake my head.

"No. I mean, have you *really* seen him. Not Taranis, but the *real* him?"

Mr. Singkham quiets. He sits back in his chair and pulls his kerchief out of his breast pocket. Another Thai design. Even though he's been in the States twenty-plus years, he's still so proud of his heritage. I admire that in a way that makes me nostalgic about my past. My mom calls me her American daughter every time she speaks to me on the phone, and even my dad, who is German born and raised but whose parents are Malian, has taken to speaking to me in English. Seeing Mr. Singkham now makes me excited to be attending the Jinju Lantern Festival as an honored guest, not as a working photographer—though, on second thought, I'm filled with dread at who I'm taking as my *date*. The murderer stuffed into superstar shape and whom I'm now being asked to spy on.

Purposefully evading my gaze, Mr. Singkham mops his forehead with his patterned kerchief and mutters unsteadily, "He has *some* trouble retaining staff . . ."

I balk. "*Some* trouble? Did you not hear what I told you? He let his last *staff* get eaten alive by rats! I woulda been dead right there on the tracks with them if I'd been sixty seconds slower!"

Mr. Singkham spares me my next explosion by not trying to contradict me. We all know I'm right. We all know that Taranis is—deep down in his bleak interior—a rotten thing. "I'm not suggesting you put yourself in danger, Ms. Neumann. I'm only suggesting that should you have another occasion to record him, you take it, and that perhaps if he affords you any liberties he doesn't afford his other staff members, you take the opportunity to snoop. He is one of the COE's most valuable assets, and we need to be absolutely certain of his treachery, and its scope, before we take any action."

I settle back into my seat. I didn't realize how far forward I was leaning. "'Snoop'?" My brows come down hard. My nails, still chipped from last Tuesday's escapade, dig into the hard leather. It looks like it's been patched with something, and I get the distinct impression that I'm not the first person to sit in this seat, wanting to tear apart Mr. Singkham like the Meinad did Taranis's face.

That seems to perk the Wyvern up. He shifts, his big ass squeaking as he plants both feet back on the floor and leans forward on his elbows. "What are you looking for?"

Mr. Singkham wipes his forehead again. "I've watched the video many times, and I can come to only one conclusion as to what they might have been speaking about and bartering over."

"Weapons," the Wyvern answers, drawing a surprised look from Mr. Singkham. The Wyvern tilts his head. "I thought it was obvious, given what we know about the Marduk and his motivations. He's been collecting weapons for years."

Mr. Singkham loses his voice. He doesn't speak. He only nods. "Our intelligence has told us that the Marduk's weapons collection is substantial. He was responsible for the raid on the SDD that took eight. Since then, our collection of nine has been reduced to four. I have . . . a *suspicion*, one I'd like Ms. Neumann to help confirm, that Taranis might be responsible for having taken some of them."

"How many does that leave you with?" the Wyvern asks, rubbing his jaw.

This conversation is so over my head my gaze can only ping-pong between the two. "Across SDD and COE safes, we now have only sixteen, though we have strong suspicion that at least eleven remain lost."

"Fuck. That means the VNA could have as many as forty-two."

Mr. Singkham nods.

My face screws up. "Forty-two?" I blurt out. "That can't be right. That would mean there are seventy . . . sixty-nine weapons total. Are there more than one weapon per person—being, whatever?"

Mr. Singkham and the Wyvern exchange a long look. A little tug-of-war takes place, which the Wyvern invariably wins when he says, "You want her in on this, you have to bring her in."

Mr. Singkham sighs. "This information is deeply confidential, Ms. Neumann. If you share this with anyone, it could risk all of humanity."

"Fuck that. Don't tell me." I shoot up out of my chair. "I already said I don't want to be involved in any of this."

The Wyvern sticks out his massive clawed foot when I try to pass by him between our chairs, blocking my exit.

I stick my pointer fingers in each of my ears. "Lalalalalala. I can't hear you."

He hardly has to move to grab my wrist, tear it away from my face, and shove me back into my seat. From there, he says casually—far, far too casually—"Monika, there are more than forty-eight of us."

"Frick!" I shout. "Don't tell me!"

"There may be as many as sixty-nine," Mr. Singkham says while I screech internally . . . and a little audibly. "We call them the Inconnus—the unknown ones."

"Sixty-seven, if we're assuming Sixty-Nine was the last one sent. Sixty-Nine and Twenty are dead."

"I don't want to know! I don't want to know!" I shout.

"It's a little late for that now," Mr. Singkham says, placing his kerchief on his desk. I glare at it, suddenly wondering how he'd feel if I shoved it down his gullet.

"Scheiße."

"Now that we have that out of the way, Ms. Neumann, help us."

My skin is tingling, my adrenaline doing that terrible thing where it makes my heart race but my mind move slow. Calculating. Calm. Easy. Relaxed in my realization that this is an adventure and I'm a junkie for it. "What do you want?"

"I want you to memorize this weapons list and see if Taranis has one of these or more in his possession." He unlocks a drawer in his desk, withdraws a green binder, and slides it across the table toward me.

I don't take it. I just scoff. "And how am I supposed to do that? It's not like he carries bulky weapons around in the pockets of his baby-blue spandex."

"I want you to search his apartment."

"And how, exactly, am I supposed to do that?"

"The two of you live in the same building, do you not?"

I gulp, my face getting mysteriously hot. "How . . . do you know that?" I ask stupidly. Of course he knows that. Everyone knows that. The only person who hasn't realized that we live in the same building is Taranis himself, because I am deeply uninteresting to him in any way outside of my ability to take his pretty picture. Hell, we've even run into each other in the lobby—twice.

Mr. Singkham gives me a droll look and exhales. "Aren't you two attending a party at the South Korean Embassy this Friday?"

I cross my arms over my chest, everything feeling so tight. "And?"

"And since the two of you live in the same building and are going on a date . . . is it not rather obvious?" Mr. Singkham's red face, more than his words, gives me insight into what he's asking me to do.

My jaw drops. I stand up in outrage, and this time the Wyvern doesn't stop me as I move toward the door. "You're a fucking dick," he says to Mr. Singkham.

"This is a matter of life and death," I hear Mr. Singkham respond.

I stand in front of the door, one hand on the cold knob. Turning around, I seethe, "I am not going to be your honeypot spy, and I am not having sex with Taranis!" I walk out on them, slamming the door behind me.

Chapter Eight

Monika

Later that night, I finalize editing a few photos from the attack at Old Sundale Station. There's one that I linger over. Fuck. I want it for my exhibit, but it's not quite right. I could throw it in anyway—it's just that good—but Taranis doesn't deserve it. The way the light his body creates illuminates the planes of his face. The blood spatter that makes him look like a dark and vengeful angel, the kind that would drag you to hell with no remorse.

I start to feel hot. The kind of heat that's embarrassing when you realize it's happening because of a picture of a guy you know better than to like.

Tucking away my own vanity, and my overactive, underused sex drive, I send the picture to Simone—still my only contact on Taranis's team—dust myself off, get into my bed, and turn on something to turn me off completely: a horror movie, the bloodiest one I can find.

Too bad the Black guy makes it to the end.

Too bad the Black guy was the villain the whole time.

I turn off the movie and lie back in my massive king-size bed complete with the most expensive sheets they had in the department store, and roll over the request made of me by Mr. Singkham. I open my phone to the final cut of the image I just edited and close my eyes with a heavy sigh.

I might have sex with Taranis—if he even wants me, which he won't.

I might also try to be a spy—if I don't get caught, which I will.

Whatever happens, there's absolutely no chance I make it out of this alive.

Chapter Nine

Taranis

Standing in my tuxedo in my office, I stare at the objects lying on my desk, still unable to make sense of them.

They don't *do* anything. At least, not anything interesting. Sharp, they might make for good fire pokers if they weren't such an unusual shape.

Even though the Wyvern has tried to keep his weapon close to his chest, everyone has seen the images Monika caught of him wielding a sword when he fought off the Marduk. A skinny, dinky little strip of metal it had appeared to be, until it caught fucking fire.

A viral meme went around from one of the pictures Monika took of the Marduk squinting at the Wyvern like he'd never seen anything more outrageous before in his life. The meme was captioned with everything from how shoppers look at the price of their grocery bills to how parents look at their toddlers. Though no one seems to remember how violent the battle had gotten after that. The Wyvern had been in sorry shape, though it was the Marduk who'd run off in the end. He'd sustained injuries I wouldn't have wanted to come back from. Which is why he contacted me so shortly after that.

I frown, my deep irritation with the Wyvern and his reversion and the COE and the VNA and the fucking Marduk at an all-time high. I handle the weapons again, and like every other time, they remain static, useless, ancient-looking things.

Frustrated, I throw the weapons onto the bookshelf behind my desk, collapse into my office chair, and lean back with my hands laced over the top of my head. Time for a little pick-me-up.

With a flick of my powers, I turn my monitor on. A series of notifications beeps in the upper right hand corner of my screen. They've been going off all day, just like they have since the first of Monika's images hit the internet. I have the files she sent me open in another window, and swipe over to them, surprised by the sensation that comes over me. It's the same shock that makes my stomach constrict and my throat work. I swallow a few times, feeling a little . . . bashful.

Most of the photos Monika took show the battleground. Bia and her fucking bat and rat army. The Meinad and her claws. But in one photo in particular, unlike the rest, it's just me, surrounded by a background so black it looks like the depths of space. I'm alight in electricity, lightning bolts crackling along every inch of my skin, blurring my silhouette. But it's my eyes that she captured.

I don't know the first fucking thing about cameras, so I don't know if it's that particular lens, its ability to zoom in, or what, but she managed to get a shot of me from the shoulders up, and my eyes are fucking blazing so bright they look like the sun. A purple sun. There's a scratch on my face, bifurcating my eyebrow, tearing down my cheek, and blood spatter covering so much of me. I look like a Titan, one to be feared by the gods.

I don't know why I like this picture of myself so much. I mean, I'll be the first to admit, I like looking at photos of myself. Anybody with a face like mine fucking would. But this? This is different. In this photo, I look like somebody I'd want to live up to.

I flip through the rest of the archive she sent me—all photos, no videos, thank fuck. If she'd seen more of what transpired after she locked herself in the electrical closet, I'd have had to kill her and leave her corpse there with those other two idiots.

I grunt, frustrated and annoyed at the lingering paperwork the SDD wants me to fill out documenting the deaths of the guards they sent. They already took my statement. I gave them nothing. What was surprising was that they weren't able to get much more from Monika, who insisted there was nothing that could have been done to save the two men. I'd say she was protecting me, but she also didn't suggest that I did anything to try to help the bastards either. She was just . . . neutral.

I don't know why, but I must have read and reread her statement and watched her recorded interview a dozen times. She was so straightforward. Hard, even. She didn't even complain that she'd been trapped in that electrical closet alone, fighting for survival. She just said it. She'd just done it. And in her interview, she showed no signs of frailty or fragility. She never stuttered once. It was such a contrast from the way she'd fumbled at my feet in the elevator, but jibes with everything I saw of her actions back at the Old Sundale Station, fighting in the dark. I sit up straighter, shaking it off, annoyed at myself for dwelling on it.

I fill out the forms required of me, though from time to time, I swipe back to Monika's pictures, feeling some kinda way about her for taking them. And then I do something I never thought I'd do in a million fucking years.

I open my email and type one out myself. I don't ask Simone to do it, or the less competent Simon. I type and then retype when I'm unsatisfied, until I have:

> Monika,
> The pictures you took from last week's heroics were satisfactory. You no longer need to collect my sign off before sharing them with the PR team.
> Taranis

I look at the draft in my inbox and frown at it. My temples feel itchy and hot for some reason. I scratch the top of my head and then huff, adding one last line to the email.

> P.S. Looking forward to tonight. Meet at my apartment at seven pm sharp. We'll leave from here.

It's six forty-five now. No way she'll be on time, but I'm looking for a reason to yell at her. I can't let her think that I'm *nice* now that she knows otherwise, can I? Yet within ten minutes, I see a fresh notification pop up on my computer screen. I click it open, brow furrowed. It's an email from Monika, and it reads:

> Here.
> Re: photos. Acknowledged.
> —MN

I frown, even angrier than I was, because I have no reason to be angry. Still, I did agree to go to this event, and even though I know it *should* please me to leave her waiting downstairs for hours, it doesn't. It coats me with a stickiness, like I've rolled around in syrup and can't get it off.

Shuddering off the strange and annoying sensations, I get up, leave my office, lock the door, and meet my photographer downstairs, only to be shocked. She's waiting for me in the lobby and—what the fuck is she wearing?

Every bone in my body stiffens as I fight not to drop my gaze, to keep it listlessly trained on hers. She's watching me, but I can read absolutely nothing in those onyx orbs. Jesus. Seeing her dolled up so close to having seen her on the battlefield covered in blood . . . *Fuck.*

"You're late," I tell her as I approach.

She doesn't respond, but turns when I do and follows me toward the glass doors of the lobby. She waves over her shoulder as we exit the building. My car is already waiting, but I don't approach the driver because I'm too busy trying to determine who she was waving at and why it bothers me.

Monika slides into the back seat of my limo. Following her in, I grunt, "You aren't wearing a coat."

She shakes her head. "Hoes don't get cold."

I snort—careful now, she might have thought that was laughter. "You better not change your mind. I won't give you my jacket," I tell her.

She simply shrugs. "I won't, and I know."

Annoyed at her for using the same tone and language with me as she did back at Old Sundale Station, and annoyed at myself for being hyperaware of the fact that she's coatless and enjoying it way too much, I pull out my phone and start scrolling . . . once again through all the pictures she took of me that chaotic evening. My body flushes with heat, and I can't help but spy on the scantily clad woman out of the corner of my eye. I worry that I may have made a poor choice in agreeing to come with Monika this evening.

Chapter Ten

Monika

Taranis stares down at his phone like every bone in his body is regretting coming with me tonight.

Somehow that helps.

I don't want to be sitting next to you, either, Arschloch, I want to tell him, but that would mostly be a lie. Taranis looks so fucking good right now I thought I was having a stroke when the elevator doors opened and I first saw him. I forgot my own name. I forgot how to speak Korean. My German and English brains also went night night. And then he'd accused me of being late, and all of it—especially how good he looks—just came together to piss me off.

I thought Taranis in a baby-blue bodysuit was the apex of attraction. Turns out, that was only because I'd never seen him in a tux. *Scheiße.* The matte black of the fabric contrasted against the silk of the . . . the . . . what's the jacket part that folds back? Whatever that part is, it folds back to reveal a differently textured, darker black vest beneath. And there's a silver chain clipped to one of the vest buttons that disappears into a vest pocket? Like . . . WHAT? Is this sexy-ass Black man carrying a pocketwatch? His shoes, his tie, his hair, his purple eyes . . . Fuck me. Fuck *him.*

The worst part is . . . I'm starting to really consider it.

My neck is hot, and I'm getting increasingly more pissed as I notice more and more attractive things about him, while this dress didn't stir even the slightest reaction out of him. Virtually none at all. For a second, I thought I saw his face tense and a vein in his forehead pop, but that was just because he accused me of being late—I wasn't.

And I *know* I look good.

This dress is sensational. It's by a Korean designer based out of New York. I had it custom fitted to my measurements, but the clever, talented bitch made the bust an inch too small. My tits are fully spilling out of the top. If I don't end the night with a nip slip—or by pissing Taranis off so much my insides end up on the outside—I'll count the evening as a win. Forget about the 007 shit entirely.

My dress is made out of silk, which means it leaves nothing to the imagination, and I'm not wearing SPANX underneath. I'm not wearing anything underneath. I worry that maybe my rolls are too . . . rolly, and for a moment I feel a thread of self-doubt I don't usually feel. Do I look . . . bad?

The soft black fabric has a shimmery finish and a slit up the side that goes nearly all the way up my thigh, and the top is low, barely held up by the thin straps that go over my shoulders and then crisscross all the way up the exposed back. My favorite part of the dress, though, are the designs stitched against it in deep purple. Dragons lunging over waves make up the bulk of the stitching, meant to symbolize the 3,800 Korean soldiers who fought off 20,000 Japanese troops during the Imjin War, preventing them from crossing the Namgang River. That's the origin of the Jinju Namgang Yudeung Festival, and even though I'm a third culture kid who's lived outside South Korea for most of her life, honoring my heritage is still really important to me.

So if Taranis doesn't like my dress, my body, my face—he can suck it, I tell myself. At least, I try.

I take a few shaky breaths while the driver peels away from the curb. She's a blond woman dressed in a boxy, slim-fitting suit, who must sense my anxiety, because her voice filters through speakers overhead:

"There's a refreshment bar on the right-hand side of the car. Just lift that black panel there."

I look up and realize the car is a limo. We make eye contact in the rearview mirror. The divider separating her seat and the passenger seat is down. "Thanks." I smile at her a little less shakily and shuffle along the bench seat until I can reach the minibar. There's a bottle of champagne—looks fancy, and ya girl never said no to expensive bubbles. I down a glass, then pour myself a second before taking a seat on the bench directly across from the bar.

"Apologies if I'm being too forward, but I just wanted to tell you, your work is incredible," the woman says.

I perk up, surprised she recognizes me or knows who I am. "Thank you."

And then she goes on to surprise me even more when she says, "I don't just mean your celebrity pics either. I, uh . . . sorry. I'm not supposed to fangirl over clients, but I saw your last exhibit at the Morrison and haven't been able to stop thinking about it. The untold stories of Black America? That photo you got of Aomawa Shields, the astrophysicist? I just . . . stunning. Your work is haunting—in a good way," she quickly adds. Her blond bob is the same length as mine, and I feel a blush creep over my chest as we make eye contact.

"I . . . Wow. I don't meet folks who know about my gallery work very often. I'm seriously touched."

She smiles more widely and it transforms her face. She's probably my age, and reminds me of the first girl I ever seriously dated. It was short and we weren't a good fit, but she was still only one of two people I've ever been with that gave me what I *liked*—tried to, anyway—and between her and my most recent ex-boyfriend, she'd definitely been closest to getting it right. That was back in Berlin, but the way her lips felt against mine is still fresh. My blush deepens.

"I opened my own gallery last year. I try to showcase photographers from marginalized communities, but I am doing my first solo exhibit in February. It's more superhero-y, but I'm hoping it'll be more of a cross between my commercial stuff and some of what you saw at the Morrison. If you want, I'd be happy to get you tickets to the event?"

"Oh my gosh, I would be absolutely—" But midsentence, the divider rolls up between us.

I jerk back, confused, and open my mouth before I feel the pressure of eyes on the side of my face. I glance over at Taranis. He's staring at me in a way I don't like. Not even a little bit.

His purple eyes blaze a little redder than usual, and his mouth is tight. "You don't need to make chitchat with the help."

Wow. "I *am* the help."

His lips turn down at the corners, and he slides along the seat until he can reach the bottle of bubbles. He pours himself a glass. "Are you drunk? This is almost empty. Is that why you're flirting in front of me?"

"What?" I glance down at my glass. "This is my second glass. And I'm not flirting," I lie.

"Do I look blind?"

"You look like someone trying to get their teeth knocked in." Oh my God. What the fuck did I just say to this sociopath?

Taranis's left eyelid twitches. I gape at him. He glares right back. "I'm your date. You flirt with her again, I will fire her. You flirt with anyone at this event, I will electrocute you both. You will not embarrass me."

Anyone might have thought he was jealous. I know Taranis better than that, and what he is, is a narcissist.

I roll my eyes and drain my glass, refilling it more out of petulance than my true desire for a third.

Time passes. This car ride is the longest of my life. Then, out of nowhere, Taranis says, "I didn't know you were a lesbian."

"You don't know anything about me."

He glares, lightning crackling across the back of the hand holding his champagne flute. "My team did their due diligence. I knew you were single when I asked you out. I wouldn't have asked to be your date if you were with someone."

I smirk. "Of course not. I doubt you'd do very well being rejected."

"You wouldn't have rejected me. And I don't care enough about you to ruin your relationship."

"Wow," I say aloud. "You are . . ." I shake my head, chuckling a little bit. "You are a sensational actor. I can't believe I fell for it."

"Don't beat yourself up. You're human. Humans aren't that smart."

I scoff again, smiling this time. "Incredible." I take a sip. "And I'm not a lesbian, by the way. I like boys too." Not that I date ever anyway. "Aliens, though?" I suck in air between my teeth. "Not my type."

He snorts, and out of the corner of my eye I swear I saw his mouth twitch just a little bit. "I'm everyone's type."

"Until you open your mouth."

"If I open this mouth to tell you to drop your top, show me your tits, lift your hips, and show me that pussy, you wouldn't hesitate."

My body turns to fire. He might as well have electrocuted me.

Our gazes lock, and despite tugging and pulling at the crackling tension between us, I can't look away. He isn't smiling at me, either, and the lack of a smug smirk makes me nervous. A little more than nervous, I admit, and I can't let him rile me like *that*. I'm not wearing underwear and don't need to leave the limo with a wet spot on my silk dress.

I clear my throat. "Fat chance." I look away, but I can still feel every place his gaze canvases my profile, searching for clues, which is odd because I'm not a riddle.

I don't plan on speaking to him again on the car ride, or at the event, or anywhere else outside of a professional setting if I can help it. But surprising me again, Taranis breaks the silence. "The pictures you took of me in that tunnel were good."

Good. It's not what I'm used to hearing about my photos, but I get the impression this isn't an employer who doles out compliments to his employees easily. I take it with a grimace that I try to pass as a terse smile. "Thanks." *Ssi-bal.* So much for not speaking to him.

"You got my email?" He's frowning again. It's a clipped, tight expression. I wonder for a moment what this guy looks like when he relaxes. If he ever even does that.

"Yes."

His mouth pulls together, his full lips shriveling. "You didn't reply."

"Yes, I did. Did you not get it?"

"Your response was two words. *Here* and *acknowledged*," he sneers.

I shift my gaze left and right. "So . . . in other words, a response?"

"You didn't read my whole email. I said I was looking forward to tonight. You said *Here*. And then you go and flirt with my driver." He makes a sound in the back of his throat that is suspiciously beastly.

"Why are you pissed off? We both know that you only asked to join me as part of the deal to get me to come work for you. It's not like you could ever be into me." Christ Almighty. Why the fuck did I say that? I sound so . . . whiny. Also, I'm not doing myself any favors if I'm supposed to be his fake date tonight and also spying on him later.

"Why didn't you say you were looking forward to it too?" he asks, all but ignoring what I just said.

"Are you for real?"

"Do I sound like I'm joking?"

"What are we even talking about?"

The car door suddenly opens. I hadn't realized we'd stopped. The driver ducks her head into the entrance and says, "Are you two ready? I can also circle the block."

"Circle the block," Taranis says at the same time I shout, "We're ready!"

Before Taranis can slam the car door shut, I lunge forward to take her hand and let her help me out of the car. Taranis edges into the narrow space at my back, his body all but lining mine, his chest bumping my ass as he ducks to follow me out. He slaps mine and the driver's hands apart.

"Be on standby," he growls at her.

She nods, keeping her gaze down, which just pisses me off, but I don't have time for that because Taranis has already been noticed.

"I really will get you those tickets," I tell her as the few photographers who are present flock toward us, along with a whole host of civilians.

There aren't many folks walking Embassy Row this time of night, but the commuters who are there collectively squeal and scream, *Ohmigawdthat'sTaranis!*

The driver looks up at me with a surprised smile. "Thank you. I would love that."

"What's your name, by the way?" I ask her, holding out my hand.

She glances at Taranis and gives me a contrite look. He's not paying attention, though, looking out toward the photographers, waving like he's the King of fuckin' England. She leans in toward me, her breath ruffling my hair. "It's Nicoleta. Thanks again."

"I'll get your number when we come back so I can send you the . . . *ooph!*" Taranis has a hold of my wrist, and when he jerks me forward, I lose my balance. I might have tumbled toward the sidewalk to give it a lovely little kiss had his body not been there to block my fall.

"What did I say?" he hisses, dropping my wrist and grabbing my hand instead. He laces his fingers through mine in a way that might look cutesy to anyone else, but the bones in my hand doth protest. "Smile," he orders.

I wince and try on a smile as the steps up to the South Korean Embassy rise before us. The meager paparazzi I thought were there suddenly triple, quadruple, flashing cameras coming out of the woodwork as we ascend alongside other formally dressed guests.

Lights flash, photographers call Taranis's name. They're calling other names too. The names of politicians I recognize, the names of high-profile businessmen and women I don't. My name, too, much to my surprise, though Taranis's above all. It occurs to me just then that even though we're surrounded by a sea of Korean and American elites, Taranis is still garnering the most notice. And he's resumed his role. For a second, I completely forgot who the world believes him to be. I'm still stuck on the fact that he thinks I'm embarrassing him by flirting in the privacy of his car—for fuck's sake. He's clearly a male used to being fawned over the *most,* and right now is absolutely no exception.

At the top of the steps, Taranis pulls me rather roughly through the gates. He wears a broad smile, perfect for the crowd, but his grip on my hand is still hard, bordering on brutal, as we make our way across the lawn and then up the final steps, where Ambassador Min-hyuck greets her guests.

"That the ambassador?" Taranis hisses between teeth clenched in that immovable smile. Men in fancy tuxedos to my left gossip behind their fingers like schoolboys, and two women walking directly in front of us glance over their shoulders, eyeing Taranis like he's a piece of meat and they're seriously iron deficient.

"Yes. My godmother."

His eyebrows furrow. "Why didn't you tell me that?"

"Ouch," I hiss as his hand clenches mine even more brutally. I stumble along after him as he cuts abruptly right, dodging a pair of gawkers and pulling me along like a yo-yo. "I thought your team did their due diligence."

His eyes meet mine, and there is no love lost between us, but too soon, he's guided me up the final steps and edged my body slightly before his as we approach the ambassador. I didn't expect him to do that. Even though it is my invitation we're here on, I fully expected *the* Taranis to take the spotlight for himself at every opportunity. Instead, he leaves a pause long enough for me to speak first as the ambassador's eyes dance between the two of us in shock and alarm.

"Annyeonghaseyo, Daesa-nim Min-hyuck," I say with a big smile, taking her hand between my two and bowing low over it. I don't get to see my own mother very often these days, so this feels nice. "You look stunning," I tell her in Korean, dipping my chin toward her formal green-red-and-white and absolutely exquisitely embroidered *hanbok*.

The older, shorter woman with graying hair gives me a demure grin in response and a very slight bow, which is a courtesy she doesn't owe me at all, given her status—not to mention the fact that the *eoyeo meori* on top of her head likely weighs a ton. It's a braided wig decorated with extravagant jeweled pins and jade plates. I got to try one on once when

I was styling a shoot for the South Korean Embassy and was told that particular one weighed eight pounds.

"It is a pleasure to see you, Monika," she responds in Korean before turning her attention to my date and switching to heavily accented English. "And you, too, Taranis, though I did not expect to see you here tonight, least of all escorting my goddaughter."

He takes her hand and bows over it deeply, but the moment he's upright again, he laces his fingers through mine once more. "I am sincerely sorry that I didn't answer your invitation. I actually did have other commitments, in that I had already at that point agreed to attend your event as your goddaughter's plus-one."

"You could have given me a little heads-up," she tells me in Korean, though I can sense the teasing in her tone. It makes my heart light. "Did you tell your mother?"

I shake my head. "I wanted to surprise her." I also didn't believe my *date* would show up.

"Well, she will be surprised," she answers, and we both laugh before her gaze switches back to Taranis again as she resumes speaking in English. "Are you two dating?"

"Oh no," I quickly jump in before I can leave the response to Taranis. "We just . . . we started working together and . . ." And what? I blank completely.

"Hit it off," Taranis finishes. His smile is so bright I have to stare up at it for a second to understand what he's saying—what he's implying. Is he . . . trying to convince the ambassador we're *actually* dating? If she tells my mom—*when* she tells my mom—my mom will tell my dad, and my parents will both lose their minds for entirely different reasons. Neither is a conversation I'm interested in having.

"I think he means—"

"Exactly what I said," Taranis states. "And we are honored to be here. If you need us for anything throughout the evening, please don't hesitate to find us. We won't take up any more of your time."

"Please do enjoy the festivities, and I will be sure to catch you inside. Thank you again for coming. Monika, we'd love to get your photo with the other honorees once all have arrived."

"Of course, Ambassador. Thank you so much for having me . . . us."

The ambassador's dark eyes switch between the two of us curiously, not a doubt in my mind that she absolutely does *not* buy that we're an item. "Of course. You'll also find Cynthia inside."

I tense, a zap of nasty electricity zipping up my spine. "Oh. She's in town?"

"She is."

I grimace. "That's so great. I'll be sure to stop by and see her."

"Please do. She is excited to see you." She isn't. I know she's not. "And she will be excited to meet your date. My daughter is a huge fan. We all are."

Fan-fucking-tastic.

"Of course, Ambassador." He gives her a wink, and I swear it brings a blush to the married woman's cheeks. "We'll see you inside."

The South Korean Embassy is a rectangular building with a massive courtyard at its center, where the party is taking place. It's absolutely stunning, and when we step into the wonderfully decorated world, I almost hallucinate that I've been transported to Jinju directly.

The hand holding mine relaxes slightly as we stand at the top of a short flight of steps looking out over the lantern-lit atrium. Lanterns hang from every tree, from ropes, from the eaves of the building, illuminating all the exterior walkways and the corridors leading inside. Different stations have been set up, and I gasp, forgetting momentarily who I'm standing here with.

"Let's go make lanterns!" I turn to face Taranis while I point off to the left. "I mean . . ." And then I shake my head. Fuck it. If he's going to be the real him with me, then I'm going to be the real me with him. And the real me? Come on. I'm a nerd. What else? "They made the little pond here a mini–Namgang River! Come on! Or do you want to check out the night market first?" I point right, toward the food stalls.

Taranis looks at me with his mouth slightly parted. He cocks his head. "I could use a drink."

"Okay, but lanterns next." It's my turn to clutch Taranis's hand fiercely as I drag him toward the *makgeolli*-tasting station.

"Hello," says the woman behind the bar dressed in a much less formal hanbok than the ambassador wears. "Have you tried traditional Korean rice wine before?"

"I love *makgeolli*—the sweeter, the better. We'd love to do a sampler."

The woman seems surprised I know what *makgeolli* is, though the moment she looks at Taranis, I'm all but forgotten. She overfills his glass, then curses, apologizes for the spill—or the cursing, I'm not sure which—and tries again, hand shaking until she manages to get two glasses filled of the syrupy, sweet liquid.

I thank her while Taranis gives her a rather scathing look, and grab him by the elbow, wheeling him around before he has a chance to ruin her night. Then I clink our glasses, pulling his focus to me. Gazes trained on each other, Taranis and I drink together. It's strange. I'm so overwhelmed by the rich tradition and the decadence of the place that I nearly forget that I hate the dude and that my real mission for the night is to backstab him—but first *tteokbokki*, spicy rice cakes.

I eat way more than my fitted dress can afford, but I'm determined to try everything. Including every possible station serving soju. I won't lie, by the time we make it to the lantern station, I'm a little more than tipsy.

I blame the soju for why I giggle—*giggle*—as I watch Taranis try and fail to fold his lantern in the right way. "You're not very good at this."

He curses, glancing around to make sure no one but me hears him. "This is stupid."

I hold up my lantern, perfectly constructed. I'm onto the decorating phase now and have started to glue some of the cut-out shapes to the sides, mostly dragons. I love dragons. "All the power in the world, and you can't make a paper lantern. Tsk, tsk. You know, in Jinju, the lantern-making station is set up mostly for children."

Taranis glares at me, his eyes flaring bright purple. If he's drunk, I can't tell. Despite his evident annoyance, mostly with me and only when no one is looking, he's been a fantastic sport about all this, smiling and signing autographs without so much as a grimace. He's even sampled everything I've offered him and participated in all the little games and activities.

"We should go through the Tunnel of Lights after this."

"Sure. Whatever," Taranis grunts, finally getting his lantern folded at the right seams. It still leans. *"Ugfff,"* he sighs dramatically.

"You're such a drama queen." He sneers but says nothing, and I can't help but laugh. "Hey, did I thank you yet?"

He glances at me sharply. "Are you making fun of me?"

"No . . ." I start, a little surprised. "I mean, I was making fun of you before, but now I'm just saying thanks. You've been . . . really great here. Even if you are pretending about all of it."

"I'm not pretending," he hisses.

I scoff and say with soju-laced confidence, "You asked me earlier why I didn't reply to your email with more enthusiasm?"

"Yes."

"You said you were looking forward to tonight, but everything else about the way you present yourself to the world is a lie. Why would I believe you in an email?"

He makes a face, then settles it into something more neutral as another couple passes by to collect the materials needed to make lanterns of their own. I think I recognize the one man as a famous Korean actor, but I don't get a good look as Taranis turns toward me and says, "I'm done with this."

"Same. Let's go put our lanterns on the lake." I pick up my lantern and watch him pick up his. Because of the small size of the pond, all our lanterns are miniature, fitting neatly into the center of a palm. It makes his look extra tiny, and I smirk as I crouch down at the edge of the water. "Here. You'll need this," I tell him, handing him a little bamboo boat.

I set my boat in the water, set my electric candle in the center, and place my lantern over it. I push it out into the water.

I watch as he imitates my motions, looking strangely clumsy. It's endearing in ways I wish it wasn't. When he finally pushes his boat out into the water and stands, he offers me his hand. I take it and let him help me up. Heat radiates between our bodies as he looks down at me sternly and I look up at him, still feeling a little drunk. That must be why I'm suddenly not finding him so irritating.

He glances between my eyes, glaring. I smile. "Do I have *tteokbokki* sauce on my face?" I wipe my lips, knowing that I need to reapply my lipstick. I didn't want to bring a purse, but the photographer in me couldn't leave the house without my iPhone at least. Luckily, I brought a little extra makeup in my clutch too.

He doesn't answer me, just continues to stare. He opens his mouth, but before he can speak, another voice cuts in: "Taranis, would you mind taking a picture?"

He's stuck, staring at me another second before turning with a wide smile. It doesn't match the downturn of his eyebrows at all. "Sure."

They snap their shots and I grab Taranis's hand. "Come on," I tell him, "let's go to the Tunnel of Lights. It's meant to be very romantic, and if people think we're having a moment, maybe they'll leave you alone. We don't have to stay much longer, I promise."

I know it's probably the alcohol and my overly relaxed state, but as I drag Taranis across the courtyard and watch him get attacked again and again by sycophants, the strangest feeling comes over me. I try to remember that he was perfectly happy to let me be eaten by rats, but as I pull him through the Tunnel of Lights and watch the red lights reflect over his skin as he stares up in what looks like consternation but that I'm beginning to understand is his version of *wonder*, I start to feel . . . sorry for him.

And that makes me worry. Because my heart is beating harder than it should be, and in this moment, it doesn't seem to care whether he's a villain.

Chapter Eleven

Taranis

Monika leaves me in the lantern-lit tunnel to go to the restroom. I stare at the lanterns—one of them, in particular. It's got dragons on it, symbols for water, and Korean script, not that I can read it. I didn't do much research before coming here, so I'm not really sure what all this means, but I noticed that Monika's got similar designs on her dress. I couldn't not notice. I seem to be hyperfocused on every fucking thing about her.

And she's annoying the shit out of me.

First, she was defensive and defiant. Then she was drunk and soft. The whiplash was unexpected and makes me nervous about her wandering off alone, even if I can see the bathroom door from here.

Wait. What? She's a human. I don't care if she's assaulted or murdered in the restroom, her blood leaking all over her beautiful dress and across the tiled floor. Fuck.

I take a step, force myself to remain calm, and then satisfy my next impulse to follow her when I remind myself that if she were murdered in the bathroom, it would reflect poorly on me for allowing it to happen. Yes, that's right. I can't let her be killed while she's my date for the night.

Besides, what if there's a woman in there she finds more attractive than me? Who am I kidding? Monika has seen beneath my shining veneer, and she's utterly unimpressed. I don't know why it's bothering me so much—so much that it's giving me a headache. I've had turbulent relationships with all my staff before . . .

I'm staring at the lantern, imagining I can see the little waves painted onto the paper surface roll, when it hits me. Usually, I can see the hatred in their eyes, the staff that finally understand who I am underneath. However, those staff all still need me. That fuels their hatred. The contracts I've bound them into, the rigid rules put in place to assure that they do what works best for me and nothing more, nothing less.

I've bound Monika up like a trussed-up cow—fuck, that's a bad analogy, and has my mind moving to other places, other bindings . . . Regardless, she doesn't seem to be fazed. She still gives me shit. Still meets my gaze. Still does her work and performs with perfection, despite my restraints. She still seems . . . calm. Like she and I are playing two different games, and for the first time in my life, she's holding more cards.

I glance at the bathroom door and exhale as Monika steps through the doorway, the tension in the back of my neck dissolving. It takes her a moment to find me with her gaze, and when she does, she smiles at me and I tense up all over again.

"Hey," she says, "is it working?"

"Is what working?" I respond, confused.

"The Tunnel of Lights? Keeping people away from you?"

She blinks at me, and I notice she's put on more lipstick. Gloss. Whatever shade it is enhances her natural one. Darker around the edges, pink in the center. Her eyes are delicately rimmed in mascara, making her naturally curly eyelashes appear thick. Her hair is cut to her chin—not a millimeter longer, not a hair out of place—and falls there in perfect waves. She has light bangs that cut across her forehead and frame her face. Her eyebrows are thick and perfectly plucked. The red lights from the lanterns bounce over her curves, making me hungry. I swallow hard.

"Hmm," I answer.

My jaw is clenched tight, my temples blazing with hatred as I'm hit with a terrible realization: I want to fuck her. I want to do terrible things to her body. I want to wreck her perfect makeup and tousle her perfect hair. Her dress is far, far too low cut for me not to want to tear it into so many pieces she'll have to leave my apartment in absolutely nothing or stay there forever.

I never fuck women who know what I'm like, preferring to maintain the illusion that I'm nice and polite and charming, even in the bedroom, and I've never had the urge to fuck an employee. I rarely want to fuck humans. Humans, by nature, disgust me.

But . . . I'm not disgusted by her.

I reach out and lash my hand around her neck. She gasps, jolting in my grip. I can feel the way her throat works, and the cords of muscle there tense . . . but then relax a moment afterward. I narrow my gaze. What is she playing at? She knows me but she's not afraid. And I hate her for that.

I hate you, I go to tell her, but those aren't the words I whisper when I open my mouth. "Your skin is so soft," I snarl, "I could tear through it with no effort at all."

Her breath is coming in shorter, hotter bursts. "It'll make it easier for Bia's creatures to devour me, then, when I get left behind next time."

I take a step to close the gap between us, bringing our bodies close. Too close. "I heard what those guys were saying to and about you. You really think they deserved to live?"

She scoffs, still so unafraid. That fearlessness will be what kills her one day, but will it be by my hand? I'm no longer sure. "I don't think they'd have won any Nobel Peace Prizes, but I definitely don't think they deserved to go down like *that*."

"Should I have just killed them myself? Ended their suffering with a quick electrical pulse to the brain?" I couldn't quite stimulate enough electricity to lobotomize someone with one internal attack—I am still missing the power that the Marduk has to corrupt from within—but

Monika doesn't know that. I give her throat a little zap, which makes her gasp in a way that does things to me.

"I wouldn't have put it past you," she whispers.

I lean over her a little farther, forcing her body to arch back. Light trickles across the bridge of her nose and reflects in her glossy eyes. They're so dark. I can't make out her pupils—if she's hating this or if she's excited. She should feel the former, but all I feel is the latter radiating from her hot fucking body. I didn't find her attractive before I knew her, but now, looking at her, I can't remember any other woman I've ever seen.

"They'd have deserved it. Like most of your fellow humans." I'm revealing too much in trying to unseat her, but she takes it all in stride.

"People aren't all good or all bad. They're a sum total of all their weird and wicked parts."

"And what are your wicked parts?"

She smiles. Her eyes are so fucking round. "Few and far between. Not like yours. You're wicked down to the bone."

I'm starting to get erect. I feel my cock stiffening in my pants, and want nothing more than to punish her for the discomfort she's causing me. "You'll pay for that," I vow.

And then this woman says the last thing I would have ever expected. She all but pants, "Please, Taranis . . ."

One of her knees buckles, and I've got no choice but to let her fall or catch her. I catch her around the waist, my other hand tightening around her neck. Her eyes roll back, and I shift forward, searing our bodies together at the hips.

My jaw drops, my eyes widen, and in the next split second, I see a new color they've never turned before reflected in miniature in Monika's glossy eyes. *Blue.* Like the sky.

Her lips part. I stare down at them. Feel the pulse in her neck go wild.

"Monika, is that you?"

An annoying fucking voice beheads the moment with a single strike.

Monika jerks in my grasp, ripping herself gracelessly from my grip and stumbling until she finds her own feet. “Oh, wow. Cynthia, hi! You . . . you look fantastic,” Monika gasps, flustered. The words sound forced and strained in ways she didn’t sound with me when we were debating her death and when I was debating whether or not to force her to her knees right here, surrounded by so many lights.

I reach out and steady her by the elbow, but she quickly yanks her arm away from me. Electricity zings up my entire arm, causing me pain at the shoulder socket. The electricity isn’t mine—I mean, it wasn’t caused by me. I frown down at my own hand, troubled by the strange color the red lights have turned my skin. My brown tone looks purple. So does Monika’s, though in a darker shade. That’s when I realize she’s put space between us, like she doesn’t want me there.

I growl low under my breath, prepared to snatch back her wrist when the other woman says, “You too. Your dress is very . . . tight.” It’s the poison in the woman’s tone that finally causes me to look up at her. She is a Korean woman with pale skin and straight, jet-black hair. Her dress is also formfitting, so I have no idea what she meant by commenting on Monika’s, but for some reason I don’t like it. I like it even less when Monika falters. She didn’t falter in the tunnels when facing death, but she falters here.

“Oh, I, um . . . yes. Yours too.” She rubs her palms down the sides of her dress and offers the woman a lopsided smile.

“My *eomma* told me you arrived and that you came with a date.” The woman’s eyes flash to me, and the look she gives me makes my skin crawl. Her bloodred lips part in a smile. “It’s a first for you, isn’t it? You never bring a date.”

Monika doesn’t reply.

“Though I did some digging and saw that you two started working together recently. It was so nice of you, Taranis, to come rescue your new employee like this. But I suppose that makes sense; you *are* the best of them.” She smiles so sweetly at me, and while I work through whatever’s going on in my arm, my temples, and my chest, I listen to

Monika suck in a small, wounded breath. "Monika, my *eomma* wanted me to come get you and tell you that they're ready for your photo op." Her face twitches, her smile off. Jealousy is an ugly monster. I can see it now. But what I cannot see is what's keeping Monika from fighting it off.

No matter. I'm used to killing. I'll slaughter it for her quickly so we can get back to where we were before we were so rudely interrupted. "Yes, Monika, why don't you go now and give me some time to get to know your *friend*." I level my gaze at the woman in the red dress and give her my best, most provocative grin.

It seems to stun the woman momentarily, because her own smile falters before picking back up in the next breath with even more brilliance. I can tell she's forgotten Monika—Monika, who is staring at me agape. I tip my chin at her, refusing to wink, because that would be too obvious. Also, what do I care that she knows that I've got this? She can go off and mope in her own despair . . . Yet why does that thought make my skin crawl?

Nodding, Monika's impossibly smooth shoulders curve slightly inward. "All right," she says, voice soft. "Yeah. Yes. I should go . . . the photo . . ." She swallows repeatedly, gaze passing between me and this newcomer; then she stalks off.

My headache explodes through my skull, and I hiss between my teeth, able to feel as Monika retreats out the door that leads to the Tunnel of Lights, like I'm holding a tether linked directly to her disappointment and it's been pulled. I balk, annoyed at her all over again. Petty human emotions. Doesn't she realize I'm doing something *nice* for her? Then again, I haven't exactly *done* anything nice yet.

Let me rectify that.

"So, you are Monika's friend?" I ask the irritating female.

She stiffens up, straightening and slamming her jaw shut. "Her godsister, in a way." She flicks her hair with her elegant fingers. "My mother is Monika's godmother, and Monika's mother is mine."

"Long-standing rivalry? That kind of thing?" I say as she leans in, the scent of her perfume invading my senses and making me choke. It smells good enough, but all it does is remind me of Monika's perfume. I hadn't noticed how subtle and smoky it smelled until now.

"Hardly." She rolls her eyes, but I don't miss the clench of her mouth. "I'm a model, mostly based out of New York and Seoul, but I'm in town for the weekend visiting some people . . ."

"And decided to take time out of your busy schedule to come harass one of your mother's honored guests?"

"'Harass'?" she says, sounding so appallingly innocent. She touches her fingertips to her chest. Through her pale skin, I can see the outline of her skeleton. "I just came by to see if my *eomma* had lost her mind when she told me that you two were here on a real date, or if it was just another one of your acts of heroism—providing permanently single Monika Kim Neumann with her very first date." She sticks her tongue out at me in a way that's meant to be cute and teasing. All it does is make me want to cut it off. "Since I can clearly see it's the latter, I'd love to invite you for a drink if you're interested in slipping away at some point tonight. I'm staying at the Beverly. It's not far."

"Did it look like I was here out of pity when you showed up?"

Her mouth curves down but corrects itself at the last second. She smiles and nods at whoever passes by behind us. I turn to face her fully, backing her into the wall of lanterns. "You looked like you were about to punish her."

"I *was* about to punish her. And now you're making me wait."

She takes a step back, the top of her head and her shoulders brushing the fabric of the lanterns behind her and making her jump. "You . . . like to punish?"

"Oh yes, I like to punish. I like to break. Does that sound like something you'd enjoy?"

Her brows have knitted. Her heart-shaped face looks stricken, but she's a determined sonuvabitch and a dogged flirt. I've met flirts like her before, who want to be able to fuck me so they'll have a story to tell.

Use me—a trait these humans have been so good at since I was a child. But I get the feeling this woman's motivation is even stupider than that. I think she wants to fuck me only so that Monika can't.

"I can do that," she says, but she's trembling. "Just so long as it doesn't hurt . . ."

"Oh, it'll hurt."

"Why are you being like this?" she finally has the courage to ask.

This is the conversation I'm used to having with my employees. The ones who finally figure out that Taranis is only a brand and his sweet smile is only skin deep. Why couldn't Monika have cowered and whimpered like this? My whole life would be so much easier. "Why are you being an ugly, jealous bitch?"

She winces like she's been slapped, and I know I've hit home. I should just torture her with my tongue, whipping words at her like this, but I'm feeling amped. The pressure in my head is getting outrageous, building, building, building. I feel like I'm going to explode, and this little petty human female feels like an acceptable outlet.

"Monika must have really done a number on you. Normally, the men and women she leaves behind don't look this pissed off." She tries to break left, but I crowd her and catch her arm.

"I thought you said she was perpetually single."

"It doesn't mean she doesn't fuck. She's a huge whore. You know she's bi, right? And she won't have a threesome with you," she adds quickly, as if that's where my mind went to first. "If you really are into her, you should know she'll probably just leave you for a woman."

A splintering pain ricochets up the back of my neck. I can't wait. I palm the side of this woman's face like a lover might and send electricity skittering all over her skin. Her mouth parts and she tries to scream, but I quickly bring her face into my shoulder in a hug while I continue to blitz her with a pain that must be excruciating.

Footsteps alert me to the presence of humans. I glance left and see an older Korean couple walking past. They smile at us. I give them my best shy smile back and top it off with a wink. They giggle like schoolchildren as they shuffle past us, and we are alone again. How lovely.

I pull her away from my jacket by the hair and see the tears pooling in her eyes. "What are you . . . What did you . . . I just came to warn you! If you really are serious about Monika, you should know she's only interested in her fancy little cameras. All she's ever wanted is to do her little art projects that everyone seems to love her for. She doesn't date seriously. She's just a huge whore. She fucked my boyfriend in high school."

Ah. And there it is. A jealousy *this* petty could have only been born from something that happened years ago.

I retreat just a little, giving this woman space—this woman whose name, for the life of me, I can't remember. I recoil my gifts from her skin and straighten, or at least I try to, but my arm, my hands, my fingernails . . . it's all pain. My eyelids are burning. I can't quite see straight.

Blinking quickly, I hiss, "Let me make this abundantly clear since you seem to be harboring delusions that I care about anything that comes out of your pretty mouth." I smile at her. She winces, her legs shaking at the knees. "I don't care if she fucked your mother and every other member of your family. I don't care if she dates men or women or those that exist in the valley between. I don't care if she wants to leave me. I don't care if she wants to have a threesome or a full fucking orgy.

"Monika doesn't get to choose. *I* decide when Monika leaves. *I* decide who Monika fucks, and for now, she fucks me and only me because I'm a selfish bastard and I don't share the things that belong to me. Monika is *mine*. For now . . ." I have no idea when I decided these things, but whether they're true or bullshit, I don't take them back. They need to be said to this annoying creature.

I straighten the silk lapel of my tuxedo and watch the woman melt. She lands on her ass on the ground beneath me, looking so stupid and small with little dewy tears trailing down her cheeks. "B-b-but why? What makes her so special?" she asks, sounding like the high schooler she once was, having the same conversation she did with her cheating boyfriend. *Grow up, get over it,* I'd tell her. But she's human, dense, committed to focusing on the unimportant.

And yet, her question does stir something inside me. Something softer than the headache radiating through my temples and shooting down the back of my neck, damn near immobilizing me. Instead of pain fluttering through my chest, I feel *pleasure*. The softest fluttering of butterfly wings brushing against all my organs.

"Because she isn't full of bullshit," I answer the woman, though she doesn't need an answer. The pain in my head spikes. "Because she interests me."

The pain comes again, this time for my legs and ass, which clenches up like I'm trying to keep in a tremendous shit. I should stop talking now, but I don't. I'm so determined to lob the head off the beast that I fail to realize the only beast I'm fighting here is me. "Because she's the most talented woman I've ever met." The words are out before I can stop them. They are the strangest words I've ever said. My head. It must be whatever's happening to my head. The pain is . . . sensational. Damn near resplendent.

I need this irritating woman to get the fuck away from me before I promise to meet her at her hotel later and instead make a deal with Bia and the Meinad to let them have their way with her in the hotel's back alley. That is, if I survive this.

I stagger back, clutching my head between my hands while the woman on the floor says, "You're an asshole." These are the words I *expect* to hear from humans. *How dare you talk to me like this? Who do you think you are?* Drivel drivel drivel. But instead of punctuating her asinine statement with any of those pitiful follow-ups, she screams. Literally screams. And damn, would she make a fantastic final girl in a horror flick.

"What?" I snarl, but I feel something happening. I feel *terrible*. My head. My fucking headache . . .

"Your head!" she shrieks again.

"Taranis?"

A soft voice startles me. I look to the right. Monika stands there, and my whole focus is attuned to the stricken look on her face as she lifts her phone. "Let me call—"

"Don't fucking . . ." *Call anyone,* is what I would have said—I don't need her reporting me to the COE for electrocuting her fake friend. Only, I start to wonder if that's what she was talking about when my vision starts to go dark and my body collapses.

I hit the hard tile on one knee, my headache fucking *splintering.* It feels like I'm being stabbed repeatedly by the Meinad in the skull over and over. I close my eyes as my hands fall out to the sides to steady myself. The tile in this hallway beneath the light of so many lanterns is ice cold. I try to use it to ground me, to remember how to breathe, but strangely all I can smell is Monika's deep spiced-and-smoky-honey-scented perfume, and all I can hear is her voice in my head saying, *Please.*

Then several images slap me in quick succession.

The first, a glimpse of a small monster with hideous, scarred skin, bright-white eyes, and horns spiraling up over his head, ending in points that are deadly sharp.

The second, a blazing flash of light.

The third, the feeling of my entire body being thrown back and forth, sending pangs of agony shooting through all my limbs, making me feel like I'm being torn apart.

And the last, a dark, demonic voice whispering terrible things in a language I've never heard spoken before but somehow understand: *Kill them all. Every last human.*

I'm blitzed by rolling pictures, too many to track, that form a patchwork quilt in my skull, a maze that I follow and follow down, down, descending into the final ring of hell before I'm able to cross the divide and fight my way to freedom.

When reality resettles around me, I'm shocked to find myself in the exact same position I'd been in. I'd have expected to be lying flat out on my back, drooling like an idiot. Instead, I'm still kneeling there, listening to the voice of an actual idiot shrieking at me in her annoying falsetto.

"Oh my God, it happened! Oh my God, did it . . . Was it because of me?" Bright laughter tingles through my pain, pulling me fully back into the present.

I lift my head, surprised that I can at all with how heavy it feels. It's like my skull was crushed between anvils or like I got sat on by a whale. I roll my shoulders back and blink my eyes open, though I can't see shit. Everything's blurry, but I rise to stand anyway. A dizzy spell causes me to reach out with both hands. One of them lands on a skinny little arm. The other lands on a shoulder that's softer than the silk she wears. I turn toward the latter.

"Easy," the voice says to me. It's deep for a woman's, and grounding. I find it soothing, and despite the tremors still rolling through my body in waves that recede like the tide, I'm able to exhale almost all my panic. Even some of the pain, too, subsides.

"Monika?" I say, blinking at her fuzzy outline.

"Yes."

My grip tightens on her shoulder.

"Are you Taranis?" a higher female voice says.

"Of course he's Taranis," Monika answers in the same breath that I growl, "Of course I'm Taranis."

"I think we should get you to the COE."

"No way! We have to show *eomma*. Taranis and I need our picture taken together!" The higher voice giggles—*giggles*. Didn't I just torture the woman a few minutes ago?

I snarl and take another step toward Monika's blurry outline, away from the annoying voice, but I stagger.

"Whoa there, big guy. Whoa! Hey, I can't take your weight."

"I'm not that heavy," I grumble, trying to find my footing. I feel like I'm moving through a swamp.

"Oh my God oh my God oh my God," the other woman squeals behind me.

"Cynthia, please! Shut the fuck up!" Monika shouts in the meanest tone I've heard her use to date. "Get the fuck out of here. And don't tell anyone about this."

"About what?" I groan.

"I think we should head to the bathrooms. I think you need to see . . . *umph*," she grunts, trying to support me as we make our way forward, but struggling.

The annoying girl squeals, "Okay, I'll go get help!"

"No! Don't go get anyone! Fuck . . . we need to get out of here quick," Monika says to me in a lower tone. I'm aware of a door being opened and bright lights washing over us. "Here. Can you see?"

I nod, and it's true. My vision has started to clear. But there's something touching the top of my head that's annoying me, and for some reason—maybe because we're clearly in a bathroom—the feeling of needing to shit has come back tenfold. Actually, it's a pressure higher up my spine than that. Like a knot sits at the base of my tailbone.

"There's something on my ass," I grumble, voice deeper and stranger than before.

Monika doesn't hesitate, the warrior in her moving with efficiency and not a hint of sexuality as she reaches for my belt and undoes it. She shoves the ass of my pants down, boxers, too, while I grab hold of the edges of a sink made out of black stone. Only, as I look down, my head thunks against something and my hands look . . . weird. My vision has cleared for the most part, so why is it then that my hands look so strange?

Whatever bathroom lighting there is in here must be off, because my hands look blue and fucking huge. "Monika, what the fuck is . . ."

"Ssi-bal," she squeals, followed by, *"mein Gott"* and "holy shit," all uttered in perfectly native accents.

"That's so fucking hot," I whisper to her, voice sounding like I swallowed gravel and chased it with a bottle of scotch.

At the same time, she shouts, "Taranis, you have a tail!"

"A what?" I glance over my shoulder. Why is my tuxedo all ripped up? Frayed stitching sprays into my peripheral vision like the plumage of a peacock.

I expect to see Monika's face. She's a tall woman—tall*ish*—and even though I'm six one, I strangely can't see the top of her head. She must be bent way over. I start to turn, but she's pulling on something on my ass and it feels fucking strange.

"Hey! What the fuck are you doing?" I zap her, only . . . the strangest fucking thing happens. Well, among the strangest. This is turning out to be a generally strange fucking evening.

She staggers back, clutching her chest. She hits the bathroom-stall door, which is closed, so she thankfully doesn't fall through it as she rights herself and blinks her eyes open at me. "I . . . You . . . you electrocuted me," she accuses, only she doesn't sound *pissed*; she sounds more intrigued.

"I didn't see anything." I frown. There were no sparks, no small flares of light to show where I'd struck her skin. I'd meant to strike her gently.

"I felt it . . . here." She points to her chest and swallows hard. "I didn't think I'd have to ask you this, but please don't kill me on accident. I'd prefer to know it was coming."

I frown harder, and suddenly something behind me lashes out angrily into the space between us. She jumps. I jump. "What the fuck?"

She points. "Taranis, I told you! You have a tail. Look in the fucking mirror!"

I turn and open my eyes. With my vision clear now, there should be no confusion as to what I'm looking at. Who I'm seeing. But I am wholly and completely fucking confused. "I . . . don't . . . understand," I say, sounding just as idiotic as the idiot I left out in the Tunnel of Lights.

"Taranis, you reverted," she says to me. There's a sudden banging on the bathroom door. "And unless you want to have to explain this to the ambassador of South Korea and every other person at this party, I suggest we get out of here before Cynthia tells too many people . . . Whoa!"

Monika starts to fall back as the bathroom door behind her swings inward, revealing the elderly, pleasant-faced Korean woman who'd walked by Cynthia and me moments before in the Tunnel of Lights. She stands in the bathroom stall now, aghast, before her shock morphs into a fear so crisp I can feel it like a breeze. I know what she's gonna do a moment before she does it—and so does Monika, who holds up both hands and says something to the woman in Korean. Doesn't fucking matter. The woman still belts out a scream that surprises me and sends a zip of lightning shooting down my spine.

Monika turns back to face me and grabs my arm. My giant blue arm hulking out of my goddamn tuxedo. Because that's what I am now. A hulk. Just as big as the Wyvern's stupid pink ass. With horns. And a . . . tail. The Wyvern doesn't have one of these. How the fuck did I get so lucky?

My tail whips around Monika's waist on instinct the moment she pushes on the bathroom door. She squeaks. My tail wraps around her tighter. It feels like . . . it feels like nothing I've ever felt before. Only that's not true, is it? Because I have felt this before, the strength of this appendage that's about as thick around as Monika's wrist at the base of my tailbone and narrows before flaring back out into a spade-shaped tip. This is the same tail I had as a boy, only I was smaller then, a soldier of Tratharine newly formed.

It's a solid strip of muscle, one strong enough to bend metal and break stone and definitely strong enough to keep Monika zippered to my side when she tells me to duck my head so I can fit my horns through the door of the bathroom and step out into a world of madness. That fucking cunt Cynthia told everyone.

The entire lantern-lit world in front of us is packed with spectators who scream and laugh and cheer the moment they see me. And all I can think in that moment of frenzy is that they're going to trample her. I haul Monika up my body, shocked that my tail can support her weight entirely, and then I start forward, intending to bulldoze my way through the crowd until I can reach the outside air, at which point I'll fly to get us the fuck out of here.

Cynthia stands closest to me and screams, "I caused his reversion!"

Attention turns to her as she waves her hand in the air. Camera lights flash, some at Cynthia now, but my attention is fully on Monika as she loops her arm around my thick neck and leans in to speak to me above the cacophony. Her lips brush my ear. A shiver runs down my spine. "Hang left. There's another way out of here."

I move without her needing to say more, down a short path that leads to the men's and gender-neutral restrooms. Monika doesn't need to guide me from here, as I already see the glowing red sign for the emergency exit: **Do not open. Alarms will sound.** I shove the door open and run.

I'm running with Monika wrapped around my body, her arms around my shoulders, her knees straining the fabric of her dress. I take the stairs in one leap, arriving at a second exit door. I pull my phone out of the inner jacket pocket of my tux that now hangs all askew over my too-large frame and dial my driver. She's waiting for us on the corner two blocks away.

Monika's panting as she grips my clothing with force. "You know, you can just drop me off here . . ."

"And let you ride *alone* with fucking Nicoleta back to your fucking place?" I could electrocute her again for as pissed as that thought makes me. I wrench open the door to the back of the limo as it glides to a stop at the edge of the curb and all but toss Monika inside. She lands on the long bench seat lining one side, her legs all tangled in the delicate fabric of her dress.

I try to slide on to the seat I'd occupied previously, but my horns are too tall and I no longer fit. I land instead on my knees on the floor in front of her. "Drive," I bark. "Take us back to my penthouse. And roll up the divider unless you want a show." I'd like her to keep it down, because I want *Nicoleta* to understand that Monika won't be going anywhere near her without me anytime soon. Monika won't be going *anywhere* without me anytime soon. Not till I'm through with her.

I feel manic and suddenly crazed as I watch Monika watch me with wide eyes. She drags her tongue over her bottom lip, and I want nothing more than to see that color smeared over my dick. I reach up to tear off my bow tie, only to find that my bow tie has already exploded off my bulging fucking neck. And then I reach for her. Monika flinches back.

"Wait, wait, wait." She shakes her head abruptly, like she's trying to clear her thoughts. "Shouldn't we be headed to the COE? Are you okay? How do you feel?"

"I don't give a fucking shit about that. About any of it." The energy rolling through me, riling me up, needs an outlet. One outlet. "Do it," I snap in the harshest tone I've ever used with her.

"Do what?"

"What we both know you've been dying to do since you first met me—not Taranis, but the real me."

Her head cocks to the side, confusion warping her features as she struggles to sit up.

"Drop your top, show me your tits, lift your hips, and show me that pussy. I know you want to give it all to me."

Her eyes round. Her lips part. Her back arches on instinct. I have half a heart to wonder if this body is even meant to breed a smaller human form, but then I remember that I don't have a heart at all. She's gonna take me if it breaks her. And then she's gonna take some more.

"Taranis, are you—"

I spasm and then I shock her, this time controlling it so that she just gets a little visible zap to the outside of her right knee.

She jerks, spreading her legs for me. Her eyes widen even more. She combs her hair behind her ear and whispers, "Your eyes are blue. Almost white."

I don't let my shock show. Don't tell her that my eyes have never shown anything but shades of purple before and the occasional red. "Don't give a shit about that. Do what I told you to do."

"You're sure?"

"Don't make me repeat myself, Monika."

She sucks in a breath, and I watch the indecision play out across her face. I try to look stern as I wait for her to decide, but my insides rattle like loose stones and I'm holding my breath. She takes too damn long—so damn long I start to wonder whether she even *wants* to fuck me anymore. I'm not the attractive human I once was, back in that elevator when she all but melted for me, and then when I had her eating out of my palm before Cynthia interrupted us.

Goddamn Cynthia. Monika wanted me to fuck her—I know she did. But now that I'm a hideous beast, what if she doesn't? I could hardly blame her.

Nerves clog my throat in a way I've never experienced before. My gaze traces the low silk neckline of her top as it hugs those perfect tits, those curves, every one. "Monika," I growl, trying to keep the desperation from my tone. I can't. Because I remember the word she whispered to me and say it now. "Please," I choke.

Monika sits up like I've shocked her—I didn't this time—and bites her bottom lip. Then her chest inflates on a breath that makes her whole body tremble. She lifts her hands to her shoulders and slips the straps of her dress down until her tits fall free. My monstrous fucking heart damn near stops beating.

Her tits are fucking glorious. Perfect and smooth, fucking deliciously dotted with fat areolas so dark they appear almost black in this low lighting. Her nipples are at attention. Perky and made for suckling. I want to bite one until it bleeds, which won't be hard because I'm distantly aware that all my teeth have suddenly sharpened. My mouth is full of fangs.

Lifting her hips slightly, she hikes up her skirt and shows me what I suspected was true all along—that she went to a public party without any underwear on—and I decide that what I told Cynthia was true: I'm going to punish Monika thoroughly tonight. And it's going to hurt.

I crawl forward, positioning myself between her knees. I tear the rest of my jacket, vest, and shirt off until I sit back on my haunches wearing only a pair of shredded tuxedo pants. Then I lay my clawed hands on her legs. My claws, made of white glitter, extend halfway up her thick fucking thighs. So fucking delicious. I feel a certain calm settle over me as I lean in and smell the fresh scent of her slippery cunt. I can see how wet she is, her arousal slicking the exposed folds of her lips.

I look up at her face.

She's so fucking excited. It makes my slowly stiffening erection rock hard. My cock strains against the tattered remains of my pants, so I free it and let my huge, pulsing fucking monster dick stand upright between us.

"Holy shit," she whispers.

"You scared? Because you should be, baby girl. This is your fucking fault. You understand that? *You* did this to me. And you're going to pay for it. You're going to do whatever you have to to make it up to me."

"Ssi-bal." Her whole body trembles.

"Tell me you understand," I say as I drop my blue lips to the inside of her right thigh and press a gentle kiss to the softest skin I've felt in this life, and in my life that came before. I remember all of it now, and I hate that I can understand the Wyvern a little bit better. Because that life feels as distant as the Tratharine planet, and so minuscule compared to this moment, right here, right now.

"I understand."

"Tell me that you'll do whatever I want you to."

"Anything," she says on a gasp.

"Tell me that you'll let me do whatever I want to you."

"Oh God, yes."

"And when you scream, you're not gonna call me by the little bitch name that I've been for the COE. You're gonna call me by the name the first humans who ever *saw* me gave me." My *host* family. They hated me. And I hated them right back. "Darius." All I can think, looking up into her bright face, filled with crazed excitement and a dash of fear, is that

I'm pissed the fuck off, this is her fucking fault, and I want to spread her out, ripe and ready for punishment, and do terrible, terrible things. "I'll give you a safe word, but you're not gonna tap out. No matter how far I take it."

She nods, and then she whispers two words that forever seal her fate: "Yes, Darius . . ."

I dive in and feast.

Chapter Twelve

Monika

Thirty minutes earlier

I grimaced through my photo shoot. Never comfortable to begin with on this side of the camera, the photo shoot seems to last an eternity, even if it's only actually a few minutes.

On top of that, it was hard not to take Taranis's dismissal personally. I mean, he can't know about my long and annoying history with Cynthia. We went to middle and high school together in Berlin, and because we were the only two Korean girls in our year, and given our mothers' close ties, we ended up in a sort of forced friendship. Needless to say, she's not the girl I would have chosen for my BFF, nor would she have chosen me for hers. To start, we didn't have the same interests or the same values. To end with, I slept with her boyfriend our sophomore year.

To this day, she hasn't gotten over it.

I'd like to say she's being petty, but stealing my date at her mom's party might just be equal payback. Fucking clever bitch. And I just . . . walked away. I should have stayed. I should have fought her for him. But I couldn't avoid this photo shoot, and I couldn't stand up to Taranis's dismissal.

I couldn't fully understand the look on his face. It was . . . creepy. And the fact that I am almost certain he'd been about to kiss me doesn't help. I was so flustered that I just left. But that's not who I am. I should have stayed and dealt with Cynthia's rude comments on the spot. I should have told her to back the fuck up, and if she didn't, I should have clawed her eyes out. He's *mine.*

At least, he's mine for the night.

The second the photo shoot is over, I book it back to the Tunnel of Lights, worried I've been away too long—what if she's doing her thing and successfully swooping in? What if he's buying it? I mean, she is the hottest woman I've ever seen in real life. It'd be tough for a guy not to waver, and Taranis doesn't have any morals. He's a narcissist at best, and at worst, a narcissistic villain and murderer.

I stand at the front entrance to the tunnel as a beautifully dressed couple heads inside in front of me. I compliment their *hanboks* in Korean and watch the surprise light in their eyes. Without a hard stare at my face, it's rare that folks suspect I speak Korean with a near-native accent.

I'm about to head in after them when it occurs to me that if I want to spy on Taranis and Cynthia, I should actually head around to the *back* entrance by the bathrooms since they're standing closer to that end. Yeah. I want to spy on them. To torture myself? Maybe. I guess.

I hesitate, debating a thousand times, and I'm still debating if this is the right move as I pass the Korean couple again on the way to the bathrooms. They both seem confused and surprised to see me again so soon as I slink past them like a creepo weirdo to the mouth of the tunnel.

I turn into the entrance, the red light of the lanterns washing over me as I stand there, ready for my gotcha moment. Though who am I kidding? If I caught them making out like teenagers in love, the only person getting got would be me.

Compromising with myself, I peek around the corner instead of jumping out like a burglar, and what I see fills me with confusion.

Cynthia's clutching her face and weeping as Taranis lords over her, words I can't quite hear ripping out of his throat. I'd expected to see them wrapped up in each other, but it looks like . . . he's torturing her. Is Taranis the narcissist doing that because she's annoying him? Or . . . is he doing that for me?

I know the answer and my stomach smashes all together and then expands like a balloon on my next jerky breath. Butterflies. Not a little flutter, but a tornado of butterflies paints my insides with warm syrup with every flap of their wings. I press my hands to my belly lest they escape as I watch Taranis release Cynthia against the lanterns behind her, lingering electrical shocks still skittering over her perfect bone structure in purple and blue shades.

Ssi-bal! What if he kills her?

I stagger out of hiding and take out my phone to record in case it comes down to a case of he said / she said, but the moment I open my mouth to call Taranis off, he takes an abrupt step away from her as if pushed by an invisible hand. His body lurches, and he grabs his head at the same time *horns* sprout out of it.

I gasp, staggering back myself while Cynthia screams bloody fucking murder, and we both watch, mouths hanging open wide, as Taranis becomes something else entirely.

"Your head!" Cynthia screams, pointing a shaking arm at Taranis as horns as white and glittery as freshly fallen snow sprout from the subtle peaks of his hairline. His brown skin takes on a bluish hue, the color rolling down his body like a flush, and he wavers where he is, like he's trying to fight against this transformation . . . and he's losing.

I take a few steps forward, my hands raised, including the one holding my phone. "Taranis?" I try, worried. Shit fucking scared. Is he . . . in pain? He looks like he's in agony. "Let me call—" Who the fuck do I call? Panicked, I start to put my recording down in favor of calling the lead COE doctor, Emily.

"Don't fucking . . ." he snaps at me, his voice loud and warped. It's so deep and dark that it scares the piss out of me, and I jump. Then I slap my free hand over my mouth as Taranis crumples in on himself.

He lands hard on the ground and I rush over to him, only to be thrown back onto my ass when a burst of energy is flung from his body. I'm thrown back toward the bathrooms. I can hear the doors slam against each other. I grab my phone; my clutch is around my wrist. I shelter my head in case another blast comes out of him, but when I look up, I'm fairly certain the damage is complete.

I scrabble over the ground toward the . . . toward Taranis. He's three times the size he was when I last blinked. His body has exploded out of his tuxedo, and did I say I thought his skin was blue before? Because now I'm sure of it. The hands he was using to hold his head have become massive and taloned—clawed. I don't know the difference. They're white like his horns, dusted in glitter, serrated on the sides, and look deadly sharp.

I'm freaking the fuck out, begging him to be all right. "Taranis, please . . . Please . . ." I keep begging him while Cynthia sits nearby shouting uselessly.

"Oh my God, it happened! Oh my God, did it . . . Was it because of me?"

That warm fluttering in my gut turns to a cold knife as, for just a second, I believe the conviction I hear in her laughter. I rebel against it, trying to focus, trying to stay calm. Did he revert because of her? Is this what happened with the Wyvern and Vanessa? Are Cynthia and Taranis in *love* now?

But before I can dig too deep down that rabbit hole, the smart part of my brain catches up to the knee-jerk thoughts. No. Fuck no, he didn't fall in love with her. Neither Taranis nor Cynthia are capable of loving anyone.

"Taranis! Taranis?" I'm scared to touch him. Scared of his claws. He releases this deep rumbling sound and, all at once, starts to unfurl. "Cynthia, help me!"

His engorged, muscle-bound arms are busting out of his tuxedo, leaving strips of it hanging off his frame in tatters. Those bulky arms lash out for stability, one hand grabbing on to Cynthia's arm—which I'm pretty sure she'd lifted only to defend herself—while the other reaches out toward me and grabs my shoulder. I'm still recording.

Taranis starts to angle himself toward me and give me more of his weight. "Easy," I grunt, struggling to accept it.

"Monika?" Finally, fucking finally, he's trying to open his eyes.

I gasp as soon as he does. His eyes . . . they're fucking radiant. The purest pale blue, a shade I'm entirely positive isn't found in nature. "Y-y-yes?"

Cynthia says more stupid things while Taranis releases her entirely. I try to encourage him once again to let me take him to Emily, but he refuses. I don't think he realizes what's happened to him, so with significant effort, I manage to get him to the bathroom. He needs to see this with his own beautiful blue eyes.

"There's something on my ass," he tells me as his head swivels on his neck. He's regaining mobility, slowly but surely, but he doesn't seem to be fully with me yet.

I'm worried about an injury I can't see, so I don't hesitate to end my recording, stash my phone back in my clutch, and reach for his belt. Under other circumstances, this might have made my heart pitter-patter. As it stands now, my heart *does* pitter-patter, but not because I pull a beautiful, glorious dick out of his pants . . .

Because I pull out a tail.

I curse in every language I know and fall back against the closed bathroom-stall door. I manage to get a few words out before the bathroom door opens up behind me. I almost crash into the *ajumeoni* emerging from the stall behind me. She shrieks, and I've got half a mind to join her as Taranis's tail starts to move autonomously. Why it wouldn't, I don't fucking know, but it reminds me of a giant boa constrictor, and I'm absolutely terrified when it wraps itself around my waist.

We stumble out of the bathroom. I'm freaking the fuck out. I want to get him to someone who might be able to be calm about all this, but Taranis is insistent that we get back to his car. Which means we have to fight our way through the press.

How fucking ironic.

Throughout it all, Taranis electrocutes my heart, carries me with his tail, scratches me with one of his claws, and bumps his horns on every-fucking-thing. I'm not even sure he's aware of most of what he's doing, and by the time we get back to his car, I'm almost positive he must have lost his mind completely. He can't be aware. He can't be fucking aware. Because he's kneeling on the floor of his car while Nicoleta pulls away from the curb, looking up at me like I'm the thing that matters most in this moment.

Not his tail.

Not his horns.

Not his blue skin.

Not his eyes the color of twilight.

We exchange words I won't remember later, because my mind is stuck on just the few that leave his lips: "Drop your top, show me your tits, lift your hips, and show me that pussy." And just like that, I don't care about any of that other stuff either.

Instead, I sit there, looking at the monster on the floor between my bare legs, who's unrecognizable to me in appearance and yet whose soul I know I've met before.

There is no *jeong* in him. There is no *jeong* shared between us—no we or oneness, no random acts of true kindness to bind us. But there is *inyeon*. Layered over years, over lifetimes, *inyeon* is a concept in Korean Buddhism that provides an explanation as to why two people may meet in certain times and certain places. It's a concept I've always found deeply romantic. Could it be *inyeon* that brought Taranis and me here and now, together like this?

Or what if it isn't *inyeon* at all, but *agyeon*—bad connections layered atop one another for so many lifetimes that our meeting here can only have a terrible outcome? Taranis is a narcissist. He's a murderer. He's bigger now and, if the Wyvern's reversion is anything to go by, more powerful. What if this leads to a dark end? Maybe we've met before and hated each other just like this so many times. Maybe Taranis's reversion leads to destruction on a massive scale. And maybe it's me who triggers it this time. Maybe we are a doomed fate.

But it doesn't matter at all if we're *agyeon* or *inyeon*. My mind and body have already decided that I'm going to do whatever he wants. I've never met a bully like this, one who *sees* me just like I see him. One who, without judgment, will give me exactly what I *like.*

"Please," he all but begs me, the single word shaking my soul.

As soon as I say the words, "Yes, Darius . . . ," he leans in and licks a line up my shaved center with his fat. blue. tongue.

I release a wild scream, only to feel a current of electricity skitter across my chest that causes me to spasm. The words any other woman might think to shout—*how dare you speak to me like this, who the fuck do you think you are, stop the car now*—don't come out. They don't even surface in my mind. All I can think is how I might have found a dom worth my time.

"Your safe word is *nirvana*," he says before licking me again. He's teasing me and it's torturous. I whimper, my back arched so badly I'm going to need a chiropractor when this is all over. "Repeat it."

"Ni . . . Fuck . . . fuck, Taranis . . ." My tits are out, my pussy's out, my dress is bunched around my waist. Taranis has shed his shredded tux, and I'm pretty sure he's pulled his cock out, though I haven't had a chance to look at it with how his tongue has been burrowing between my folds, working me up toward a monstrous crescendo.

He slaps my tits hard enough to make me scream. Bright, hot pain flashes through my chest. He might have held back, but not by much, and I fucking adore him for it. Oh no. Oh God. He's going to have me wrapped around his giant claws before the night is through.

I bite my bottom lip and whimper as tears swim in my vision. He glares at me sternly, and I know I've done something wrong, deserving of punishment. *Please, God, yes . . .*

"Do you not understand simple instructions? What did I tell you to call me?"

"Darius," I whisper, realizing my slip.

"Since you can't even get that right, don't make another goddamn sound in my presence until I give you express permission. Watching you humiliate yourself for my pleasure, like you humiliated me by bringing me to this goddamn event, is the only thing I want from you right now."

I'm so wet. I have half a mind to be humiliated anew by the fact that I'm going to leave a huge puddle on this seat that Taranis, the bastard, will inevitably make someone else clean, but I can't speak. He told me not to. Instead, I watch and wait as he pulls on my right arm until I'm lying down, sprawled out on my back across the long bench seat. This time, when he opens my legs, placing the right over the back of the seat and draping my left knee over his shoulder, and ducks his head back in between them, he avoids the risk of impaling me with his horns.

They're huge, his horns—at least a foot long each, maybe more. They stand straight out from his head, unlike the Wyvern's, which arch down first before curving up and ending above his crown in terrifying points. And Taranis's spiral. The spirals catch the light and make the glitter coating them look like diamonds. They're beautiful. But I can't focus on them now because his tongue is long as hell.

I take the hard thrust of his tongue in silence, every nip of his sharp teeth on the soft skin of my thighs terrifying. Every dizzying ministration of his lips over my clitoris, my vulva, my every little inch leaves me paralyzed. I'm sweating with the effort it takes to stay quiet, writhing on the bench seat, opening my mouth wide, and, as the first orgasm hits, giving in to it with rapture.

Electricity shoots through my body at the same time that the orgasm blasts through my lower half. I'm embarrassed by how quickly I come, but not embarrassed enough to somehow stop it even if I could have. Pleasure thrusts itself over me like the tide over the shore. I can't do anything about it. I also can't stay quiet anymore.

I scream, shouting Darius's name amid a chorus of curses that I'm sure can be heard by Nicoleta up front. I'm hotter than an ember. I'm shaking all over, spasming as the orgasm drifts away from me. I call it back, but Taranis—Darius—has released my clit from his lips and is yanking my hips forward, moving his mouth lower, all the way to my asshole. I feel super uncomfortable and squeeze my knees around his shoulders, but he sends little shocks across their outsides, and I cry out.

He slaps the outside of my lowered thigh *hard.* "You're just a stupid little whore, aren't you?" he says, his voice raspy. His face is blockier than it was, his features sort of similar but all wrong, and for a moment when our eyes meet, I try to jerk away from him, like he's a strange monster I've never seen before.

I bite my bottom lip and whimper tragically, tears along the seams of my eyes. I don't think he'd have any way to tell, but they're tears of happiness. He knows what I *like,* and what I like is being a sub. A true sub—not that I've ever had the chance.

I've only had two partners in the past I've felt comfortable enough to ask for what I want. My girlfriend had a hard time giving me commands with any authority and was uncomfortable tying me up. Her discomfort made me uncomfortable, so after the first couple times, I just stopped asking . . . and went back to what worked for both of us.

One boyfriend I had—fucking prick—took it too far. He punched me—*punched* me—like he'd just been waiting for the go-ahead. I'd kicked him out and never talked to him again.

In Darius's arms, I feel so fucking safe. Oh, the irony. The bitter bloody irony. I am still 100 percent certain Taranis would have no trouble leaving me in an abandoned subway station, but I am equally sure that when it comes to this, Darius wouldn't let me drown.

"Answer me, whore," he hisses in this new throaty tone that makes my libido roar.

I all but scream, "Yes!"

His eyes blaze such a violent white that I have to blink away the brightness, which appears blurry through the tears that now fall over my cheeks in earnest. "And you can't follow instructions worth a damn. Tsk, tsk, tsk." He makes the sound instead of simply clicking his tongue against his teeth and then brings one clawed finger to my face, where he gathers up just a single tear. He brings it to his tongue and licks it clean, unimpressed and unmoved by me. "What did I say about speaking without permission?"

I can't answer, so I only nod.

He makes another cruel expression, and it's only then that his gaze finally drops to my exposed breasts, still ringing with the sting of where he hit me. He bites his bottom lip, and the fact that I don't pass out right there should earn me my next Peabody. "You need significant training, don't you?"

Please. I nod again.

"You need a firm hand, don't you?"

Oh God, yes.

"You've never had anyone train you before, have you?"

I shake my head. And it's true.

His mouth ticks to one side to reveal sharpened teeth. "Just a disobedient little whore."

Yes. I lick my lips.

His gaze canvases my every inch as mine does his. His blue body is sculpted and muscled and huge, marked by patterns too neat to be scars. I can't quite make them out, but I also don't have time to spare for them. Not when my eyes drift down.

"You have five minutes to help me decide if you're worth it." He leans back, throwing his arms out to the sides as he leans against the seat behind him, his huge naked body spread out over every inch of the limo's floor.

His cock juts up into the space, and I am . . . floored. I've never seen an appendage like it. It's too long and too thick, and there's a strange bulge around the middle that I don't totally know what to do with. But when he beckons me forward with two fingers and says, "Get on your knees and unhinge that jaw. Come be a monster's whore," I've never moved faster. And as I clamber over his blue tree-trunk thighs, I remember what I told Mr. Singkham before I stormed out of his office.

I lied.

Monster's whore is the only thought on my mind. Spying on Taranis and bathing in holy water can come after.

Chapter Thirteen

Taranis

She drops to her knees like she's paying the penance a lifetime of sin has cost her. I know in that moment that she won't need five minutes.

She crawls over the short distance separating us, hands landing on my thighs. There isn't space enough for her to fit between my legs, so she simply straddles one, her knees pressing into my skin in a way that should hurt, but doesn't with the thick padding of fresh muscle separating us. I don't think about it. Can't think about it as I watch her, wholly entranced, approach this *thing* that I'm calling my dick now. Never seen a dick like it, but holy fuck if it doesn't feel as sensitive as it did. Maybe more so as her fingers lightly work the shaft.

I tilt my head back, concentrating on the roof of the car. If I look down at her for even a fucking second, I'm 1,000 percent sure I'll come in my pants before she can even get her mouth on me, and I want to feel her mouth fucking bad.

To say I'm more shocked than I've ever been would be the understatement of a lifetime. I'm more shocked now than when I sprouted horns out of my head half an hour ago. I should have known. I should have fucking known. Of course the first human I've ever been remotely impressed by would *also* be the perfect little sub to control.

I haven't fucked anybody in a long time. The women who want me want to use me for my status, and I use them for the brief pleasure they provide in return. I hate humans. Fucking despise them. And yet this one here? Who smells like smoke and honey? With eyes that glitter like gems when tears fill them? This is not a face I will likely forget.

The desire comes over me—true desire, unlike anything I've ever felt—to give her exactly what she wants. To see this powerful woman—a woman who rages head-on into war, armed with no supernatural abilities, nothing but a fucking camera—on her knees for me? So desperate to suck my cock she can't help the needy, mewling sounds she's making? *Fuuuuck.*

Touch isn't new to me, but hers feels like it as she handles my cock so carefully—at first. Exploring it, she moves her calloused fingertips over the ridges and veins, the strange bulge around the middle, the fucked-up almost pointed head. I grind my teeth together, the pain in my jaw worse than the fresh pain of new horns on my hairline. I don't give a shit about my horns anymore. These crazy fucking appendages can wait. Because I can feel Monika's warm lips pressing dewy pecks along the underside of my dick.

I am a dick.

I'm a bad fucking dude.

I shouldn't touch her at all, not till I know how all this new shit works, but I don't care. I don't care about any of it right now. All I care about is fucking her. Maybe keeping her too.

Monika doesn't hesitate. Her fearlessness doesn't falter here in the face of this new challenge. Instead, she moves steadily, easily, like she's practiced on a thousand monster cocks before this one. She rubs my dick over her mouth, down her right cheek, eyes closed, lips parted. I have to peek when her tongue sneaks out to taste the base of my shaft, as far down as my literal blue balls will allow.

I fight for control. Her hands are pressed to my inner thighs, prying them apart, but there's nowhere to fucking go. I'm too goddamn huge, as big as that pink prick. And the worst part is, I can't even make fun of his bubble gum–colored skin anymore, because mine is baby blue. How freaking adorable.

"God-fucking-dammit!" I cry out. It's too much. It's all too fucking much.

Monika's deep throating the head of my cock and the curve of the tip means it's gliding easily down the back of her throat. The chick has got no gag reflex. Fuck yeah, I'm keeping her. Keeping her until I'm done.

She's working as hard as I've ever seen her. She's not a fucking quitter. My abdomen is clenched. She slowly releases my cock from her mouth and looks at its length for a few moments, her eyes wide. I groan. Not with abandon, but with impatience. She's making me wait. She lowers her head again, and I can feel her tongue licking down, down, down my nutsack. She opens her mouth wide and sucks on one of my testicles, using her hands to try to fit them both in her mouth.

I can't help the purr that comes out of the back of my throat. It's an inhuman sound I've never made before. I swallow three times but fail to control it. She pants when she pops up for air, but only for a quick breath. Then she spits on the head of my dick, returns those precious lips to my balls, and uses her left hand to stroke my erection like a goddamn pro.

I'm not going to make it. I wanted so badly to hold out for five minutes, only so I could punish her right, but I'm not going to. My eyes fly open. I tip my head upright. I want to see every-fucking-thing, so I blast the limo's inner lights, cranking them till blue lights shine bright.

Too fucking close . . . I grab the sides of her head and lift her off my balls to my erection. "Suck," I tell her.

She obeys immediately. The moment her mouth suctions around the head of my dick, I'm doomed. I force her to deep throat me, grabbing her around the neck so I can feel the bulge of my cock against my hand through her skin. She gags, drooling around my cock. Messy, messy, messy . . . Fuck! I grab the hair on the back of her head and wrench her off me. I stare into her eyes. Her pupils are fully dilated. She looks up at me like I'm the villain she's waited her whole life to find.

Her cheeks are flushed. Her neck is exposed. My gaze drops down to it, imagining so many imaginings that it's hard to know which one to execute first. My dick down her throat again, so deep she can't breathe? Between her tits so I can watch her struggle? Or do I lay waste to any desperate plans and simply rip that slit up the side and fuck her on the floor right here?

"You remember your safe word?" I ask her.

She nods.

"Good little whores have good little safe words. And they remember to use them." My voice is a threat.

She nods.

"Say it."

"Nirvana. I won't forget, Darius." She licks her lips. "But I won't use it."

For fuck's sake. I can't wait. "Get on your back and spread your legs. I'm gonna fuck you with this monster cock now. You good with that?"

She whimpers as she nods, maneuvering herself onto her back while I rise up on my knees. I lift one of her legs onto the bench seat, making just enough space for me to lower my hips to hers.

"Good girl."

Her palms are pressed to the carpeted floor beside her hips. She looks scared. *I'm* fucking scared. But I don't dare let her see it.

I sweep my palm over her forehead, pinning her head to the floor. "Hands around my neck. Eyes on me." She obeys quickly, and I lose the tenuous hold I had on my sanity.

Her lips touch mine and the moment is disastrous. I can't remember kissing a human before this, and now that I have, I want to do it all the time. Electricity, energy, whatever the fuck moves through my back, starting at my heels, warping my feet and forcing me to kick off my shoes as something happens to them. For fuck's sake. My legs ache. My tail snaps through the air. I can't control it. It slides between Monika's thighs, the tip circling my own shaft, maneuvering the head of my cock to where it needs to be.

"Fuck, Monika." Up on my forearms, I've got both arms bracketing her shoulders. I'm arched so we can stay eye to eye, nose to nose, as the head of my cock finds her opening. Her thighs are shaking so badly. She's crying in a way I find so fucking tender. I hate humans. I hate them. But remembering that she's a human whom I'm also supposed to hate is difficult. I sigh. There will be time for hate later. But not now. "Scream for me this time," I whisper.

She moans. Her jaw shakes as the strange tip of my cock finds her center and slips easily between her lower lips, then spears the heat of her lower body.

"Fuck," I groan.

"How does it . . . feel?" she hiccups.

I should punish her for speaking, but I'm too absorbed in the sensation of her body taking mine. She's electric lightning, so goddamn wet. I slide into her easily . . . at least for the first few inches. "So different." I push in deeper, watching her face twist in pleasure at first, and then pain a moment after as I thrust into her another few inches. "Fuck. This is fucking incredible."

She whimpers, and I remember that while the head of my cock may be narrow, it expands rapidly to the size of a fucking Gatorade bottle. Monika grunts as I meet resistance. I'm not even halfway in. We haven't even gotten to the bulging middle part of my dick yet.

"We're gonna work slow," I tell her, gripping her more tightly, like I'm scared she's gonna try to run. And I am scared, but not of that. I'm scared knowing she couldn't run if she tried. I could really hurt her. And the selfish bastard in me wants this more than once. "You okay with that, baby?"

She sniffles, but her gaze recenters on mine. "Yeah. Yes. It hurts a little, but I can take it." She licks her lips.

"Good girl." I kiss her forehead. Like I've lost my damn mind. But I can't take the action back, and I'm not sure that I want to when she gets that faraway look in her eyes—a distraction I take advantage of to edge another half inch forward. We groan in unison.

I drop my lips to hers and kiss her *sweetly.* I peck at her mouth, dewy and full. She tastes like she smells. Spice and honey and smoke. My lips move over hers, and there's so much of us pressed together. I roll my head to the side and taste more of her, moving across her cheek to her jaw to her ear. "You're just my filthy little cum bucket, aren't you?"

She gasps and tips her hips up into mine, letting more of me inside her until we finally reach the bulge around my monster cock—whatever the fuck it is.

"When I'm finished with you, you're just gonna be a loose hole," I growl into the shell of her small ear. "Too used for anybody else to want to fuck you." I drop my lips to her throat, tilting her chin back with my claws. My hand covers her face almost completely. I wish I were shorter than this beastly inhuman size so I could suck on her tits from here. For now, I'm left to just watch them glisten with sweat. She glitters as much as I do.

"This is only for tonight." It's a lie, but I'm sinking into her body and this moment too deep, in a way I worry I'm not gonna be able to pull back from. "We're still gonna hate each other tomorrow."

"Yes, Darius . . ." she hisses.

"For now, you're just mine to do whatever I want with. To do . . ." But I thrust and her inner walls clench around my dick. "Relax for me, baby girl."

"Augh . . ." she cries out, and I can feel her trying.

I rake the tips of my claws down her chest over her tits. I flick her nipples, and her eyelashes flutter wildly and her body relaxes just enough for me to be able to shove my way forward, past the bulging center ring of my dick, until I'm fully seated inside her.

"*Scheiße*, Darius!" She starts to whisper in German and then in Korean. Her head thrashes to either side, and I work quickly, suckling on her neck, the soft cartilage of her left ear, the tender space behind it. I breathe in the scent of her hair as I start to thrust shallowly into her body.

"Oh my God, oh my God, fuck . . . Darius . . . *ssi-bal* . . . *ssi-bal* . . . *ich kann nicht mehr* . . . I'm going to . . . it's . . . *zu früh* . . ."

And then the little whore surprises me when her back arches, her fingernails dig into my neck, her tits thrust up into my chest, and then her thighs turn to stone around my hips. I can feel her feet kick against my shins. She coils her ankles around my calves and squeezes everything so fucking tight.

This isn't going to end well for me, I think, and it doesn't. It's fucking *excruciating* trying to hold out, make this last, and not come with her.

"Darius, Darius, Darius," she pants. "Yes! Please . . . *bitte* . . ."

I know one thing for certain: The way she says *please* is something I'm never going to forget.

Just for tonight, I repeat to myself, yanking on her hair and staring into her glossy eyes. Tears track from their corners. I catch them on my tongue as her pussy tries desperately to milk my cock and I try desperately to hold on. I'm fucking lying. Just for tonight, my ass. Better yet—*her* ass. Fuck, she's so tight already, and I'm so fucking huge. This is sick. I'm a monster, and despite that, she's still so hungry for me.

She meets me desperate breath for desperate breath. Her hands are all over me, in my hair, gripping my horns, scraping down my back. I grab her wrists and pin them to the floor above her head, and she makes a wild keening sound as the peak of her orgasm passes. Her hips lift and I keep my pace steady, concentrating hard on the feel of her inner muscles squeezing around my length. I suck hard on her ear, and she vibrates as she falls apart, her body limp and useless under mine. I take the opportunity to gather both of her wrists in one hand and pin them to the center of her chest. I'll need bindings and rope, maybe a ballgag and spreader bar. Cuffs. So many restraints . . . for the next time.

I kiss her ferociously, thrusting harder now. My desperation mounts. My body starts moving jerkily, and she wrenches back, gasping for air. I let her draw in a single breath before I pull her back. I take her mouth, kissing hard like I'm excising poison from a wound. I taste everything she has to offer, and then take more she doesn't. I growl, the purring in the back of my throat getting louder. "I can't . . . I'm going . . . Come again with me, Monika. Please." *Please.*

"Y-y-yes, Darius . . ." She gasps, tears coming fast now. She doesn't use the safe word, and I know this woman well enough not to worry. She can take care of herself. "Darius, please . . . don't stop, Darius . . . don't . . ." I never used to like the name the humans gave me, but it sounds fucking good on her whispered breaths, spoken like a treasure.

I hold her wet right cheek in my palm and watch her face as I whisper, "I won't stop. You're doing so fucking good. You're perfect."

She screams, her back arching like she's possessed. We collide in thunder, and somewhere in the midst of it all, I get both arms wrapped entirely around her, both legs too. She can't move and she's locked against my mouth, screaming against my fangs as she comes again.

My forehead blazes and the muscles in my lower back bunch. My mouth hangs open, suspended while that deep, terrifying purr slips out of my throat. My chest sinks down onto the massive pillow of her tits while my dick jerks and twitches. She squeezes around me and I roar into the curve of her neck. All her soft curves fit my hard lines perfectly. I melt and she takes. She gives and I absorb.

"Holy fuck," I growl, trying to pull out of her as a surreal sensation sweeps me. Something happens down there . . . Something must be . . . wrong . . .

"No, Darius, no . . . don't pull out . . . stay." She grabs me with every ounce of strength she has. It isn't much against mine, but I don't need more encouragement. I piston my hips forward, slamming against her so violently it makes me grimace. I know I'm gonna leave bruises all over her and I'm sorry for it. But not *that* sorry.

I open my mouth to say something—apologize? Remind her this is just for the night? Tell her it isn't and that I'm going to chain her to my bed for the rest of forever? Ask her if she has any fucking clue what the fuck is going on? But I don't. My orgasm blasts through me, and I come without ever finishing the thought.

Cum erupts from the head of my erection and I damn near black out. I can feel my semen entering the searing heat of her body, warming it even more. She spasms underneath me and I hold her fucking still, locking her in my monstrous embrace as I bite down on her shoulder. She cries out, kicking her feet, but the safe word never comes out of her mouth; she simply clutches me to her body while she shakes and shudders. I think she might be coming once more.

The walls of her core clench around my cock tighter and tighter—so tight I start to panic. I open my eyes, not even realizing I'd closed them. My gaze finds her tits, her magnificent, massive tits, dotted by black nipples. I want to eat her whole. I fucking want . . .

What the fuck is happening?

Glancing down her body past her tits, I yank down on her bunched dress. There's a bulge in her soft stomach that wasn't there before. That's my dick. That's my fucking dick!

I jerk, trying to move back, but she locks her legs around me and issues a stern command that has me fighting for stillness, holding steady as I continue to come for her, filling her to the point that I can feel it leaking out of her and dripping down my nutsack.

The roar that comes out of my mouth is inhuman and obscene as I empty and empty and empty. I've never come so hard in my life, I'm sure of it. I've never come for so long. I've never felt a pussy so tight. This doesn't feel . . . real. This feels so right that it feels wrong.

I lift one hand above my head to brace against the seat while my left foot braces against the seat behind me. I push as hard as I can against both, hoping to clear my thoughts, come back to reality, but I'm fucking gone. My chest heaves. I pant against her neck. Her dress is still bunched around her waist, and I hate it, wanting it off. I want to do this all over again without anything between us.

The release took too much—*is* too much. As my orgasm starts to recede, the prickling sensation crawling over my skull fades with it. I unlock my jaw and all my straining muscles and try to withdraw from her, but I can't.

"You're stuck," she pants into my ear. She sounds strained, whimpering in a way that worries me. "I think . . . your dick swelled up inside of me."

"Fuck." That would explain it. Though it is explained by nothing at all. "I should have . . . gone to see Emily . . ."

She laughs this maniacal, crazed, and desperate laugh that makes me nervous. I blink quickly, trying to come back to myself. Turns out, that isn't a good idea either. The scattered pieces of my mind have been shoved together and reassembled in no order I can make sense of.

I open my eyes and take in the sight of her blood. "I bit you. Fuck." I lean in and lick the bloody droplets marking the smooth curve of her shoulder and upper arm. "You're mine. Gonna tie your filthy whore body up." I'm hardly lucid, half coherent. But I'm full of a need that hasn't yet been sated. "You don't need this dress anymore," I say, reaching down her body and ripping the garment free with my claws.

She jolts but doesn't protest. Her whole body trembles. Her hands clutch the floor of the car. Her mouth is wet with spit. Her shoulder is wet with blood. Her thighs are wet with cum and slick.

We lay there panting, my lips moving over her face. I can't stop kissing her. I can't control anything about this moment. "You're a filthy girl," I say against her mouth. "Absolutely disgusting."

She kisses me back, struggling to keep up. I like the taste of her lips when they're soft and supple like this. When she's so weak.

"I think . . . I can pull out of you now," I say, and I do.

We both groan at the sudden sensation of me leaving her heat and look down at my cock, draped across her low belly, spattering residual cum across her dark skin. My cum is *white*. Not cream, but white. And glittery, like my claws and my horns. Fucking ridiculous. More alarming, however, is the huge ring that's still deflating halfway down my penis.

"Did I just have that inside of you? Fuck . . ." I quickly curl up onto my knees, lifting hers in the process. I hold her hips up and inspect her folds, finding the white, glittery cum smeared over her skin tinted pink. "Fuck, you're bleeding. Gonna take you to Emily . . ."

"No, no . . . no, I feel okay." She laughs lightly, and it's that laughter that convinces me to believe her just a little bit.

I look up at her face. "You're coming up to my penthouse. Forever."

"I thought you said it was just for the night?" Her lips are open and smiling. Her eyes are shut.

"It's for however long I want."

"I don't want to be . . . locked up . . . in your sex dungeon forever . . ." She exhales, looking like she's either dead or on her way to sleep.

"You gonna fight me off?"

"Would it help?"

"No. You're mine to do with what I want."

She smiles dreamily, and my heart does this funny thing it's never done before and clenches up in my chest. My whole fucking torso clenches. I rub my thumb over her ridiculously soft mouth, and the long-standing beliefs I've held in my mind start to move in random patterns, occasionally crashing together, like distant planets or falling stars. Everything is incinerating.

"Then sex dungeon it is, Darius."

We've been parked for so long, the driver's been gone a minute. Luckily, this is my private garage. The only concern I have is making it to the elevator without anyone seeing Monika's body on the security cameras. "First, filthy girl needs to shower and eat." I slap her outer thigh before throwing the scraps of my clothing around her body and slinging her over my shoulder.

I crawl out of the car with her draped over my back. She hangs there helplessly. The only sign of life from her is the little kiss she places along my spine that damn near incapacitates me.

"There's only one rule," I say in a rough snarl as I stalk across the concrete on newly clawed feet, making it to my private elevator. The lights are bright and make our bodies look like pure carnage in the mirror. I don't care. All I can do is stare at her ass, where my cum weeps down her inner thighs. My mind goes wild. "Nasty little whores don't get to walk in my apartment. You either get carried or you crawl."

She emits a little gasp but does not surprise me at all when she whispers, "Yes, Darius."

Chapter Fourteen

Monika

I let that monster do things to me I've never even imagined in my wildest fantasies.

He tore apart his own damn sheets to make bindings and tied me up, legs and arms spread. I let him shower me off, brush my hair—and my teeth—watch me pee, and even though I was too sore to take him again in my pussy, I let him come in my mouth twice. Once, I even let him slip the narrow head of his cock in my asshole and fill me up there.

His cock swelled every time and I tried my best to soothe him by squeezing the thick band of muscle wrapped around the center with my hands, lap at it with my tongue, or simply let him thrust between my thighs as a proxy for being inside me. I wanted him inside me again, but he vowed that until he and I both saw Emily, the answer was no.

I let him make me a midnight quesadilla out of the most magnificent cheese I've ever eaten and then feed it to me bite by bite on the ground while he sat in a chair above me, like I was a dog.

I let him spank me, bite me, devour me like a cannibal. My ribs and hips hurt from how hard he pulled on my skin, and I know he'll leave bruises that I'll see in the morning light. I'll relish all of them. I even like the bandages on my shoulder, weeping with blood from where he bit me in the car. His mouth is full of fangs. My eyes are full of stars.

I'm going to masturbate to this for years, I think as I sit in his kitchen, alone in the dark. I woke up thirsty as fuck and in a fair amount of discomfort. Taranis—or Darius?—had the foresight to grab my clutch. I found it in the melee of tattered clothing scattered around his bed upstairs, and go through it now, finding an ibuprofen packet I've had in there for months and taking it gratefully. I wash it down with ice-cold water and go through the images I took on my phone as a way to keep me awake and from thinking about things too critically.

I may be a dead girl walking, but I'm also . . . confused. Trying to decide if I should slink back to my own apartment four floors down—ass naked—or . . . or what? Taranis told me this was only for one night, and he's sleeping like the dead, face down on his king bed that, beneath his new size, now looks like a twin. Is the night over? I mean, it has to be. I can't give any more. I ache down to the bone in the best of fucking ways.

He also said it was forever. I shiver and look down at my phone screen, where my thumb's been hovering over a button I've been reluctant to push this whole time. Pushing that last ludicrous thought aside, I press play.

The video starts with Taranis electrocuting Cynthia and ends once we hit the bathroom, right before I pulled his tail out of his pants. I didn't take any pictures, not one single photograph. That doesn't mean the internet isn't flooded with other pictures of Taranis as the monster upstairs.

I know I need to send his PR team something. New contacts forwarded to me by Simone have been blowing up my phone all night wondering what the fuck happened since Taranis isn't answering his. I'm surprised they haven't sent anyone to bang on his apartment door yet—though, given what happened to the last SDD troops who got too close to him, I don't blame anyone for not signing up for that mission.

I can't send them the whole video. I can't show them Taranis literally torturing a human woman, so I crop out that bit. What's left, though? Well, that makes me cringe, my toes curling into the footrest of the hard wooden barstool beneath me. I take another sip of water and wonder if my pride can handle it. Because the clip *without* the torture bit makes it fully look like he *did* revert for Cynthia, especially when she screams those exact words. There's nothing else to suggest why he reverted in the video. I can't even hazard a guess, and I was there. Cynthia theoretically should have a better guess than I do, but she's an idiot and vain.

Another email from Taranis's PR team pops up on my screen. Well, shit. I open it up and see that Mr. Singkham has been cc'd and has even responded, begging for any update I might have, even though it's two o' clock in the morning.

I shiver. It's cold in here. I should go. *I should stay. But stay to fuck him or stay to do some spying?*

I glance around his apartment. It's so cold, and there isn't much in it. No obvious neon signs that say LOOK HERE FOR WEAPONS. If I were going to spy, now would be the time to do it. But spy on Darius? After what went down between us? *Augh.* No. I can't think like that. I can't think with those kinds of feelings. The night is over. I have no expectation I'll ever see Darius again. Tomorrow, I'll go back to my dealings with Taranis. *Ssi-bal.*

Fuck it. I hit send at the exact same time I decide to get up and do a little snooping—one second before a voice crashes over my head like a brick.

"What the fuck are you doing?"

I drop my phone, and it clatters noisily over the black granite countertop. I turn around on my stool, phone immediately forgotten as I see him standing at the top of his staircase, leaning against a banister made out of metal and glass, which means I can see everything through it. Everything.

And *gawd.* The monster dong hanging between his legs makes my mouth water even as warning sirens go off in my head: MAYDAY MAYDAY MAYDAY. Even soft, it's not an appendage to scoff at. It's an organ to gasp at. And it's not soft right now. It hardens the longer

I stare at it. I wonder—not for the first time tonight—how that thing ever fit inside me and how I can make it fit inside me again. I whimper.

Taranis's eyebrows pull together, and if I weren't so distracted by the anaconda between his legs, I might have taken more time to appreciate how everything about him has changed, including the shape and structure of his once-beautiful face—everything except for his hair. He still has the tight fade he started the night with. The thick, well-groomed eyebrows. The eyelashes curling above eyes that continue to glare at me now.

"You gonna answer me, or do I have to come down there?" The threat makes my knees clench.

In a whisper that sounds like some fair damsel and not like my usual deep smoker's pitch, I say, "I was thirsty." *I wasn't about to spy on you. Not one bit.*

I watch his whole body relax, softening. His forehead unfurrows, his shoulders roll back; he relaxes his stance and his grip on the railing in front of him, letting one hand drop down to his cock. Fuck me. "You shoulda told me, baby," he says in a tone I've never heard him use. He sounds . . . nice. And not nice like Taranis the public-facing Champion nice, but *nice* nice. Just nice. "I didn't want you leaving my bed."

Just for tonight. Just for tonight. I'm a spy. I'm a spy. 007 and all that shit.

I gulp hard and watch as a look of consternation crosses his brutalist features once more. "How'd you get down here? Did you walk?"

I should lie. I *really* should lie. Instead, I nod.

"Oh, baby girl. Wrong answer." He suddenly lifts from the ground, little flares of light traveling over his skin—skin I'm starting to notice is newly marked with glittery designs that I can see only when he lights himself up from within. They're startling swirls, all over his body. Beautiful, even if nothing else about him is. Delicious? Absolutely. But beautiful? Not anymore.

He comes to a stop a few feet in front of me, hesitating like he's nervous about something.

Nervous? Taranis? Ha. What a joke.

"Why are you looking at me like that?"

I shake my head. "N-nothing."

"Spit it out."

"You . . . you just look really different."

"No shit."

"That's not what I mean," I sigh as I gesture to his body. "I mean your face. Your features. The Wyvern's face didn't look different after his reversion, but yours does."

He gives me a dull look. "You mean I'm ugly."

I consider lying, then shrug. "Well, compared to the way you looked before . . . yeah."

His eyebrows rise to his hairline before a slow smile starts to creep across his boxy face. He's got a boxer's nose now, with a ridge in the middle; a squarer, flared jaw; a fuller mouth. In its most relaxed state, he still looks mean. Like his insides have finally started to reflect on his outsides. And the fact that I still find him the hottest thing I've ever come across, I know says more about me.

I open my mouth to ask him how he's feeling after . . . all of it . . . but before I can get a word off, he starts laughing. "You're such a bitch."

I grin wider than I ever have in my life, at least that I can remember, and when Taranis starts laughing in earnest, these deep belly laughs that sound totally at odds with his typically harsh demeanor, I start to laugh too.

In the darkness of his massive flat, we stand there naked, facing each other, laughing so hard we can't catch our breaths. He leans onto his forearm on the kitchen island, his body surrounding mine. His heat crashing against my heat. The intoxicating smell of his body mixing with the smell of his cum and my sweat. I tip my forehead forward and place it against his burly chest. He cups the back of my head with a hand covered in claws. And we keep laughing until finally, Darius jerks my head back and presses a quick peck to my mouth. "You're going to pay for that," he whispers.

"Please, Taranis." I'm panting again, the little monster whore that I've become.

"No." He grabs my neck. Squeezes. I look into his eyes and watch the blue lighten even lighter than it was until it shines nearly white. "You call me *Darius*."

"Darius . . ."

"Not just for tonight, but from now on."

Then he swings me up over his shoulder, still chuckling like a male I don't even recognize, for more reasons than one, and I can't help but think that I might be in big, big trouble.

Chapter Fifteen

Monika

A familiar sound grates at my eardrums, a sound that can only be one thing. I jolt upright—or try to—but Darius's limbs are heavy, pinning me. His arm locks over my back and his knee digs into my thigh. "What are you doing?"

I squirm. "My phone. I think my mom's calling."

"It's the middle of the night. Call her in the morning," Darius grumbles, sounding more like his old self, and deeply annoyed.

"My mom is hyperorganized and knows what time it is here," I say on a yawn. "She wouldn't be calling if it weren't important."

"Fine. Crawl," he orders me.

"I'm not going to crawl," I laugh, choking on the sound. "Punish me when I get back." And in a fit of insanity, I turn over to face him in the bed and quickly dive in to give his cheek a peck.

His eyes fly open and he looks at me. Just stares.

"What?" I whisper, feeling a little self-conscious, and then even more so when he doesn't answer. "I'll be right back."

I shove at him as best I can until I'm able to stumble out of the bed to his walk-in closet. I don't want to call my mom back while wearing nothing but my birthday suit. Especially not after the night I've had. If she knew even one of the things I got up to tonight, she'd likely hire a hit squad to kidnap me back to Berlin and never let me out of her sight.

As quietly as I can, I ravage Taranis's walk-in closet, grabbing the first T-shirt and sweatpants I see, and book it downstairs. My phone rings again as I make it to the island.

"Annyeong, Eomma," I say, trying to keep my voice light.

Immediately I know something's wrong. My mom's voice is strained as she says slowly, in Korean, "I am sorry for calling you so early your time, Monika, but Cynthia has been involved in a terrible car accident and can't get through to her mother. Can you please go to the hospital to check on her?"

No. Absolutely not. I hate that bitch. "Of course, *Eomma*."

"I know you two don't have the best relationship," she says, surprising me by acknowledging it for once. "But she sounded really afraid. I thought about flying in myself." That shocks me to my core.

"What did she say happened?" I ask as I book it down the hall. I consider going upstairs to tell Darius I'm leaving, but I can hear the sound of his snores. Instead, I take the hallway to the left, finding the floor plan familiar even if his penthouse is three times the size of my three-bedroom. Our places share that, in part, but absolutely nothing else.

His foyer is cold and unwelcoming, just like the rest of his penthouse. I push the button to his elevator, my mom still talking until the connection cuts out. "She was so excited when she caused Taranis to change into his other *shape* . . ." my mom says, lacking the word for *reversion* in Korean that would mean the exact same thing. She cuts back in when I hit the lobby. " . . . she took interviews for hours." I wince, hating that more than I have a right to. Taranis isn't mine, even if I'm starting to feel something for Darius. "She only wrapped up an hour ago when she drove herself home and was hit by a truck. It didn't stop. They didn't catch the driver . . ."

"She drove herself?" I ask, slipping into the back of a car Marsha—Taylor's cheerier, older white-lady counterpart—hails for me, shooting a curious look down at my bare feet. “That doesn’t sound like Cynthia.” I wasn’t even confident she had a license; her mother’s people always drove her everywhere.

“No, it doesn’t, but I guess she was so excited she thought it was a good idea.” My mother curses, making me gasp as the car zips away from the curb. She never curses. “Sorry, *Schatz*.” I stick out my bottom lip, feeling suddenly overwhelmed as she uses the German pet name my father uses for me. “I’m just stressed. She sounded so strange when I spoke to her. I just want you to make sure she’s okay.”

“I can do that. She’s at Sundale Central Hospital, right?” It wasn’t the fanciest hospital, but it had the best emergency room in the country.

“Yes. She broke both of her legs in the crash and got a concussion.”

I wince. “That probably explains why she sounded so weird.”

“Yes, you’re probably right.”

“I’ll call you as soon as I speak to her, and I’ll try her mother’s assistant in the meantime.”

“Thank you.”

“I love you, *Eomma*.”

“I love you too, Monika.”

I get the strangest feeling that she’s relieved to be able to hear my voice. Which just makes me feel like shit. My mom was panicking and Cynthia, for all her faults, was hurting, while I was getting that good monster dick.

The car glides to a stop in front of the hospital, and I don’t bother to check my appearance before going to the front desk for Cynthia’s room number. The nurse shakes her head, then seems to do a double take at my ID, eyes widening as she says, “You’re Monika Neumann?”

I nod. “I am. Can I see Cynthia?”

“Well, she’s meant to go into surgery in less than an hour . . . but I suppose if you’re quick . . .”

“I’ll be quick.”

The Indian woman with twice as many curves as I have rises and quickly leads me down a series of hallways, some bustling, some eerier than others. “I saw the pictures you took of Cynthia and Taranis tonight.”

"Pictures?" I didn't take any pictures, just that one video.

She nods. "At first, I thought it was so romantic, but then I wondered if something wasn't wrong, considering that Taranis hasn't so much as called to check on her." She gives me a curious look, asking questions I'm not going to answer.

"I haven't seen the pictures. I just sent a video to the PR team." The nonanswer doesn't seem to please the woman, who gives me a pout. Luckily, we soon arrive at a door with a whiteboard mounted to the front that reads *Min-hyuck, Cynthia.*

"You have twenty minutes. Don't make me regret this."

"I won't." I hustle inside, the door clicking shut at my back.

Cynthia and I stare at each other. She's way more alert than I expected her to be. She's hooked up to IVs and has her legs wrapped in thick layers of gauze all the way up to the thigh and all the way down to her feet. They hang suspended off the bed in these sad-looking gurneys. And she doesn't look pleased to see me. In fact, she looks downright terrified.

"Cynthia?" I say hesitantly, like I'm speaking to a wounded animal, which, I guess, in a very real sense, I am. "You okay?"

She rifles desperately through the front pocket of the oversize hoodie she's wearing. It's not hers. She doesn't own an oversize anything. Her fingers are fumbling as she pulls out a phone—a phone that looks like it was brought here straight from the nineties. The little brick of a Nokia is gray, with buttons and no touch screen. I shake my head. I don't understand what's happening.

My voice is laced with confusion as I take a step toward her uncomfortable-looking bed. "My mom was freaking out. We haven't been able to get hold of your mom yet."

"I don't want my mom to come here. I just want you to take this before they come back." She sniffles and starts to shake, glancing around the room as if she expects the walls to open their mouths and eat her up. "Take it. Please. I should never have gotten involved. I should never have tried to steal your man." She starts to weep openly, and . . . she's not a cute crier. It's the ugliest I've ever seen her, and that, more than the sight of her two mangled legs, is what strikes fear into me and even a little bit of compassion for her.

I approach the side of her bed and place my hand on her arm. She bows her head and cries in earnest, her face puffing up and turning red. She pats my hand, and I place my other hand awkwardly on the top of her head. Touching her like this makes me realize I don't have anywhere near as much experience as I should comforting people. This feels all kindsa weird. Shit. Am I just as out of touch with humanity as Taranis is? The thought gives me the heebie-jeebies. So does touching her hair. The worst part is that I expected her to push me away, but she doesn't. Instead, she just sobs there for another couple minutes.

"Don't cry . . . You'll be okay. They'll do the best work on your legs. You won't even see the scars."

"Scars?" she wails. "I'm gonna have scars?"

"No! I just said you won't be able to see them! They probably don't . . ." My voice fails me because the nurse did just say she needs to go into surgery. How do you perform surgery without cutting anything open?

"You're such a bitch . . ."

Not the first time I've been called that tonight. "So I've been told."

"You should never have posted those photos."

"What photos?"

"Don't play dumb!" She shoves me off her, but before she does, she slaps the plastic cell phone into my palm. I curl my fingers around it on instinct while she reaches back into her sweatshirt pocket and pulls out a snazzier device. She unlocks it and turns it toward my face. "These pictures. The ones you took of me and captioned *Only real love causes reversions.*"

"Yuck. No, I didn't. Gag." I scroll through the slideshow, horrified at the images. If the cropped video I sent was capable of making it look plausible that Taranis went through his reversion for Cynthia, these stills hammer it home.

There's a short clip of him dropping to his knees in front of Cynthia; then the next still is of him on his feet, blue and busting out of his tuxedo. The following image is of him with his hand on Cynthia's arm, and the final image is of Cynthia's face and the pure elation written across it. It doesn't matter that you can only see a little piece of Taranis's blue profile or that his eyes are closed in it, Cynthia's face says enough. She's completely in love.

I'm too busy being annoyed at what the PR team did with my video to notice the like and comment count. When I do, I nearly lose my lunch, and that's a pity because I don't get a chance to eat *tteokbokki* very often. There are two million likes and thirty thousand comments, and this was only posted two hours ago.

"Shit," I hiss, my stomach dropping through my toes, which curl into the tiled floor. I still don't have any shoes on. Jealousy rears its head in my loins—that's not right. *Scheiße.* That's too many body parts in one sentence. I can't even think of a good metaphor.

The sudden urge to sit comes over me—sit and stare at what I've done—but Cynthia's sobs have petered out. She snatches her cell phone from my limp grip and wipes her nose on the sleeve of her sweatshirt, which, the longer I stand here, I start to notice carries a man's scent. And it's not Taranis's.

"Yeah, shit. Take it down."

"I can't," I start to say while the taste of regret coats my tongue, and then I'm hit by the wrongness of her request. "Wait. Why would you want me to take it down? You're famous. You were taking interviews all night . . ."

"I said take it down, please."

I take a chance and, instead of retreating, sit on the edge of her bed and watch the way she winces away from me. "What happened tonight?"

Cynthia sniffles and sniffles some more. She wipes her eyes and glances around again at the walls, and she's not looking at me as she starts whispering, "It wasn't a car accident."

"What?"

And then it all comes out in a rush. "I was driving out of town, to my *eomma*'s estate in North Sumnerville." The wealthiest suburb around Sundale and where her mother lives—that all tracks. "I was feeling myself and wanted to listen to the radio longer, to see if any of my clips had started to play." That tracks too. "I took Old Highway 68. I was almost home when somebody appeared in the passenger's seat." That . . . doesn't track.

I'm about to interrupt with a litany of questions when she says, "I screamed—of course—but they grabbed the wheel. We went off the road, and I saw that we were about to hit a tree, but all of a sudden, we weren't there anymore. We were somewhere else. It was dark and cold. They put me in a chair, and then the Marduk was there. He asked me how I . . . caused Taranis's reversion." She starts to hiccup while all my blood runs cold.

"I told him it wasn't me. I told him that Taranis electrocuted me—he doesn't love me," she spits. "But he saw the pictures." She limply tosses her phone into her lap. The screen is unlocked and that last picture of her beautiful, happy face is shining up at us, making a mockery of the moment. "He said that if I was lying and wasting his time, he would hurt me. I told him that *you* took and posted the pictures—not me." That bitch. "But he didn't care. He asked me where you lived. I told him, and that seemed to piss him off too. He told me that if I went to the police or told anyone at the COE or SDD, he'd kill my mom. And then they broke my legs. I must have passed out, because the next thing I remember, I was in the hospital."

I shiver all over. Behind me, the door opens. "Ms. Neumann, the OR doctors are ready for Cynthia. It's time for you to leave," the nurse tells me.

I nod and slide off the bed, aghast and horrified and struggling to process. "Why the phone?" I ask Cynthia.

She shakes her head. "He just said to give it to you. He put me in this sweatshirt because I didn't have any pockets." She shudders just then and suddenly becomes frantic in her effort to tear it off over her head. She throws it at me. "Get rid of it."

I nod, and even as the nurse says my name sternly again and again, I hesitate and then rush forward, thinking of one more thing. "Can you tell me anything about the place they took you? Or who the other one was with the Marduk?"

Cynthia's eyes shut. She shakes her head. "Dark hair, olive skin, I guess. Maybe Greek or something. They weren't that tall. I'm not sure if it was a man or woman. Only wearing black. Smiling a lot, so fucking smugly."

"Ms. Neumann!"

"And the place?" I whisper, grabbing Cynthia's hand and forcing her concentration to my face.

She opens her eyes and shudders as she says, "I don't know. Some kind of warehouse. It could have been anywhere."

The nurse shoves me back with force as two other people move into the room and drop the arms of Cynthia's bed. They start rolling her toward the door. Just before she passes through it, she turns her head to look at me and says, "I smelled the sea." And then they wheel her away from me.

The nurse gives me an admonishing finger shake before escorting me back to the front desk and then all but kicking me out of the hospital. I stand there under the brightly lit emergency awning as people filter past me, none looking too worse for wear, except for a woman about my age holding a bloody towel to her mouth and being escorted by her absolutely frantic-looking boyfriend. I'm still staring after them, back through the automatic doors of the hospital, when an unfamiliar buzzing picks up in my pocket.

I fish out my phone. Don't see any notifications. And then I withdraw the *other* one. There's a text. With fingers that feel like sausages as they bumble around, smashing down half a dozen buttons, I open it.

Meet me at Habesha Cafe. 4am. Or

Or what? That's how we're playing it these days? Not even an *or else*? Just an *or*?

I snort out a breath of nervous laughter and think through my options, finally landing on just one. I call a car and head to Habesha Café. That *or* really did it for me, and I'm not interested in getting my or anybody else's legs broken.

I call my mom as I sit in the back of the car, the driver giving me weird looks and keeping his mask on as if he's afraid I'm going to infect him with whatever I got at the hospital. To be fair, with how tired I am and how messed up I look, I appear as if I could be carrying any number of infections. I give my mom a brief update, tell her about Cynthia's surgery. She thanks me and promises to keep trying Ambassador Min-hyuck, and I promise, albeit reluctantly, to check back in on Cynthia in a day or two.

As I hang up the phone, the car pulls up to a normally well-trafficked city street that's currently dead, as it's still pitch black out. I don't have a key, I don't have an ID. I don't even have underwear. I get out of the car shakily, offering the driver an extra tip of a hundred bucks if he'll wait around the corner for me. He agrees, but when I give him a number to call in case I'm not back in thirty minutes, he tells me he doesn't want any trouble and drives off.

Thanks, dude.

I stare at the coffee shop door for too long before opening it. There's a light on in the back and movement coming from the kitchen, but that's not what draws my focus. My focus instead falls on a giant behemoth of a male seated at a dainty little mosaic table directly in front of me.

"Monika," he says, his voice low and even. "Have a seat."

"I think I'll stand."

Suddenly, I'm moving—being pushed by an invisible hand. Wind gathers at my back and flings me forward. I land on my stomach on his sweatshirt on the table, my head hanging off the end and almost in the Marduk's lap.

His hand crawls over my back, down my sides to my sweatpants pocket. I open my mouth to scream. "Don't scream." He speaks before I can follow through on that idea and rips the wind straight from my lungs. I can't breathe and clutch desperately at my neck while the Marduk reaches over my body and does something to my pants. "Sit," I hear him order, but at a distance. I can't hear anything over the sound of whooshing in my ears. And then I'm thrown unceremoniously back.

I land in a hard wooden chair, which tips back on its legs, threatening to fall before righting itself with a bang. I hold on to my seat, my heart pounding, and when I look up into the Marduk's cold black gaze, he raises a blond eyebrow and releases me.

I suck in air like I'd been drowning. I *was* drowning. I know this supervillain has power over wind and thunder, but I didn't think it worked like that. *Ssi-bal.*

After coughing to clear my throat, I swallow repeatedly, a funny taste in my mouth that I hope never to experience again. I wait, gaze raking over him, trying to pick up clues . . . something . . . anything! That's when I see what's lying on the table between us. What he pulled out of my pocket.

He glances down at my phone. "Why don't you unlock it for us?"

I can't do that. We both know that I'm recording all this. I don't respond.

The Marduk simply tilts his head. "Doesn't matter either way." And the phone suddenly explodes from within, bursting apart into thousands of microscopic pieces, never to be salvaged, the recording I'd been taking gone with it.

We wait a moment, staring at each other, before I break the silence. "Nice coffee shop." I'm still gripping the edges of my chair like it's the only thing that's going to keep him from flinging me into Oz.

"I think so."

"Why am I here?"

"The better question is, why are you late? It's almost four thirty. We'll have to do this quickly, and I don't have time for questions. I know that your little friend is not the key to Taranis's reversion, unless torturing her a little bit somehow triggered it. I also know that you were there since you took the recording. What caused his reversion?"

I simply lick my lips and shake my head. "I can only tell you what I saw," I opt to answer, rather than telling him the truth that Cynthia got her legs shattered for—I don't know. "I saw Taranis torturing Cynthia, electrocuting her while she sobbed. I saw her fall, and then the next thing I know, Taranis is falling beside her and rising up again twice as large."

"And what did he do afterwards?"

Me.

I feel heat rise in my cheeks but am proud of my even tone as I say, "Panicked. He was out of it. I managed to get him out of the South Korean Embassy and to his car, which took him back to his place."

"And yours. The two of you live in the same building."

"Correct."

The Marduk swipes his sweatshirt off the table between us, and as it falls, he does the last thing I'd have hoped he would. His gaze drops to my clothing. He inspects it for all of two seconds before lifting his nose to the wind. A slight breeze wafts from behind me, pulling in his direction, and his mouth starts to form a grin. "My, my. Monika, do you have a thing for villains?"

I heat further, harder, hotter, all the way down to my toes, which curl into the cold floor. I don't say anything.

The Marduk leans back in his tiny chair and strokes his beard. His gaze keeps me pinned in place. His arms are tattooed all over in wild symbols that frighten me for reasons I don't understand. I've got chills rushing over every exposed piece of my skin—not that he's looking at me like that. He's got a detached, almost clinical way about him that makes me afraid in a way Taranis never has.

"I take it you are his key, then."

"I don't know what that means."

"Only that I'll have to change my plans and let you leave alive."

Alarm bells are ringing. The choir sings, *"DANGER DANGER WARNING WARNING."* "You're leaving?"

"Unfortunately, yes. You're free to go. I've learned all that I've needed from you."

"And you're not going to threaten me? Break my legs if I go to the COE or whatever?" I don't know why I'm giving him ideas. I'm just . . . confused. My adrenaline is keeping my voice calm, but my hands still shake. I'm not . . . cut out for this world. Human-size conflict, I seem to be able to handle, but this is some big inhuman-size shit.

"No. If you're Taranis's key, and I suspect you are," he says to me from the door, "then it wouldn't do me any favors to hurt you and alienate him. He's one of my most useful allies and now the most powerful being on this planet."

I'm surprised to hear the Marduk admit as much, and I watch him stand in the doorway, darkness washing over him like a pall. It's too dark outside still, sunrise an hour off. This morning, however, feels even darker than most.

The scent of roasting coffee fills my lungs as he watches me and I watch him. I can think of nothing useful to say, nothing useful to ask, and so I chirp, like an idiot, "He is?"

"Yes. He's fully reverted and number Six."

A little bell jingles as he leaves, his hands in his pockets. I think he might be whistling a tune as he makes his way down the street.

A clanging in the back coming from the kitchen startles me. I pick up the Marduk's sweatshirt for no reason I can think of and follow the path he took on the sidewalk. I need to call a car. I need to calm the fuck down. My vision is blurring and my hands are starting to shake real bad. I feel completely adrift and in way, way the fuck over my head.

I don't understand what the Marduk's just told me, and the one person—being—I wish I could confide in is the one who might be first in line to tear off my head. If the Marduk is right, and I've got no reason to believe he isn't, Taranis really is the bad guy. I can't tell him any of this. I can't even call him now for a goddamn lift.

Sniffling pitifully, I reach into my pocket to grab my phone and pull up any and every transportation app—whichever one can get me home fastest. But what I pull out isn't my phone. It's the little brick that the Marduk gave me. The one without internet. Because my phone got exploded.

I stand on the street, look up at the putrid gray sky, and shout at the top of my lungs, *"SSI-BAL!"*

I'm so fucked.

Chapter Sixteen

Taranis

She ran out on me. That little *hussy*. That was always one of my favorite words my white human host family taught me.

I'm angry and irritated as I rush through a shower and pull on clothes. But . . . I'm also pleased. And the rugged combination of emotions confuses me . . . and makes me irritable all over. Standing in front of the mirror does not improve my foul disposition.

I'm still the same monster I was last night, and I look even more ridiculous in the soft morning light. For starters, I'm still blue. My horns and the claws on my hands and the talons on my feet are all white. Like a children's art project, they look like they were dunked first in Elmer's glue and then into a vat of glitter. I have fangs. Not a dainty set of fangs like the Wyvern has that affect only his back teeth, but a mouth full of them. My front teeth are pointy. And the worst part of all, I'm almost as big as that hideous pink creature. And definitely more hideous.

My face *is* a different shape. Monika was right about that. Was it the ugly composition of my features that drove her off? My clawed hands come insecurely up to my cheeks. My brow, cheek-and jawbones stick out too much, making the unusual glow of my eyes even more startling as they lie in shadowy hollows of my face. They're not purple anymore, but blue, with only the slightest purple tint as I stare into them now.

Frowning, I go to my closet only to find that it's been ruffled. One of my T-shirts is missing off the hangar, and the drawer where I keep my rarely worn sweatpants is ajar. Hmph. At least she left in my clothing. *That has to count for something,* I think as I pull a T-shirt on over my head and proceed to shred the hell out of it on my horns. Not that it would have fit.

I huff out a sigh, abandoning any hope of wearing a shirt and moving on to pants. I can't come close to slipping my talons through the leg of my jeans, so I go to my sweats. I can pull them on with minimal tearing, but they only come up to my shins. Like fucking capri pants.

Irritation blasts through me, and a huge ball of electricity swells from my chest. Fuck. I stumble back, away from the full-length mirror, caught off guard by my surging powers. But after the initial shock wears off, I grin. I may be uglier than sin, but my powers are magnificent. I can feel fresh energy storming through my body, waiting to be unleashed. It makes it easier to recall the strange dreams that plagued me last night—an expansion of the visions that crippled me the moment I reverted—and remember exactly how to use my powers to their fullest extent.

Training on brutal battlefields made of black sand, the Elders watching over me as I attacked and was attacked again and again by monsters who could shift into wind, who had claws and hooves and horns, who could cause pain with nothing more than their will.

I shiver and frown, remembering so much about my *childhood* and finding it utterly unsatisfying. Not because of the violence. No, that I rather liked. But because on Tratharine, there was nothing that was mine. A collective army, we fought, slept, and ate together as we worked to protect a violent population that had few redeeming qualities. Babies were birthed in centers by magical machines that engineered us. Badly injured and disabled Tratharine were killed the moment the Elders deemed them ineffective.

I was among the top soldiers. I was counted among the ten the Elders confided in and depended on most. I was number Six.

I stretch out my arms, admiring the way the symbols glitter over them in the light. Symbols meant to bind me to my weapon and, more importantly, to the Elders whose magic created them. I shudder. The Elders had—*have*—more power than the lot of us soldiers combined. Though the Marduk still fights in their name and honor, I don't want them here on this planet. I don't want to invite creatures so powerful that they not only lay waste to humanity but also have the ability to rule over *me*, even in this form with all my newly acquired power.

I want to be out from under the COE—that motivation has not changed. I don't need a new master.

As I watch myself in the mirror, I realize that, like this, I'll have no problem killing Mr. Singkham and Ms. Lemon, if needed, and taking over the COE. I am also no longer sure I'll have an issue with the Marduk. I can take him now; I'm quite convinced of it. And if my memories ring true, then he needs to die. Without him, the Elders won't make it to this side.

There is just one other thing I must do first: Find and punish Monika Neumann.

First Monika, then Mr. Singkham's cleverly engineered death—a simple internal electrical charge should do it. Everyone will think he had a stroke instead. Then the Marduk and any minions who may remain loyal to him. Then destroy all the weapons. Fuck, kill, kill, destroy. Easy peasy.

Feeling quite content with my plans, I strut in my fucking capri pants to my office. First things first: I need to find her address. As my dick swells at the memory of last night, I also decide that second on my list before killing Mr. Singkham is going to see the doctor to make sure I *can* continue fucking Monika with wild abandon with this new magnificent dick. It makes me wonder if I should shower—yes. Did she shower? I would have heard it. Which meant she really left my penthouse in the middle of the night without a bra or drawers on, my cum and her slick crusted all over her.

Did strange men and women see Monika's pert nipples poking through the thin fabric of my T-shirt? Did they look at her bare toes curl, curl, curling as the pleasure crashes through her, and she's fully restrained, incapable of escaping my hold as I slam into her over and over and . . .

Fuck.

I rub my hand roughly over my face as I enter my office and find her file. It sits in a locked drawer underneath my built-in shelving unit, right beneath the shelf that holds my strange silver weapons. I glance at them as I wrench the drawer open, and curiosity has me reaching out to touch one of them. I brush my fingers over the metal, which isn't like any metal I've ever felt before. Almost rough, it carries a preternatural chill, like it's trying to warn me away from it. Like it isn't even mine.

I frown as I pick one up and pull it on. I did some research. In the human world, there exists only one other weapon like it: the katar. An ancient Indian weapon, it fits on my hands like gloves. There's a trigger mechanism inside that I can squeeze and the single blade pops into three.

Now that I've reverted and have regained my memory, I remember the Elders bestowing this weapon onto me. I could use it on Tratharine just fine without a key, but for whatever reason, here on Earth, the key is required both to find the weapons and activate them. The Elders could not have designed this system to be more fucking complicated. When activated, lightning would shoot out from the tips of each blade of my weapon, so powerful that one single strike to the chest could kill any incoming opponent. I could simply stand at the top of a hill and eradicate an entire approaching army one by one.

That's why the Wyvern is only number Sixty-Two in our hierarchy.

I grin at the revelation, then frown again as I remember that the Marduk is number Four. I cannot allow him to revert, or I might struggle with phase three of my *fuck, kill, kill, destroy* mission. Especially considering that the weapons remain dead in my hands on this planet, nothing more than useless scrap metal. I frown. Is this weapon . . . even mine? What if he offered me a poor man's replica?

"Of course he fucking did," I grunt, clearing my weapons from my desk and tossing them onto the shelf behind me before returning to Monika's file to find her personal information. "One problem at a fucking time." Fuck, kill, kill, destroy. I need to keep my priorities in check.

I pull my phone out of my pocket and, ignoring far, far too many notifications that I have no intention of dealing with now or later, I call her. It goes straight to voicemail. Concern mounting alongside suspicion, I try again. And then three times more.

"Stupid bitch," I curse, my chest heating with embarrassment. She's going to see those missed calls from me and what's she gonna think? That Darius is some desperate fucking loser?

Lewd and lucid visions of how I'll punish her for ignoring my calls flood my thoughts and make me harder than the goddamn paddle I'm gonna whoop that ass with. Oh, how I'm gonna punish her . . .

I glance down at the file, which is stamped with a black-and-white photo of her face that I tear out and shove into the pocket of my sweats *like a psycho* and come to the bit with her address. "No." I blink at the paper. I blink again, and anger hits the nape of my neck. "That fucking . . . *liar*."

I know I'm being irrational as I slam the paper down on my desk and move out of my office, kicking the door shut behind me. I return to my living quarters, heading straight past the couch I fucked her roughly on last night and rip open the glass doors that lead to my balcony. I take flight without bothering to shut the doors behind me, circle the building, find the four floors down from mine, and touch down onto the most bizarrely decorated balcony I've ever seen. There are carpets out here, bright pink and orange, and so many plants I nearly trip over one in my haste to make my landing.

Batting back the feathery bush, I rip open the door to her balcony, my irritation spiking to dangerous levels as I find it unlocked. I may have aerial precautions installed to notify me of any incoming intruders, but she doesn't. "Stupid, reckless woman . . ."

Even though I *should* feel better knowing that she didn't leave my—*our*—apartment building in the dead of night, I don't. Because when I take a tour of her apartment, I find room after room of spectacularly blinding color and horrific decorations . . .

But no. Fucking. Monika.

Where the fuck would she have gone, and when? Did I not have a conversation with her that ended in me fucking her with my tail about how naughty girls who walk around my place when they were expressly told to be carried or crawl don't get to leave my bed? Ever again?

I grunt as I enter her bedroom and plant my hands on my hips, looking down at a bed that's covered in a hideous green duvet that's not even slightly rumpled. She didn't sleep here last night. Where the fuck did she go? Who was she with? My tail swats at the air violently. Maybe tail-fucking her in the ass would have sent a clearer message.

As my mind rages with worry—*anger*, I mean, not worry—the sound of elevator doors gliding open pulls my attention around, my entire body moving with it. That better be fucking Monika, and if she's with anyone else, so help me . . .

My *horns* crackle with electricity as I step out of her bedroom, cut down the hall to her living room, cross it, and see her in her little entryway. "You dare," I hiss.

She screams before she glances up, her eyes puffy and her hair mussed. I have a full-body reaction to seeing her standing there in my oversize T-shirt and black sweats that entirely swallow her curves, and what I feel is . . . unsure. I don't feel like myself at all.

The electricity that passes through my horns makes my shoulders roll back. I come alive, inhaling so deep I feel it in my toes. And then lightning skitters out in a cloud around me, a huge burst that makes Monika scream a second time. I exhale and the lightning cloud reabsorbs into my body, disappearing as quickly as it came. I'm moving forward the whole time, my paces long. Her apartment is big, but still smaller than mine, and I make it to her in seconds.

She's standing up, whatever rags she was holding in her hand now discarded at her feet, her mouth fumbling over words. I grab her by the throat, rage lighting like a match down my spine. Pushing her back against the closed elevator doors, I bring our noses nearly to touch. Against her lips, I exhale, "You dare run from me?"

While she chokes on some sort of excuse, I open the elevator doors behind her with a flick of my gifts and push her back toward the empty free fall. She screams, "Taranis!" Her eyes fly open wide and she grabs on to my forearm, and I frown, not liking the feeling that she's called me *that.* Darius held her trust last night—a trust Taranis has never so much as touched. I want it back.

"Darius," I whisper.

Her pulse pounds beneath my palm, and I don't like that either. She's been calmer in front of greater adversaries before, and I decide then that I'm not sure that's what I want to be to her anymore.

"Darius," she repeats.

I drag her into the foyer and whirl her body around, pressing her into the concrete wall. My gaze sweeps her face. Her eyes are all bloodshot. She hasn't slept.

Her expression shifts, but I don't take the time to read it. I press my mouth to hers, fully open, tongue seeking. My hard body softens the instant I feel her stiff limbs melt for me. I gather her up, spreading her thighs around my hips and grinding my cock against her center.

"Why didn't you answer your phone?" I say on tortured breaths.

"I . . ." She shakes her head. "I lost it."

"You *lost* it?" I hiss. That's a lie if I've ever heard one. I grab her hair and wrench her head back. *Easy,* I remind myself.

She whimpers, scrambling, "I . . . left it in the cab."

"What company? I'll have my people get it back." My gaze is narrowed and heated. I don't know why she's lying to me. Where was she?

"Don't bother. The guy was an asshole." Her hands are on my chest, beating on it pitifully. "Please . . ."

"No. This is not the *please* I want from you." I shake her head.

She winces, gloss forming on her eyes, and I don't like that either. I grind my hips against her harder, and she gasps and licks her lips. But when I lean in to meet her heat, she contradicts herself and begs, "Nirvana."

I jerk back. "What?"

"Nirvana," she says, sagging in my grip in a way that spells defeat with all capital letters. I've never seen her like this before. So . . . drained. "I want to—you know I want to be a monster slut for you. But I can't take a punishment right now, Taranis . . ."

"Darius," I snarl.

"It's hard to remember you aren't Taranis when you're yelling at me."

I release her hair and she lifts her head. The strain in her expression bothers me more than I like. My whole body stiffens. Like *I've* been electrocuted. I stroke the outside of her bare arms. She's cold as ice. "What happened? And don't lie."

She shifts her gaze from side to side as if debating lying, then exhales. "Cynthia got into a car accident last night and landed in the hospital. My mom was calling me, remember?"

I frown, hardly remembering that at all.

"My mom was so stressed I didn't even bother stopping at my apartment to get shoes or my wallet. Or my car." I start to set her down, but the moment her feet hit the ground she winces. "Ow."

"You're hurt?" The next breath she takes is shaky, and my stomach bottoms out at the sound of it. "Don't you dare cry." My front teeth are clenched. My spine is ramrod straight. "How are you hurt?"

"I'm not, really. My feet are just really sore. I walked here."

"From where? Which hospital?"

"Central . . ." she says slowly.

I fucking choke. "That's three miles at least." My horns alight.

She rears back like I really am gonna hurt her, and I. Hate. All of it. "It's not a big deal. Cynthia is okay . . . except for two broken legs . . ."

"I don't give a fuck if Cynthia's okay." I struggle to control my volume as I snatch her up in a cradle hold and carry her down the hallway toward her living room. "I don't care if Cynthia got turned into a fucking toad or was kidnapped for ransom."

Monika winces when I say that.

"You don't even like her," I add.

"I did it for my mom. She was really freaking out. And they haven't been able to get hold of Cynthia's mom. I'm glad I went."

"You should have fucking told me. Texted me. Something." Holding her with one hand around her back, my tail beneath her knees, I use my free hand to grab her by the cheeks.

"You're right," she says through lips puckered like a fish's. "I just . . . didn't think about it, and I didn't want to wake you up. You were snoring."

I squeeze a little harder. "I don't snore." She grunts out what sounds dangerously like a laugh even as tears surface again in her eyes. "Stop that."

"Sorry," she says when I release her face, opting instead to comb her unruly hair behind her ear. "I'm just really tired. We can talk about whatever you came to talk about in a couple hours. Please. I just . . . need sleep."

"Shut up, Monika."

"What?"

"Just stop . . . talking." I'm speaking through clenched teeth, and my hands are tense. She winces as my claws dig into her body, and I spasm, my anger self-directed as I grumble out an apology. I carry her across her apartment, back to her bedroom and the en suite bathroom—which is even bigger than mine, I find.

I set her down on the marble countertop between the his-and-hers sinks. The fact that only one sink has anything surrounding it pleases me in ways I refuse to acknowledge. I run the bath, stoppering the tub. It's a claw-foot—must have been custom installed, because my tub is built in and looks totally different. Everything about her place is eclectic, at best. There are crystals and candles lined up on little golden stands all around the outer edge of the tub. I think about lighting them but find my ears burning at the thought.

Instead, I return to her and watch her try to focus on me with bleary eyes. She's swaying where she sits, exhausted in a way I don't fucking like. She looks nothing like the woman I had underneath me last night. She looks like that tough woman's soft insides. It's . . . hard to look at. She's way too vulnerable, and when I tap her hip and she lifts it, giving me space to pull her sweats down and then off, the electricity burning in my chest burns hotter and releases from my horns in a burst.

Monika jumps. "What was that?"

"Nothing." I glance at the mirror behind her and see that my eyes are a color they've never been before. White. And they're blazing. "Arms up."

When she lifts her arms, I peel the shirt off her, noticing that she's still covered in my scent. I'm reluctant to bathe her for fear that it'll fade. And then I decide I'll just make sure to give her a reason to smell like me later. And every other day.

I blink and realize I've got one palm pressed to the side of her face, cradling her cheek. My jaw clenches as I glance down again at her naked body, reminded that she left the house without a bra, underwear, or socks. She must have been really scared. And I was upstairs sleeping more soundly than I've ever slept in my life. I firm my grip and yank her off the counter more roughly than I intended. I all but toss her into the bath.

"I'll be outside," I mutter quickly. "Shout if you need anything, and don't fucking drown." I slam the door shut behind me.

I'm on edge as I enter her kitchen. I'm surprised to find it well stocked. I start cooking quickly—a simple Western omelet with ham, green peppers, onions, and grated cheddar, a few spices, and buttered toast. I don't want to linger. I'm not hearing as much noise coming from the bathroom as I feel like I should.

I'm damn near running, her steaming plate in hand, as I reenter the bathroom. She's standing on her shaggy bath mat, water dripping down her body. My mouth dries and I don't like it. I don't like anything about this. I don't want to have these impulsive, automatic reactions toward her, but I'm clearly a sex-starved lunatic who lost his mind last night in the courtyard of Sundale's South Korean Embassy.

I set her plate down long enough to grab a towel off the golden hook shaped like a paw and wrap it around her. I dry her off clinically. Well, as clinically as possible. I don't breathe as I drop to one knee and slide the soft towel up the insides of her legs. Then I drag it over her bruised inner thighs and swollen mons quickly, taking an extra second to spread her lower lips just to make sure she's not bleeding. Relieved to find that she's not, I tip my chin up and plant a lingering kiss on her beautiful mound, sucking her lips into my mouth quickly before releasing her.

She whimpers and sways forward, trying to catch herself on my shoulder, but I'm already standing up, hanging her towel, and carrying her back to her bed. I lay her against an armada of brightly colored pillows, wrench the blankets down and then back up over her lap. I place her plate on her thighs, hand her a fork and a glass of water. And then I sit on an appallingly garish aqua-colored velvet love seat positioned near the full-length window.

The curtains are parted now, letting in early-morning sunlight. It's seven thirty. At least, it was when I last checked. I should still be asleep upstairs in my bed, and so should she. I glare at the offensive way the sunlight caresses her bare skin, tickles her face. Her hair is combed back away from her forehead. I don't know what she ordinarily does with it, but I can see it starting to dry puffy. I open my mouth, about to offer to help her with it, but then clack my jaw shut immediately when she takes her first bite.

She moans. The sound is brief, and low. It stirs a feeling deep in me. Not a sexual feeling this time, but something just as satisfying. I *cooked* for her. I've never cooked for anyone.

"This is really good," she says softly. Far too softly. "Thank you, Darius."

"Darius," I say, correcting her on instinct when that was what she called me in the first place.

She smirks. "That's what I said."

"Good," I grunt, emotion rushing through me. If that was weird, she doesn't seem to notice.

She resumes digging into her omelet right away, a quickly muttered, "Thank you, Darius," her final word on the subject.

And absolutely destroying me.

I sit there like a sycophant and watch Monika's eyelids grow heavy. Her shoulders eventually stoop, and she drops her fork in the center of her plate. She damn near licked the plate clean, and I dislike immensely the pleased way I feel as I take it away, force her to down half her glass of water, and then tuck her under the sheets.

My desire to crawl under her hideous bedspread is strong. She's so weak and soft, pliable and desirable. My fearsome warrior has shed her armor, and I'm surprised to find her so trusting underneath. She doesn't kick me out. She doesn't do more than smile at me sleepily as she rests her head on her pillow wordlessly. She doesn't use words she doesn't need.

Instead, she lets me watch her fall asleep.

I sit there far too long after her breathing has deepened and her eyes have begun to twitch underneath closed lids. She has long eyelashes, I notice, with a strong natural curl. She looks good without makeup. And without a bra. I just want to touch and caress.

Pretending to have some self-control, I get up, clean the dishes I used to cook for her, and step out onto her balcony with my irritation in check. I pull my phone from my pocket and dial a number I dread.

He answers on the second ring. "What do you need, Taranis?"

"Presumptuous of you," I growl, slamming Monika's balcony door shut and then pulsing electricity through the lock until it melts. Though the odds of anyone but me breaking in via her balcony are slim, they aren't nothing. Since I live in the building, I actually have air sensors built in to detect any incoming flying objects—creatures—that would dare approach. But if I'm not on-site and she is, there's still the reality that the sensors could be triggered, and I might not make it to her in time to stop anyone from doing . . . something. And they just might, now that she's captured my interest, as I'm sure the entire world likely knows after last night.

The deep voice on the other end of the line chuckles. "I can't imagine any other reason you'd be calling."

"Meet me at Habesha Café in twenty minutes."

A surprising response makes me immediately suspicious. He answers quickly. Too quickly. "See you soon."

Chapter Seventeen

Darius

Nineteen minutes later I'm sitting in the familiar coffee shop, watching the largest male on planet Earth step through the glass front door. He has to duck in order for his horns to enter, just as I did one minute earlier.

Amid the crowd of mostly East African patrons—none of whom seem to be interested in taking either of our pictures—it takes him exactly no time at all to find me seated alone at a table that, relative to our sizes, looks like it was made for children. I sit in the wooden chair, my body overflowing its edges. I gesture to the Wyvern to take the only other seat at the table available to him, an obnoxious hanging macramé chair shaped like an egg that swings from the ceiling.

The Wyvern approaches me with one black eyebrow cocked, his eyes a pleasantly light pink as if he's the happiest motherfucker on this blue rock. He points a black-and-red claw at the hanging egg seat, while I wonder what kind of deranged sociopath of a woman lets this repugnant offspring of Hellboy and a shark marry her and whether I can get my woman to do the same.

"I'm not gonna fit that."

"I got you this." I kick a small wooden block nested beneath the intricately tiled tabletop toward him. It's about one foot square. He frowns at it and opens his dark-pink mouth, but a female voice beats him to it.

"I have another chair, sir, if you need something a bit larger?" A woman speaking in slightly accented English steps up behind the Wyvern, lifting a sturdy-looking wooden chair.

The Wyvern looks surprised. I imagine it's because she called him *sir*. Every idiot on this dumb planet knows his name. More than mine, even. I mean, he's recognizable as ever, looking like a gigantic, vengeful pink Easter bunny.

"Thank you, ma'am," he replies after his shock wears off.

She grins wide enough to reveal her white teeth. The front two have a little gap between them. She sets the chair down, removing the little stool, then takes our orders without using a pen and paper. I try to make mine extra complicated just to bother her, but she's seemingly unfazed. Her long braided hair sways near her low back as she turns with that stupid smile still on her face.

The Wyvern glances over his shoulder as he scoots closer to the table. "Why'd you want to meet here?"

"They don't stare here."

The Wyvern's eyebrows scrunch. He sweeps his gaze over the coffee shop's dozen-plus patrons and, seeing that they're all engaged in conversations of their own—or heatedly playing backgammon—he makes an impressed face. "Okay. But why not at the COE?"

"Those nosy morons don't need to take pictures of every fucking thing I do, and I'm not here on official COE business. I'm here to talk to you."

The Wyvern's expressions are too fucking expressive. I can't stand it. I can't stand him. He's smiling slightly, his fangs pressing against his bottom lip. He looks like an idiot. If he weren't pink and enormous, I'd think he were human for all the goddamn stupid looks he's giving me.

"So, I take it you want to talk to me about your reversion?"

"Obviously."

"A woman changed you too?"

I feel my cheeks burn. "It would seem."

"Cynthia, right?"

"Yes, right," I say, distracted when the barista or owner or whatever deposits our drinks on the table in front of us. I wonder about something as I watch the tall, willowy woman move away from us, tripping twice on chair legs.

"It was a good thing you poached Monika, then, I guess, since she introduced the two of you at the event last night. Was that the first time you met?"

"Yes, yes, yes. Monika . . . What?"

The big oaf shrugs, looking amazingly stupid sitting in that perfectly normal-size chair, reminding me that I'm only just smaller than he is and likely look equally as stupid. "The pictures she took last night were pretty cool. It was insane to see you revert on camera—at least a little bit of it. And Cynthia seemed thrilled too. Totally over the moon for you."

My own expression screws up as I try to make sense of his English, if that's what he's even speaking. Wondering if things might be clearer if I speak to him in Tratharine, I do. "What the fuck are you talking about?"

His eyes widen. He makes a face. "Tratharine?"

"You speak it too."

"I do," he answers in Tratharine before switching back to English. "But I prefer English."

Strangely, I do too. The Tratharine I knew once feels like it belongs in that rusty crypt I dug it out of, a crypt that I'd like to keep locked. In English, I continue, "I don't have any idea what you're talking about. What the fuck are you talking about Cynthia for?" Cynthia is turning out to be the bane of my existence. Insulting my girl, calling her out of bed, making her walk across town barefoot, and now interjecting herself into my conversation with the Wyvern, distracting the both of us. I will add her to the list of people to kill too. Fuck, kill, kill, destroy, kill—but hers must definitely look like an accident. I can't have Monika irritated with me, as it'll set back my progress in the fuck department.

My horns crackle. He glances up at them, and twin puffs of fire billow from the tips of his. "You . . . don't like Cynthia?" He cocks his head like I'm no longer speaking English or Tratharine, but Mandarin.

"Of course I don't like Cynthia! Last night I tortured Cynthia! Why would you think I like that foul, annoying woman?"

I regret asking the moment he pulls out his phone. He opens a social media app and shows me my own latest post. It has six million likes. Six fucking million.

I snatch the device out of his hand and feel anger infuse my irises. In the screen of his phone, I see them reflect purple before bleeding fully red. I feel my left eye twitch and surging electricity sweep my bones as I take in the image on the screen before me.

Me. On one knee at a woman's feet. Her gazing at me in pure rapture.

A photo Monika took.

The phone screen turns black. A crack appears down the middle. Having ruined the device, I take it all the way and crush it into pieces that fall down around my fist.

The Wyvern doesn't even blink. He just reaches into his pocket and pulls out a second, identical device. "Don't worry 'bout it. Happens all the time. At least to me." He chuckles, like we're friends. We're not friends. I'm going to tear him apart.

"Who . . . How . . . What the *fuck is this?"*

"The picture?"

"Yes."

"Of you and Cynthia?"

"Of me and that annoying bitch!"

My fingers fly over the keys of my own phone. My hand shakes as I fight the urge to crush the damn device. I send an angry email—just the one—before returning my attention to the beast sipping daintily on his coffee across from me. He's wearing a white T-shirt, presumably size XXXXXXXL. Absurd fucker. Claws or not, I'm going to gouge his eyes out.

"I didn't revert for Cynthia. I had just finished torturing her by electrocuting her face when I reverted. Monika's photo seems to have conveniently left that part out."

The Wyvern sets his coffee cup down. Some sweet-smelling concoction covered in cinnamon. "Interesting."

"Tell me about your reversion," I snap.

"I'm sure you've read about it in the papers. I got grilled like a flank steak by the COE, SDD, and every damn news outlet in Sundale."

I nod. "You woke up one morning and looked like . . . that. You found yourself in love with Ms. Theriot and all that mushy shit."

He laughs. "Yeah, something like that." And then shakes his head and leans in a little closer. "It was a lie."

That perks my attention away from the horrifying photo on my phone—the one I don't know how to take down because I don't know my own goddamn social media log-in credentials.

"Not a complete lie. All that shit did happen overnight. And then the next morning, when I met with Emily—"

"The doctor?"

"Yeah."

"What did she have to do with it?"

"Nothing. And at the end of the day, Vanessa didn't *really* have anything to do with it either."

"Explain."

"Look." He leans forward and plants his elbows on table. His fingers drum over the colored tiles, forming the face of an Ethiopian woman looking out over a sunrise. "I got my memories back from Tratharine. I remember what our lives were like before. We were soldiers. Bred for combat and trained young. Every single part of our lives was violence. They didn't even give us names, only numbers meant to keep us in line and keep us fighting to be stronger. The lower numbers were the strongest . . ."

"I'm Six."

He laughs. "'Course you would focus on that, you narcissistic fuck. The Elders sent us with a mission to conquer and, once the battlefield had been leveled, open the gates so they could arrive and set up a new world order, enslaving the remaining humans and starting a new breeding ground for soldiers that would then go on and take over another planet, enslave a different people, and on and on and on, and for no fucking purpose other than the accumulation of power—but they made a mistake."

Curious, I find myself leaning in toward him too. I imagine that we look like high school kids sharing gossip—if high school kids were seven feet tall, sometimes pink, sometimes eggshell blue. "What?"

"The Elders bred us for violence and thought we would revert with a violent trigger, that a spike in pain or rage would bring our original forms and our memories back. They expected that we'd land on an alien planet just as violent as ours—or worse." The Wyvern is grinning wildly now. He even has the audacity to laugh. "But the humans? They *welcomed* us. There was no pain. No violence. So our original forms had to find new triggers—at least, that's mine and Emily's best guess."

"And so when you got all lovey-dovey with your little boo thang, it was strong enough to break the spell?" I sneer in disgust. "Just a real-life Cinderella story, aren't you?"

"I told you before, that wasn't it. Love came later. But my reversion didn't happen when I told people it did. It started way before then. The second I met Vanessa, I had an attraction to her. A normal attraction, anyone would have to someone they found good-looking. But then something happened. It was small." His face twists, nose crinkling. He looks away from me, and his tongue presses against the inside of his cheek, like he's struggling to puzzle through something. "It was so small it shouldn't have mattered . . . but it changed everything."

"Stop being so damn cryptic. The fuck happened?"

"She fell." His gaze flits to mine, and a bright, bright iridescent white consumes his eyes. It's so bright I can't even see his pupil. The runes on his skin seem to glow, forming a map that leads to a treasure I don't think is meant for me. "She fell and my first instinct was to catch her." A wind comes from nowhere and gives me the fucking chills. "I damn near trampled people to get to her, just to slip my palm under her elbow and make sure she didn't hit the ground. I didn't want to see her hit the ground . . ."

A sticky, creeping sensation, like tarantulas migrating, crosses my chest. My memories dance, and no matter how hard I try, I cannot force them to focus on any of the visions I had of my native land. I cannot recall any of the urgent, pressing things I've got going on with the Marduk or my weapon or the fallout I'm going to have to deal with from seeing that terrible post on social media. I can't even remember the way Monika's curves looked, bathing in the bright lights of my bedroom—I didn't let her dim a single one, preferring to fuck her under a goddamn floodlight because I wanted to see everything . . .

My memories come down to one.

The feeling I had when Cynthia started talking shit about Monika. All fluttering eyelashes and bright smiles. Fucking cunt. And how every instinct in my body had been . . . not to defend Monika . . . but to correct the other woman. She'd been wrong, flat-out, talking down on Monika when she's the most impressive woman I've met in my life. And so I'd done something strange and out of character for me. I . . . said something nice about somebody.

I knew in the moment I opened my mouth that I'd been in situations like this before and done and said nothing. I hadn't been compelled to. So why then? Why now? Why over this woman who, just days before, I'd felt nothing for?

My memories are tugged to the vision of Monika pulling herself out of the Old Sundale Station tunnel like it was no biggie . . . And then again, seeing the pictures she'd taken of me. Then when she responded to my email with two words and, after, showed up at her godmother's gala in that dress. And how she'd been living in my apartment building this whole time and never thought to bring it up like it was no fucking thang . . . She was just—*is* just—too much. She's too fucking cool for me.

The sex part hadn't even factored when I stood up for her against those untruths. Her little camera had more power than a cannon. More power than me too. And so I'd been selfless. Just for a second, less than five breaths. The words I said couldn't be revoked, and neither could their consequences.

I'm rubbing my chin absently when the Wyvern breaks my focus. "You did something, didn't you? Something completely different for you."

I nod.

"It wasn't torturing Cynthia, either, was it?"

I shake my head. "I said something nice."

The Wyvern nods. "Not much, but for you, that would do it . . ." He starts to laugh.

"I said something nice about Monika."

And then the Wyvern's grin turns absolutely feral. He looks like the cat who ate the canary. "No shit?"

"No shit."

He chokes. "You and Monika?"

I nod. "She's mine now."

"Fuck." The Wyvern rubs his face. "I can't decide if Vanessa's gonna be pissed or find this real cute."

"Why would she be pissed?"

"You kidding? Monika's way, *way* too fucking good for you. You two aren't even in the same league."

I send a burst of electrical current to whack the Wyvern in the face. He curses and rubs his jaw, then sends a fireball flying back. I feel for his insides—a gift I know only a few of us in the Tratharine army possess. I find his mind, and I send a little electrical pulse between his temples that causes his entire body to sit up straight.

He blinks at me, shakes his head, blinks again. "Fuck," he says. "That's like what the Marduk—"

"Yes."

He frowns, sitting back. "Has reverting changed sides for you?"

"Like it did for you?"

"Yeah. My girl's good, so I want to be good too."

Huh. The way he says it makes it sound so simple, but my situation is more complicated than that. My girl is neutral. She takes pictures of the good and the bad. "Nah," I tell him. It's not a lie because I'm not changing sides because of Monika. I was never a hero.

He gives me a dark, skeptical side-eye. "That right?"

"Yeah."

"And have you found your map?"

"What map?"

He gestures to his arm, to the runes that seem to be lightly carved into his granite skin. "Led me to my weapon." He tilts his head as his gaze moves over my bare chest. How the fuck is he sitting here, the better dressed one between the two of us? He's a slob, last I checked. "Yours are different."

I nod, stretching out one arm between us. The glittery patterns that form over my skin only turn bright white in natural light. "Yes. Seems like it. What do the weapons do? Other than open a gate for the Elders to pass through when combined."

"What weapons do," he answers with a shrug. "Have you found yours?"

"Map didn't lead me anywhere," I tell him, and there's truth in it.

He picks his coffee cup back up and squints. "Bullshit."

"Whatever."

He repositions himself in his chair and cocks his head. "Look, Taranis, I don't care if you're lying to me. I don't care if you have your weapon. I don't care if you're dating Monika, and I don't care if you're a hero or if you're a villain. All I know is that if I have to kill you to ensure that the Elders don't make it here, I will."

"You can't, Sixty-Two."

He just shrugs. "Maybe. Maybe not."

Feeling strangely magnanimous, I decide to give him something. "I don't want the Elders here either." My tail lifts to curl around my cup of coffee. My arms remain crossed as I sip from it. "I don't like having a master. And since you've been absolutely annoying, I only have one last question."

"Shoot." He tosses some bills onto the table. What looks like forty bucks. I glance at it, and he says, "I've got a sugar mama."

"How do you get the weapons to work?"

"Thought you didn't find yours?"

"Theoretically," I say with emphasis, "how would one get their weapons to work?"

"Yours doesn't?" He's wearing another damn smile, this one more mischievous than any of the others.

"Theoretically, no. It doesn't."

"Then maybe, and I'm just theorizing here . . ."

"Of course." Fucking annoying monstrous prick.

"Maybe your weapon doesn't belong to you."

The Marduk. That fucking dick. I *knew* it. Why I ever thought he'd give me my own weapon, even though I gave him his, is fucking stupid and so am I for harboring the trust I had in him. After all, he is a villain.

"What?" the Wyvern asks me.

"Nothing," I hiss, annoyed all over. My cell phone bings with a notification that the meeting request I put in has been accepted. My body tingles from head to toe, and I know my skin is crackling with lightning.

"Damn. Something's got you hot and bothered."

"I'm late for a meeting."

"With who?" he asks as I stand.

"Someone who's going to get what they deserve." I pause, glance down at him sitting there smiling while my blood boils in my veins. "Thank you for the coffee. You look like a giant cotton candy."

He just laughs as I stomp away. "When you're mad, you look like a grape."

Chapter Eighteen

Monika

Darius's office is way smaller than I thought it would be. That should be comforting, but it isn't. Somehow, the size of the room makes the whole space feel twice as intimidating. It feels like a prison. The ceiling is low. The gray walls are covered in dark-gray shelving. Open shelves decorate the upper half of each wall and showcase books and carefully placed bobbles. Closed shelves decorate the lower half of each wall.

A massive concrete desk stretches nearly all the way across the room. A computer sits on it, but where a keyboard should be are two sheets of paper, one of which is decorated with black text I can't read from here, the other of which looks like it might be a photograph laid upside down.

Darius sits behind his desk, a blue monster with white horns that shoot up taller than I stand. He's showered and shaved but still shirtless. Not that I'm complaining. I'd say if I did have one complaint—and I do—it would be that his fingers are steepled and pressed against his lips and he's glaring at me like he just found out I killed his childhood hamster.

"I'm a little surprised you called a meeting and didn't just break into my apartment again." What's more surprising was that he let me postpone it. The original meeting request came in for yesterday, but I accidentally slept through it and had to ask him to reschedule for the next morning. He did without complaint.

He doesn't respond. Hmm. The topic of the meeting wasn't provided in the calendar invite, so I thought playful banter might have been on the agenda, but I guess not.

His eyes bleed a darker and darker purple the longer I stand there. I'm wearing normal human clothes again after spending all day yesterday naked in bed, nursing my aches. I saw another calendar invite pop up for me after this one, scheduling me to meet with Emily and another doctor named Viola, who's meant to give me a pap. Even though I haven't had that visit yet—it's scheduled for tomorrow—I can't deny that I'm feeling a little hopeful Darius might be up for another session later . . . or now . . . if this meeting is a sex workshop. I thought it might be when I got the invite. Now I'm feeling less sure. He looks like he's going to eat me. And not in the fun way.

My hands are empty, making me wish I lived in the era of briefcases just to give myself something to hold. Even worse, there isn't anywhere for me to sit. The chair Darius sits in is the only one in the room.

I glance around. Darius's eyes are so bright, flashing blue and purple and white. "Why are you here, Ms. Neumann?"

I swallow, but there's not a doubt in my mind he can hear me lick my lips. "You called for this meeting, Darius."

His eyes burn. His horns crackle with electricity. "And why did I call for this meeting?"

"I'm not really sure anymore . . ."

His palm slaps down onto the desk so loudly I jump. He pushes one of the papers toward me ever so slightly, prompting me to edge forward and take a look.

I creep toward his desk and see a familiar still from the video I took at the South Korean Embassy printed on the paper. It's from his socials, the one of Cynthia's face looking the picture of happiness. The less-than-crisp shot gives me bubble guts while simultaneously making me want to tear out her hair.

"Is this what you saw happen the night of the gala?" he asks me in a voice that's way too calm.

I meet his gaze. It's bright purple again, bringing out the menace in his monstrous face. I tuck my hair behind my ear, glad I had time this morning to rewash and dry it. He focuses too intently on the movement of my hand as I bring it down to my stomach, then shove it into my sweater pockets. I'm wearing leggings and a low-cut, formfitting black V-neck. I didn't want it to totally look like I was here for the D, so last minute I threw a chunky pink sweater over all of it. I'm suddenly regretting not having worn my bulletproof Press vest from our last mission. I don't look professional, and I don't look equipped for war either.

I scratch my neck with my other hand and roll out one ankle. I'm wearing slip-on shoes that I hope to hell he doesn't notice are actual house slippers. "Um . . . no. Not all of it."

"What did you see?"

"I saw you holding Cynthia in a hug first, except you were electrocuting her, I think."

"And did you capture that on video?"

I nod.

He slams his hand down on top of the paper again and crumples it into his fist. "Then why did my PR team post this shit?"

"It's . . ." It's obvious. The alternative would make him look like a psycho killer. This makes him look like a swooning romantic. " . . . for your image, you know. Your brand. As Taranis. She makes you look good here . . ."

He sweeps his arms across his desk, sending everything to the floor, including his computer. I jump, genuinely afraid. "Did you like seeing this post?" he asks me, seething. I don't understand it.

I hesitate, debating how much power to give him here. But there is no other alternative to the truth. I shake my head.

He stands up to his full height, and holy fuck, I forgot how tall he is now. His horns nearly touch the low ceilings. "Well, I fucking *hated* it. Take off your clothes."

"I . . ." I waver. Even though this is maybe what I thought I came here for, he's making me way too nervous. "I don't think it's a good idea to mix the personal and professional stuff," I try, voice weaker than I've ever heard it. Because how can I forget how good that omelet was yesterday morning, or the fact that he cleaned up my apartment after? He was nicer to me than anyone's been in a long time. And he's the villain whom I'm supposed to sabotage.

"Take off your clothes and come here."

I know the safe word. It's on the tip of my tongue. But I remove my sweater instead and shut the fuck up. My shirt goes next. My leggings and slippers. My underwear, socks . . . bra . . . I stand in front of him feeling self-conscious. He's still in sweatpants, after all . . . though he doesn't stay in them for long.

He drags them down his thighs and steps back from his desk, his bare ass bumping into a cluster of metal pieces that make a jangling sound when they're shoved together. "Come here." He gestures at me with two fingers. His claws are longer than my hands.

Swallowing hard, I step across his bare concrete floor. Like the rest of his house, there's no carpets, no signs of life. Just a cold box that feels like a tomb. I move around his concrete desk until he's close enough to grab me. He doesn't. Instead, he glances down at the surface where the incriminating photo once was.

"You had my permission to share your pretty pictures without my first right of refusal for less than a day." He grabs me by the back of the head and guides me to stand in front of him, then pushes my head toward the desk. I lower with no resistance, hissing lightly when my perky nipples press flush against the cold concrete. He grabs my hands and locks them at my lower back. He prods at my pussy with a knuckle, undoubtedly finding me wet already, then makes a very male, primal sound before kicking my legs apart.

"Your poor decision-making leaves me no other choice than to rescind the liberty I gave you." Something cold trickles over my asshole.

My eyelashes flutter. I can't imagine a less romantic place to be in than this room, or anywhere else I'd rather be right now.

"I'm sorry, Darius . . ."

"Don't fucking speak." He wrenches open a drawer under his desk and pulls out a stress ball for me to see, one marked with the logo for the COE. He shoves it into my mouth. "If you want to say the safe word, you're going to have to scream it loud."

Without any other prelude, I feel Darius insert something not at all as small as it should be into my ass. I jolt over the desk, but Darius kicks my feet even wider and presses down on my wrists on my lower back. He doesn't say anything as he shoves whatever it is a little farther in.

A vibrator? Dildo? It's wiggling inside me, so I know that's not it. It's not a finger because those are all clawed. I can't figure out . . . *"Mmmph,"* I groan, my eyes rolling back as the huge head of whatever it is finally makes it past that outer ring and my tight anus squeezes on the thinner shaft of his . . . tail. Holy fuck. It has to be.

"Mmm," he groans, and that strange purring has picked back up in his chest. "Tight." He starts to thrust his tail in and out of me and it *hurts*, but it also feels so fucking fantastic. I'm not going to come from it, though, and I could cry. If he would just touch my clit a little bit, for a second, I'd erupt.

A few minutes pass. I'm writhing and shaking on the table while he tail-fucks my ass. My tits are so unhappy, pushed against this hard desk. I could cry at the injustice of it. And then the bastard at my back has the nerve to whisper, "Fuck it."

I feel something prod my pussy lips, and I scream around the foam gag in my mouth as Darius shoves the head of his dick inside me in one smooth motion. He rocks against me and, within a few heartbeats, has himself fully inserted in both my holes. He doesn't wait. He starts to fuck me fast, riding me hard enough he's going to leave bruises on the tops of my thighs where they're hitting the edge of the desk. He doesn't fuck me anywhere near long enough for me to be able to come, as I twist between the pleasure and pain of it. And I'm a sick, sick girl because even though I could have chosen to spit the ball out of my mouth at any point and said the safe word, I don't. Because more than I'd love to come right now, I love being owned like this by him.

Tears wet my lashes. Tears of the most exquisite delight. *I make a terrible spy,* I think, sobbing around my gag as Darius's shallow thrusts start to get sloppy and his hand on the back of my head tightens. *"Augh . . . fuuuuck,"* he groans and that's when I feel the telltale swelling of his cock inside my body. Combined with the added pressure of his tail in my ass, I panic, lifting on my tiptoes, but there's nowhere for me to go. He keeps me pinned as he roars out a curse and then drops over my body.

I can feel the hot splash of his cum inside me and hear the lascivious squelching sound as he continues to rock against my body. The sensations make my eyes roll back and my nostrils flare. His cock expands around the middle, and I pray, as my hands clench, that I'm well worked out enough from the first time that I don't tear.

He lies over my back, propped up on his elbows, his head hanging down over the top of my head. His lips brush over my crown again and again, biting and tasting my hair and the shells of my ears. His claws trace lines around my bandaged shoulder. The wounds left by his teeth are still there but scabbing over quickly.

"Where I bit you will leave scars," he says against the side of my face. He takes my ear between his fangs threateningly but doesn't bite down hard. "And when they fade, I'll bite you again to leave more scars in the same place. Maybe I'll leave them all over your body so that everyone who looks at you will know who you belong to."

I shudder as his cock twitches inside me. His tail is calm inside my ass. He's so still the pain is gone, and I wish for a ludicrous second that we could stay locked like this for an hour.

I sniffle and he bends around me to speak against my nose. "Why did you crop out the part where I hurt Cynthia from your video?" His hand is on my neck, squeezing gently.

I feel so used, so treasured, so adored. He plucks the ball out of my mouth, spit coating my mouth and dribbling out of the corner. "I . . ." The truth is so *embarrassing*. It reveals too much and I can scarcely give it voice.

"Tell me."

A light, feathery whisper slips out between my teeth. "I wanted to protect you."

He shivers. *Shivers*. He doesn't speak. His hips surge against my ass a little harder, and the prickling pain inside my body makes itself known. But then his hand . . . his huge hand . . . starts working its way around my body, wriggling between my soft stomach and his impossibly hard desk. He somehow manages to squeeze beneath my weight, and two of his huge fingertips find my clit. He starts to brush over it fast and hard. My hips buck. My eyes squeeze shut.

"Does it hurt?" he whispers.

I shake my head, then nod. "A little." I'm wet enough, the lube and cum more than enough to make his touch rub smooth. But he's going so fast there's absolutely no buildup. And the pressure makes my ass clench on instinct, and that reminds me that he's still got his tail shoved in there deep.

"Good. I wasn't going to let you come at all. Did it occur to you that I don't want my fucking picture taken next to that goddamn hussy? Answer me."

I shake my head, panting, gasping, wishing I could push myself up off the uncomfortable desk, but his back is there, caging me. Also . . . *hussy*?

"That's right. I didn't. And if you take my picture next to another woman again that isn't you, I'll kill her."

My eyes fly open. I can't see his because he's using his chest to smother me. I'm so close I can't bear it. His fingers squeeze my clit, pinching it hard, and that's what does it for me. It hurts, but it's enough. The most deliriously magical and simultaneously horrible orgasm I've ever had rips through me, making my whole body clench up around his tail and dick. The pressure is surreal and the orgasm floats through my body, leaving a tingling behind that scrapes out my insides and reorganizes them to his liking.

When I come to, he's picked his torso up off my body, though his cock and tail are still firmly seated. "Sign this." He slaps my ass hard enough to jolt my whole body against the concrete. He lifts my right wrist and then drops it onto the desk.

"Wh-what?" I pant, my gaze scanning over the document he shoves underneath my cheek. My eyes are unfocused until I blink.

"It's a contract amendment, rolling back the allowance I gave you to communicate directly with my PR team and adding in that you no longer have my consent to take my photo without prior permission."

"B-b . . . No!"

"And when you're finished, sign this." He holds up a document in my line of sight that can't be mistaken for anything other than the large block letters printed at the top: Marriage License.

"What!" I scramble, trying to pick my head up off the desk, but he shoves me back down.

"Sign these. And when we're done here, you're going to give me your phone so I can send them the full video. They've already taken the other post down, but I'm going to need to make sure that it's clear to the world exactly how I feel about Cynthia."

"You can't do that," I wheeze. "You'll look like a villain."

"I *am* a villain. And only you know just how villainous I am." His tail wiggles in my ass, and I clench my cheeks around it. He slaps them one, two, three, four times in quick succession. It's so rough that I cry out, horribly tortured by the sting. It makes me want to do terrible things. Sign whatever he wants and beg him to do more to me.

No! No thinking with the coochie! My eyes water and I heave, "I can't sign that, Darius. I can't take your picture in battles if you want my permission first. That just . . . doesn't even make sense."

"Good thing that after you sign this," he says, fluttering the pink marriage certificate in front of my face, "you won't be going into battle anymore. You'll be tied to my bed, and that's where you'll stay."

"Are you serious?"

"Do I sound like I'm joking?"

"You aren't my only contract."

"I will be once I kill Mr. Singkham and take over the COE."

I freeze. "What?"

He bends back over me. "I am tired of being controlled . . ."

"But that's exactly what you want to do to me!" I rasp, squeezing my inner muscles around him, causing him to jerk. He doesn't answer. "You can't own me. That's not how this works." He still doesn't answer. He knows I'm right. He knows that the balance of this relationship relies entirely on my consent, on my limits and my wants. "And as for that other contract amendment, no."

"Yes," he counters, wrapping my hair up in his fist and lifting my head from the desk high enough that he can bend around me and meet my gaze with those burning purple irises.

"It's not realistic. You want my sign-off, fine, but I can't get preapproval in the middle of a battle, and I'm not going to sit on the sidelines. That's where I was with the Wyvern and why I took your contract in the first place. Also—I can't believe I even have to say this—you can't kill Mr. Singkham and take over the COE."

"Why not?" His horns crackle, and behind him, I see the metal pieces on his shelf also flaring with violent color. He doesn't seem to notice. And the very conversation we're having now is why I don't say anything about it.

"Because there are other ways to get out of a contract," I tell him, voice laden with implication.

"Like what?" he seethes, nostrils flaring.

"You can just leave. Like I'm going to leave." Once I get un-impaled from his hard appendages. "I'm not signing anything."

"You really think you can try to intimidate me?"

I scoff. "Of course not. You've got me pinned to your desk with your tail and your cock. I like you, Darius," I groan as I try to push myself up on shaking arms. He surprises me this time by letting me up, but then wraps his arms around me and falls back into his chair, his cock and tail still firmly wedged.

"Oof," I whimper even louder, head rolling back and hitting his chest, which heaves with rage and aggression and need—at least, those are all the things I'm feeling. "I like you. You have to know that. I admired Taranis as a hero, but I actually *like* you, Darius. You can't put me in a cage unless it's in your bedroom and we're still using safe words." His hands come around my stomach, one of them palming my right breast. I can tell his dick has softened enough to pull out of me, but he makes no move to do that. "And if you don't like your cage, just leave it. There's nothing binding you there. You don't have to kill anyone. You have more money than God. If you signed a lousy contract when you became a hero, just fix it.

"I might not be able to fix mine, because you have me outmanned and outmuscled," I grunt, trying to free one of my arms so I can reach back and touch Darius's face. I stroke his cheek. He moves where I want, coming closer to me until our cheeks are pressed together. "But you can't stop me from taking other contracts if you stop putting me on the good missions."

He cracks his fist on the edge of the desk, and the sound of thunder clacks through the room. "Do you have any idea who you're talking to? I won't let them put you on other contracts." He snatches the papers off the desk and holds them up. "Sign them."

"I won't."

"Sign them, or I'll break your arm so you can't hold up a camera."

"I'd rather get eaten by rats."

With no warning, Darius shoves me off him so that I lie splayed over his desk, his cock and tail ripping out of me in a way that makes me cry out in pain. He storms out of his office, slamming the door so hard at his back that a few books and bobbles fall off the shelves behind me, and so do the weapons that were on the lowest shelf.

Wincing, I stand upright and turn around. I glance at the weapons on the ground, feeling proud of myself for standing tough despite feeling like I just had my insides scooped out. My pussy is gaping, and so is my ass. Both are clenching and winking, desperate for more of what Darius had.

I bend down and stroke my finger along one of the weapons. Lightning flares beneath my touch, but doesn't hurt me. I place them back on the shelves carefully, hoping that he figures his shit out but also understanding that this is shit only he can figure out.

I learned a long time ago that I was no one's therapist. I get to choose how I let folks treat me, and even if I want to be put in a cage by him, I don't want to be caged by him. If that's a line in the sand we can't erase together, then I'm going to leave and let our lawyers and our good friends at the COE settle the fallout.

He has to understand that I'm a photographer. I'm an artist. For better or worse, trying to disentangle me from my life's work would be like trying to use chopsticks to pick all the salt out of the ocean.

The hero always saves the damsel at the end of the story, and if this was going to be the end of ours, then hell—nobody said I couldn't play both parts. After all, as he's said himself, he's the villain.

And once he finds out that I've been spying on him, he's going to do worse than break my legs or throw me off the top of our building. The bullshit contract amendment and the little pink paper I've folded up in my pocket won't mean anything. Because after my confrontation with the Marduk, and after hearing from his own mouth that he plans to kill Mr. Singkham, I've got to start taking my spy duties seriously.

Chapter Nineteen

Monika

The web of lies may have begun with Taranis, but it ends with me. That's what I keep telling myself as I sit down with Mr. Singkham, my last encounter with Darius replaying itself in my mind. I'm so uncomfortable, sore as hell, and my meeting with Emily and the COE gyno definitely did not help. She was ecstatic when I told her that Darius and I had been *intimate,* and even had a name for what happened to his penis when it . . . expanded. She called it *knotting*.

I had a little bit of tearing, and she asked me way too many questions about why my asshole looked inflamed. She gave me cream for all of it, a prescription for extra-strength ibuprofen, and the courage to keep having sex with Darius if I'm enjoying it. And I am enjoying it. Even if I want to give him a lobotomy.

Entirely breaking doctor-patient confidentiality—or maybe that doesn't even exist for the COE—she let me know that he was clean and that I didn't need to worry about pregnancy because he'd had a vasectomy. Huh. Emily also told me he hadn't been in yet, but she asked me to encourage him to come see her. She wanted to have a look at all his shiny new bits. I snorted and wished her luck. If he didn't want to see her, he wouldn't come to see her. Nothing I could do to change that.

"This is what it looked like?" Mr. Singkham has a binder open on his desk in front of me. He's sitting in the chair next to mine rather than across from me, excitement oozing from him like he's a little boy on Christmas Day. Wait—do they celebrate Christmas in Thailand?

I glance over at him and see that his full concentration is on the laminated sheets. "No. It's not a long sword. It's short. Two of them."

"You think he has two separate weapons?"

I shake my head, then shrug. "There were two of them, but they were identical."

Mr. Singkham releases a long, thoughtful sound, stroking his chin. "Back to the thumbnails." He flips pages until he arrives at a set of two-by-two-inch images, each one depicting a separate "weapon" against a backdrop of plain white. Some of them don't much look like weapons, though. Most of them don't look like much at all, but there are a lot of them. Two dozen at least.

"Shouldn't I just focus on the ones that have been stolen?"

"These are the ones that were stolen."

"Oh shit." I shake my head and go back to the pictures. They look hardly more useful in battle than kitchen utensils. "The weapon I saw was sparking blue and white."

"And you say it started to radiate energy because he was upset with you for the social media post?"

"I mean . . ." I reply, shifting in my seat, my face growing surprisingly warm. The marriage license crinkles in my pocket. I flap my hands. "I don't know. He was angry and it was glowing. Whether the two things were related, I couldn't hazard a guess." It also sparked after he left, but for whatever reason, I don't mention that.

"Fascinating. Just fascinating."

"What is?"

Mr. Singkham looks at me. He's grinning. "That he's managed to turn his weapon on at all. We haven't had a Champion who's been able to do so yet."

"What about the Wyvern?"

Mr. Singkham gives me a funny look, then silently shakes his head. "There's . . . more to it than that."

When it doesn't seem like he'll say more, I look back at his book. "You know who these all belong to?"

"Some were found in the backs of the pods of the Forty-Eight that crashed, but less than a dozen. Eight, I believe. The rest, we haven't a clue. And the Champions don't feel anything in particular when they approach the various weaponry that would give us any indication who the weapon might belong to or what it might do." He adjusts his tie. It's red with little blue comets—the pods falling from the sky.

I feel uncomfortable giving this information to Mr. Singkham without Darius's knowledge, and I'm worried I acted too hastily. In the last seventy-two hours, I've watched the guy who I grew up idolizing turn into a gigantic blue beast, fucked him, dealt with my godsister getting her legs broken by the Marduk, met with the Marduk—who I'm pretty sure was going to kill me until he found out I was Taranis's key, whatever that means—and then been fucked again by monster dick after being presented a series of contracts meant to strip me of autonomy and bind me to him.

I haven't admitted it out loud, but the truth is that I'm scared. I don't know what to tell to whom. I don't know who to trust. What to feel. What I've started to feel for Darius is in complete conflict with what I feel for Taranis. For a minute there, lost in the expanse of his blue skin, I thought that Darius might be surging as his dominant personality, but after our last meeting, I'm concerned that Taranis is winning. And I don't trust Taranis. Especially not after hearing his talks of murder.

I swallow hard, sparing Mr. Singkham a glance. Does he really deserve to die? He might be a shrewd businessman at the end of the day, but does that qualify him for the casket? If Darius is looking for an out, he has other options. Or is Taranis simply looking for a reason to make a grab for even more power?

"Anything on this page?" Mr. Singkham asks, pointing to a new sheet. The weapons are all rusty and dark, some too difficult to hardly make out.

"Is this an axe?" I ask.

"We aren't sure."

I grunt at the photograph of a weapon that looks like an axe blade but has a handle in the shape of a circle. "Terrifying."

"I certainly wouldn't want to see it in practice—at least, not in the hands of a villain."

"Me either."

"Any others look familiar?"

"No . . . these aren't swords. This is a whip." Black and dull and utterly uninspiring looking. "Wait. I think . . ." I drag the binder closer to me and squint at a rusty red thing. It does seem to be the right shape . . . and the markings look almost familiar . . . "The color is wrong. Do you have anything bigger? Closer up?"

"Yes, of course." He flips a few pages farther, and I recognize the weapons on first glance.

My finger stabs down on the large images taking up the full-page spread. "It's that one."

"The wrist swords."

"Yes. They were the same shape. Not the same color, though. These look kinda rusted and dim. His were bright white and, like I said, buzzing with electricity."

Mr. Singkham immediately moves around his desk, leaving me with the binder. He fires up his computer and starts typing furiously. An email to the SDD head? Sending the Navy SEALs to arrest Taranis right now? Or just taking notes? "Incredible." He shakes his head.

"Are you going to . . . confront him?"

"Yes."

I tense. "Are you sure that's a good idea?"

"We have no concrete proof that Taranis stole these weapons, so I'd like to see if there isn't a way to convince Taranis to come to us willingly with this." He pauses typing and shoots me a glance. "You could be exceedingly helpful in convincing him to come in."

"No thank you."

He grunts. "Then I may need to consult the SDD president, Ms. Lemon." He frowns. "It could be dangerous."

"And yet, you asked me to do it?"

Mr. Singkham has the decency at least to blush. "Did you see any other weapons in Taranis's possession?"

"Nope." Whew. At least I can admit that in the negative. But what to do with the other information I have on Taranis? Before accusing him point-blank of conspiracy to commit murder, I know I need to talk to *Darius* first.

"This is fantastic work, Ms. Neumann, simply fantastic. I cannot thank you enough. If there is anything else you might have come across or any other information you have for me, please do let me know."

I hesitate, debating. "There is . . . something."

His eyes ping to mine. His fingers once again freeze over the keys.

I exhale and rub my face roughly with one hand. "I visited my godsister, Cynthia, yesterday in the hospital." Was that even yesterday? *Quatsch.* Time has ceased to have any meaning anymore. "Sorry—Saturday," I correct. "Anyway, it was after the video stills I took were posted to Taranis's socials."

"Oh yes, I did hear about that. I reached out to the South Korean ambassador to wish her my condolences on her daughter's injury." He turns to face me fully, elegantly arraying his arms over his desk. It's wood—glossy and dark and warm. His whole office is full of light up here on the thirty-fourth floor. A stark contrast to Taranis's evil lair. Which is annoying. Because I'd still rather be there *bent over his desk, tits mashed into the concrete, tail deep inside my ass, knot fully inflated inside me, pinning me*. I snap out of it with a start, my whole body heating.

Mr. Singkham gives me a discerning look. "I also was a bit confused as I thought that the pictures of Taranis and Cynthia seemed rather . . . *lovey-dovey*, to use the American expression, but that's not the impression I got from the ambassador." I make a face. Mr. Singkham quirks his head. "Something tells me there is more to the story."

"The images were clips from a video I sent Taranis's PR team. They were cropped—made to appear that way—but the reality was much different." He electrocuted her. "There is no love between Taranis and Cynthia. He's since taken the post down and is fairly pissed about it." Fairly. Mildly. Hardly at all. Ha.

"Oh." Mr. Singkham's eyes suddenly grow large. "Oh my."

"Cynthia wasn't in a car crash either. She was kidnapped."

"Kidnapped? By whom?"

"The Marduk and an ally of his. They wanted information about Taranis's reversion, but when they realized she wasn't . . . the cause of it . . . he broke her legs."

Mr. Singkham emits a curse in a language I don't speak.

Still, I nod. "She's pretty freaked out, but she's safe. The Marduk and whoever was with him let her go after. They were the ones who dropped her off at the hospital."

"My God."

"She did say one thing I think might be worth mentioning. I asked her about the place they took her when they interrogated her and then broke her legs. She said it was a warehouse that smelled like the sea. I know that's not a lot to go on, but I've been thinking a lot about it, and I did a shoot at the docks once as part of an exposé on forced sex work and human trafficking that passes through Sundale. I can't see how it would be possible for an underground ring of supervillains to hide out there, but it's the first place that came to mind. I just . . . thought you should know."

Mr. Singkham stares at me with his lips ever so slightly parted. I think he might be drooling.

"Mr. Singkham? Can I . . . be dismissed? I've had a hell of a week." *Weeks*. Not to mention, I still have a pile of unanswered emails and clerical work to do for my February gallery opening. Plus, feelings about an annoying alien to contend with. And a marriage license in my pocket.

Mr. Singkham nods, but as I rise to stand, he speaks carefully, like he's saying the words out loud as he puzzles through them. "Not the docks, Ms. Neumann. The harbor."

"The old Sundale harbor?"

He nods. "It could be. We have reason to suspect there may be VNA activity in that area. The fact that your godsister called it a warehouse narrows it down even more. We *may* have reason to launch a covert mission, Ms. Neumann—one that might uncover a fair cache of the Marduk's hidden weapons. This information may be helpful for our cause."

"Good," I exhale, relieved. "I'm glad I could help." I start to leave—try to leave. I don't make it two feet.

"Ms. Neumann, the COE may need your help again."

I groan and stare up at the ceiling, wondering what I did so wrong in my past life to deserve this level of excitement. *Okay, universe, I know I asked for thrills, but could you tone it down a bit?*

Mr. Singkham turns away from his computer to give me his full, undivided attention. I want none of it. "We have been developing plans for the Wyvern to lead a contingent of COE officers to investigate our findings. We have scouted a few locations so far but haven't found more than traces of the VNA's presence. If your lead proves to have merit, this could be a big coup for the COE. And regardless, we need coverage, even if the mission turns out not to recover anything of direct value. There is a lot we're missing relying solely on bodycam footage. I would like you to accompany the next mission and document their findings, whatever they may be."

I groan and sulk toward the exit. "Fine."

"Excellent. I'll send word when the plan comes together and it's time for your troop to leave. We also may need to interrogate your friend, Cynthia."

"Give the girl a break," I say, but not just for Cynthia's sake—also because I don't want her confessing that the Marduk gave me a cell phone that I can use to contact him and may or may not kill me if I share that information.

Mr. Singkham's face screws up. "We can wait, but if our next mission proves fruitless, we will need to speak to her. In the meantime, do let me know if you have any trouble with Taranis. He's not to know about these plans for now."

I nod, understanding that entirely. "Taranis is giving me grief about my contract, but I think we might be able to work it out. If not, then I may need to get my lawyers involved."

Mr. Singkham frowns. "You've been doing exceptional work, and he has no idea you captured that footage of him with Bia and the Meinad, correct?"

"No, he doesn't know about that."

"Then what seems to be the problem?"

"I . . . uh . . . It's just an issue with him trying to get approvals . . ." And marry me. I shake my head. "I think I can handle it, for now."

"Well, keep me in the loop. We don't have him on assignment for the next few weeks, for obvious reasons, which means you shouldn't have much contact with him. Though I appreciate the information you've been able to provide about him, I don't want you engaging if it's at risk to your safety or general well-being."

"Right. I'll just stay away from Taranis for now." And I'll try to stay away from Darius too.

Chapter Twenty

Darius

I'm lying buck-ass naked on the rail of my balcony, contemplating life, the universe, and everything, my hands locked behind my head, my feet crossed at the ankles. *Just leave*. It's been two days since she said those words to me. I haven't seen her since. I haven't seen anyone since, but somehow it's not seeing her that's bothered me more.

I reach up and twiddle my horns. I'm starting to like them. The sun shines down on my skin, warming me. I still haven't been to the COE, even though they've called me incessantly since my reversion. I will need to go see Sandra and her design team eventually because I need something that fits, especially if I want to be seen in public again with Monika.

And I plan to.

The online chatter, I haven't paid much attention to, though the couple times I've tried turning on the TV, I've seen those irritating images of me reverting alongside Cynthia's elated face. There's a lot of speculation about what's gone on between us. The world seems very aware that Cynthia is in the hospital with two broken legs and that I haven't gone to see her. It's the first time I've seen negative press about myself hit the big screen and it feels . . .

It feels liberating.

I grin slyly up into the sun, baring my fangs to the clouds as if in challenge. I think I have decided. I may not have figured out my entire life, but I have figured out my next few days. Fuck, kill, kill, destroy is feeling a little less . . . optimal now that I've got Monika's annoying words ringing through my head. I might need to amend them.

Fuck Monika.

Marry Monika.

Destroy the weapons.

The Marduk can live, so long as he stays out of my way. As for the COE? I suppose I could consider leaving it intact. Or just leaving it.

I'm about to get up and descend a few floors to act on parts one and two of my plans when the phone in my pocket starts buzzing with a sound it's never made before.

I pull out my phone and stare at the red warning light flashing, taking up the entire screen. INCOMING . . . AERIAL OBJECT INCOMING . . . INCOMING . . . I glance out at the Sundale skyline over my right shoulder and cock my head as the next breeze sweeps my skin, cooler and harsher than the last. I can just barely make out the speck of golden color traveling toward me at an alarming rate, and I smirk, sitting up on the rail, my tail curling around it for balance.

Interesting.

I watch the golden imbecile materialize in sharp clarity, his clothing rippling over his body in the wind he creates as he dives like a bullet straight toward me. For whatever reason, I don't feel compelled to stop him.

The weight of his body hits me from the front with full force. I had the presence of mind to slide my electric glass balcony doors open or else we would have gone straight through them as he tackles me onto the polished concrete floor of my living room. I'm able to form an electrical current around myself that buffets some of the impact, though it doesn't help when the Marduk straddles my chest, lifts a fist, and then hits me. The bastard punched me in the face!

I can't remember the last time I was punched. Clawed and daggered, shot and set aflame, sure, but punched? Like a human would punch another human? It's the shock of it that keeps me from doing anything, and I'm horrified to find that being punched in the eye actually *hurts*.

"Ow!" I yowl, shoving a lightning-filled hand against his chest and sending him flying off me and back onto the balcony.

The sunlight glints off his appallingly golden hair. He looks like that ugly lion from the story of the girl who went to the magical land and murdered a bunch of people. I always liked that girl's deceitfully carnivorous energy, though I never understood why she kept so many friends missing essential body parts.

"You *dare* attack me in my own home?" I gasp.

He advances on me, coming to lord over me, and grabs me by the throat, but only because I let him. It's very strange, being so much larger than he is now. "*You* dare . . ."

"I dare? I dare what?" Even if I'd been blindfolded, I'd know who it was by the smell. He smells like rain, and the sound of thunder accompanies him. I meet his gaze and see that his eyes are black with red streaks. Hmm. They don't often get red with me.

His hand clenches around my throat. Wind batters me from all sides. But that's fine. I know I could kill him now in . . . one, two, *three* ways very easily. I could electrocute his mind until he was nothing but a vegetable, or I could stab my claws through his stomach, root around in there a bit, and pull his heart out through his bellybutton, or I could do both simultaneously.

"Why did you go to the coffee shop?"

The fuck? "Excuse me?"

"What did you do there?" His eyes bleed red in their totality.

Meanwhile, I feel my own shoulders relax down my back. "Oh my."

He roars and the wind causes my ears to pop. Spots fill my vision, and I laugh as he throws me across my living room and I hit the far wall. Pain ricochets through my back. I float to the floor, landing on one knee, a wide grin on my face exposing my newly sharpened teeth.

The Marduk advances on me, white face darkened by his rage. His tattoos seem to swirl on his skin as the wind picks up in the room. If my foyer looked like Monika's, he'd have turned it upside down by now. As it stands, there's nothing here but two pieces of heavy furniture.

"If you go near that coffee shop again, I will—"

"You will what? You know that I'm only letting you rough me up as a courtesy." I rise to stand, my dick flopping about. I place my hands on my hips and laugh. "I could kill you here and be done with you forever."

"I know that, which is why I have contingencies in place should I fail to return. You touch me, and Bia finishes what she started with your girl."

"Excuse me?" I hiss, voice soft. Dangerously soft.

The Marduk's eyes flare. His fists hang heavy at his sides. He's in a black tee and black jeans, black boots, no coat. "Don't go back to that coffee shop. That's where I meet with the Tratharine I need to meet with. I don't need you *Champions* cluttering the space, and until you officially change sides and make your new allegiance to me and the other true Tratharine public, I don't want you there. Ever. Are we understood? You do this, and Monika will be fine. I already met with her and had the chance to scatter her body parts into a thousand pieces and, as a courtesy to you, left her intact."

My right eye twitches. I feel electricity skitter up and down my back. I don't speak, don't respond to his threats. Don't let the anger I feel toward Monika for meeting with the Marduk dismantle me entirely. I merely watch him disappear into the sky and listen as my cell phone alarm finally stops blaring, warning me of an incoming projectile.

And as I stand there, wishing I'd have struck him dead and worrying over the reason that I didn't, I let the plans I'd been ruminating on earlier change yet again. Fuck, marry, destroy, *kill*. Or kill, destroy. Either way, the Marduk cannot and will not live.

Chapter Twenty-One

Monika

It's been three days since I—or anyone—has heard from or seen Taranis, so needless to say, finding him standing in too-short sweatpants with a hole cut in the ass for his tail to pop through in the middle of my bedroom as I get out of the shower is . . . unexpected. I shriek.

Taranis exhales heavily. He blinks a lot in a way that makes him look really soft and almost approachable for a seven-foot-tall alien monster, and then he has to go and ruin it by opening his giant mouth. "Good, you're finished. Put this on. Let's go."

He tosses some clothes onto my bed—he must have gone through my closet and picked something out, and I can't say I'm not impressed with the selection. But considering it's the middle of the day on a Thursday, I can't imagine where I'd need to wear these thigh-high boots and this formfitting sweater dress, especially when he's dressed like that.

"Um . . . what are you doing here?"

"Picking you up for our date."

"What?"

"Get dressed. I'll wait."

"We're fighting," I remind him.

"Yes, excellent. Now, get dressed. I'll wait for you outside."

I'm so bloody confused. I start to drop my towel, and he immediately covers his eyes. "It's nothing you haven't seen before," I say in a low voice.

"Yes, but we're leaving, and if I open my eyes and see you in all your glory, we won't. So put this shit on, do your hair or whatever the ladies do or don't, and come on. You have five seconds."

I scoff and watch him bumble out of my bedroom, knocking his horns into the doorframe and cursing before he ducks and tries again. I chuckle, and then I start to wonder whether I should bring up the contracts he gave me earlier this week or ask him if he's okay or just . . . what the fuck is happening? But I don't do any of that. Instead, the idiot I am—the same idiot who agreed to go on missions for Mr. Singkham or spy on Taranis or even become a war photographer in the first place—pulls on the sweater dress and thigh-high boots and follows the world's greatest double-crossing superhero-villain to wherever he wants to take me.

And where he wants to take me?

The circus.

"Are you serious?" I ask him as Nicoleta pulls up in front of a venue guarded by a high fence, behind which stands a massive white tent, with people dressed all kinds of crazy flocking to it. I start to laugh as he ducks out of the car and offers me his hand.

He's got a grumpy face on that relaxes when he pulls me toward him and then hooks his arm around my waist and holds me even closer. "It's supposed to be fun."

"It's the circus."

"It's a circus for grown-ups."

"Then why are there so many kids here? And why am I the only one dressed up?"

"So ungrateful."

He pinches my ass hard, and I laugh as he walks me toward the VIP line while everyone else in the general line watches us agape. I offer passersby wary smiles, but it's hard to even notice them when Darius doesn't. Instead, he acts like this is all totally normal. Like he's a regular guy ordering popcorn from the vendor, who about looks ready to piss herself at the sight of him.

The people-pleasing Taranis is nowhere in sight either. He waves off anyone who tries to ask him for pictures or an autograph, and when he leads us to our seats under the big top, I laugh when he realizes the seats are too small for him.

"You're also blocking the eleven rows of seats behind you," I tell him, starting to stand back up. "Let's go stand at the back."

"I'm not going to stand at the back," he huffs, and before the squadron of frantic ushers can try to accommodate him, he grabs my hips, hauls me onto his lap, and starts to *lift*. We rise up into the rafters, him still in a chair position, me still seated on top of him. He floats us over to where the light crew stands on a metal walkway and takes a seat at an empty place amid the employees—one without any railings. I've never been particularly afraid of heights, and I'm not afraid at all right now. I probably should be. He's so hot and cold—one minute he's asking me to marry him, the next he might just push me.

"Popcorn? Wine?" he asks me, warm breath on my neck, his strong arms circling my waist.

My arms prickle with goose bumps. "Yes," I say breathily.

He hands me both, and as the circus starts and acrobats leap and spin onto the stage, I no longer think I might be in trouble. I know for *certain* I'm in trouble.

After the show, he flies us home, unwilling to wade through the traffic that Nicoleta is caught up in trying to get out of the parking lot. We land on the balcony of his penthouse, my limbs all a little shaky from holding on to him as tight as I was. He seems to realize this and sweeps my feet, then carries me inside. He sets me down on the barstool in front of his kitchen island before moving around it with confidence and opening up his fridge.

"You were right," I say with a chuckle. "That was an adult circus."

"I told you."

"I was expecting clowns and animals. I'm glad there weren't either."

He smiles as he turns toward me, his hands filled with peppers and round blocks of mozzarella. "It's a variety show, technically. Not a circus."

I nod and then shiver, residual chills from flying shooting up my arms. "I about lost my lunch when that guy stood on the other guy's shoulders on a bicycle and went over that tightrope."

Darius nods absently, too busy watching me with concern. "You cold?"

"A little. Mostly just still wound up from flying." I smile at him. "It was a lot of fun."

His lips part a little, and then he shakes out of it. "Let me get you a blanket."

He returns a moment later with the comforter off his bed. He throws it all around me, and I laugh. "You don't have a blanket?"

"Why would I need a blanket?"

"For comfort?"

"I'm comfortable." I don't believe him at all, given the furnishings in his flat, but I don't say that.

"What about for your lady friends you bring over that might not be?"

"I don't bring lady friends here."

I find that unbelievable too. "Yeah, right. You're the world's most eligible bachelor—well, I mean, you were." He glares and tosses a piece of chopped tomato at me. "You probably have a whole stable of lady friends."

"I don't, and even if I did, that's where they'd stay—in the stables. You're the only person who doesn't work for me that's come to my place."

"I do work for you."

He frowns. "You know what I mean."

I don't speak. I can only smile at him shyly as I tuck my windswept hair behind my ear. I'm sure it's sticking out in every direction at this point, but he doesn't look at me like I'm insulting the aesthetic of his place. He looks at me like he's . . . absorbed.

"You want eggplant Parmesan or chicken Parmesan? Got Parmesan that needs eating."

"You're cooking for me again?"

He nods. I watch his hands work deftly with the tomatoes, not so much as pinching their fragile skins with his hands. It's like he's always had claws.

"Mmm . . . eggplant. Can I help?"

He hesitates. "Sure."

He slides me a cutting board, and soon enough we're working side by side on his kitchen island. I'm still swathed in his comforter, which smells deliriously like him, and he's standing on the corner adjacent to me. He grates Parmesan and I slice eggplants while his red sauce starts simmering. The smell of garlic and fresh basil swirls around us, making his place feel a little homier than it did.

"You cook?" he asks out of the blue, his tail constantly in motion and stirring the air behind him in a way I find oddly soothing.

I snort. "Definitely not. I'm more of a whatever-I-can-eat-that's-fast kinda gal. It's nice to have a home-cooked meal. I . . ." My voice breaks like a prepubescent boy's. I clear my throat and try again. "I really liked my omelet."

He stares at me for a beat too long, then nods and looks away from me quickly. We lapse again into a nearly pleasant silence. Nearly. There's so much between us left unspoken, but I can't seem to find the courage I need to bring it up. Or maybe I just don't want to break the spell of the moment. This is nice. Maybe the best date I've ever had.

"I take it you cook often?"

"I do."

"I took you for an in-house-chef kinda guy."

"I had one for a little while. He sucked, so I fired him. Couldn't make a simple ratatouille." He clicks his tongue against the backs of his teeth, his brow furrowing in memory.

I can't help it. I wish I could but I can't. I bark out a laugh that has him bumping his shoulder against me in what was supposed to be a light gesture but nearly throws me out of my seat. "Shit, sorry," he chuckles.

I laugh harder.

He smirks and places the eggplant slices on paper towels layered over kitchen towels and instructs me to salt them. I don't understand why until I start to see little beads of moisture start to condense on the tops of the eggplants a few moments later. We flip them.

"You like heat?" he asks me as he starts to layer the thirteen-by-nine-inch baking tray.

"Yessir. The Korean in me came out stronger than the German, in that way."

"Your dad is German?"

"He is. Born of Malian parents. Hence the melanin." I got a lot more color from my dad than my mom, even if my hair texture came out very different from both of theirs. For no reason I can think of, other than the fact that Darius is also Black, I add, "It's not that easy being Black in Germany. Or Korea. Or really anywhere, for that matter."

He snorts. "Guess I don't have to worry about that anymore."

"I'm sorry," I say, laughing loudly and unattractively. I tuck my hair behind my ear while his brow flattens. He gives me a dull look, but there's a humorous glint in his eye. "That was pretty good."

"I still can't fucking believe it."

"What?"

"Turning blue." He opens the oven, and a gust of warm air billows out of it. He slides the covered pan inside and sets the timer, then shuts the oven door. "Some stupid shit."

I laugh and he shakes his head, gets two ornately carved crystal wineglasses out of the cupboard, places them on the counter. He then slides open a dark-gray farm-style door on the left wall that I incorrectly assumed was a bathroom. It's not. It opens into a walk-in wine pantry. I whistle.

He smirks and grabs a bottle, returns to me, and pours me a glass. "You like red?"

"Yeah."

"We better be talking wine only, I hope." He clinks his glass against mine while I work to puzzle together his words.

When it finally hits me, I laugh again. "I don't have a crush on the Wyvern, if that's what you're asking."

He grunts and doesn't answer, just sips his wine and watches me sip mine. I don't know what it is, but it's good.

"Do you think it's inevitable, all the Champions and villains eventually changing colors and getting big?"

"We're supposed to change, all of us. The way we look as humans is just an illusion implanted by the beings we left behind on our home planet. Made it easier for us to blend in and be accepted by the humans."

"You're saying if you'd ended up on a fish planet, you'd have ended up a little goldfish?"

"A shark." He snaps his fangs in my direction and I flush.

"How do you know all that?"

"I've been remembering details of my life before." He looks uncomfortable. "We got forty minutes; wanna sit at the table or the couch?"

I glance at the couch. It's such a glossy leather that it looks like you'd slide right off it. Then again, the dining chairs are made out of stiff wood.

"What?" he asks, almost in a growl.

"Nothing. Couch looks . . . okay."

"What's wrong with my couch?"

"Nothing, let's sit," I say, sliding off my stool, but when I turn toward the couch, he's standing in front of me, blocking my way.

His fingers are on my chin. *Scheiße*, his claws are massive. "I know you haven't accepted the fact that you're mine yet," he says to me, sending feeling skittering all the way through my bare toes that's infinitely more powerful than any of his lightning bolts. "But I don't wanna be enemies either. I wanna know what you're thinking. Not gonna get mad and yell at you again. I learned my lesson the last time."

Well, shit. This is uncharted territory. I don't trust him as far as I can throw him, which wasn't far before he turned blue and grew to almost seven feet. Feeling untethered and way too comfortable after the date and the wine and the wind, I blurt out, "Your couch sucks."

"What?"

"All your furniture sucks. Your place sucks."

He gawks at me like a fucking kid. "You're kidding. This is a multimillion-dollar penthouse."

I point at that hideous leather thing on his floor. "Your couch looks like a giant bar of soap. And your dining chairs look like they were made to torture heretics in the Middle Ages."

"Excuse me? These are three-thousand-dollar-chairs designed by Peter Olvanson."

"You just made that name up, and even if Peter existed, I'm pretty sure he hates you. The most comfortable spot to sit in your house is on this stool, and it doesn't even have a backrest. What kind of masochist has a chair that doesn't have a backrest?"

His eyes narrow even farther. He takes a step into me, his abs brushing my knees and forcing me to look straight up if I want to keep his gaze. "Your apartment looks like a flea market."

I scoff. "It's cozy, colorful, and maximalistically decorated."

"The best interior decorator in the country designed my space."

"Does she hate you too?"

"No." But his full lips twitch.

I grin and point a finger up at his mouth. "Aha! What did you say to insult her, and how far into the process were you?"

He grunts. "Two days."

"And had she procured the couch yet?"

His blue-purple lips purse even farther until I can't see their fullness at all. "No," he growls.

My head falls back as I laugh again. Hard. "She's an evil genius. I think she and I would be friends."

"You're an asshole," he says.

"*You're* the asshole. You're a villain."

And then his huge hand comes and cups the side of my face. In a dark, demonic voice, he murmurs, "Oh no. I'm a far more complex, far more terrible creature." I shiver, eyes opening as I look up into his. They radiate the most spectacular white light. "I'm not a villain. Not a hero either. Like you, I work on my own. Don't have time for Boy Scouts or merit badges."

I chuckle, shoulders shaking. "You're two-faced."

"Which one of my faces do you like better?"

He's joking, but I actually have an answer to that. I reach up and stroke his cheek. He flinches and it fills my chest with a scary tremor. He's not a male used to being touched, is he? At least, not with gentleness. "This one."

"That's a lie." He grabs my wrist, then tilts his mouth into my palm, kissing it and sending feeling coursing through all my bones. "I saw you damn near pass out when I turned on the charm back in that elevator."

"Maybe. But this is a face I'd do a lot more than pass out for," I admit like a fool. But it's worth it to see the surprise on his face.

"Yeah?"

I nod.

"Like what?"

And then I blurt out, "Try to trust. I don't trust Taranis at all. But I'm starting to trust Darius."

His hand strokes down to my neck. His face looks . . . I can't interpret his expression at all. He looks pissed, but his touch is so soft.

"Thank you for tonight," I say. He doesn't respond, just watches the movement of his hand over my skin. "Your eyes are so bright."

"Sounds about right."

"Right?"

His claw flicks over my collarbone gently. He exhales, and then exhales deeper. "Okay," he says calmly. Far too calmly. His gaze meets mine again and is so bright it's impossible to hold it without squinting. "Okay."

"Okay what?"

"Let's go to your place."

"We can hang out on my balcony. I have those heater things that are terrible for the environment, but, *shh*, don't tell anyone."

He rolls his eyes. "Who would I tell? I don't have friends. And I know damn well you don't either."

The strange realization hits me, and I shrug at the truth of it. And then we both start moving at the same time, except we're moving in opposite directions. "I thought we were going to my balcony," I say.

"We are. But I'm not going to take the elevator all the way down to the lobby and then take the other elevator all the way back up just to go down four floors. Come on."

Instinct and curiosity have me trailing after him as he snatches the wine bottle off the counter, gripping it in the same massive hand as his glass. As he approaches his balcony doors, they slide open automatically. I wonder whether it's his gifts doing that or he's just a lazy fucker who had automatic sliding glass doors installed in his penthouse.

We're high up on the thirty-second floor, and even though I'm on the twenty-eighth, my balcony faces a different direction—west instead of the more highly coveted south that his faces. Actually, I observe as I step out into the wind, his balcony wraps all the way around his penthouse. Lucky sonofabitch.

I'm smiling giddily, still wrapped up in his comforter as he wraps his burly arms around me and lifts us up together from the floor of his balcony. "Eyes on me," he whispers in a low voice, making my stomach clench as I'm distinctly reminded of the first time he said those words to me.

He goes silent then as we round the building to the west side and start to descend. "You know I'm not gonna drop you, right?"

"I don't think Darius would drop me, no," I reply right as a particularly loud siren sounds way beneath our dangling feet, making me jolt. "But sometimes I don't know who I'm speaking to—Darius or Taranis."

He's quiet again for another pause, this one long enough for him to finish his descent and touch down lightly onto my balcony, covered with a bright pink-turquoise-cream-and-yellow outdoor rug. Even though my plants are thriving in the day's lingering sun and I've got fancy self-watering cans rigged up, I've been concerned because my balcony door has been jammed for the past few days and the maintenance guy couldn't fix it.

"I wouldn't let you fall." The way he says it so simply feels so unlike him.

I turn on the heater, then take a seat on my finest outdoor sofa, a plush pink poof of a thing. He hands me a glass and pours me wine, then sets the bottle on the low table between us.

Instead of taking a seat on the sofa beside me, he drags a dark-red papasan chair over, making space for it between my petunias. They blossom bright purple and white behind him. Feels fitting. I must be making a face, because he makes one back at me and grunts, "You gotta stop smiling at me like that."

"Like what?"

"Like I'm *cute*."

"I'd tell you you are cute, but you already know that."

"I don't wanna be cute to you."

"What do you want to be, then?" I ask genuinely. "My hero?"

He rubs his chin and shakes his head. "The villain you say yes to."

"Yes?"

"What'd you do with the marriage license I gave you?"

I choke, wine literally spraying from my lips. He doesn't so much as flinch. I cough to clear my throat as best I can and sputter, "That was a power play. You don't . . . actually want to be married. You want to control." I set down my wine.

He lifts his. His serrated claws rattle the glass. "Maybe I want both." He drains his glass and I drain mine. He pours us both some more.

I swallow hard. "Why did you . . . why did you come for me today?"

"Because I wanted to. Why did you come with me?"

"Because I wanted to." I smile softly.

He stares at me for another while. Another long while. The sunset has started its descent and bathes his skin in twilight. The blue appears plum in this light. It's breathtaking. He's breathtaking. Far more beautiful than he ever was as a human right now to me. Because that human was fake. And this version of him is starting to feel real.

"I've been thinking . . ." He sits up and clears his throat.

"Thinking? Uh-oh. That sounds ominous."

He rolls his eyes. "I didn't like how we left our meeting."

"I didn't like anything about that meeting."

"That's a lie." He cocks an eyebrow and an edge of his mouth.

I heat but refuse to dignify that with an answer.

He sets the bottle down on the wooden live-edge table positioned between us. He sits abruptly forward on the lip of the papasan chair, and I'm honestly surprised he doesn't tip the whole thing over. "I won't kill Mr. Singkham."

"Oh, good. I'm glad." I sound sarcastic, but I really am.

"And I won't change your contract." He rubs his chin.

"Good . . ." I start—I should have waited for him to finish.

"I'm gonna annul it. I'm quitting the Champion shit."

I spit my wine out again, and this time it splatters the table between us.

He glances down at it. "Am I gonna need to get you a bib?"

"For real?"

"Yes. You've spit out more wine than you've drunk."

"Not about that," I mutter. "The, ya know . . . no-more-heroic-photo-ops thing?"

"Don't act so surprised. It was your idea."

I shake my head. "I definitely didn't think—"

"I'd quit?" He stares off into the distance, huffing through flared nostrils. "I didn't either. I've been Taranis so long. Thought it might be easier to take over the COE, be *the* Champion. But you were right. I don't want strings, I don't have to have strings. It's gonna take me some time to figure out who I am without 'em. And nobody ever said I didn't want my picture taken anymore."

"Figures."

"But just by you."

I smile at him, feeling proud. I'm used to being complimented on my photographs, but not like this. This feels . . . different. More personal. More tender in ways I'm not sure either of us hardened souls is used to.

"And the murder thing? Does that mean Mr. Singkham's off the hook?"

"For now," he grumbles, sounding displeased.

I laugh, irrationally elated that the male I'm starting to really crush hard on has admitted that he might *not* want to murder my boss. The list of things wrong with me might be getting longer, but I can't deny that right now I'm happy.

Without prompting and without warning, I stand up from my little couch, drop my blanket, and go to him on the papasan chair. He leans back as I take a seat in his lap, curling up there into a ball against his chest. I peck his lips one at a time, watch his eyes close as he breathes out a sound that is pure satisfaction.

I kiss my way along his jaw and against his neck, whisper, "I see you. And I like what I see."

"This ugly mug?"

"Everything."

He shivers a little and when his lips part, I dive in, kissing him in earnest. We make out until my jaw starts to tire. It's sweet, though, filled with none of the explosiveness of our earlier couplings. And it's nice. I daresay I'd go so far as to call it *romantic*.

After a while, it's Darius who extracts us from the slippery slope we're sliding down. He gives me a series of quick pecks along the temple and says, "I gotta go check on the eggplant. Can you get us some plates from your place, unless you want me to bring my masochistic ones?"

"Sure . . . Oh wait, no. My door is stuck. I can't get in from the balcony, so just bring your plates—and also don't abandon me here," I tease.

He gets that pissed look again, his brows furrowing.

"I'm kidding," I add.

But he just shakes his head, and when he kisses me next, it's so different from any kiss he's given me before. It's different from any kiss I've ever had. It's pure tenderness. Just the press of his soft purple lips to my mouth. His lips are cool, but his tongue snakes out to lick my bottom lip just once, quickly, and is so warm. I'm smiling and my eyes have closed. I didn't mean to shut them. It just feels nice.

"I know I'm an asshole, but I wanna be your asshole." There's a pause. My eyes fly open. Our gazes lock. "That didn't sound right."

I buck with laughter, my whole body convulsing with it. I catch myself on his T-shirt, clinging to it as tears fill my eyes. Through my own laughter, I can feel his body shaking with laughter too. "You're an idiot," I cackle.

"Wanna be that for you too," he says in a low voice, but his arm comes around me and his mouth presses against the top of my head. He starts to stand, my body still cradled in his grip. "I don't know how not to be a villain, baby girl, but I'm not gonna let you fall."

My heart squeezes. I want nothing more than to tear it out of my chest and give it to him as an offering.

"You believe me?" he asks, taking a step back and stroking his claw lightly over my cheek.

I nod. "I do. At least, I'm going to try. I also want to help you figure out what else you want to do besides Champion stuff. What you want to do as Darius."

"I know you will, baby." He reels me back in and plants a sloppy kiss on my forehead. "In the meantime, I'm gonna work on not tearing my hair and heart out every time you go on assignment, all right?"

Tell him. Tell him about the spying. Fuck. If there was ever a time to confess, it would be here, now. I open my mouth. "All right." *Womp womp wommmmmmp.*

"I am warning you, though, someday we're gonna talk about that *other* contract you refused to sign." Without waiting for a response, he leaves me with a hammering heart.

He flies off, returning a few moments later with a steaming tray of eggplant Parmesan. He dishes it out, and the salty, savory taste and the incredible smell distracts me from more dangerous conversations as we slip into easier ones.

He keeps the wine flowing, and we talk late into the night about everything and anything. He tells me about his prim and proper "host" family, who were wealthy and status driven and so ecstatic to have a Champion for a kid that they treated him like a shiny trophy. I understand why he hates them.

I tell him about my family and what it was like growing up as a third culture kid. Well, we both were, in a sense—a fact that bonded us further.

We talked about the Champions, speculating over who will turn next, and if any of the villains might. Hearing him talk about the Wyvern and Mr. Singkham and Ms. Lemon makes me laugh, despite my misgivings—*my lies*. He holds them in very little regard. I tell him I kinda like the Wyvern, and he admits that he kinda likes the big idiot too. We talk until the sunset burns away the light and indigo comes to cover the world. As night truly settles over us, I invite him inside, like a horny idiot. Instead of accepting outright, he wrenches open the door to my balcony, shoves me inside, and kisses me in that tender way.

"I'll see you tomorrow," he whispers against my lips as I swoon toward him.

"What's tomorrow?" I ask dazedly after him as he heads to my balcony and gathers our dirty dishes and the tray with the rest of the eggplant Parmesan.

"I'm taking you on another date." He pauses over the threshold.

"You should let me take *you* on a date."

He cocks his head, considering giving up control . . . and I watch as he finally gives in. "Okay. Okay, yeah."

"I promise it won't be torture," I say, wondering if I should take him to an art gallery, dinner, a slasher flick—my favorite—or something else entirely.

He just grunts; then, before he leaves, he says, "Better not be, or you won't like your punishment."

I'm giddy as a schoolgirl until I check my phone—my new phone—and see an email marked URGENT from Mr. Singkham waiting at the top of my inbox.

> Ms. Neumann, the details for your next mission are attached.

Shit. Next Friday. Five p.m. And I still haven't told Darius about any of it.

Chapter Twenty-Two

Darius

The next week passes in a blur. I see Monika every damn day, and now that she's gotten the all clear from Emily, every damn day I also fuck her.

She takes me on dates. Last Friday, she took me to see some horror movie that might actually be the worst film I've ever seen. The only thing that made it bearable was the way Monika laughed hysterically anytime anybody died and talked through all of it. Saturday, we realized we share a competitive streak and played a dozen board games. I won, I punished her. She won, I punished her. Sunday, we got breakfast and I forced her to let me join the call when she videoed her parents. Monday, she had to work and I had to wrap up some shit.

I got the design team to make me enough clothes to last me months. Tuesday, I convinced Monika to send me the full video of the night that I reverted. I made my assistants hand over the log-in credentials for my social media accounts and posted the full video myself. I then recorded a short follow-up video telling the world I was resigning as a Champion. Not wanting to waste extra effort typing up something original, I sent Mr. Singkham the same video with the subject line: TWO SECONDS NOTICE. Wednesday, his team tried to contact me, going so far as to come to my apartment building, but this is *my* apartment, not the

COE's, so I simply called the cops while I flew on outta there with Monika on my arm and took her to dinner.

Earlier today, Monika took me to her art gallery for the first time. I was surprised. Don't know why, since it was her idea, but Monika doesn't seem to mind I'm no longer a Champion. Her gallery is impressive, even if the exhibit isn't her artwork. Her confidence gives me confidence. Her confidence in *me* erases any hesitation I might have had that resigning was the right choice. I don't start imagining new projects and activities for myself yet, for now I'm simply content to be.

Lying out on my balcony again in a way that's become second nature, I text my girl: What are you wearing?

She responds a few seconds later with a picture of herself in the nude. I reach under boxers especially tailored to my size—my last parting gift from the COE—and start to jack off. I wonder, if I come over the edge of the balcony, what poor sap it'll fall on thinking it's bird shit. Ha. I never realized such small tortures could bring such simple satisfaction to me. This new life as Darius might just prove to be *fun*.

You're fucking incredible. Hate that you're working. Can't wait to have you all to myself tomorrow night. I send her a picture of my hard cock against Sundale's impressive skyline.

She does not respond satisfactorily. About that. I messed up. I have a photoshoot for the Wyvern and Vanessa. Can we do Saturday?

Rage permeates my being. My urge to text the Wyvern, Vanessa, Mr. Singkham—to cut power to the entire damn COE power grid—is so strong the lights in my own penthouse flicker. I set my phone down in a rage, take several deep breaths, and bring the lights back. The poor sap that was about to get cummed on is spared. This time.

I *don't* storm her apartment, bend her over one of those ridiculous colorful couches she has, and spell my name in bright-red handprints on her perfect round ass. Instead, I simply exhale anger and respond to her text. OK. Look at that. Growth.

And I'm rewarded for my sacrifice. I'll make it worth it, promise.
I smile. Expect punishment.

I'd expect nothing less.

I grin up at the sky, liking this life already.
This life as Darius.

Chapter Twenty-Three

Monika

I shouldn't have canceled on Darius. That's all I can think to myself as I lunge, falling hard on my forearms.

"RUN!" The word is ripped from the lungs of the heavily armed, heavily tatted COE officer who's been assigned to me. Unlike the SDD jerks I met at Old Sundale Station, this COE officer is cool. The whole group of twenty-six tactical officers has been really kind and helpful, leading me to believe that the problem either lies with the SDD or with Taranis. He may just be unpopular enough that he was assigned the biggest dickheads on purpose, or only dickheads volunteered to team up with him. Whatever the case, I'm grateful for the non-dickhead officers with me now. They're keeping me breathing.

Officer Ortiz grabs me by the strap of my bulletproof vest, the one with Press half burned off the front after the Wyvern got flung off his feet and his flames went wild, lashing into me like a whip. It was either that or be burned by acid. And the acid's still coming.

Ortiz grunts as she pushes me out in front of her, likely taking the hits that seem to have been intended for *me.* The creature chasing us is spitting acid, and even more alarmingly, I don't know who he is. He's a lean creature with dark-brown skin and locs that travel all the way down his back. But his locs look like they might've been floating from the little of him I glimpsed before all hell broke out.

His face isn't among those I've photographed, and I've taken pictures of almost every single member of the Forty-Eight—the good, the unaffiliated, and the bad. It makes me think of what the Wyvern and Mr. Singkham told me in that very first meeting. There may be more than forty-eight. There may be as many as sixty-nine of them . . . And out of the ten—possibly up to fifteen—aliens attacking us, I don't recognize anybody.

We're down at the old Sundale ports. When Sundale won the bid for the relocation of the COE headquarters fifteen years ago, industry in the city—on the entire East Coast—went up a hundredfold. The ports were revamped and moved just south of the city where there's more available coastline. These ports have been in disuse ever since. There was talk of building a boardwalk here with parks and shops, but there were issues with land stability, so the project was tabled, never to be revisited again.

Now we're inside the smallest of the six warehouses, the one where Cynthia was potentially tortured, fighting for our lives as we race back up the ramp to reach the main level. The COE was right to follow Cynthia's lead: The villains *are* using this space as an evil lair. The problem with that? They were prepared. It makes me wonder if Cynthia wasn't taken and released for this exact reason . . .

I was led here. We all were.

Some sort of signal we didn't discern must have been activated, because by the time our team descended the ramp from the ground level to this watery, half-submerged basement, there was a crew of villains lying in wait. Our team, meanwhile, is composed of the Wyvern, two dozen humans with guns, and *me.* We may not be outnumbered, but we are outmatched significantly.

I feel a burn on the back of my left calf and miss my next step. Ortiz hooks her elbow under my arm, spins around my body so that I'm moving forward while she's moving backward—running, mostly carrying me—her gun drawn and blazing. She fires and the sound is explosive. I close my eyes on every bang, even as I try to keep filming.

A wave of heat assaults my front, and I know that the Wyvern is doing his best to wield his fire to protect us, but it's so wet down here, and one of the beings must have power over water, because the fire hits the water and dies instantly. And then *whoosh*. I try to glance over my shoulder, snapping pics like a social media star desperate to catch a glimpse of just anything, when the Wyvern roars, *"EVERYBODY DROP!"*

I hit the ground, dragged there by Ortiz, whose body half covers mine. My forehead scrapes the concrete underneath me. I can feel another body drop to the ground next to me, warming my right side before pain skewers the back of my calf, like a knife lodged there in a spot I can't reach.

I scream and that's when I realize it's a collective scream of all the humans close to me. A huge roar sounds and I look up, panicked, my heart beating like a snare drum. I whip my camera around and manage to capture a shot of the Wyvern throwing a metal barrel at the acid spitter advancing up the concrete ramp. It hits him in the face and chest, sending him flying backward.

Another two aliens step forward. Water rises around a male with tanned skin and straight black hair. He throws a fist forward and water pummels the Wyvern.

"Ortiz!" I shout, pointing at the Wyvern.

She's already up, though it looks like it costs her great effort. The man on her other side is up, too, moving a little faster. Both of them fire. I take their pictures with steady hands, adrenaline keeping me steady even through my injuries. My left leg is dragging on the ground, so I lift my right into a crouch for better stabilization and watch a female with light-brown hair and freckles step up between the two male aliens, a smile on her face that's absolutely terrifying. And suddenly a wall of smoke appears, making my vision hazy. I can't see through or past it.

"Fuck off, number Thirty-Eight!" the Wyvern roars.

"You attacked *us,* number Sixty-Two," the female calls back. "You may have fangs now, but don't be disappointed that we bite back."

Out of the hazy wall that may be real or imagined, a figure darts in a blur, launching itself at the Wyvern. The Wyvern throws up a wall of flame, and the blur vanishes. I switch my Nikon to record, even though the lighting is terrible, and sweep my lens around the cloudy space.

There's a scream to my right. I glance up, but I can't see anything besides COE team members dressed all in black, pointing their weapons down the ramp but not firing. If they're seeing only the same gray haze that I'm seeing, there's nothing to fire at.

A grunt to my immediate right has me swinging my camera around. The sticky, wet world clings to my skin. My hands may be steady, but my legs are shaking. The guy that was next to me, kneeling right there with his gun at the ready, is *gone.* Just—poof!—disappeared. And in his place kneels an alien with white, tan skin. They're looking at me. Smiling at me. Right at me.

My fingers move on autopilot. I switch to stills. I take their picture. It's a perfect shot. They look perfect in it. Short dark hair, looking styled in the humidity rather than watered down. Their arms are exposed in their black T-shirt. They have on black pants. Lots of heavy silver jewelry. They look like they could be Mediterranean—Greek, even—and I know instantly that this is the other villain who was involved in hurting Cynthia. I suck a breath in through my teeth.

"You seem important," they whisper to me, their lips a dark pink, almost burgundy. "I think I'm going to kill you. Gotta cover my bases, after all." They reach for me and almost touch my cheek and this deep, primordial instinct way down within me, coming from places my ancestors drew on for their own survival, tells me that if they touch me, it'll be the last thing that ever happens to me.

My secondary identical Nikon Z9 camera hangs on a strap around my neck. It has a 50mm lens—so a little heavier than the 24mm I'm using now. I rear back, tumbling ass over foot, removing the strap as

I fall. I swing my camera at the being as hard as I can. My camera connects with their cheek. At the same time, I feel something heavy drop onto my shoulder.

"Hold still!" Ortiz shouts in my ear. And then I see the barrel of her long gun thrust out before me. She aims at the being's chest and pulls the trigger.

The ringing in my ear is sensational. It lasts long after the bullets pass straight through the empty place where the terrifying teleporter once was. They're gone now, no trace left, my camera gone with them. I don't think I have many pictures on it, but I don't like that they took it.

"LOOK OUT!" Another member of the COE team. "RUN!" I look up to see that the cloudy atmosphere has shifted. Instead of fog, I see a wall of water—and it looks very real as it rips toward us.

Hands are on my shoulders, Ortiz's and another's. They're dragging me up. Everyone is running.

There's suddenly a short spear flying past my head. "They're firing darts!" someone shouts.

"Location?" someone else cries out.

"Ceiling!"

My feet pedal backward as fast as they can, trying to keep up with Ortiz and the male without sacrificing a shot. If photo evidence of these beings' existences is all we get out of this, at the cost of the human lives already lost, then I can't stop.

I glance up, and sure enough, there's a female dangling there like a flying fucking fox, launching short wooden daggers out of her wrists. I take her photograph. Ortiz cusses in her whispery Guatemalan Spanish. The other guy who's got a hold of my other shoulder curses in Mandarin.

The dart-wielding female has black hair and wild, wild red eyes. They're pointed directly at me, and I don't move fast enough when she swivels her arm toward my left eye. Ortiz trips, and it's that accident that saves my life. The sting of the wooden dart against my cheek lets me know I'm still alive.

I don't realize how close to death I am. No one ever does in the moment. Because all you can do in a life-threatening situation is worry about the next step and the next and the next that will keep you breathing.

I run up the ramp, my camera flashing, until I'm eventually dragged out into the daylight where huge black SUVs and Humvees stand by waiting. One of the Humvees—the one I was headed toward—explodes. It explodes not in flame, but like a balloon. Pieces of the car slam outward, and the people who were driving the car are torn apart in the wreckage. Metal chunks and body parts go flying, and I'm slammed down onto the ground again, this time on my back, so hard my head rings with a tinny sound as it hits the concrete.

Moans and screams rise up. I hear sirens on the breeze. It must be the COE calling in reinforcements. Or the SDD. Please, let it be the fucking Navy SEALs or the goddamn army.

I glance to my right and see Ortiz on the ground next to me, open my mouth, and remember not to scream. I remember that I've been in combat environments before, remember that I've seen bodies, remember that a scream could be the difference between me living and me drawing the next barrage of fire. Ortiz has a huge piece of metal sticking out of the side of her head. I realize she didn't pull me to the ground underneath her. When the car exploded, she was taken down by the shrapnel.

I turn my face so that I'm staring straight up ahead at the sky. It's a sunny Sundale day, darkened only by the shadow that moves across it. Overhead, the Marduk flies past. Fire chases him, but it's like he's walking on top of it, some wind pressure I can't quite feel pushing the fire back . . . and then *whoosh*. The fire cascades toward me.

I roll onto my stomach. Warmth heats my body through my bulletproof vest, terrifyingly. For a split second, all I can think is *This is it, the end, and I do* not *want to go like this.* Being roasted alive is nasty business. I squeeze my eyes shut tight as the temperature gets so hot that I buck against the ground, trying to escape it. Tears wet my cheeks and my hands covering my face. *I'm going to die here.* And then the fire recedes. There aren't hands on my body this time, pulling me up. I don't know how many people are still alive. But I know that I want to be.

My sneakered feet kick at the ground, skidding, skidding, skidding until my toes finally gain purchase. I lunge, my whole torso boneless as my lower half does all the work in keeping me up. Something hits the back of my vest. Something else hits my shoulder. I barely feel it. I've been in war zones before, but not like this. Never like this.

My job is supposed to be neutral, but the sacred bonds of presshood are not being respected here. I feel targeted just as much as any of the fighters around me. And even in highly violent combat environments where danger was a risk, I've usually been more shielded, kept slightly farther back from the front lines. I've never been on the *final* line after all the other lines have fallen.

A few other soldiers have gotten up off the ground and are firing as they retreat toward the remaining SUVs. Meanwhile, the villains under the Marduk's watchful eye are just picking the rest of us off one by one.

I slam my palms against the nearest SUV at the same time another COE officer collides with the car right next to me. I glance at him, but he's not paying attention to me. He's ripping off his helmet.

Are you okay? I shout to him in my head, because my lungs have seized up and my voice doesn't work. My voice doesn't work because he's turned to face me and his eyes are bulging out of his skull, and as I watch, his head just . . . explodes. His eyes pop out of his skull, bouncing off my armor-plated chest. His mouth opens and blood pours out, spraying my face.

I glance up at the sky and see the Marduk staring down at the man on my right. A wave of fire swallows the Marduk up for a moment, but it's battered back. Was he . . . aiming for me?

Another SUV explodes. I can't risk trying to get into the one closest to me now.

I open the passenger's-side door and shout at whoever might be inside, "GET OUT! RUN!"

I hear the driver's-side door open at the same time that the passenger's-side door is ripped off its hinges, right out from under me. I'm caught up in the blast, thrown off my feet and away from the melee. I hit the concrete of the parking lot between this cluster of port buildings and roll, roll, roll.

My forearms scrape over the ground on every turn, but I don't stop to assess any of my wounds. They feel minor right now. Instead, I stagger up onto my knees and watch as the Wyvern and the four remaining COE members stand up against one, two, three, four, five, six villains I can see emerging from the hazy mouth of the tunnel to join the Marduk. We don't stand a chance. We're all going to die if we don't run.

"GET THE FUCK OUT OF THERE!" I shout at the top of my lungs to anybody left. "EVERYBODY RETREAT!"

I'm not a member of this army. I'm not trained for this. One of the cardinal rules of my job is to keep my mouth shut and take pictures, but I know Vanessa too well to watch her fiancé get exploded to itty-bitty pieces.

I see the Wyvern hovering not far from me, keeping his eyes firmly on the villains. "Roland, if you don't get the fuck out of here, Vanessa is going to murder you and then come for me!" My voice is a tortured shriek. "Get those fighters out of here!"

I watch the indecision. The Wyvern throws a few more balls of flame toward his adversaries, but it's only to ward off incoming darts, water, and wind. He roars, and in a move so fast my camera can't capture it, he grabs the four remaining COE fighters in his arms and takes flight.

There's a small trailer parked on the far side of the parking lot. I run toward it and see the Wyvern's huge shadow on the ground following me. I round the trailer, expecting to be able to grab hold of the Wyvern's foot and hitch a ride out of here, only to find *six* COE soldiers positioned here hiding. All six of them point their guns at me.

I squeak and lift my hands, one of them still clutching my camera fiercely, the reflex more automatic at this point than anything.

The Wyvern touches down onto the ground. "Lower your weapons. We don't have time to wait here. Monika, come with me."

"No, I'm not a threat. They aren't targeting me," I say because it's logical, not because I actually believe it. "You're better off grabbing as many of these fighters as you can and hauling ass out of here. The rest of us will scatter. Run like hell." My face is on fire. I smell blood and burning hair. My body zings with adrenaline and electricity.

Electricity. I should have told him. I should have fucking told him! Because all I can think is that I really fucking wish Darius were here.

"I'm not a match for these fuckers. Not this many." The Wyvern looks beat. His chest heaves with each breath. He's got blood running down his cheek, and when he turns, I can see he's got darts pegging his entire left side. "I can't keep you all safe." He glances around at the lot of them.

"We were called in for reinforcements by the COE. SDD reinforcements are said to arrive in ten," an older woman with a tan, weathered face clips. "We can hold them until then."

"You can't. There are too many, their powers too strong. And they may have reinforcements coming themselves," the Wyvern groans. He glances up at the sky. "The Marduk is here. He'll have a hard time killing me by himself, but together with the rest of them, they could and will. I'm the biggest threat to them there is." He glances again at me, his irises dancing with fire. "Monika, come with me now. Vanessa would kill me if I let you get hurt any more than you already are, and I don't need to tell you what Taranis will do to me."

"I'll be okay," I pant. "We're going to run. They won't chase us into Sundale. Once we've cleared the ports, we'll be safe." I say the words like I believe them, and for a moment, when his gaze hardens and he nods at me once, I nearly do.

"We'll give you cover. Take the injured with you," the commander of the reinforcements barks at the Wyvern.

He doesn't hesitate. He can't afford to. Not when the windows of the shack behind us explode outward.

The Wyvern grabs three of the four bodies he brought here, the fourth opting to remain back and help the rest. Meanwhile, I'm being grabbed again, this time by the commander, who shoves herself in front of me and starts firing, throwing commands out as she runs.

The gunfire has its intended effect. The villains, super as they may be, aren't immune to bullets. I see that several are bleeding, and the teleporting individual hasn't reappeared, thankfully. The Marduk is struck when one of the COE members shoots up at him, and it's that small window that gives the Wyvern—and me—the time we respectively need.

The Wyvern bullets toward the sun, carrying the injured three. I make it to the next building and follow the corrugated-metal siding until I finally reach the back corner. Only two more buildings separate me from the road. Once I get to the road, I'll officially be out of the port district. Once I get to the road, I believe the villains won't follow me. *Ssi-bal*, I hope.

"I think we're almost there," I shout, turning around, but the commander who had been right at my back is on the ground, screaming as acid eats at her face below her helmet. I charge forward to help her, but she's gurgling up blood, her body twitching as lifelessness quickly comes over her. My gaze is trained on her body. I take a picture, my lower half shaking when I spy a shadow on the ground. And it's approaching.

"Why don't you come out and take my picture? I promise, I'll smile pretty for you," a male voice coos. He's not far now, not nearly far enough.

I turn and run—not toward the road, I'll never make it—but to the closest building.

The warehouse doors are unlocked. Some are missing altogether, but this one's hanging ajar. I enter it in a rush, light streaming into the big open space in patches. It's cluttered, and errant sunlight catches upturned crates, barrels, old broken machinery that was left behind. I just pick a patch of light and run toward it.

As I'm crossing the space, I hear a door bang behind me. I'm already at the opposite end of the warehouse, at another door—this one locked. There's a broken window to my right. I climb up on a few boxes to reach it, then use my camera body to smash what's left and haul myself outside, tearing up my thighs on broken glass. The drop is far, but I manage not to break anything as I land on the concrete below, then run some more.

I don't have a sense of which direction I'm going, only that the sound of bullets is growing intermittent and fading to the background. I hope that means they're running away, not that they've been caught by something.

Sweat drips down my spine. The buildings turn from metal to brick. They don't look inhabited, and when I run past the mouth of a dead-end alleyway, I can see a cluster of houseless men looking out at me. They flinch when I come to an abrupt stop.

"Hide," I hiss, trying to keep my voice as low as possible. "Hide!"

I start to run again, but one of the men calls out. "Come hide with us!"

I hesitate, but not for more than a moment. My lungs burn, my thighs shake so badly it's a miracle I'm still standing. I turn around and the three men motion me forward. They're moving toward the back of the alley, which terrifies the shit out of me because I don't see an exit. And then one of them charges ahead of the rest and shoves a massive green garbage bin to the side, revealing a small hole that leads down into the brick building's basement.

He slides inside and gestures for me to follow, going so far as to hold my waist so I don't collapse when I hit the ground. It's a far drop. The other man follows, but the final man shoves the garbage bin back into place.

My hand shakes as I point. I start to ask about him, but when I turn, one man's pale face shines in the dark. He lifts a finger to his lips and I don't say a word, but I exhale in relief when I realize there's also a hole in the garbage bin large enough for the remaining man to wriggle through. He drops down onto the ground, and the three men guide me silently across a dry basement cluttered with objects I imagine might belong to these men or others living here with them.

They take me to a crawl space I would have never noticed was there. It's covered by an old air-conditioning vent, which they remove and replace once we crawl inside. And not a moment too soon either.

There's a banging sound. Loud. It sounds like an explosion.

"Where'd you go, little pretty camera girl?" an echoey voice calls. The same acid spitter as before. "Taranis's little key. The Marduk isn't happy with him," he tsks. "Not happy at all now that he's removed himself from the game. Which means you're *fair game*."

The men are all completely still. The world around us is dark. So dark. Too dark. Panic I hadn't felt before starts to seep into my pores, my flesh, my bones. I can't see anything, and I don't dare move to pull out my phone or my camera. I'm lying on my stomach, my forehead pressed to the cold, dry concrete below me. I have the chills, and I can't seem to stop shivering. I think I might be bleeding somewhere. I don't even know.

"I want my fucking picture taken," the same voice roars. There's a banging sound. Tearing. The fucker is destroying anything and everything he can find.

I feel so sorry I came to hide. I should have kept running. I shouldn't have risked these men's lives. I can't believe none of them have thought to turn me in yet . . . and then one of them grabs me.

I jolt.

He has me by the arm. I try to pull away, but his dry, cracked palm shifts up my wrist to my hand. He holds it, squeezing it, and I realize he's trying to reassure me. There are tears on my face as I press my cheek to the concrete, facing him. I squeeze his hand back.

I hear the male rage in the other room. He's not giving up. "I know you're here!" He shouts and bangs and shouts some more, "When I find you, I'm going to burn your eyes out of your skull! You have no idea what you've seen, and if you share those photos with a single soul, we will never stop hunting for you!" A few more loud sounds and then, in a quieter tone, the male voice says, "You've been warned."

His stomping feet get quieter and quieter. I hear the sound of ringing metal that I can only hope—pray—is him kicking a garbage can as he leaves. *Please leave.*

I'm suddenly finding it hard to move. My breaths are too shallow. There . . . there might be something wrong with me. Or maybe it's just the dark. Maybe it's my crashing adrenaline. All I know is that there's a sudden disconnect between my thoughts and my actions, and all I can do now is squeeze the hand of the man lying beside me. I squeeze it with everything I got.

My eyes close, rendering the darkness complete. I wish I could call Darius.

Chapter Twenty-Four

Darius

There's banging on my window. My sliding glass balcony door, in fact. I had expected it, given that my phone and home alarm went off in a brilliantly loud blaze—I increased the volume after last time, expecting a repeat attack. What I don't expect, however, is that it *isn't* the Marduk.

I get up from my office chair, where I'd been researching colorful rugs, and head to my living room, where I stop dead. The Wyvern stands with his fist on my glass. His fist is streaking blood.

I rush forward, my feet carrying me without thought. I use my powers to slide the door open before him. He staggers into the room, and I experience another bout of shock as he falls forward, letting me catch him and bring him to my couch. I have to carry way more of his weight than I expect to have to, and as I stare down at his pink skin, I notice scrapes and deeper cuts all over his back.

"What the fuck happened?" He looks like he's been chewed up by a much larger beast and spit out. But his eyes are clear. They're blazing.

"Have you heard from Monika?" His teeth are clenched. He releases a pained moan when he tries to lean back. I pull him forward to see that his whole left side is covered in short wooden darts. I start to pull them out, uncaring for how he grumbles, when his words finally catch up to me.

My fingers freeze around a dart. It's wet and bloody beneath my fingers. "What did you just say?"

"Have you seen or heard from Monika? I was with her and COE forces. I dropped off the injured and tried to call her," he pants, unable to catch his breath, "but she's not picking up. Her phone just rings and rings."

I stand up, my hands dropping away from his bloody body as all the blood in *my* body rushes to my feet. I'm cold. Numb. Colliding thoughts vie to take precedence, and I can't focus on any of them. "She was with you and Vanessa at a photo shoot for your wedding."

"No. What? She's part of a secret mission. She was sent with us to document it," he coughs. Blood comes out in his hand. "Fucker. That fucking acid fuck."

"Acid?" I hiss, dazed.

He doesn't answer, but says, "She made it out of the ports, but nobody's heard from her since. The COE officer with her was found dead. The SDD forces finally arrived, but by then the Marduk and the Inconnus were already gone, their base completely destroyed. I think they might have had Sobek involved, because the entire old port was sunk." He looks up at me, the kindling in his eyes ever ablaze. "I thought she might have called you. Or come to you first." He tries to stand. I shove him down.

My mind is on fire. I reach into my back pocket, withdraw my phone, and call the woman who ditched our date and lied to me. The phone rings and rings and rings, then goes to voicemail. *"Hi, you've reached Monika Neumann . . ."* she says in the blandest tone I've ever heard.

Every word jacks up my pulse. I haven't ever felt like this. This clenching in my chest. This cracking in my ribs.

I head to the window. "You need to go see the medic. And she better fix you up good, so that way I can kill you next time I fucking see you."

My mind has yet to accept the possibility that something bad has happened to Monika, despite the way the Wyvern looks. It veers in that direction and then retreats. I keep my jaw locked and my mind focused on the next steps. The Wyvern said the old docks. That's where I head.

The sky is bright and that pisses me off. It has no right to be this nice a day as we creep toward November. Not today. Not when my mood is bleak enough that every light in every building, every streetlamp, every car headlight flickers as I float overhead. I'm not moving at my maximum speed, and that pisses me off too. I can't afford to miss her.

My hands are clenched into fists that feel weighted like stones. I struggle to lift them from my sides. I don't know what to do with them. Her phone rang and rang and rang, but the last three times I tried to call her, it went straight to voicemail. She's hanging up on me on purpose. Why? What's she doing now? Where is she? Did the Marduk take her?

The thought shorts in my mind, and my hands flinch. I reach into my back left pocket for a burner phone I rarely use. I hesitate, debating calling him, as I round a low block of crumbling brick buildings and begin my descent. I'm forty, twenty feet up from the sidewalk when, right in front of me—no more than half a block away—a woman steps out of a narrow alley.

"Monika!" I roar, my voice louder and harsher than I mean for it to be.

Her neck snaps up, our eyes connect, and I fall. I've never fallen before while flying. Never lost control. But I do now. All the concentration in my being sharpens on the cuts and abrasions all over her body. Her hair is matted in blood to the left side of her face.

I hit the sidewalk on both knees surrounded by a cloud of electricity. Pain radiates up my thighs, but it's fleeting. I could have broken both kneecaps and it wouldn't have stopped me from staggering upright toward Monika, whose expression is utterly indecipherable. Her eyes are big and wide, like she's surprised to see me, her lips gently parted. Blood glistens on their insides.

She's wearing all black, a bulletproof vest covering her chest with the half-burned word PRE decorating the front of it in large, blocky white letters. She's got a camera in her hand and is walking down the street like everything is normal. Like she's just out and about taking photos on a casual autumn stroll, never mind the fact that the knees of both of her pant legs are torn open, revealing bloodied legs.

"Hey," she says to me.

Hey. The fact that she remains alive after such a glib response is a testament to my control. Perhaps my lack thereof. If I could have controlled the schism between my heart and my powers, she'd certainly be dead by now, electrocuted in one swift surge to the heart. Because the alternative is too much to bear. Just take her out of *my* misery. I can't . . . be . . . on this planet . . . if she's . . . also on this planet *and* capable of being injured . . . like this. And as my entire universe comes crashing down, everything I've ever known boiled down to a single bloody beating heart—*her* bloody beating heart—she has the *audacity* to say *that* to me now?

Hey.

I want to strike her, thrash her, bend her over my knee . . . but when I close the distance between us and reach out to touch her, I don't do any of those things. My claws start at her widow's peak and, so gently as not to touch her, I push her hair off her forehead. It's wet with the blood that drips from the curling tips.

The skin on her forehead and nose has been rubbed raw, like she had her face pressed against a massive cheese grater. There's a cut on her left cheek, and when I cup the back of her head with one hand while the other continues its sweep down her neck, I feel that the back of her hair is crispy and hard, as if burned.

I open my mouth and words sit bunched all along the length of my tongue, clogging the back of my throat. They congeal into a solid mass, and when they erupt, they erupt as one. *"Hey,"* I clip. The word is hard and angry.

She doesn't flinch. Instead, she blinks at me and holds up her camera. "I didn't get much usable footage."

"What?" I whisper much more softly, but in just as harsh a tone. Is she insane? She's talking to me about her fucking photos?

"I d-didn't . . . I think some of the pictures might be . . . The one . . ." She's touching her chest now, feeling around her neck for something. "My other camera . . . It's gone. I should go back and look for it." She physically starts to turn from me, and as she does, I see that she's got a fucking stake three inches long sticking out of the back of her right shoulder. Against the Wyvern's skin, the darts looked small, like beestings. Against her size, they look like fucking javelins.

I catch her wrist and pull her back around to face me. My gaze narrows as I focus more intensely on her eyes. Fuck. Her pupils are fully blown. My fingers circling her wrist suddenly become aware of the frenetic nature of her pulse. Even though the temperature hasn't dropped below sixty, her skin is clammy and as cold as ice.

"Monika, I'm taking you—"

"AAAAHHH!" A sudden burst of human wailing jolts my attention to the alley. I stand up straight and wrench Monika behind me, but the men charging me are older, wearing baggy clothing over their thin frames and unshaved. All three are white and over fifty. One of them has a chain in his hand, and the other two hold planks of wood.

I give them each a zap, a light jolt of electricity, which causes them to buckle and drop their weapons.

Monika makes an odd sound. "W-wait . . . they helped me!"

The man who was leading the charge looks up at me, and then at Monika past me. "You passed out. We left to make sure the coast was clear, but when we came back you were gone. Are you okay?"

"Oh, I'm fine. I lost my camera but . . ."

My brain lights on fire. She's so far from fine. I'm wasting my time here with this. "She's going to be fine," I say in a rasped hiss. I've never felt more violent, and yet, if what Monika says is true, I owe these men her life. "You helped her?"

They nod.

"What happened?"

"Champions—" one starts.

"Villains," another corrects.

The one who spoke first nods. "They were attacking these military folks. We ran off to hide, but she showed up alone, so we took her in. One of the villains came and smashed up our spot pretty good, but we didn't let him find her or us."

"She passed out," another says, this one with a long, white beard. His jaw clenches again and again, and his pupils are enlarged. He has track marks between his fingers. "We were worried, so we went out to try to find help. She gave us her phone, wanting us to call D—"

"I called her a dozen times. Why didn't you answer if you had her phone?"

"We didn't know what kinda trouble she was in."

The third man says, "The only name she gave us to call was Darius. But no Darius called. Just superhero names—Taranis, the Wyvern, and folks from the COE. We got spooked that those mighta been some of the supers fighting, and turned her phone off."

My body hardens; my heart is harder. I swallow stones and struggle to speak through them. "I will find you again," I tell them, looking each of the three of them in the eye, "and repay you for what you did for her." I wrap Monika up in my arms as carefully as I can and start moving up into the sky.

One of the men shouts after me, "Didn't do it for pay, but we'd like to know she's okay. She don't look so good! Got some shit on the back of her legs that looks bad!"

That's the last thing I hear from the three men before the wind gobbles up their words and I'm left to the nightmare-inducing sound of Monika's shallow breaths and frantic heart.

Chapter Twenty-Five

Darius

The COE has a fully equipped medical department, but not an emergency department. There is a small, private hospital the COE sends its armed staff when needed, and it's where I take Monika now.

She's walking and coherent when I drag her through the sliding glass doors. The lights flicker off before I manage to concentrate hard enough to turn them back on and keep them on. By then, all eyes have turned to us.

The nurse behind the triage desk is standing and pointing. "Did she come from the ports?"

I nod.

Instead of asking us to sit and wait—which we wouldn't have anyway—she shouts across the space, "Code four-oh-eight! We have another burn victim!"

Two human doctors come flying through the double doors to our left a moment later, a stretcher between them. "Where was she hit?" the man doctor asks me, moving around Monika while she just stands there.

"Her shoulder," I answer.

The woman doctor shakes her head, her short braids tied tight at the nape of her neck. "The dart wound isn't what we're concerned about. We're concerned about the acid."

"Oh, that," Monika says, like she's speaking to us from somewhere else. "My legs mostly. Maybe my back? It feels hot." She shrugs.

I almost pass out. Right there, in the center of the triage, where regular human folk with regular human ailments sit and watch as they wait, the doctors draw enormous metal scissors from their scrubs and begin cutting Monika out of her clothing, starting with her pant legs.

Fuck. FUCK!

The tops of Monika's thighs are completely torn up, shredded by what looks like claws. Even that is not enough to move the doctors. Instead, they make panicky sounds when they see the backs of Monika's calves covered in gooey pustules and scattered red blisters. It's revolting. They keep going, carefully pulling Monika out of her vest and then cutting off her shirt, working carefully around the dart. They even cut off her sports bra.

"She's okay to lie flat," the female doctor says after examining her front. "There are first- and second-degree burns on her back from where her vest overheated, but nothing on the front."

"Acid?" the man doctor asks.

"Nothing on her front. Only her thighs have visible wounds and abrasions."

"Agreed. We're safe to proceed." The male nods his agreement, and together they lift Monika off her feet and place her face down on the stretcher. The male takes her camera away from her and hands it to me absently. Without a word, they start to push her down the hall, talking about her legs. It's only when they're ten paces away from me that I realize they were wearing thick black gloves I've never seen doctors wear.

I take a step to follow them, but the hospital doors slide open behind me.

"Please, help him!" The watery voice belongs to a woman. A woman who looks absolutely tiny standing next to the monster beside her—the pink monster who was just sitting in my apartment.

I turn and watch as the entire process repeats itself as if in slow-motion. The Wyvern is grunting, sounding much more coherent than Monika did. "She okay?" I hear him ask me as if through water. My brain ain't working right.

I shake my head, nod, shake my head a second time. "No. Acid."

"Yeah," he says as he tries to lie on a stretcher. His legs hang off the end. "That's why I'm here too. The darts and the water, I could deal with, but the acid . . ." He roars and I see he has the same blisters and sores on his chest that Monika does on her legs. He coughs, bloody spittle wetting his lips.

Fingers grab hold of my arm and just as quickly release. Vanessa charges after the stretcher, but two new doctors block her path as she tries to follow her fiancé. "Did you touch the acid?" one of them asks her.

She shakes her head, and with a simple cursory sweep of Vanessa's body with his gaze, the doctor nods once. "We're going into surgery. We'll come get you when he's out." The doctor looks over her head at me. "Do you intend to wait for the woman you brought in, or is there another contact we can notify for her?"

"I'm her contact," I say, voice so soft. *The only name she gave us to call was Darius.*

"We'll let you know when she's out." He must see something on my face that gives him pause. He hesitates instead of following the stretcher past the double doors down the hall to the unknown. "She's going to be all right. They both are." His gaze strays to Vanessa before quickly returning to mine. "Just try to stay calm. Have patience. The acid is . . ." A voice shouts at him from behind the swinging double doors. He turns. "Please stay in the waiting room!"

Vanessa wavers on her feet long after the doctor disappears. Finally, after far too long, she turns. She's sobbing, and when she comes to me, her arms are outstretched, leaving me no choice but to catch her. And I surprise myself. I hold her in my arms and let her sob all over me, leaking her disgusting human fluids all over my tee. My white T-shirt makes the inky red blood look so much more gruesome. It's Monika's blood, and it's smeared across my hands too, turning the tips of my fingers purple.

I let Vanessa grab my T-shirt and twist the hell out of it as I escort her to the waiting room and find us two seats, far enough in the back that we won't be stared at but still in a position where I can see the waiting room doors. I want to know the second there's information.

I let Vanessa lean her temple on my arm and squeeze my wrist so tight her little nails leave marks. I let Vanessa whisper to me about how they're going to be okay and ask me if I have any idea what the fuck happened and just . . . chat to me even though I *hate* humans. I let her do all these things because I need it. I need it so fucking much.

"You heard the doctors. They're going to be okay," I say, my voice strangling on the final word.

Vanessa tips her face to look up at me. She blinks, her eyes big and brown and red and watery. She bites her lips. "You really do care about her, don't you?"

I hesitate, consider lying—it's none of her fucking business. Except I don't. "Yes."

She rubs her nose. She has brown eyes. I've never noticed that she has brown eyes before. I've never noticed anything about her, really. "We all thought you liked Cynthia for a minute."

"I don't."

She releases a desperate, watery laugh. "Yes, we saw the full video you posted where you electrocuted her. Are you really done being a Champion? You were always everyone's favorite."

"I don't want to be everyone's favorite. I want to be *her* favorite."

"I can see that." She inhales shakily and glances toward the door, but there's a plant at her eye level that blocks us from sight and that she can't see over.

"I'll tell you the second somebody comes in," I offer her unexpectedly.

She loops her forearm between my body and my bicep and squeezes my upper arm tight. "Please."

"The Wyvern told you I liked Monika already, though, didn't he?"

She nods. "Yes." She doesn't even try to lie.

"Did he tell you about this mission?"

She whispers, "I thought he was invincible." Tears continue to drip from her eyes. "I feel so stupid."

My claws clench into my artfully torn jeans, designed by Sandra to fit over my massive thighs and lupine feet. They're now speckled with dirt and blood from when Monika's legs were pressed against me. "Not as stupid as I feel. Monika *lied* to me about where she was going. She said she was going to take pictures of you. She didn't tell me shit."

Vanessa just nods like that's okay. I growl in the back of my throat and open my mouth, but before I can speak, Vanessa says, "Of course she didn't tell you. You're the bad guy."

"What the fuck?"

"The Wyvern and I know that you're working with the Marduk. Monika told us. She's the one who found out in a recording she took of you talking to the Meinad and Bia. So of course she didn't tell you about the mission. You might have tipped off the Marduk—or worse, joined him." She looks up at me and she's crying in earnest now, and it tears through the tattered remnants of my soul. "She didn't tell you because even though she knows you're the villain, it doesn't matter to her."

"What?" I choke.

She offers me a smile—a smile in the face of her scandalous accusations—and then she squeezes my arm again. "She likes you back." She sniffles and turns forward. "She must have been trying to protect you. If she hadn't been, the COE could have led you into a trap." She tenses and turns to me then, placing both of her hands on my arm. "You won't, will you?"

"Won't what?"

"Fight against Roland? Fight with the Marduk?"

"No," the answer comes through my teeth like a hammer hitting nails through concrete. No word I've said has ever been truer.

Vanessa exhales, seeming to take my word, though I've given her no reason to trust it. "Good. I didn't think there would be so many of them. Roland told me that there were thirteen, including the Marduk."

"Which villains?"

She gives me a look. "The unknown ones. The Inconnus."

I blink at her. And because we're here, sharing this private moment that exists outside of time, a moment with no consequence, Vanessa tells me everything she knows. Everything Monika knew. About how Monika was the one who got the information from Cynthia about the Marduk's location—about how Cynthia wasn't in a crash but actually had her legs broken by the Marduk. All I can think is all the ways that Monika lied to me. And all I can think is what she said to me when she sent that cropped video to my PR team. *I wanted to protect you.*

This can't stand. None of it can. The punishment I have in store for her will be epic. Though nothing will compare to what I have in store for *him.*

A prickly feeling that creeps across the back of my skull tells me that Monika wasn't at the ports by accident, and if the Marduk was there, he could have easily ensured her safety but didn't. He's declared war, and I think I know the reason.

"I didn't have time to ask Roland what the powers were of the beings that attacked them, but he did tell me that Three was there, a being that can teleport." She glances at me sideways and shivers. "They attacked me about six months ago."

Attacked her? Roland's woman?

My vision starts to go red. I don't know Vanessa. She's a human. I should hate her. But in this moment that stands so far outside of time, I can no longer see the reality that existed before I plonked down beside her in this shitty plastic chair—I don't. I feel protective of her, and when she next squeezes my arm, I squeeze hers back.

"Monika's so fucking badass," Vanessa says, and it's so unexpected I snort. My light laughter causes her to jump, then smile. She relaxes a fraction after that.

"She is."

Vanessa nods, though her expression sobers quickly. "And she's lucky too."

"What do you mean?"

"Roland told me that something like fifty COE and SDD fighters were sent in." She blinks and then looks around at the empty room, occupied only by two other individuals. "Haven't you wondered why this room is so empty, Taranis?"

I haven't. Not once. I shake my head.

"They all died," she whispers. "The Marduk killed everyone. Only Roland, Monika, and five others made it. Three of them Roland carried here by himself before going to your apartment . . ."

"Miss Theriot?" a booming voice calls.

I jerk and Vanessa jumps to her feet. "Is he . . . ?"

The nurse nods, a smile on her face. "He's impatient to see you." She gestures Vanessa forward, and for a second, I'm instantly forgotten.

Then Vanessa surprises me. She turns around, hooks an arm around my neck in an awkward hug, and whispers against my cheek, "Be good."

And then I'm alone, left to wonder how the fuck Monika survived, and what in the hell Vanessa means.

Chapter Twenty-Six

Monika

"You stubborn idiot, wake up." The voice is familiar to me, but I'm not sure who it is. I have a feeling I know them, but I can't quite make the link to their name in my mind. Then my eyes blink open, and I see the prettiest face I've ever seen, one belonging to my arch nemesis.

I frown. "What are you doing here?"

"Checking on you." Cynthia sits below the edge of my hospital bed, and she's shifting back and forth in a way I don't understand. As my mind clears of fuzzies, I realize she's sitting in a wheelchair.

"Oh . . . shit. How are your legs?" I cough. There's air flying into my nostrils through little tubes. I've been treated for work-related injuries before, but only minor scrapes and bruises. I've been to the hospital, but I've never been *hospitalized* before.

Cynthia's face gets all pink. "Fine. I mean, I'm hardly healed at all, yet here you come, stealing my spotlight again."

I chuckle and then groan. "Sorry. I mean this with my whole heart when I say this—I definitely did not intend to."

She laughs a little at that. "I just, um . . . You came to check on me, so I thought I'd return the favor."

"Thank you."

She runs a hand through her hair and then holds it out to me. "Truce?"

I grin. "Truce." I use all my strength to lift my right hand and clutch hers.

Cynthia glances across my body, and my gaze swivels to follow hers to find whatever she's looking at.

"Ow," I hiss. There's a shooting pain in the back of my neck when I try to turn. Ugh. Feels terrible. Actually, my whole body feels terrible. I try to move my arms, but they feel weighted even though they're lying at my sides atop a plush blanket, untethered. Huh. This doesn't look like a hospital blanket, and I know for damn sure that no truce in the world would have convinced Cynthia to bring it. That's one step too far.

I carefully look up to see the person—being—standing at my other side. Darius has his arms crossed, his clawed feet stamped apart on the tiled floor, a completely blank look on his face.

I flinch. "Oh shit. You're here."

When he exhales, his already wide nostrils flare even wider and his horns crackle with blue light. He doesn't speak. My mouth opens to say something to defuse what looks like an imminent eruption, but I can't get anything out. He's *pissed.* Is he . . . gonna kill me?

"What happened, Monika?" Cynthia's voice severs the tension, which is ascending to dangerous heights. "It wasn't . . . because I gave you that phone, was it?"

I tense. "I . . ."

I try to think back to what happened, remembering the lower floor of the dockyard collapsing into the sea, running up the ramp, being dragged, a female hanging from the ceiling, shooting darts at me, the burn of the acid up the backs of my calves, the sound of bullet casings hitting the asphalt, the wind whipping shards of an SUV through the air, the squelching sound when larger pieces connected with skin, and then . . . the Wyvern asking me to come with him, me telling him no, and then . . . running. So much running . . .

"Answer the question," a dark voice growls.

I flinch a second time and try to offer Cynthia a small smile. "It wasn't . . . you . . . You didn't do anything wrong," I say, settling for that.

She exhales. "So what was it, then? Where did you go?"

"Well, we did go down to the docks." I watch her face pale, either in guilt or because she's remembering her own abduction—I can't be sure. "I can tell you that the COE was going on a mission to uncover . . . something. They already had info on the docks, so your lead wasn't what . . . it wasn't . . . your fault. I promise." I squeeze Cynthia's hand. "And it wouldn't have mattered anyway. It was a trap. The COE forces—*we*—were ambushed, and even though there were so many of us, it wasn't enough."

"Even with the Wyvern there?"

I nod. "He was doing all that he could, but there were too many of them—"

"Who is 'them'?"

"Villains. Led by the Marduk. They had incredible powers. The COE forces didn't stand a chance. Even the Wyvern was badly injured by them."

"They say he's just down the hall. Please tell me it's your last mission. At least for the sake of my spotlight," she smirks, trying to lighten the mood and succeeding.

I smirk, closing my eyes as I remember the feeling of taking off around the edge of that brick building, sprinting through an old warehouse, the door clattering open at my back, the feeling of heat tearing through the skin on the tops of my thighs, ignoring that, the wind cooling the blood on my face as I keep on running, just . . . running until eventually a piercing darkness is followed by scattered blue light. My smile falls. "I can't promise it's my last one, but—"

"It's your last one without me," the dark voice booms again.

I glance over at Darius and wither beneath his stare.

"That's, um . . . good. I guess. I'll, uh, give you two some privacy," she says, wheeling herself toward the door. "I'll come by and see you later. There was an infection in one of my legs, so I'm still in and out. Do you want me to call your mom?"

Surprise makes me forget about Darius's brooding rage for a moment. "That would be great. Tell her I'll call her in an hour or so, after I talk to the doctors."

"Sure."

"Thank you."

Cynthia just shakes her head while offering me a smile more genuine than any she's ever given me. "You're lucky to be here. As my *eomma* would say, *God must see you out of the corner of his eye.*" Then she wheels herself out of the room.

"Well, how about that," I croak, trying a smile as I turn toward the room's only other occupant.

He doesn't so much as flinch. He simply steps forward, muscles in the L's of his jaw flaring and pulsing like he's chewing on his words before he speaks.

"I know you're mad," I blurt out, but my gaze takes that opportunity to drop to his outfit and widen my eyes at the sight of it. He's wearing a ruined white T-shirt and distressed jeans, both of which are covered in stains that look like blood.

"What happened to you?" I ask without thinking. If I had, I might have avoided the scathing look that crosses his face as he stomps over to the side of my bed, places both palms flat on the mattress on either side of my head, and crackles electricity at me. It just passes along his horns, but it feels very directed. Distantly, I can hear whatever monitors I'm hooked up to start to beep louder.

"What happened to *me*?" he hisses. His breath smells like bad coffee. I don't know why that makes my chest feel cluttered. It seems like such a human thing. It also lets me know that maybe, just maybe, he's been hanging around here for a while. "I was by myself, in my office, shopping for hideous rugs to decorate my apartment with to your liking when I was accosted by a giant pink idiot who kindly informed me that you were not, in fact, taking nauseatingly romantic pictures of him and his partner eating fucking cake, but that you were part of a supersecret mission to uncover a VNA base and that, in the process, were ambushed by the Marduk and at least ten of his minions whose powers are terrible and unfamiliar and that forty-five of fifty COE officers were killed and that the only other survivors of the entire ordeal, besides that handful of officers, were the nearly-impossible-to-kill monster with power over fire, and *you*. The war photographer.

"I was understandably upset," he says, pulling back and snatching a bottle of water off the side table next to my bed.

He upends it into his mouth, and as I watch his throat work, I lick my lips and whisper, "Upset because you were worried about me or because I lied to you?"

That was apparently the wrong thing to say.

He throws the half-drunk water bottle across the room. I jump and try to sit up, but he looms back over me, the sudden scent wafting from him reminding me of the winter. A steaming cup of coffee in front of a window overlooking a forest covered in snow. His eyes blaze purple, but seem to clear the longer he stares, mellowing back into blue.

"*Upset*, because when I went to go look for you, I had no fucking idea where exactly you were—if you were even alive, if the Marduk had taken you. You didn't tell me shit."

He suddenly closes the distance between us, his mouth moving to the crook of my neck. He's so warm. I gasp as that warmth moves through my entire body, settling between my hips.

He nibbles on my throat, careful not to move the cord carting oxygen to my nose, making me feel even more lightheaded than I should. His hand moves to my opposite shoulder, and he gently traces his claws down the outside of my arm. "And when I finally found you, you looked like you'd been mauled by a pack of rabid hyenas."

"Where . . . where was I?" I ask him, truly unable to remember.

He pulls back, staring between my eyes. "Wandering the streets. Three homeless men had hidden you successfully enough to keep whoever had been chasing you from finding you—"

"Oh shit! I remember them! Are they—"

"They will be well taken care of." He closes the distance between us and presses his lips passionlessly to mine, like the movement was automatic more than intentional. Like he just needed to kiss me. I need him too.

He stands up and rubs his hand down his face, walks to the end of my bed, where he presses some kind of button that causes the whole bed to whir and sit me a little more upright. I stutter, "D-does that mean you're going to kill them or like . . . give them a reward?"

He's still glaring at me, his eyes swirling with purple and white, indecision made visible.

"I hope it's the latter," I whisper. "They were really brave, helping me like they did."

"They were."

"So . . . you didn't kill them?"

"I didn't."

"That's cool."

"You know what isn't cool?"

I could list a thousand things. Instead of playing dumb, I try, "Me spying on you?"

"Try again."

"Me . . . telling Mr. Singkham about your weapon? I saw it in your office."

Surprise lights in his eyes before he narrows them. "Try again."

"Me . . . meeting up with the Marduk after Cynthia got hurt?"

"One more time, little girl."

I wince at the condescension, still not knowing what he wants to hear from me. I shake my head.

He growls mean and low. "I'm upset because you told me you were going to try to trust me. Because you told me that you *knew* Darius wouldn't let you fall. What happened to that? Or did it mean nothing at all?"

I shrink into myself, a sad little turtle. He's right and I'm wrong. I don't like being wrong. And it makes me realize just how fragile my trust truly is. I gave it to him with strings attached when I'd meant it as a gift. Most days, I feel pretty tough, but maybe I'm only strong when adrenaline laces my blood. Maybe when it comes to everything else, I'm a coward. He said it once—we're both alone, we have that much in common. But maybe where he's alone because he hates everyone, I'm alone because I suck at trust. But I *want* to trust Darius.

"I'm so sorry, Darius," I whisper. "I should have told you. I was just scared."

"The fact that you think I would hurt you pisses me the fuck off—"

"Not physically," I say, cutting him off. "I just . . . putting my trust in you, only for you to turn around and tell the Marduk . . . I couldn't risk it."

"So your plan was to lie to me so I couldn't lie to you first?"

"No. I couldn't risk giving you my trust and having you break my heart."

His face falls. Everything stills except for my medical machines, which frantically continue to beep.

He steps up to the bed and places his hand on my cheek. I look up at him, gnawing on my lower lip. When he says nothing, simply stares between my eyes, I blurt out, "I'm not any good at this, Darius."

He inhales, then inhales even more deeply. His stained and tattered shirt stretches over his muscles, and he looks like he's about to burst . . . until his eyes close and he arches over my body, blocking out the awful white hospital lights behind him. He kisses the top of my head and just breathes for a second while I cling to his wrist, hoping against all hope that this isn't it . . . that he doesn't leave . . .

He withdraws and his stare is hard again. Hard and mean. I worry about what to say, what to do, what paltry promises I can offer to convince him that this time when I tell him I'm going to try to trust him, the words are actually true. But before I can get a word off, he pulls a phone out of his pocket. An old Nokia brick. "I take it you have one of these somewhere in your possession?"

I nod and whisper, "The Marduk wanted to meet with me after he hurt Cynthia. He backed off when he realized I was your key."

Darius hisses, "We had a recent confrontation ourselves. He must have changed his mind about granting you clemency."

I swallow hard.

"I'm not going to be mad that you and I have been double-crossing each other's double-crosses. I wanted to be, but I'm struggling to be angry with you in general when you look so fucking pathetic in this hospital bed and when I'm so deeply in love with you."

I clench up and then bubbles burst through me. "L-love?"

He nods.

I try to smile, though it's hard to grin against the grim expression he gives me in return. "I love—"

"No. No . . . Don't say it. You can say it after I fix this."

"After you fix what?"

He rounds the bed, his massive blue body crackling with lightning as his eyes bleed a color I've never seen them before—blood red. He grabs the back of my head and then kisses the bandages over my forehead. "Everything."

Chapter Twenty-Seven

Darius

It's two days more until Monika is cleared to come home. Though her wounds were mostly superficial, the acid was of an inhuman compound the doctors had never encountered. They had Monika stay the extra days to ensure there weren't any side effects—and for the annoying COE doctor, Emily, to take photos and samples so she can run tests and, more importantly, come up with something to counteract the worst of the side effects, namely the boils. They spread slowly and continue to disintegrate through whatever substance they hit. Emily is fairly certain that if left untreated, they'd chew through skin to the bone. I try and fail not to think about what Monika's legs would have looked like if I hadn't found her in time.

Meanwhile, Emily's excited jabbering in the face of Monika's—and my own—distress awarded her a couple electrical zaps. Small ones, of course. Nothing to cause permanent damage. After all, if we're going to get a useful antidote out of her, I'll need her brain intact.

I shoot a text to Simon from the back of my limo. I sit there, shifting uncomfortably as my tail rubs against the squeaky leather. Why is it so squeaky? I hate it. Monika's right: All my furniture is uncomfortable. Even in my damn vehicle. At least I already took care of my apartment.

"What are you thinking about?"

"Nothing," I lie, squeaking against my seat again as I glance down at Monika's legs. She's wearing hideous sweatpants her annoying godsister brought her that are bright orange and tattered at the hem—Cynthia truly could not have chosen a more hideous pair. But not even their hideousness is enough to abate the rage that shoots up my spine at the thought of the bandages that lie beneath the ugly fabric. Like the carcass of a dead animal on the side of the road, too gruesome to look at, too gruesome *not* to look at, I can't stop staring at every one of her wounds down to the littlest scratch. Every one of her stupid fucking bandages affects me.

The limo is huge. Doesn't matter. I'm sitting so close to her the outsides of our thighs are zippered together. She tries to edge farther away from me, likely unimpressed with my answer. "Don't," I snap.

"Are you going to be an asshole forever?"

"Yes."

I feel the temperature of her body rise, and lean in to plant a kiss to her temple. I like the way she leans back in to me too much. I like it even more when she says, "I'm really okay."

"I know."

"You don't have to be an asshole."

"I'm your asshole, remember?"

She doesn't rise to the jibe and instead quips, "You don't have to go on a rampage."

"I know. But I like violence."

She grips my knee and I place my hand, three times the size of hers, atop it. "Don't start a war."

"I'm not starting anything. I'm going to end it."

She sighs. "Will you at least let me in on your plans?"

"Like you let me in on so many of yours?"

She huffs, unrepentant, and with her injuries I can't even properly punish her yet. "I thought we agreed that wasn't the play? That we were going to trust each other from now on?"

"I just have one more move." And while I may trust Monika, I don't trust that she wouldn't try to stop me if she knew what it was.

She makes a sound that, on any other day, would have gotten her turned over and turned out. I'd have shackled her wrists to the arms of my desk chair and let her kneel there all fucking day, putting that mouth to better use than those irritated fucking sounds. "When you're out of those bandages, I swear to God you won't be able to sit for a month."

"You don't believe in God."

"I am a god. I believe in me."

"So you're swearing to yourself?"

"You got a mouth I want to fill." I rub my own jaw, irritated with myself and fucking furious with her and just damn . . . scared. "You must have knocked some attitude loose when you hit your head."

"I'm sorry that I don't want to be talked to like an inconvenience for the rest of my life."

"For the rest of your life?" I raise an eyebrow and actually look at her—try to—but she's still got a white bandage taped to her forehead and another to her left cheek. It didn't look like that serious a cut, but it was deep. They gave her nine damn stitches. Five surface, four underneath. Her face is still all bruised and swollen, which doesn't make it any easier when she smiles bashfully up at me. "Let's start with today first," she says, her eyes locking on mine.

I look away quickly and rub my face again. I want to reach over and grab her fucking thigh, but there's stitching zigzagging all across her goddamn legs. There's no part of her I can touch without causing her pain. "I'm going to take all your days as soon as I find where you hid that paperwork."

She makes another annoying fucking sound that makes me want to hear her beg to be taken from the back. All damn night. This time it's a little laugh as if she doesn't believe me. Her laughter turns quickly to a groan when she shifts position.

"How bad's your pain?" I snarl.

"Not bad. Everything feels better after showering. They offered me codeine, but I said no. It freaks me out, so I just took the Motrin 600 and the antibiotic Emily prescribed for my legs . . . What are you . . ." She doesn't finish.

"Divider up," I call out, and Nicoleta complies while I unbuckle my seat belt, kneel on the floor of the limo, and carefully spread Monika's bandaged legs.

"Are you serious?"

"Stop me if you want to stop me," I tell her, tearing a hole in the crotch of her sweats. She's not wearing anything underneath.

Her palms come down on the top of my head. They're bandaged too. The right one also has stitches.

I don't think about it as I gently pull her hips forward on the seat and spread her exposed mound with my fingers. "Fuck, you're pretty," I whisper to her heat. She's on fire. I blow on her lips gently and her back arches. "Don't you dare fucking move. You stay still."

She's unshaved here after three days in the hospital, and I can smell the generic soap on her skin. It's all heavenly to me because she's still here, despite everything. Her breathing is hard, and I know this is a bad idea. She should be relaxing, shouldn't she? I don't know. I didn't ask her doctor about sex. But she's not injured here, one of the few places she isn't, and I need this. I need her not to hurt, not to make any more of those sad, whispery sounds, even if just for a few minutes.

I spread her mound, spread her lips next. So pretty and dark brown, almost black, they flower a lighter brown at their center, and when I spread her even farther open, pink way in deep. It's that pink I'm going for. I lick a line through it and then open my mouth wide and inhale it all. My tongue enters her body, reaching for her G-spot and coming up short. So I bring my tail around the side of my body and slide the tip up the inside of her thigh. It's long enough to enter her, and I'm surprised by the stimulating sensation I feel jolt through my own body as I start to fuck her fast with the thin limb while my mouth retreats to work her outer skin. My tail is getting more sensitive.

I nibble on her mound, suck on her clit, feel as her pulse jacks up way too high, and before I'm really sated, I finish it. I fuck her so fast with my tail she screams, and when I suck next on her clit, *hard,* she comes undone. She comes for me and I feel a little better when she shivers and sighs contentedly. Before I'm ready, I pull away.

I sit back on my heels and rub the slick from her body down my chin and neck. "I can't stand to look at you . . ." I choke, my dick as hard as a goddamn tire iron in my jeans. I reach down and stroke myself once, twice, then shove the offending appendage down my goddamn pant leg. My tail is another story.

"Darius . . ." she starts, still panting.

"When you're hurt like this. I don't fucking like it." My tail swats at the air, droplets of her orgasm spraying over the seats of my limo. It's a good way to part with the vehicle, I decide. One last hurrah. I'm gonna sell it in the morning.

"Your car?" she says.

Didn't realize I'd spoken out loud. "Yeah. Gotta downsize," I say, lifting up and giving her a quick kiss before plopping down beside her. I ignore my angry erection entirely. "Now that I've taken a serious pay cut."

She snorts and reaches out to place her hand on my thigh. "I, um . . . That was . . . Should I . . ."

"You don't wanna finish that sentence, or you're gonna piss me off all over."

"I . . . Sorry."

My head rolls on my neck before I lift it to lazily look at her. "You?"

She bites her bottom lip.

"You're some kinda something. A lion until you have an orgasm. Then you become a sweet little kitten."

"Fuck off." She pushes my shoulder.

I laugh and try again—try harder—to look at her. My gaze moves over her face. The taste of her satisfaction on my tongue makes it easier. "You said you weren't good at this," I tell her softly, imploring her through gaze alone to understand what I mean when words seem so difficult to piece together. "This is hard for me, too, but I want to be good at it."

Her blush gets deeper. She nods quickly and gives my thigh a little squeeze. My tail rolls up the inside of her ankle and she jolts. "Does it hurt to sit on that thing?"

I groan. "You're an idiot."

We ride the rest of the way to our building in companionable silence, and when we arrive, I help Monika gingerly exit the vehicle after Nicoleta opens the car door for us. "It's good to see you're okay, Monika," she says.

"Thank you," Monika answers, and for whatever reason, I'm feeling less jealous when Monika smiles at her. "And, uh . . . sorry again for this time. And last time . . ." Maybe that's why.

The woman smiles even as the tops of her cheeks tint pink. "No problem. I'm just glad you're all right."

"Thanks." Monika blushes again, and I can't stand it because it's so fucking cute.

I want to wrap my arm around her, but she's got deep stitching in her shoulder—over thirty of them where the dart went into her.

I've been doing an excellent job of repressing the urge to call the Marduk and tear his face off so far. I know I *will* tear the Marduk's heart out of his chest and I know exactly how I plan to do it, but I am not doing shit until Monika's better, until the Wyvern is recovered, and until the COE has a plan to protect them in case of inevitable retaliation. Because when I go for the Marduk, he will suffer as he never has. And as someone who is fast friends with rage, I know that the Marduk will want his vengeance after I enact my plans. I will need to use that instability in his emotions to break him entirely, and cut the head off the feral animal he is so I can mount it on a pike on my balcony.

My overall master plan has been rewritten: Kill, fuck, marry, destroy. So long as I can keep my dick in check, the Marduk dies first, before everything.

I texted Simone in the car to meet us at my penthouse. She's been around, coordinating the movers, and is there when the doors open up. She smiles at Monika but waits to speak until I do. It's been a preference of mine since the dawn of our working relationship, but I find myself suddenly annoyed by it.

"You can talk, Simone. And you don't have to wear a uniform. Tell Simon not to wear a uniform either. Just tell him to dress however he wants. And get me a new car. I want something comfortable. Custom made, of course. I still want to have a privacy divider. And a soundproof interior. For . . . reasons."

Monika chokes. Simone is taking notes, but Monika has her looking up when she interrupts, "Your name isn't Simone, is it?"

She glances at me. When I don't say more, just frown, she chuckles lightly. "No. It's Raven. Taranis's other assistant isn't Simon either. It's Davíd."

"Simon and Simone?" Monika elbows me in the ribs. "You're absurd."

"I'm working on it." I grimace at *Raven* and say, "Did you see the contract I sent you?"

"I did."

"And did you decide?"

Raven nods quickly, surprising me. "I'm interested in staying on, particularly within the new terms." A raise being one of them. Fixed hours being the other. No longer on call and no longer required to manage a tenth of my previous schedule being the last key amendments.

"Good," I say, trying to keep the surprise from my voice. I assumed she wouldn't be interested, even with the added perks. I'm no longer a Champion and I'm generally an unpleasant creature, and yet, here she is.

"She's your PA?" Monika asks.

"Yes."

"I thought you were quitting?"

"Except where cases of my girlfriend diving headlong into danger are concerned."

Raven snorts. Monika shakes her head, "Good grief."

"Yes, that's what you're causing me—grief. Now, let's get you settled onto my new couch." I push her down the hallway, muttering over my shoulder to Raven as I go, "Please also get rid of these doors. I don't like them. They aren't *comfortable*. And get that designer in who said something about giving my walls texture—whatever that means."

"Are you redecorating?" Monika asks, trying to look over her shoulder at me but her bandages get in the way. I grab her by the top of the head and turn it forward.

"Yes. Someone I happen to like told me my apartment was uncomfortable, and since I'd like her to make this her permanent residence, I am having it tailored to her liking."

Monika stumbles. "You . . . didn't have to do that."

"I wanted to," I answer, catching her elbow as I guide her to my living room. "My things were designed by someone who hates me and I never even noticed. I want things to be warm. I want to make this feel like a home for you."

"Well, I like the rug you've got here and in the foyer. Reminds me a lot of the one I have. Very colorful. Already the space feels warmer. And, ooh! You started the fireplace," she says as we enter the living room area. It's here that she comes to a dead stop. "Oh. My. God. Are you fucking serious?"

"Are you hungry? I was thinking of making saffron risotto, but if you don't like risotto, I also have ingredients for broccoli-cheddar soup. The doctor said you might have discomfort chewing with your facial stitching . . ."

"YOU ROBBED MY FLAT!"

"Risotto it is." I pull out the ingredients I'll need and set water to boil.

Monika is still standing in the center of the space, in the no-man's-land between the living room area and the kitchen. The kitchen is still black, but I wanted her opinion on what colors to paint it first before going all out. The living room, however, is an explosion of hideousness that I rather like. Her yellow couch looks like it's made of Big Bird's skin. It is also *her* couch.

"What . . . what did you do?"

I sigh. "I spent hours looking at furniture and decided that nothing I could select would be better than what you already selected for yourself, so while you were at the hospital, I had Simone and Simon move it all up here."

"Their names are Raven and Davíd, and what do you mean 'all of it'?"

"I mean all of it."

"ALL OF IT?" Her voice ends on so high a note I strain to make sense of it.

"Yes. All the furniture, anyway. I have a few spare guest rooms that aren't decorated yet—I don't really have guests, if you can believe that. I figured you'd want to turn one of those into your photo-developer room—Do they call that a red room? Am I making that up?—and another into an office, if you need one. Or we can share mine. I won't need it much anymore."

"You . . . you!" She storms up to me, coming around the island, which is her first mistake. She comes close enough to grab, which I do, taking her by the back of the neck. The shortened, burned strands of her hair still haven't been trimmed and have an odd texture against her coarse, wavy hair. Her hair has so many textures. Curly, wavy, some straight pieces near her ears.

I card my claws through her hair, tilt her head back far, and kiss her for all she's worth. I kiss her in anger and rapture. I kiss her mostly to distract her, and it works. She relaxes in my arms, her own fists falling slack around my wrists.

I walk forward, forcing her to back up until we round the kitchen island and enter the living room, where I press her down onto her soft Big Bird couch, spread her legs, and use my mouth to bring her to orgasm once and then again. I wait until she's boneless before pulling back. Her lips are wet with my spit and her cum, and her vulva and clit are swollen. It's a lascivious sight that's hard to ignore. I fight against my hardened abdomen and the erection demanding attention. I'm about to leave her there to nap or relax and return to the kitchen to prepare her food when she reaches out and grabs my pant leg, her fingernails exciting my nerves as they trail over the bare skin of my knee.

"Please, please, Darius."

I catch my breath and hold it. "I'll be back with your food."

"Please, I'm begging you. Feed me."

"You're injured . . ." I choke.

Her palm skims the front of my pants, moving over my zipper roughly. "I just want to swallow."

Fuck. "If I let you swallow, will you forgive me for the furniture?"

Her eyes widen. She hesitates, but then I undo my zipper. "Yes," she gasps as I pull my blue cock free. "Did you know they call this a knot?" she says, sliding her finger around the hardened ridge of my shaft.

"Who calls it that?"

"Vanessa and Emily. Vanessa learned the word from her romance novels."

"You don't read romance novels?"

She shakes her head. "I read political biographies and books about cameras. The hottest thing I've read lately was a review of really, really big lenses."

I snort. "I like you."

She looks up at me with a grin. "I like you too. Now, give it to me." She sticks out her tongue as far as it will go, and I'm too weak to do anything but exactly what she's asking. I start to stroke myself and her eyes flutter as she watches my every move. It's such a poor replacement for her mouth, hands, ass, pussy . . . but it'll have to do for now. Until she's healed, has entirely forgotten she once had an apartment four floors down from mine, and the Marduk is no longer a problem. If I have to hypnotize her with sex, so be it.

"Fuck," I grunt as she starts to whimper my name, begging me to come on her, in her, fill her with my knot. "You make such filthy fucking sounds."

I use my right hand to stroke my shaft while my left hand reaches down to her breasts. I fondle them through her sweatshirt, use my tail to massage my testicles, and collapse onto one knee on the edge of the couch, putting my cock just below lip level. Releasing her tits, I use two hands to cover the knot. Grunting, I choke, "Open your mouth."

She opens her mouth, such an obedient little whore, and sticks out her tongue as far as it'll go just as the release hits me like a truck. Cum erupts from the tip of my cock in a bright white, with a slightly silverish hue. It hits the side of her face before I manage to shove the head of my dick into her mouth. I don't stuff her fuller than that, even though I want to.

I empty and the sight of her throat working so rapidly to swallow load after load just makes me come harder, in a more violent stream. Sweat beads on my hairline. Electricity buzzes up my horns. My tail's tip rings my balls and squeezes, and I damn near have a fucking stroke when she suctions her lips.

I must come for five hours. Maybe it's only five minutes, but it's both the longest and shortest five minutes of my life. Because when it's over, there's cum all over her mouth, dribbling down her chin, wetting her lips, and dripping onto her sweatshirt.

"Fucking Christ," I hiss.

"Can I lick your knot, Darius?"

Fuck yes. I remove one hand and bring my knot to her mouth, let her lick the cum from it and suck on as much of it as she can until finally, it starts to recede. "Goddammit," I say when I'm finally able to let go of it without it feeling extremely sensitive, so sensitive it borders on painful. I drop down onto my back and lie on the bright turquoise-pink-yellow-and-tan carpet I robbed from her apartment.

After a few minutes of silence, in which the only thing audible are our labored breaths, she finally says, "Fuck it. Keep the couch. I want the knot."

I laugh. "Deal."

Chapter Twenty-Eight

Monika

The days pass. Eleven of them, to be precise. I've lost the forehead bandages, I've gotten the knot three times, and I've had exactly zero in-person meetings with the folks at the COE, courtesy of my new live-in boyfriend, who's been fielding all my phone calls.

The only time I've seen Mr. Singkham and my other contacts at the COE was at the funeral hosted for the COE combatants who were lost in the battle against the Marduk. It was a miserable, bleak affair. It rained in Sundale that day. The only bright spot was what happened afterward. In a strange twist, Vanessa and Roland ended up coming to our penthouse for dinner. And, in an even stranger twist, Darius cooked for everyone. He didn't even grumble about it, too much. It felt almost like . . . he was buttering them up. Maybe even buttering me up. But for what?

Maybe for the renovations. More of my stuff keeps arriving to his penthouse every day, and the worst part is that the buttering is working. Anytime I think about going back to my own flat to get something, check on something, do some work, have some alone time . . . I get back massages, or delicious snacks, or my pants ripped off and stuffed full of blue monster dick. It's hard to stay focused. It's forced me to reconcile a shocking truth: I would have moved out if I wanted to.

"How are you feeling?" Darius asks, voice gravelly this morning.

I smile and arch my back as he prowls up my body on the bed. "Good. Especially after that."

"You seem better. Your stitches are healing up, *jagiya*."

The shock of hearing him call me by a common Korean term of endearment—one heard often in my favorite K-dramas—hits me this time like it does every time. I know he does it to unseat me, and I smile. "God, I'm so into you," I tell him as sunlight filters in through the semitransparent blinds.

"Don't I know it, *meine Liebe*. Now, get up. I got sheets to change."

I feel strangely nervous as I get up and hobble awkwardly to the bathroom. I hover in the doorway as I watch his naked blue ass fuss over a pillowcase. I think his horns might have gouged a hole in it somewhere in the midst of our morning escapades—another one. I squeeze my legs together and clear my throat. He glances up at me with that same annoyed look he gave the pillowcase.

"I really did mean it . . . what I said," I say, swallowing past the lump in my throat. "I know it's been a short time, just a few weeks, and like . . . we fight a lot, but I . . . I want to lick the cum off your knot until I'm eighty, or a hundred, or five hundred, or however long humans live."

Darius stands upright. His penis looks freaking gigantic, even soft, as it flops against his leg. "My eyes are up here, baby girl."

I clear my throat and switch my weight between my feet. I expect to see him laughing at me—smiling, at the very least, but he's just staring at me with that annoyed look reserved for pillowcases that have offended him.

"I turned blue for you, baby."

My mouth runs dry. "Yeah?"

"Yeah. Don't ever doubt this." He gestures between us. "Not ever. I may not say or do shit like I'm supposed to, but I'm gonna make sure nobody ever gets in our way again."

I squint. "What's that supposed to mean?"

"Nothing." He winks and blows me a kiss at the same time. "Go take a shower. You smell like dick."

"You're an asshole."

"And you're gonna lick mine later for saying that," he calls out, making me laugh as I shut the door between us.

Chapter Twenty-Nine

Darius

All right, so the plans got a little muddled. *Fuck* came first since self-control was lost in the haze of Monika giving little precious pieces of her heart to me, but now that she's healed, we're about to be back on schedule.

Fuck, kill, marry, destroy. Easy.

I text the Wyvern. He's good to go, as aware of the *kill* portion of my plan as I intend for him to be. Mr. Singkham and the COE forces he was able to wrangle up, and the SDD forces he had to borrow to make up for the deficit in his staff, are also aware of . . . some aspects of this plan. The parts that matter.

Then I text Vanessa. I had Vanessa organize a brunch with Monika—one Monika is nearly late to after our morning's activities. Doesn't matter. I have plenty of time, and this shouldn't take long.

I sigh, relaxed. I'm driving. It's an odd sensation. I haven't driven a car myself in a long time—since I first got my license. A rather useless affair, considering I can fly. But I don't need to be spotted by the peons, so flying is out of the question today. It's 11:00 a.m. exactly. Everything is right on schedule.

I turn on the radio, curious to hear the news. It's all about me, of course, though the bright irony of it all is that for the first time in my life, I'm not trying to get press and don't even care. It's liberating. I should have tried this whole don't-give-a-fuck-and-quit thing a helluva long time ago. I smile while the radio presenter drones on, roll down the window, and let the sun stroke my horns and freshly shaved hair.

"And still, it's been two weeks and Taranis has yet to make a public statement beyond what he posted to social media. Since his initial post declaring that he would be stepping down as a Champion, the only follow-up information we've learned is from COE president Mr. Singkham, that personal reasons have caused Taranis to consider taking some time off . . ."

Time off? Time off! Mr. Singkham. Tsk tsk tsk. If he doesn't quit with his obfuscations, he might just have to rejoin the master plan lineup and die after the Marduk.

"So, is Taranis simply stepping down as a Champion, or is he joining the villains? Forty-Eight expert Maya Lin is on the line with her thoughts . . ."

I lift my phone, the one I haven't used in weeks, the shitty little Nokia burner, and place a call to the only number in the Rolodex. It rings and rings and rings before cutting off. I wait with a small smile on my face. By the time I place my next left turn, he's calling me back. Our typical arrangement.

"Interesting," he says as soon as I pick up. "I didn't expect to hear from you."

"Well, here I am."

"It would seem so."

I can't hear anything in the background. I wonder where he is, decide I don't care, make my next turn. I'm almost there.

"Are you calling because you've suddenly decided to join my team after the Champions' last tragic loss? I'm sure you heard about it. The Villains Network is offering competitive compensation packages." His voice is sardonic and nasty and mean.

I grin. "I did hear about that, actually. I happen to be *close* friends with the COE photographer that was on-site."

A slight pause before he answers. "I see." I wonder if my tone is making him nervous yet. If it's not, it soon will be.

"She takes lovely photos, doesn't she? So many clear images of the surprising members of your *team*." I whistle theatrically as I find a parking spot directly in front of the building I'm going to enter. What luck. "I'm surprised you let her go, considering the information she gathered."

"It wasn't for lack of trying," he says with a sigh. "She is rather *wily*, your key."

"And knowing she is my key, you still went after her, injuring her quite badly. Here I was, thinking we had an unlikely, if not rather amicable, alliance." I shift my car into park and glance out the window. I cut the power to the building, watch as people panic, surprised, and then slowly filter out until it's empty.

Almost.

"Alliances shift, Taranis. You should know that better than most. And your girl has an unfortunate amount of information on my friends. I'm not going to be able to let that go. In fact, if you weren't hovering over her like a shadow, I might have had to do something about her already."

"And that's exactly what I've called to talk to you about." I open the door to my car, cross the sidewalk, and head into my favorite coffee shop in all of Sundale. "You see, I can't have that."

"I'm not sure you have anything to bargain with, seeing as you already gave me my weapon and you no longer work for the Champions," he grunts. "You're reverted and still just as useless to me as the Wyvern, in an entirely different way."

"You're right: I am quite different than the Wyvern. He looks so good these days in a cape." The bell dings as I step inside the space.

"Cape's no better than a collar, if you ask me."

"On this, I happen to agree."

I smile as the owner of the shop comes rushing through the doors that lead to the back. She's holding some electrical cables in her hands but drops them when she looks up and sees me, trips over the bundle, and goes down between two tables in a tangled web of cables and long, willowy brown limbs.

I walk over to her as she looks up. She's going to speak, but I lift a finger to my lips, successfully quieting her. I drop into a crouch, sitting on my heels. I note that she is rather pretty. Large lips, dark pink around the edges, lighter pink in the middle. Clear dark-brown skin. Goddess braids that go down to her mid-back, even in a ponytail. She smells like honeydew melon, even beneath the coffee-ground scent that clings to her.

"So, did you call to discuss new VNA uniforms, or was there something else you'd rather tell me?"

"Yes, let me get to the point. The point is that I actually think I *do* have something of interest to you, outside of weaponry, intel, and excellent taste in uniforms." I hand the phone over. Out loud, to the woman, I tell her, "Say hello."

Her manicured eyebrows pull together over a nose that gently slopes from a shallow brow. "Hello?" she says. Her voice is slightly accented. Very pretty. Even the gap between her front teeth is cute. *This is going to be fun,* I think with no small amount of pleasure, but a great one.

And any doubts I may have had that this was the right plan, or even a moderately good one, are erased by the Marduk's response. For the first time since I've known him, he doesn't have one.

"What's going on?" she says to me, handing the phone back.

"Why don't you put it on speakerphone, darling?"

Confused as ever, and so naive and trusting, she does as I ask.

"Now, you see, my friend, if you don't give me your word—a word that I *believe*—that Monika will be left alone for the rest of her human life by you, the villains, and any and all of your minions, I will be left with no choice but to take matters into my own hands and repay the kindness you showed my woman to yours, with even greater kindness." I smile to show all my fangs.

The woman is nervous, but still doesn't seem to realize the danger she's in. She just stares up at me, wide eyed, even as I send the lightest electrical current tittering over her skin, causing goose bumps to rise on her arms beneath her stained yellow apron and white T-shirt.

The Marduk chuckles. It's forced. "The Habesha Café owner isn't my woman. The fact that you'd think that shows you're a fool. And besides, you think your *girl* would like it if you did something villainous to another human woman?"

"Oh, my dear old friend, you underestimate Monika—at least, you haven't seen her response to the power of my new magical blue dick."

I grin at the woman and waste no time in sending a surge of electricity straight through her bones, electrocuting her from the inside. A few volts higher would incapacitate her entirely. Her whole body spasms, nearly jolting off the tiled floor in a position that's utterly grotesque and inhuman.

Her mouth is closed and I frown. I release her. "Perhaps that was too much. You couldn't hear her scream properly. What if I isolate the electrical burns to her feet? That will make it harder for her to run from me should she get that idea."

I strike her legs with electricity and this time achieve my desired effect. She folds in on herself, reaching for her sneakers, and releases a bloodcurdling shriek that makes even the hairs on my neck rise up. The smell of burning fabric and skin reaches my nose.

I pause while she labors to catch her breath. In the desperate silence, I muse, "My powers are so much more sensational now that I've reverted." I comb my fingers across the top of the woman's hair. "I guess I have the Elders to thank for that."

The coffee shop girl screams as I pass that lightning through her stomach, chest, and back. I bend her legs, twist her bones, and when I'm done I grab her by the back of the throat, stand, and begin dragging her limp body behind me out of the building to my car.

The Marduk's breathing has become labored. He isn't speaking, so I press, "Have I made my point, or would you like to hear more?"

"No, please! Please!" she screams from the floor of the back seat after I toss her in. She tries to rise, but I give her a little zap between her temples to keep her grounded. She releases a pained moan.

Through the sound of her sobs and shrieks, I hear a voice, as loud as it can be, shout through the rinky-dink little phone, "Enough!"

I cut off the flood of pain I'm causing this innocent, rather pleasant young woman. Well, I cut it off *after* I give her one final zap. *"Auck!"* She's crying now, tears streaming down her cheeks as she cradles her head between her arms and spasms on the floor.

"You've made your point," the Marduk says, voice gravelly as he struggles to regulate his breath.

I chuckle lightly. "I'm so glad I have your attention and have given you some idea of what it felt like to come upon my female wandering the streets of Sundale with dart wounds in her back and acid crawling up the backs of her legs."

"This female has no value to me."

I smile. "Then you'll have no problem with me torturing her. Who knows? Maybe I'll break both of her legs. I am, after all, learning from the best."

"What do you want?" he snaps at me.

"A deal."

"You can't possibly. You could never trust that I would simply give you my word not to retaliate. You must know that I will end you and your female for daring to threaten me."

My cheek tics. I blast his female with a harder voltage than any I've used thus far. She releases a wild shriek and then quiets abruptly, now unconscious. "Hmm. That may have been a little harsher than I intended."

"I will tear you apart."

"The funny thing is that your tone and your threats are rendered somewhat comical by the fact that this shitty burner makes you sound like a chipmunk. Now, this is how this is going to go. Are you listening?"

"I'm listening."

"Sweet Lemlem is alive—did you know that was her name? I certainly didn't until today. Luckily, it's written on her little name tag, which might prove to be a good thing for her, as I don't know what condition her brain will be in when she wakes up, but I don't really care about that."

"You stupid, insolent motherfuc—"

"Now, I have no way of guaranteeing that you'll leave me, Monika, and Monika's family alone after I release Lemlem, so I really only have two options—well, three, if I'm being creative. I could kill her in a simple act of retribution—it would bring me some satisfaction, but it would put Monika and me in a difficult position.

"Option two: I could release her to you and hope you'd keep your word. But that wouldn't be enough, as you've accurately pointed out. So I could release every piece of information I know about keys and the villains you keep hidden, our weapons and how you plan to use them to build the Elders' gate and unleash hell on Earth. I have Monika's photos and the Wyvern's testimony too. Then I could tell the world about you and our little coffee shop owner. See what these pathetic, fickle, violent humans do with the information. She might never be safe again. At the very least, she'd be hounded by reporters, possibly detained by the SDD and the COE, who would assume she'd be close to you, know your whereabouts and your plans. It would ruin her life in one easy move."

He starts to interject, but I speak louder: "Or, third—and this is my most creative idea so far—I could sell her into the black market sex trade. I'm sure a woman who's fucked the Marduk would likely fetch a high price. Since you'd have to spend the next months or even years tracking her down, it would buy Monika and me a little time . . ."

"You motherfucker," he hisses. "None of those are—"

"If we go with option two, I *could* keep all of those pretty little pieces of information to myself as collateral, and you and Lemlem could ride off into the sunset . . ."

"Or I could find Monika now and tear off her arms."

"Lemlem would die first. And very painfully, I might add. Do you know what electrical currents do to the human brain? Not pretty," I tsk. "Not a pretty sight at all."

"I will not let you threaten me like this. The woman means nothing," he roars.

"Oooh, wrong answer. You're going to have a difficult time recovering Lemlem or obtaining Monika locked down within the heart of the COE building. Until then, I think I'll keep Lemlem here in their labs for safekeeping," I laugh, lying through my teeth as to our whereabouts.

"They would never let you harm a civilian."

"I'm *Taranis*, sweetheart. I can do whatever I please. I'll tell Lemlem you say hello when she wakes up—*if* she wakes up. It's unclear. She is awfully still . . ."

"You—"

I hang up on him just as I turn into the parking garage of my building.

It takes me no time at all to drag Lemlem into the penthouse elevator, into my flat, over the new brightly colored foyer rug, and into my office—the only room in my penthouse still devoid of color, and the only one still biometrically coded and steel reinforced. Of course the Marduk could get in if he wanted, particularly with Three's help, but my alarms are all active, including on my phone, which should give me enough time to return once I know he's coming. Not that I suspect he'll think to come here. The more likely outcome—the one I'm betting on—is that he will have Three tear apart the COE, where we'll be waiting for them.

I relish the thought as I bring Lemlem to the manacles I mounted to my ceiling. The chains dangle low. I spent time thinking about the exact type of manacles I'd use and decided that, since I didn't know the full extent of the powers of Marduk's minions, I'd use all of them. So after the manacles, I fix her wrists in rope, then duct tape, then plastic zip ties, then in handcuffs I stole from the COE.

The mount to the ceiling is made of iron, and the chain that connects her hands passes through it first. Because she's still passed out, she's draped all over my floor now that I've moved my desk out of the way. I keep my chair out of her reach as well. If she does wake, she'll have no choice but to stand or possibly lose her hands—she won't have much circulation with them affixed as they are and stretched above her head. She might not even end the day with working hands if she doesn't wake up soon, but that's not my problem. I promised the Marduk his female in exchange for mine's safety, but *an eye for an eye* is my motto and my woman was burned with acid and fire, half drowned, beaten, scraped, and shot at—electrocuted and ruined hands is the least I can do to reciprocate.

I leave her draped over the floor. No water. No food. I check her pockets and she doesn't have a phone on her. So I leave a note taped to the inside of my office door before I shut it, lock it, and leave the same way I came in.

I head to the COE building, enter the compound, as planned, through a service entrance, and what I find there pleases me. "Has he arrived?" I ask, slipping from my vehicle to the tune of SDD armed guards nervously approaching. Their boots make muffled thumps against the concrete below the COE campus.

A male guard with skin as white as mayonnaise steps forward to meet me. Blech. I hate these goons.

"We're being circled, but they haven't made contact yet, sir." *Sir.* My eye twitches when he calls me that.

"How many, soldier?"

"We aren't sure. One of them is using a cloaking shield to muddle our direct lines of sight, a lot like what happened the last time the COE was under attack and the Wyvern and Mr. Singkham were kidnapped. What we've picked up on the cameras is that there are either four or six of them. Two males and either two or four females."

"One of them is the Marduk, I'm assuming?"

"We haven't been able to detect his presence yet."

"Hmm." I don't like that. I want this done quickly.

We take the elevator up to the ground floor. The campus has been cleared. I'm shocked the COE was willing to go to such great lengths to assist me in this assassination—I mean, apprehension—especially since our recent breakup, but I'm guessing, based on what they know about the Marduk and his army, it was deemed a worthwhile endeavor.

Mr. Singkham meets me in the central lobby of the primary building, black-clad officers fanning out behind him like a flock of geese and he, the mother hen. "We have a sighting, but the Marduk seems to be retreating."

I snarl, "And the others?"

"Advancing."

"Fuck." I come to a complete stop, the lights of the large marble lobby flickering as a thought comes to me. "Do you have descriptions of the ones advancing?"

As Mr. Singkham speaks, he gestures to the woman on his left. She holds up her wrist. There's a small tablet affixed there in black armor. "We're having trouble seeing who is advancing with the naked eye. We had a similar issue during the COE breach six months ago when the Wyvern and I were abducted from the premises by the one called Three. We learned then that the distortion was being caused by this female. She is number Thirty-Eight." The woman pulls up an image of a curvy, freckled female at Mr. Singkham's signal.

I memorize it. It's not much to go on, grainy as it is and taken through a smoky haze, but whatever. White. Dirty blonde, maybe brunette. If I have to kill several white blondish females before getting to the right one, so be it.

"However, we learned that the illusion doesn't affect camera footage. They must also know that, because they've been doing a good job of remaining in motion. So far we've been able to take pictures of three of them, excluding the female. We have this male," he says, drawing up a picture of a male with pale skin and bright-yellow hair. "We don't have an ID for him. And these two females." He shows me pictures that make me smile—well, not so much smile as bite my front teeth together to show all my fangs.

"Fantastic."

"Fantastic?"

"Bia and the Meinad."

"We had suspicions but weren't yet able to identify them. The pictures are so out of focus . . ."

"It's them." I relax my shoulders. "I saw them recently. They almost killed me and I almost let them kill Monika. But I've learned a few tricks since then." I stand up straight and roll out my neck. "Open the front doors."

"We aren't ready to attack yet," the female says. She must be the commander here.

I turn to face her and give her a grimace. She frowns at me when I say, "You may not be, but I don't work for you and I don't care. Open the doors, please." I boop her nose with the tip of my finger. She slaps my hand away. I don't mind. Because I've already pivoted to boop Mr. Singkham. He stares at me like I've grown extra heads.

"We shouldn't be overconfident," Mr. Singkham says, taking a step away from me and adjusting his suit. "Bia and the Meinad are among the most powerful, and I've seen firsthand the chaos that number Thirty-Eight can cause."

"Shush. Open the doors. I don't want or need your people to come with me. I will do this on my own."

Everyone exchanges skeptical looks.

I roll my eyes, push past Mr. Singkham, and push through the wall of black. "I know we haven't been properly introduced, but I am not the male you once knew as Taranis," I shout over my shoulder as I head to the reinforced-steel doors that have been drawn shut on the other side of the sliding glass. "I am no longer that grinning idiot. I am number Six, one of the most powerful members of the Tratharine army, and I am pissed the fuck off."

I push my powers through my limbs, and realizing that the mechanism that controls both the glass and the steel doors is electronic, I open the doors myself. Natural light floods the space, bouncing off the cavern of white marble surrounding me. I glance at my phone briefly before tucking it into my pocket. The Wyvern should be arriving imminently with my female and his own. They'll be going straight to the lowest level of the security building. Three will likely be able to enter but will have a hard time making it past thirty guards and the Wyvern, and will only be able to teleport help in from the outside one villain at a time. And there will be four fewer helpers left after I'm through with these walking corpses.

I step outside. The breeze is calming. The sight of three Tratharine flying toward me is not. It's exhilarating.

They touch down on the sidewalk just beyond the high fence marking the perimeter of the COE campus. The gate is open, but they don't enter.

"Please, don't be frightened, it's just us." I slam the silver steel doors shut at my back, blocking anyone from attempting to intervene. It's not that I worry for their safety. *I* want to be the one to kill these creatures. No one else. After denying myself the pleasure of killing the Marduk's woman this morning, my murderous instincts need some appeasing.

I gesture them forward. "Come in, come in. You're more than welcome. And, Thirty-Eight, you're welcome to come out of hiding."

She must be curious—either that or confident—because when Thirty-Eight shows herself, I find her only ten feet from me, standing on the nice paved pathway that leads up to the COE building. Green grass spreads out on either side, marked by curving, cobblestone pathways dotted with benches for miserable human employees to sit on when contemplating which flavor sandwich they'll eat that afternoon. Humans and their sandwiches. Such odd lives these peons lead. Yet somehow distinctly more interesting than these idiots, who run around after weapons they can't even use at the bidding of masters they only half remember and who may never even make it here—who, given the way the reversions have been affecting the only two of us who have reverted so far, won't.

Thirty-Eight glances back at the others and gestures them forward. "Nineteen, Twenty-Three, Fifty-Seven."

I smile at the others, gaze flitting over Fifty-Seven and Twenty-Three—the Meinad and Bia, respectively—before landing on the unfamiliar male. "Apologies, I don't think we've met."

"I'm Terrasinth." The ground begins rumbling beneath my feet. "I control the earth. I could cave the COE building behind you quite easily and kill your precious humans."

"Oh my, how special of you. I think I might remember you. You were number Nineteen, weren't you?" The male doesn't answer. He doesn't know. I shake my head and laugh. "Were you there helping the Marduk at the ports two weeks ago kill all those pesky little COE humans?"

"I was," he says, his chest puffing up.

"Good."

His eyes glisten a silverish brown. How pretty. "Why did you call the Marduk here?"

"He didn't tell you?" I laugh, planting my hands on my waist. "Wow. What a fearless leader you have. He didn't tell you that he found his weapon and his key?"

That seems to startle the four of them. Thirty-Eight glances at the others. The Meinad and Terrasinth continue glaring at me. "You're lying."

"I wish I was. Do you know what his key is?" I shake my head, laughing in earnest now. "It's a human woman. *Another one*. This is starting to get despicable, don't you think?"

"I should have killed yours when I had the chance," Bia hisses like a snake.

I clap. "You are so right. You should have. You also should have killed *me* when you had the chance." I gesture toward Bia and the Meinad, who I can feel begin rumbling with their own powers. "Because do you know what's going to happen now. No? My, my, the Marduk truly doesn't give a fuck about you, does he? Did he not even tell you that I'm number Six? And I'm going to torture the fuck out of all four of you?" And so I do.

Before the Meinad can attack and before Terrasinth can open the ground beneath me and before Bia can summon her army of bees or snakes or polar bears or what-have-you, I send electrical currents through each of their bodies, a hundred times sharper and stronger than any I sent through the Marduk's woman. A thousand times.

My body radiates with a terrible and awesome power that causes my feet to lift from the ground and my entire being to pulse with electricity. Lightning shoots from my horns, scattering around me like rain, piercing the chests of each of my adversaries, their hearts, their stomachs, their brains.

I decide I'd like them to die in half an hour on the dot, make sure it lasts long enough for them to know how upset I am about all this. A few times, they each try to call upon their powers to save themselves. Some little snakes come wriggling up out of the ground, I'm attacked by a flock of birds at one point—but they all slam against the electrical field like pigeons against glass. Terrasinth topples several trees and the entire ground quakes long and violently enough to sink some of those pathetic human bench seats—good riddance anyway—and at several points my vision grows hazy with whatever illusions Thirty-Eight tries to toss my way.

Pointless. Were they not even listening? I am number Six, currently the most powerful being on this planet except perhaps for Monika who, as loath as I am to admit, controls my heart and my hand. Who am I kidding? I love to admit it because loving her is the most fun I've ever had.

A final flare of bright electric intensity radiates through my bones, causing them to burn with exertion as light flashes off my body so bright and wild I hear glass shattering in the building behind me. The streetlights on the block flicker, and then the whole grid goes dead . . . and so do the four supervillains who had the audacity to threaten my woman, lying on the grass and concrete.

My powers flicker and coalesce around me, folding back around my body like a cloak. My muscles sing with aches and a little pain. My neck cricks when I roll it out; so do my ankles and clawed toes. I have a slight headache, but overall, I sigh contentedly as I touch back onto the now-charred front walkway of the COE. Nearly the entire front garden and steps are scorched earth.

I go to the bodies, checking them for any final signs of life. Finding none, I give Bia one last swift kick to the side of her head, dust off my hands, and walk back through the doors of the COE building.

"Well, that was easy." Easier than even I thought it would be, especially considering that the Marduk never showed. "Sorry about your lights," I add, too lazy and tired to turn them back on.

Mr. Singkham stares at me, jaw agape. "You . . . you . . ." He's standing between two soldiers who hold a larger tablet between them. I imagine it contains the video feed of what just transpired between the four villains and me—at least, it *did*. Now the screen shows black, just like all the other tech in the building.

"Enjoy the show?"

Mr. Singkham's jaw continues to work.

I pull out my burner phone. "I am disappointed the Marduk didn't show. I'll just give him a quick call to let him know what I did to his people, which will hopefully inspire him to come give us a visit. While I'm busy with this, can you find some sort of device to call the Wyvern? I'd like his support for when the Marduk gets here."

Mr. Singkham is still staring at me like he's never seen me before in his life. The truth is, he hasn't. Only one person on this planet and any other has ever truly seen me. He blubbers two or three times before he finally forms words that are comprehensible. "He—he—he never showed."

My thumb claw hovers over the talk button on my burner. I look up. "What?" I snap, fully prepared to kill Mr. Singkham next should he give me another answer that causes me even the smallest amount of displeasure.

"We've been calling, but we haven't heard from the Wyvern, Ms. Theriot, or Ms. Neu—"

I rip my own phone out of my back pocket only to find it dead too. The damn burner is the only one that seems to have survived this. I quickly use it to place a call to Monika's number, but it just rings and rings.

Dread rolls over me. *No.* It's not possible. The Marduk can't have gotten to her. The Wyvern was with them. They should have been here half an hour ago . . .

I go to call again, only for a number I do recognize to pop up across the screen. It may be Monika's, but as I answer the phone, my blackened heart fully expects to hear the Marduk's smug tone flood the line, and braces for that eventuality.

Instead, the voice I do hear shocks and soothes me, even as it screeches in ire. "Taranis Darius Marcel Smith, did you seriously chain an Ethiopian woman up in our office?"

"Yes," I exhale, relief coating my bones in syrup. "Are you okay?" She doesn't sound distressed or harmed, but I can't know for sure until I see her, hold her in my arms.

"No! The Ethiopian woman . . ."

"Yes, yes, yes. Where is she now? I am assuming you released her?" I ask, rolling my eyes.

"Of course I did. But the 'where' she is might be a little trickier to answer. Where are you?"

"Out battling villains," I say, frowning. "Why? What happened?"

"Uh, well . . . I was out battling villains too."

My hackles rise. "WHAT?"

"I'm good. All good. But I have to tell you, I've had the strangest day."

"Where are you?"

"At home." *At home,* she says. Not *at my place*. At home.

There's an easing in my chest that makes my shoulders soften down my back. "You safe?"

"Yeah, the Wyvern's here and I've got my weapons—Vanessa's got hers too."

"Your weapons?"

"Just . . . come here . . ."

"What the fuck did you do?"

"I was a good girlfriend and fixed all your shit. Where are you?"

"I'm out . . . being a good boyfriend and getting revenge for you."

"Good God. If this is going to work, we're going to have to set some serious boundaries, *Taranis*," she hisses, using the name for me I now know she only uses when she's pissed off. Pissed off but still fighting for me.

"Whatever you want, *jagiya*," I tell her, ignoring Mr. Singkham's protests and taking to the skies.

Chapter Thirty

Monika

One hour earlier

"So you're telling me that the weapons actually belong to *us*? And we're the keys to unlocking them?" I say, flabbergasted by everything Vanessa's told me over brunch.

The Wyvern is supposed to pick us up to take us to the COE building for some meeting Darius called, but Vanessa's got me way too hyped, so I convinced her to show me her weapon—a weapon currently stowed in the trunk of her car because I persuaded her to let me photograph her with it when we go pick up the weapon I spied in Darius's penthouse that Vanessa claims belongs to me.

"Exactly," she says, nodding animatedly and ignoring the Wyvern's next call.

"But I saw it lighting up with electricity when Taranis was pissed."

"Were you also pissed?"

I stop to think about it as I give her my key fob to get into the penthouse garage. "I was."

"Maybe it wasn't responding to him, but to you."

"Hmm." That gives me something to think about as we pile out of her SUV and head toward the elevator. I notice Taranis's car is gone, which is odd, because most of the time he just flies if he's on his own.

Vanessa extracts her sword from the trunk, glancing up at the ceiling as she does.

"Don't worry. No cameras down here," I explain. "Taranis took them out after . . ." *The first time he pulled me naked out of his limo.* "He's just insanely private. He'd rather be robbed than be spied on."

Vanessa and I ride up in silence. Her phone starts ringing again as we reach the penthouse floor. "I've got to take this, or he's gonna freak." She rolls her eyes and brushes the back of her wrist over her cheek as she lifts her phone to her ear. "Hey!"

"Are you fucking kidding?" says the voice on the other end of the line, one I can hear clearly. "Where are you?" He sounds pissed, though not quite as pissed as I'm pretty sure Darius would be if I dipped out on him in favor of a ridiculous plan with one of my girlfriends. Not that I have many of those. Well, not that I *had* many of those. Vanessa's starting to feel like a promising candidate. And Cynthia, while not exactly promising, is at least a candidate.

"It's right through here," I tell Vanessa as I approach the closed doors to Darius's office. He hasn't used it once in the past few weeks, so I'm a little surprised to find it locked. Luckily, I'm coded to all the penthouse biometrics now.

I press my palm to the panel beside the door. It clicks and swings slightly inward. I push it the rest of the way open and come to a dead. fucking. stop.

Vanessa slips into the room behind me and screams.

On the phone, I can hear the Wyvern shout, "The fuck is going on!"

"Oh my God. Taranis has like . . . There's a woman tied up to the ceiling . . . hanging from the ceiling. She's dead!"

"I don't think she is," I say, clapping my hands over my mouth as the woman starts to cough.

"Auooow," she groans, and I rush forward, grab a chair shoved against one wall, and start to drag it. It makes a screeching sound over the hard,

sadly rug-less concrete floor in here that has the woman wincing as she tries to open her eyes, right her head on her neck, and focus.

"Hey, I'm not gonna hurt you," I feel the need to say as I push the chair up against her back and then carefully race around her body and try to pull her up onto the seat. She's taller than I am, though, and starts to struggle, so Vanessa sets down her sword and comes to help me.

Together, we manage to get her seated. We back away from her and I glance at Vanessa, who's got her pink-painted nails pressed to her mouth. Her cheeks are puffed out. She looks like she's gonna burst.

"How . . ." I start.

"I told Roland where we are. He's coming."

"Good." I should call Taranis and ask him WHY, but I want to get the woman down first.

The woman croaks, her head resting on the back of the chair. She swings it around and blinks her brown eyes open. Seeing us, she starts, "Who—who—who the hell are you people?" And then she squeals, "Are you with the guy? With the lightning?"

"I . . ." I try again, but I'm about to shit myself in shock and confusion.

"We're . . ." Vanessa starts. "I'm . . . dating the Wyvern. I'm his fiancée."

Vanessa has one of the most recognizable faces in America at the moment, but the woman gives her a dead-eyed blink. "Who is the Wyvern?"

Vanessa and I share a glance before I sputter, "Are you in shock? Or like . . . injured?" Maybe that explains why she doesn't seem to recognize the most famous person in the world.

"Yes," she moans. "Some monster . . . came into my coffee shop . . . and then *electrocuted* me. I thought it was Mr. Taranis—he's come into my coffee shop before—but why would he do this to me? He's never tried to hurt me before . . ."

"Oh my God!" Vanessa says in the same breath that I shout, *"Mein Gott."*

Flustered, panicked, guilty, and confused, I flap my hands like a bird. "Let's . . ." And then the adrenaline starts to kick in and my pulse settles. I speak and my voice is sharper than it was. "Let's worry about the why *after* we get you out of here. Vanessa, can your sword cut through that metal?"

"I'll try." Vanessa lifts her weapon, and the moment she touches the hilt, the blade comes to life.

The woman screams. I offer her paltry reassurance as Vanessa whacks and hacks away at the steel beam connecting the woman to the celling. It doesn't work.

Vanessa's sweating as she says to me, "Where's your weapon?"

I glance at the bookshelves. Taranis shoved his desk in front of them, but I can still reach the strange objects I identified from Mr. Singkham's book.

I withdraw the short wrist swords and slip them onto each arm. There's an inner handle inside each object, and the moment I grip them, twin blades shoot out of the sides of central blades, making me and Vanessa and the captive woman all jump. And then we scream as a collective when my wrist swords suddenly erupt in electricity that doesn't burn me at all.

I wave my arms around in a panic and get lucky, because my right arm is pointed at the ceiling when I inadvertently squeeze the blade-release mechanism inside the hilt a second time and a blaze of lightning releases from the tip of the central sword and hits the ceiling above the woman's head.

"MOVE!" I shout, and the woman just manages to dive forward out of the chair as the entire ceiling crumbles, the huge metal hook her chain is looped through falling with it. She lands on her face on the ground, and when I race over to her, she immediately recoils. "I'm so sorry!" I shout. "I've never used these before!"

I fling the lightning hand swords off my wrists and don't bother gathering them as they clatter against the wall, shooting off a couple last errant sparks before becoming dull, lifeless alien antiques once more. I drop down onto my knees next to the poor girl and roll her onto her back.

"I'm gonna go grab a glass of water and some towels," Vanessa shouts, dashing out of the room and thundering down the hall, her sword in hand.

Meanwhile, I help the woman sit up. She's whimpering, cradling her hands, which look swollen and uncomfortable. They've turned a darker brown, almost purplish color.

"Christ almighty," I hiss. "What on earth? Why would Taranis do this to you?"

"I don't know . . ." She wipes her nose with the back of her wrist as I prop her against the wall. She tries to tuck her feet underneath her and cries out, pained.

"Hey, stop moving. Is it your feet?" I ask her.

She bites her lips between her teeth, closes her eyes, and nods.

"I'm gonna take your shoes off. What's your name?"

"Lemlem," she whimpers.

"Lemlem, I'm Monika. I'm the girlfriend of the guy who did this to you," I admit, feeling a little weird about that confession. Tears track down her cheeks. "I am so sorry. I can't understand why he'd do this . . ."

"He tortured me," she cries out as I untie her chunky black sneakers and gently pull them off. I take her frilly yellow socks next and try not to puke at the sight of burns—electrical burns—open and weeping on the soles of her feet. My stomach heaves. I choke.

"Okay, I'm going to . . . go get . . . someone." Someone way more equipped to deal with injuries than me. "Actually, I think we should get *you* to someone. Vanessa, grab me a couch pillow!" I gently stretch out her legs so the soles of her heels no longer touch the ground.

"What?" I hear a drafty reply from way too far away. Where the hell is she?

I need to call Taylor to get an ambulance. We need EMTs up here.

I reach for my phone to do just that when Lemlem sniffles. "He . . . I think it has something to do with a guy that comes into my shop—my coffee shop."

"Who?"

"Just this guy named Max." Max? Who the fuck is Max? "He comes in almost every day. He's the only white guy that does."

"Vanessa, where are those towels?" I shout.

"What?" She sounds even farther away when she responds too many beats later.

I turn my attention toward Lemlem again and shove the insane manacles farther up her wrists, away from her hands, trying to give them a little relief. "I'm gonna try to undo the plastic and rope ones. There are scissors . . . let me grab them. Tell me more about this . . . white guy. Is he somebody you're dating?"

She makes a whimper and a snorting sound in the same breath. "No. You think my mama wouldn't kill me if I brought a guy like that home to Addis?" She balks again for good measure while I retrieve the scissors and cut through the plastic around her wrists first.

"I mean, my guy's blue. A white guy seems all right from where I'm sitting," I tease, trying to lighten the mood.

She shakes her head. "No! No, not . . . *Aaawwww!*" she screams.

"Sorry!" I have to leverage the thick metal blade of the set of scissors against her wrist in order to apply enough pressure to get through the plastic. *"Scheiße!"* I finally get through. "I'm so sorry. So what is it about the white guy your mom wouldn't approve of?"

"Tattoos . . . Ow!" As I do the other wrist, her face twists up and her toes curl, which must cause her even more pain, because she starts to tilt to the side. I catch her and help her back into a sitting position. I massage her wrists while she says in a pant, "My mama always thought that white guys with that many tattoos were bad for business." Her head falls back, knocking against the wall. Her ponytail sags, her goddess braids frayed. Her lips twitch. "I thought he was cute, but we never talked much. He asked me one time if he could come host business meetings during my set up as early as four a.m. I told him sure. I didn't mind so long as he didn't make many demands. He never did. He was always pleasant and nice."

My own heart is beating a thousand miles a minute. I am starting to get concerned that maybe, just maybe, we should have just gone to the COE headquarters like the Wyvern and Taranis asked us to instead of making this pit stop.

"Is he blond with a thick beard? Looks like a Viking? Black eyes?"

Her eyebrows furrow. "Yes. You know him? Your boyfriend met with him in my shop once. Before he was blue."

"I got the towels! I found some bandages too!" Vanessa says, storming into the room, bright and optimistic, while my world crumbles around me. She must see something in my expression, because she tilts her head, her pretty puffy curls like a cloud around her. "What is it?"

I whisper-hiss, "I think this is the Marduk's key."

"What?" Vanessa comes a few steps forward, but I never get a chance to repeat myself because an alarm starts blaring from somewhere I can't see, and a moment later, two bodies suddenly appear in the small room between us.

Wind, like a vortex, smashes through the space, slamming me against the wall beside Lemlem and tossing Vanessa out the door and onto her ass in the foyer. *At least there's a rug there,* I think rather helplessly as I place one arm across Lemlem's body. The other hand falls out to my right side and bumps fortuitously against my weapon. *My*. Weapon.

I slide it onto my wrist while the Marduk does a slow turn of the room, and I watch the expression on his face as it finally falls to Lemlem. Key or not, it's clear by the tightening of every muscle in his body that she means something to him. And she has no idea who he is.

He's frozen solid, and the being who arrived with him—a being I recognize from the docks—shouts, "Four. Four!" When the Marduk doesn't move except to blink, his harsh, bleak expression so focused on Lemlem that I don't have any idea what he's thinking, the being who I know now to be Three takes a menacing step forward.

Lemlem shrieks.

The Marduk throws his arm across Three's chest to stop them from advancing, but I don't give a shit about that. I've already leveled my weapon at Three's chest and pulled the inner trigger. Lightning flares from the tip of my weapon and slams into Three fully, hitting the Marduk's arm first. Both beings go cantering back.

Three hits the opposite wall and surges forward, pissed, but as they advance on me and the Marduk stands slightly off to the side near Taranis's desk, angrily admiring the blackened stain on his arm where I tagged him, it's clear they've both forgotten Vanessa.

Vanessa releases a battle cry as she flies into the room, her sword blazing. "Fuck you!" she wails like a banshee, and I tilt my head in shock—I don't think I've ever heard this girl curse before. And then my jaw drops open completely when Vanessa swings her sword.

Three is reaching for me or Lemlem or us both, but a thin strip of flaming metal cuts through their forearm just below the wrist. There is only a little blood because the blade is on fire and sears the wound shut.

Lemlem screams as the disembodied hand falls onto her outstretched shins. She tries to pull her legs back in, but her feet are still all messed up.

Three turns to attack Vanessa and releases a carnal roar. Their inky-black hair stands on end. Their eyes are red and bright, expelling red light onto their cheeks. Dressed all in black, they move as a blur toward Vanessa, who squeals, but I'm ready. I fire another round into Three, hitting them in the side. I fire another round at the Marduk while I'm at it, but Lemlem grabs my arm, pulling it down so that I hit the Marduk in the thigh instead of the chest.

He turns his gaze to me, and it, too, bleeds red.

He charges forward, but Lemlem throws her arm across my chest. "Stop! All of you, stop! Please! Don't hurt her—either of them. These women saved me. I might have lost my hands if they'd been any later." She lifts them up and winces, sniffles. "Ow . . ." She curses in a language I can't interpret.

The Marduk looks at me, looks at her, looks at me again. He lunges toward me, and I lift my weapon, but she grabs it with both of her useless hands and shoves it toward the ground. "Don't hurt him," she says.

"Are you crazy?" I screech back, struggling with the aloof woman who clearly wouldn't be able to recognize danger if it was plastered all over every page of the internet and also waltzing every day into her coffee shop. "This man is the ultimate supervillain!"

We're sort of fighting for the weapon, though the fight is rather pathetic. Her hands may hurt her, but somehow, her long limbs are getting in my way. I can't wriggle my weapon free.

And then Vanessa screams. Three has gotten back up and is running toward her.

"No!" Lemlem shrieks.

"Let go of me!" I shout, panic clogging my throat as Three disappears after Vanessa through the doorway.

The next few seconds happen so fast that I can't track them. Something in the foyer causes Three to shout in pain. The Marduk has a hand raised in that direction, leading me to believe it's his doing. The Marduk then lunges out of the room, into the foyer, and returns with Three.

He drags Three over to where I'm sitting. I try to block him from reaching Lemlem, but he shoves me out of the way with a powerful blast of wind. I hit the leg of the desk, and when I blink my eyes open, the Marduk has a hand on Lemlem's outstretched leg but is looking at me.

"Tell Taranis that we're even."

"What does that mean?"

"It's over, so long as he doesn't come looking for me."

"What? Wait. Where are you going? You can't take Lemlem with you!" I shout, but the Marduk is whispering in Three's ear, and a pained, enraged Three roars before suddenly the Marduk explodes into a burst of black smoke, and the three of them disappear like they were never even here.

I'm completely frozen where I'm lying twisted on the floor. I glance up when Vanessa crawls into the room on all fours, looking absurd and diabolical carrying a flaming sword while wearing a pretty sundress. "Are they gone?"

I nod. "I think so." My heart is pounding. "You injured?"

"Nope. You?"

I take a moment to check myself and conclude, "Nope."

"What did the Marduk say to you?"

"I think . . . Lemlem might have convinced him to leave us alone."

"Lemlem? The girl Taranis tortured?"

I make a sound—it's sort of like laughter, but a hysterical version. "Yeah. I guess, uh . . . his plan worked?"

The sound of glass shattering in my living room has us both screaming, scrambling to our feet, gathering our weapons, and running into the foyer. The Wyvern is there, his horns fully blazing, his eyes a dark red—until he looks up and sees his girl.

"Hey!" Vanessa says cheerily. She sets down her sword carefully against the wall. "So, something kind of crazy happened, but it's all good now. No need to panic . . . *eep*!"

The Wyvern wastes no time in rushing over to her, gathering her up in his arms, and squeezing her until she's barely visible in his muscular chest.

Giving them their privacy, I reenter Darius's rather destroyed office, set my weapons down on the desk, and pull out my phone. My chest blazes with too much adrenaline, but my voice is even as I dial Darius's number. His phone goes straight to voicemail, but I notice that I have a missed call on my own phone from an unknown number. I try it, and it's Darius's voice I hear.

Before he can speak, I tilt my eyes up at the hole in the ceiling and shout, "Taranis Darius Marcel Smith, did you seriously chain an Ethiopian woman up in our office?"

"Yes," he says, unrepentant before his voice fills with strain. "Are you okay?"

"No! The Ethiopian woman . . ."

"Yes, yes, yes. Where is she now? I am assuming you released her?"

And why, exactly, does he sound annoyed by that? Oh, right. Because my boyfriend is a psychopath. "Of course I did. But the 'where' she is might be a little trickier to answer. Where are you?"

"Out battling villains. Why? What happened?"

"Uh, well . . . I was out battling villains too."

"What?" he damn near shrieks. My heart fills with little lumps of emotion that should be battered back by the knowledge that my man—my beast—kidnapped and tortured an innocent woman today, but isn't. So what does that say about me?

"I'm good. All good," I say, glancing at Vanessa and the Wyvern making out in my hallway. I shake my head, roll my eyes, and plant my butt on the desk next to my weapons. I slide the left one onto my wrist and watch lightning travel up and down the beautiful, intricate markings that decorate its every inch. "But I have to tell you, I've had the strangest day."

And the worst part? I didn't get any of it on camera.

Epilogue

Darius

Three months later

I'm spellbound. I stand in Monika's crowded gallery surrounded by peons staring up at my favorite portrait. I find them much less irritating than usual, because today, even though they are sycophants, they are *Monika's* sycophants, and here for her. These artsy-fartsy types are hardly paying me attention.

"Do you see her use of light here?" some idiot wearing a beret says to his human companion as they shuffle up close and point at my picture. "Astounding. It renders the composition so much more accessible, despite the subject matter. Would you excuse us?" she huffs, irritation lacing her tone, until she looks up. When she sees me, her eyes widen, her lips part, but instead of the usual *Ooh, Taranis, can I have your autograph?* she rolls her eyes and tuts. "That's the subject. I don't know what she sees in him." The woman is whispering to her friend, but I can still hear her clearly.

I give her a little zap as she edges past me, and she jumps and rubs her ass, glancing over her shoulder suspiciously before disappearing into the crowd.

"*Mein Gott*, what are you smiling like that for?" Monika's voice pulls my attention down. She looks fucking radiant tonight, dressed all in dark-green satin that hugs every one of her delectable curves.

I slip my clawed fingers around the back of her neck and pull her toward me. "I'm so damn proud of you," I tell her, leaning down for a kiss.

She pulls back, denying me. "That's not your *I'm so proud of you* smile. That's your *I'm going to hurt someone and enjoy it* smile. I thought we talked about this?" Her pink-painted lips are drawn into a tight circle—one of my favorite looks she gives me.

I love when she's irritated with me. It usually means I get to beg her forgiveness in the only way I know how. My hand on her ass, which is where I place it now. "I didn't hurt anybody."

"Promise?"

"Sort of."

She groans. "Is this what I get? Half-truths? I thought we were done with the lies after your last secret plan almost backfired and got me killed and *my* last secret plan definitely backfired and almost got me killed?"

I smirk. I don't know that I'll ever outgrow the lies entirely. After all, Monika still hasn't noticed the trackers I've placed in her phone, car, wallet, camera bag, and two of her cameras.

I lift her feet from the floor and hug her against my chest. I'm in a gray suit with a dark-green shirt and green silk pocket square to match. Despite the clash with my blue coloring, I don't want there to be any mistaking who I'm here with tonight.

I kiss her gently on the mouth, then kiss each of her cheeks. "How much?" I whisper in her ear.

I feel her body tense up against mine. So responsive. I crave her. "How much what?" she asks.

"For the picture?"

"This one?" She laughs. "You really are full of yourself . . ."

She pulls back and takes a look at the image that's got me so entranced. She's right. It is a picture of me, of my face, but it's so different from all the rest. The title of her exhibit is *Aliens Among Us*. As predicted, it's a gallery of images of superbeings, but in positions and poses that aren't conventionally shot.

My least favorites are the images she was granted permission to use from the battle at the ports. A single shot of a dart in focus, with a woman hanging from the ceiling behind it, blurred, is the one I hate most. That dart is headed straight for the camera and she still has the scar on her face to prove it.

But my favorite of the images is this one here, and not because it's of me—many of them are. This is a picture she took of me at her dad's barbecue. Her parents came into town and hosted a barbecue with members of their family from New Jersey, mostly Malian Americans, but also blended and ranging in age from two to eighty. There must have been about forty of them—cousins, cousins, cousins, and cousins who I'm pretty sure weren't even technically related.

In the photo, I'm standing at the grill, wearing an apron. I don't have a shirt on underneath, so you can see my blue skin shimmering in the light, patterns drawn across it in glittering white swoops and swirls. They match the patterns on my weapon. But it's not my alienness that matters at all in this photo. It's the light, the way it hits my chin and chest, illuminating the stains on my apron, the charcoal smears on my arms.

I'm laughing like an idiot in this picture. I just look so . . . silly. So stupid. So much like a peon. I can't even remember what I was laughing at anymore—maybe something one of her drunk-ass uncles said, I can't be sure. But I do know that I've never seen me like that, and I like it more than a proud male like me probably should.

"This isn't even my favorite," she says. "Why do you like it?"

"It's not that I like the way I look in it," I say against her lips. Staring into her eyes, I can see the light from my own reflected onto her cheeks. And it's bright white. A color that I now know means total and utter infatuation. It's sickening. "I like the way you see me. Nobody's ever seen me like that. Not even me."

She grins. "That might be the nicest compliment I've received all evening."

"Well, I take *that* as a compliment, considering how many compliments you've likely received tonight. After all, you are *the* Monika Neumann."

A gloss covers her eyes and she bites her lower lip. She reaches in between her breasts, confusing me for a moment until she withdraws a piece of jewelry, simple and so perfect a platinum that it shines nearly white. She holds it out between us and swallows hard. "I was hoping you might consider becoming Mr. Darius Neumann, if you'll have me."

It hits me like a brick, and I forget to breathe. When she gives me a slight laugh and nudges me with her knee, I realize she's expecting a response. "Are you . . ." But I can't speak.

She withdraws something else from between her tits. A folded square that looks badly beat. It's the same marriage license I threatened her with all those months ago.

"Holy fuck, are you asking me to marry you?"

"Yes," she laughs and then chokes up. "Am I allowed to say it now? Now that it's all finished?"

She's been asking and I've been telling her to wait, unsure of what the words would do to me. But I nod now.

"I love you," she tells me.

"You're fucking insane," I growl. "But you're the only one crazy enough for me, baby. I love you too."

"So does that mean you'll marry me?"

I dip Monika low to the ground and kiss her deeply enough that the peons around us start to whistle. I give them all a collective zap that will undoubtedly earn me a punishment I deserve, and I couldn't be more ready for it. A lifetime of it.

Against her parted lips, I whisper, "I do."

ACKNOWLEDGMENTS

I really cannot start these acknowledgments without thanking the author community that rallied around me for the release of book one. Having bestselling authors whose books I've admired for years reach out to me proactively to ask if they can grab ARCs, blurb my book, join me for events, and help boost me in any way that they can shows how powerful the romance community truly can be. To name a few, I'd like to thank Katee Robert, Ali Hazelwood, Kenya Goree-Bell, Zea Kayleigh, Kimberly Lemming, Nikki Payne, Laura Thalassa, Natalie Ashee, and Anna Fury.

The same goes for the indie bookstores, clubs, and subs that reached out. Y'all are incredible for working with me when I had no idea what I was doing (and still don't) in this whole trad world. The Yakima Book Co & Traveling Book Bus, Mis Amores, Flame & Fable, Dog Eared Books, Slow Burn, Burn Bright, and Tropes & Trifles to start!

Thanking you readers should be OBVIOUS because I am grateful every day when you drop into my DMs ranting about something that happened in one of my books in the BEST possible way. The way y'all make me squeal over words I wrote is EVERYTHING.

Black readers, y'all get an extra shout-out. There's nothing easy about being Black in this world or in this industry, but y'all prove time and again that we step up for each other. That we are not a monolith. That Black books SELL. That Black bodies are just as deserving of adoration and adulation in fiction as in real life, and so worthy of love.

And thanks to all of you, my first trad book ever ended up becoming an INSTANT #9 *USA Today* bestseller! I still cannot even believe it!

Thank you to Montlake and the Talcott Notch team that got me here. Lauren, Amy, Kristi, Nadia, and the larger teams—it has been an absolute pleasure working with y'all in every way. I couldn't have asked for a better entry into this whole Big Trad universe.

Sam, Natasha, and Meg: Thank you for being assistants extraordinaire.

Katherine, Ajira, and Lo: Thank you for your camera help! You seriously unlocked a whole new knowledge level for me.

And lastly, I really can say that I would have accomplished absolutely nothing if not for my family. Mom and Dad, for being extra parents to my toddler. Hubby, for doing everything else while I struggled majorly through the mini burst my career has taken in tandem with being a pregnant toddler mama.

And to my toddler, the baby in my belly, and my fur baby, thank you for making my life so damn hard and keeping the fight alive in me. Y'all are my everything.

ABOUT THE AUTHOR

Elizabeth Stephens is the author of *All Superheroes Need PR* in the Supers in the City series and often gets lost in places that don't exist. With a growing backlist of over fifteen titles, her work is best known for diverse casts, tough heroines, wacky world-building, and villains—or beasts—who get the girl in guaranteed happily ever afters. When she isn't tip-tap-typing away, you might find her enjoying the outdoors of the Pacific Northwest or traveling and making adventures of her own with her husband, tiny humans, and doggo, King Louis. For more information, visit www.booksbyelizabeth.com.